THE
LINCOLN
MYTH

THE
LINCOLN
MYTH

★ ★ ★

A NOVEL

STEVE
BERRY

RANDOM HOUSE
LARGE PRINT

All rights reserved.
Published in the United States of America by
Random House Large Print in association with
Ballantine Books, New York.
Distributed by Random House LLC, New York,
a Penguin Random House Company.

Cover design: Scott Biel
Cover image: Travel Images/UIG/Getty Images

The Library of Congress has established a
Cataloging-in-Publication record for this title.

ISBN: 978-0-8041-2121-7

www.randomhouse.com/largeprint

FIRST LARGE PRINT EDITION

Printed in the United States of America

10 9 8 7 6 5 4 3 2 1

This Large Print edition published in accord with
the standards of the N.A.V.H.

For Augustus Eli Reinhardt IV
A special young man

ACKNOWLEDGMENTS

Thank you, Gina Centrello, Libby McQuire, Kim Hovey, Cindy Murray, Jennifer Hershey, Debbie Aroff, Carole Lowenstein, Matt Schwartz, Scott Shannon, and everyone in Art, Promotions, and Sales. The Random House team.

To Mark Tavani and Simon Lipskar, thank you for another great job.

A few special mentions: Grant Blackwood, a supertalented novelist, who helped with some of the early plotting; Meryl Moss and her extraordinary publicity team (especially Deb Zipf and Jeri-Ann Geller); Jessica Johns and Esther Garver, who continue to keep Steve Berry Enterprises running smoothly; John Cole at the Library of Congress for arranging an enlightening visit; and John Busbee, in Des Moines, who introduced me to Salisbury House. A special thanks to Shauna Summers, a fine editor at Random House, who helped with all things Mormon (though any mistakes that remain are mine).

As always, to my wife, Elizabeth, the most special of all.

I've dedicated novels to parents, children, grandchildren, an aunt, my old writers group, my editor, agents, and business associates. When Elizabeth and I married, included in the package was Augustus Eli Reinhardt IV. At the time he was four. Now he's a teenager. Eli worships his mother and his father. But I'd like to think he holds a small place for me, too. Like Cotton Malone, I'm not the most cuddly guy in the world.

But that doesn't mean we don't care.

So this one's for Eli.

Any people anywhere, being inclined and
having the power,
have the right to rise up and shake off the
existing government,
and form a new one that suits them better.
This is a most valuable, a most sacred right—
a right, which we hope and believe, is to liberate
the world.
Nor is this right confined to cases in which the
whole people
of an existing government may choose to
exercise it.
Any portion of such people, that can, may
revolutionize,
and make their own of so much of the territory
as they inhabit.

ABRAHAM LINCOLN
January 12, 1848

THE
LINCOLN
MYTH

PROLOGUE

★

Washington, D.C.
September 10, 1861

Abraham Lincoln kept his temper under control, but the woman standing across from him was taxing his patience.

"The general did only what all decent people believe to be right," she said.

Jesse Benton Fremont was the wife of General John Fremont, United States Army, the man in charge of all Union military affairs west of the Mississippi River. A Mexican War hero and renowned explorer, Fremont had received his latest command appointment in May. Then, a month ago, with the Civil War raging in the South, he unilaterally issued a proclamation emancipating all slaves of Missouri Rebels who'd taken up arms against the United States. That was bad enough, but Fremont's edict went even farther and declared that all prisoners of war would be shot.

"Madam," he said, his voice low. "Is it truly your husband's view that any captured Rebels be killed?"

"These men must know they are traitors to their country, and traitors have always been put to death."

"Do you realize that once that is begun, the Confederates will shoot who they hold of ours in retaliation. Man for man. Indefinitely."

"Sir, we did not start this rebellion."

The clock on the mantel told him it was nearing midnight. A note had arrived at the presidential mansion three hours ago, its message concise. Mrs. Fremont brings to the president from General Fremont a letter and some verbal communications, which she would be glad to deliver with as little delay as possible. If it suits the president's convenience will he name a time to receive them this evening or at some early hour tomorrow.

His response told her to come immediately.

They stood in the Red Parlor on the first floor, a chandelier burning brightly. He knew of this imposing woman. The daughter of a former U.S. senator, highly educated, raised in Washington, D.C., schooled in politics. She'd defied her parents and married Fremont at the age of seventeen, eventually birthing five children. She'd supported her husband during his explorations of the West and was there when he served as military governor of California and as one of that state's initial U.S. senators. She'd campaigned with him when he became, in 1856, the first presidential nominee of the new Republican party. He came to be known as the Pathfinder, and his candidacy had reawakened popular enthusiasm. And though he lost to James Buchanan, if Pennsylvania had voted differently he would have been elected.

So, for Lincoln, as the first Republican party president actually elected, appointing John Fremont commander of the West had been an easy choice.

Now he regretted it.

He wondered if life could be any worse.

The immense pride he'd felt in March, taking the oath as the sixteenth president, had been replaced with the agony of the Civil War. Eleven states had seceded from the Union and formed their own confederacy. They'd attacked Fort Sumter, forcing him to blockade all Southern ports and suspend the writ of habeas corpus. The Union army had been dispatched, but suffered a humiliating defeat at Bull Run—that crushing blow convincing him this conflict would be long and bloody.

Now Fremont and his grand emancipation.

He could sympathize with the general. Rebels had soundly defeated Union forces in southern Missouri and were advancing northward. Fremont

STEVE BERRY / 6

was isolated, with limited men and resources. The situation demanded action, so he'd placed Missouri under martial law. Then he'd gone too far, ordering the slaves from all Rebels freed.

Neither Lincoln himself, nor Congress had been so bold.

Several messages, and even a direct order, to modify the proclamation had been ignored. Now the general had dispatched his wife to deliver a letter and plead his case.

"Madam, there are considerations here far beyond those of Missouri. As you have reminded me, a war rages. Unfortunately, the issues that divide the opposing sides to that conflict are not so distinct."

Slavery being the main misunderstanding.

From Lincoln's standpoint slavery simply was not an issue. He'd already thrown the secessionists an offer, telling them that they could keep their slaves. They could even raise a new flag, send representatives to Montgomery, and have their confederacy—provided they allowed the collection of Northern tariffs in their ports. If the South became free of tariffs, Northern industrial interests would be crippled, the national government would be rendered broke. No armies would be required to defeat it. Tariffs were the country's main source of revenue. Without them, the North would flounder.

But the South had rejected his overtures, firing on Fort Sumter.

"Mr. President, I have traveled for three days in an overcrowded train, the weather hot and miserable. It was not a journey I enjoyed, but I came because the general wants you to understand that the only considerations relevant are those of the utmost importance to this nation. Rebels have taken arms against us. They must be stopped and slavery ended."

"I have written to the general, and he knows what I want done," he made clear.

"He feels he is at the great disadvantage of being opposed by people in whom you have every confidence."

A curious retort. "Who do you mean?"

"He thinks that your advisers, men closer to you than him, have a better hold on your ear."

"And that accounts for his disobeying my orders? Madam, his emancipation proclamation does not come within the range of military law or necessity. He has made a political decision, one that is not his to make. Just a few weeks ago I sent my personal secretary, Mr. Hay, to see the general, who asked him to modify the part of the proclamation that freed all slaves in Missouri. No answer was given to my request. Instead, the general has now sent you to speak to me directly."

Even worse, Hay's reports had made clear that

Fremont's command was rife with corruption, his troops on the verge of rebellion. Not surprising. Fremont was stubborn, hysterical, and rash. His whole career had been one fiasco after another. Back in 1856 he'd ignored the advice of political experts and made slavery that presidential campaign's main issue. But the country was not yet ready for such an uprooting. Sentiment wasn't right.

And it cost him a victory.

"The general's conviction," she said, "is that it will be long and dreadful work to conquer the Rebels by arms alone. To secure the support of foreign countries, other considerations have to be recognized. The general knows of the English feeling for gradual emancipation, and the strong wish to meet that feeling on the part of important men in the South. We cannot allow that to happen. As president, surely you know that we are on the eve of England, France, and Spain recognizing the South. England on account of her cotton interests. France because the emperor dislikes us—"

"You are quite a female politician."

"I am not ignorant of the world. Perhaps yourself, a man who barely laid claim to this great office, should be mindful of other people's opinions."

An insult he'd heard before. He'd won the 1860 election thanks to a fracture in the Democratic party, which stupidly had offered two candidates.

Then the upstart Constitutional Union party chose another of its own. Among them the three garnered 48% of the popular vote and split 123 electoral votes, which allowed his 40% and 180 electoral votes to claim victory. True, he was but a lawyer from Illinois, the extent of his national experience one term in the House of Representatives. He'd even lost the 1858 Illinois race for the U.S. Senate to his longtime nemesis Stephen Douglas. But now, at fifty-two years old, ensconced in the White House with a four-year term, he found himself at the center of the greatest constitutional crisis the nation had ever faced.

"I must say, madam, that I cannot be unmindful of others' thoughts, as I am barraged by them every day. The general should never have dragged the Negro into this war. This is a conflict for a great national object and the Negro has nothing to do with it."

"You are mistaken, sir."

He'd allowed this woman some latitude, mindful that she was merely defending her husband, as a wife should.

But now the Fremonts were **both** bordering on treason.

"Madam, the general's actions have caused Kentucky to rethink whether it will stay with the Union or join the Rebels. Maryland, Missouri, and several other border states are likewise reconsidering their positions. If this conflict be about the freeing of slaves, then we shall surely lose."

She opened her mouth to speak, but he silenced her with a lift of his hand.

"I have not left anyone in doubt. My task is to save the Union. I would save it the shortest way under the Constitution. The sooner the national authority can be restored, the nearer the Union will be the Union as it was. If I could save the Union without freeing any slave, I would do it. If I could save it by freeing all slaves, I would do it. If I could save it by freeing some and leaving others alone, I would also do that. What I do about slavery, and the colored race, I do because I believe it helps to save the Union. What I forbear, I forbear because I don't believe it would help to save the Union. I shall do less whenever I shall believe what I am doing hurts the cause, and I shall do more whenever I shall believe doing more will help the cause."

"Then you are not my president, sir. Nor would you be the president of those who voted for you."

"But I **am** president. So take this message back to the general. He was sent west to move the army to Memphis and keep advancing eastward. Those are still his orders. He shall either obey them or be removed from his post."

"I must warn you, sir, that it could be hard if you continue to oppose the general. He could set up for himself."

The federal treasury was empty. The War Department a mess. No Union army anywhere was
prepared to advance. And now this woman, and
her insolent husband, were threatening revolt? He
should have them both arrested. Unfortunately,
however, Fremont's unilateral emancipation had
become popular with abolitionists and liberal Re-
publicans who wanted slavery ended now. A bold
strike at their champion could be political suicide.

He said, "This meeting is over."

She threw him a glare, one that said she was
unaccustomed to being dismissed. But he ignored
her sneer and stepped across the room, opening
the door for her to leave. Hay, his personal secretary, was on duty outside, as was one of the stew-
ards. Mrs. Fremont passed Hay without saying a
word, and the steward led her away. He waited
until he heard the front door open, then close, before signaling for Hay to join him in the parlor.

"That is an impertinent soul," he said. "We
never even sat. She gave me no chance to offer her
a seat. She taxed me so violently with so many
things that I had to exercise all the awkward tact I
have to avoid quarreling with her."

"Her husband is no better. His command is a
failure."

He nodded. "Fremont's mistake is that he iso-
lates himself. He does not know what is going on
in the matter he is dealing with."

"And he refuses to listen."

"She actually threatened that he might set up his own government."

Hay shook his head in disgust.

He made a decision. "The general will be removed. But not until a suitable replacement is found. Locate one. Quietly, of course."

Hay nodded. "I understand."

He noticed a large envelope that his trusted aide held and motioned toward it. "What is that?"

"It arrived late today from Pennsylvania. Wheatland."

He knew the location. The family home of his predecessor, James Buchanan. A man vilified by the North. Many said he paved the way for South Carolina to secede, blaming that act on the **intemperate interference of the northern people with the question of slavery.**

Strong, partisan words from a president.

Then Buchanan went farther and said that slave states should be left alone to manage their domestic institutions in their own way. Northern states should also repeal all laws that encouraged slaves to become fugitives. If not, then **the injured states, after having first used all peaceful and constitutional means to effect redress, would be justified in revolutionary resistance to the government of the Union.**

Tantamount to a presidential endorsement of rebellion.

"What does the former president want?"

"I did not open it." Hay handed him the envelope. Scrawled across the front were the words FOR THE EYES OF MR. LINCOLN ONLY. "I respected his wishes."

He was tired, and Mrs. Fremont had sapped what little strength remained from a long day. But he was curious. Buchanan had been so eager to leave office. On Inauguration Day, during their carriage ride back from the Capitol, he'd made his intentions clear. **If you are as happy in entering the White House as I shall feel on returning to Wheatland, you are a happy man indeed.**

"You may go," he said to Hay. "I'll study this, then be off to bed myself."

His secretary left, and he sat alone inside the parlor. He broke the wax seal on the envelope and slid out two pages. One, a parchment—brown with age, water-stained, dry and brittle. The second, a soft vellum, newer, the black ink fresh, in a firm masculine hand.

He read the vellum first.

It is a sorry place, the country which I left you, and for that I apologize. My first mistake was declaring at my inauguration

that I would not become a candidate for
reelection. My motive was pure. I wanted
nothing to influence my conduct in
administering the government except the
desire to ably and faithfully serve and to
live in grateful memory of my countrymen.
But that proved not to be the case. On
my return to the White House the day I
accepted the oath a sealed package awaited
me, similar in shape and size to this one.
Inside was a note from my predecessor, Mr.
Pierce, along with the second document
I have enclosed. Pierce wrote that the
enclosure was first given to Washington
himself, who decided that it would be
passed from president to president, each
man free to do with it as he saw fit. I know
you and many others blame me for the
current national conflict. But before you
criticize any further, read the document.
To my credit, I tried in every way possible
to fulfill its mandate. I listened carefully
to your speech on Inauguration Day. You
called the Union explicitly perpetual in
name and text. Don't be so sure. All is not
as it seems. My initial intentions were not
to pass this on. Instead, I planned to set it
afire. Over the past few months, away from
the turmoil of government and the pressures

of the national crisis, I have come to believe
that the truth should not be avoided. When
South Carolina broke the Union I stated
publicly that I could be the last president
of the United States. You openly called that
comment ludicrous. Perhaps you will see
that I was not as foolish as you thought. I
now feel that my duty has been faithfully
executed, though it may have been
imperfectly performed. Whatever the result,
I shall carry to my grave the belief that I at
least meant well for my country.

He looked up from the sheet. What a strange
lament. And a message? Passed down from president to president? One withheld by Buchanan
until now?

He rubbed his weary eyes and brought the second sheet closer. Its ink had faded, the script more
stylish and difficult to read.

Signatures graced the bottom.

He scanned the entire page.

Then read the words again.

More carefully.

Sleep was no longer important.

What had Buchanan written?

All is not as it seems.

"This cannot be," he muttered.

PART ONE

ONE

✯

One glance and Cotton Malone knew there was trouble.

The Øresund, which separated the northern Danish island of Zealand from the southern Swedish province of Scania, usually one of the busiest waterways in the world, was light on traffic. Only two boats in sight across the gray-blue water—his and the fast-approaching profile of the one slicing toward them.

He'd noticed the craft just after they'd left the dock at Landskrona on the Swedish side of the channel. A red-and-white twenty-footer with dual inboards. His boat was a rental, secured at the Copenhagen waterfront on the Danish side, a fifteen-footer with a single outboard. The engine howled as he plowed through the moderate surf, the skies clear, the crisp evening air devoid of breeze—lovely fall weather for Scandinavia.

Three hours ago he was working in his bookshop at Højbro Plads. He'd planned on dinner at the Café Norden, as he did almost every evening. But a call from Stephanie Nelle, his former boss at the Justice Department, changed all that.

"I need a favor," she said. "I wouldn't ask if it wasn't an emergency. There's a man named Barry Kirk. Short black hair, pointy nose. I need you to go get him."

He heard the urgency in her request.

"I have an agent en route, but he's been delayed. I don't know when he'll get there, and this man has to be found. Now."

"I don't suppose you're going to tell me why."

"I can't. But you're the closest to him. He's across the water in Sweden, waiting for someone to come get him."

"Sounds like trouble."

"I have an agent missing."

He hated to hear those words.

"Kirk may know where he is, so it's important to secure him quickly. I'm hoping we're ahead of any problems. Just bring him back to your shop and keep him there until my guy comes for him."

"I'll take care of it."

"One more thing, Cotton. Take your gun."

He'd immediately gone upstairs to his fourth-floor apartment above his bookshop and found the knapsack beneath his bed, the one he always kept ready with identification, money, a phone, and his Magellan Billet–issued Beretta, which Stephanie had allowed him to keep when he retired.

The gun now nestled against the small of his back, beneath his jacket.

"They're getting closer," Barry Kirk said.

Like he didn't know that. Two engines were always better than one.

He held the wheel steady, his throttle three-quarters of the way engaged. He decided to max out the power and the bow rose as the V-hull gained speed. He glanced back. Two men occupied the other boat—one driving, the other standing with a gun.

This just kept getting better and better.

They were not yet halfway across the channel, still on the Swedish side, heading diagonally southwest toward Copenhagen. He could have taken a car, crossing the Øresund Bridge that connected Denmark to Sweden, but that would have taken an extra hour. Water was faster and Stephanie was in a hurry, so he'd rented the bowrider runabout from the same shop he always used. Far cheaper to rent than to own a boat, especially considering how little he ventured out on the water.

"What do you plan to do?"

A stupid question. Kirk was definitely annoying. He'd located him pacing the docks, exactly where Stephanie had said he'd be waiting, anxious to leave. Code words had been arranged so they both would know they'd found the right person. **Joseph** for him. **Moroni** for Kirk.

Odd choices.

"Do you know who those men are?" he asked.

"They want to kill me."

He kept the boat pointed toward Denmark, its hull breasting the waves with jarring lunges, throwing spray.

"And why do they want to kill you?" he asked over the engine's roar.

"Who are you, exactly?"

He cut a quick glance at Kirk. "The guy who's going to save your sorry ass."

The other boat was less than thirty yards way.

He scanned the horizon in every direction and spotted no other craft. Dusk was gathering, the azure sky being replaced by gray.

A pop.

Then another.

He whirled.

The second man in the pursuing boat was firing at them.

"Get down," he yelled to Kirk. He ducked, too, keeping their course and speed steady.

Two more shots.

One thudded into the fiberglass to his left.

The other boat was now fifty feet away. He decided to give his pursuers a little pause. He reached back, found his gun, and sent a bullet their way.

The other boat veered to starboard.

They were more than a mile from the Danish shore, nearly at the Øresund's center. The second boat looped around and was now approaching from the right on a path that would cut directly in front of them. He saw that the pistol had been replaced with a short-barreled automatic rifle.

Only one thing to do.

He adjusted course straight for them.

Time for a game of chicken.

A burst of gunfire cut across the air. He dove to the deck, keeping one hand on the wheel. Rounds whizzed by overhead and a few penetrated the bow. He risked a look. The other boat had veered to port, swinging around, preparing to attack from the rear, where the open deck offered little cover.

He decided the direct approach was best.

But it would have to be timed just right.

He kept the boat racing ahead at nearly full throttle. The second craft's bow still headed his way.

"Keep down," he told Kirk again.

No worry existed that his order would be disobeyed. Kirk clung to the deck, below the side panels. Malone still held his Beretta but kept it out of sight. The other boat narrowed the distance between them.

And fast.

Fifty yards.

Forty.

Thirty.

He yanked the throttle back and brought the engine to idle. Speed vanished. The bow sank into the water. They glided for a few yards then came to a stop. The other boat kept coming.

Parallel.

The man with the rifle aimed.

But before he could fire, Malone shot him in the chest.

The other boat raced past.

He reengaged the throttle and the engine sprang to life.

Inside the second craft he saw the driver reach down and find the rifle. A big loop brought the boat back on an intercept course.

His feint worked once.

But would not again.

Nearly a mile's worth of water still lay between them and the Danish coast, and he could not outrun the other vessel. Maybe outmaneuver, but for how long? No. He'd have to stand and fight.

He stared ahead and grabbed his bearings.

He was five miles or so north of Copenhagen's outskirts, near the spot where his old friend Henrik Thorvaldsen had once lived.

"Look at that," he heard Kirk say.

He turned back.

The other boat was a hundred yards away, bearing down. But out of an ever-dimming western sky a high-wing, single-engine Cessna had swooped down. Its trademark tricycle landing gear, no more than six feet clear of the water's surface, raked the other craft, its wheels nearly smacking the driver who disappeared downward, his hands apparently off the wheel as the bow lurched left.

Malone used the moment to head for his attacker.

The plane banked high, gained altitude, and swung around for another pass. He wondered if the pilot realized that there was an automatic weapon about to be aimed skyward. He headed straight for the trouble, as fast as his engine allowed. The other boat had now stopped in the water, its occupant's attention totally on the plane.

Which allowed Malone to draw close.

He was grateful for the distraction, but that assistance was about to turn into disaster. He saw the automatic rifle being aimed at the plane.

"Get up here," he screamed to Kirk.

The man did not move.

"Don't make me come get you."

Kirk rose.

"Hold the wheel. Keep us going straight."

"Me? What?"

"Do it."

Kirk grabbed hold.

Malone stepped to the stern, planted his feet, and aimed the gun.

The plane kept coming. The other man was ready with his rifle. Malone knew he'd have only a few chances from a bumpy deck. The other man suddenly realized that the boat was coming at the same time as the plane.

Both a threat.

What to do?

Malone fired twice. Missed.

A third shot hit the other craft.

The man darted right, deciding the boat now posed the greater problem. Malone's fourth shot found the man's chest, which propelled the body over the side and into the water.

The plane roared by, its wheels low and tight.

Both he and Kirk ducked.

He grabbed hold of the wheel and slowed the throttle, turning back toward their enemy. They approached from the stern, his gun ready. A body floated in the water, another lay on the deck. Nobody else was on board.

"Aren't you a ton of trouble," he said to Kirk.

Quiet had returned, only the engine's throaty idle disturbing the silence. Water slapped both hulls. He should contact some local authority. Swedes? Danes? But with Stephanie and the Magellan Billet involved, he knew partnering with locals was not an option.

She hated doing it.

He stared up into the dim sky and saw the Cessna, now back up to a couple thousand feet, making a pass directly over them.

Someone jumped from the plane.

A chute opened, catching air, its occupant guiding himself downward in a tight spiral. Malone had parachuted several times and could see that this skydiver knew the drill, banking the canopy, navigating a course straight for them, feet knifing through the water less than fifty yards away.

Malone eased the boat over and came up alongside.

The man who hoisted himself aboard was maybe late twenties. His blond hair appeared more mowed than cut, the bright face clean-shaven and warmed by a wide, toothy smile. He wore a dark pullover shirt and jeans, matted to a muscular frame.

"That water is cold," the young man said. "Sure appreciate you waiting around for me. Sorry I was late."

Malone pointed to the fading sound of a prop as the plane kept flying east. "Someone on board?"

"Nope. Autopilot. But there isn't much fuel left. It'll fall into the Baltic in a few minutes."

"Expensive waste."

The young man shrugged. "The dude I stole it from needed to lose it."

"Who are you?"

"Oh, sorry about that. Sometimes I forget my manners."

A wet hand was offered.

"Name's Luke Daniels. Magellan Billet."

TWO

★

KALUNDBORG, DENMARK
8:00 P.M.

JOSEPE SALAZAR WAITED WHILE THE MAN GATH-
ered himself. His prisoner lay semi-conscious in
the cell, but awake enough to hear him say, "End
this."

The man lifted his head from the dusty stone
floor. "I've wondered . . . for the past three days . . .
how you can be so cruel. You are a believer . . . in
the Heavenly Father. A man . . . supposedly of
God."

He saw no contradiction. "The prophets have
faced threats as great as or greater than those I face
today. Yet they never wavered from doing what
had to be done."

"You speak the truth," the angel told him.

He glanced up. The image floated a few feet away, standing in a loose white robe, bathed in brilliance, pure as lightning, brighter than anything he'd ever seen.

"Do not hesitate, Josepe. None of the prophets ever hesitated in doing what had to be done."

He knew that his prisoner could not hear the angel. No one could, save for him. But the man on the floor noticed that his gaze had drifted to the cell's back wall.

"What are you looking at?"

"A glorious sight."

"He cannot comprehend what we know."

He faced his prisoner. "I have Kirk."

He hadn't received confirmation yet on what happened in Sweden, but his men had reported that the target was in sight. Finally. After three days. Which was how long this man had lain in this cell, without food or water. The skin was bruised and pale, lips cracked, nose broken, eyes hollow. Probably a couple of ribs broken, too. To increase the torment a bucket of water lay just beyond the bars, within sight but not reach.

"Press him," the angel commanded. **"He must know that we will not tolerate insolence. The people who sent him must know we will fight. There is much to be done and they have placed themselves in the middle of our path. Break him."**

He always accepted the angel's advice. How could he not? He came directly from Heavenly Father. This prisoner, though, was a spy. Sent by the enemy.

"We have always dealt with spies harshly," the angel said. **"In the beginning there were many and they inflicted great harm. We must return that harm."**

"But am I not to love him?" he asked the apparition. "He is still a son of God."

"Who are you . . . talking . . . to?"

He faced the prisoner and asked what he wanted to know, "Who do you work for?"

No reply.

"Tell me."

He heard his voice rise. Unusual for him. He was known to be soft-spoken, always projecting a placid demeanor—which he worked hard to maintain. Decorum was a lost art, his father had many times said.

The bucket of water lay at his feet.

He filled a ladle, then tossed its contents through the bars, soaking his prisoner's bruised face. The man's tongue tried to savor what little refreshment it could find. But three days of thirst would take time to quench.

"Tell me what I want to know."

"More water."

Pity had long abandoned him. He was charged with a sacred duty, and the fate of millions depended on the decisions he would make.

"**There must be a blood atonement,**" the angel said. "**It is the only way.**"

Doctrine proclaimed that there were sins for which men could not receive forgiveness in this world, or in the world to come. But if they had their eyes opened, made able to see their true condition, surely they would be willing to have their blood spilled in forgiveness of those sins.

"**The blood of the son of God was shed for sins committed by men,**" the angel said. "**And there remain sins that can be atoned for by an offering upon an altar, as in ancient days. But there are also sins that the blood of a lamb or a calf or a turtledove cannot remit. These must be atoned for by the blood of the man.**"

Sins such as murder, adultery, lying, covenant breaking, and apostasy.

He crouched down and stared at the defiant soul on the other side of the bars. "You cannot stop me. No one can. What will happen is going to happen. But I am prepared to show you some consideration. Simply tell me who you work for and your mission, and this water is yours."

He gathered up another full ladle and held it out.

The man lay flat on his stomach, arms extended,

wet face to the floor. Slowly, he rolled over onto his spine, eyes to the ceiling.

He and the angel waited.

"I'm an agent . . . for the . . . Justice Department. We're all . . . over you."

The U.S. government. For 180 years it had been nothing but an impediment.

But how much did his enemies know?

The man rolled his head toward him, tired eyes focused tight. "Killing me will accomplish . . . nothing, except bring you . . . more trouble."

"He lies," the angel said. "He thinks we can be frightened."

True to his word he slipped the ladle through the bars. The man grabbed the offering and tossed the water into his mouth. He slid the bucket closer, and the man shoveled more liquid down his dry throat.

"Do not waver," the angel said. "He has committed a sin that he knows will deprive him of that exaltation he desires. He cannot attain it without shedding his blood. By having his blood shed he will atone for that sin and be saved and exalted with God. There is not a man or woman who would not say, 'Shed my blood that I may be saved and exalted with God.'"

No, there was not.

"There have been many instances, Josepe, where men have been righteously slain in order to atone for their sins. I have witnessed scores of people for whom there would have been a chance of exaltation if their lives had been taken, their blood spilled as a smoking incense to the Almighty. But they are now angels to the Devil."

Unlike this emissary, who spoke the word of God.

"This is loving our neighbor as ourselves. If he needs help, help him. If he wants salvation and it is necessary to spill his blood on the earth in order that he may be saved, spill it. If you have committed a sin requiring the shedding of blood, do not be satisfied nor rest until your blood should be spilled so that you might gain the salvation you desire. That is the way to love mankind."

He stared away from the apparition and asked the prisoner, "Do you seek salvation?"

"Why do you care?"

"Your sins are great."

"As are yours."

But his were different. To lie in search of the truth was not a lie. To kill for another's salvation was an act of love. He owed this sinner eternal peace, so he reached beneath his jacket and found the gun.

The prisoner's eyes went wide. He tried to retreat, but there was nowhere to hide.

Killing him would be easy.

"**Not yet,**" the angel said.

He lowered the gun.

"**We still have need of him.**"

The apparition then ascended until his form disappeared into the ceiling, the cell left dull, as it had been before the light appeared.

A kindly smile played on his lips.

His eyes shone with a new light, which he attributed to heavenly gratitude for his obedience. He checked his watch and calculated back eight hours.

Noontime in Utah.

Elder Rowan must be informed.

THREE

★

Senator Thaddeus Rowan stepped from the Land Rover and allowed the sun to soak him with a familiar warmth. He'd lived in Utah all of his life, now its senior U.S. senator, a position he'd held for thirty-three years. He was a man of power and influence—important enough that the secretary of the interior had personally flown out to escort him today.

"It's a beautiful place," the secretary said to him.

The southern half of Utah belonged to the federal government, places with names like Arches, Capitol Reef, and Bryce Canyon. Here, inside Zion National Park, 147,000 acres stretched from northwest to southeast between Interstate 15 and Highway 9. The Paiute once lived here but, starting in 1863, Latter-day Saints, moving south from Salt Lake, displaced them and gave the desolate locale a name—Zion. Isaac Behunin, the Saint who first settled here with his sons, reported that **a man can worship God among these great cathedrals as well as in any man-made church.** But after a visit in 1870, Brigham Young disagreed and dubbed the locale Not Zion, a nickname that stuck.

Rowan had flown the 250 miles south from Salt Lake by helicopter, landing inside the park with the secretary, the local superintendent waiting for them. Being chairman of the Senate Committee on Appropriations came with many perks. Not the least of which was the fact that not a dime of federal money was spent on anything, anywhere, unless he okayed it.

"It's magnificent country," he said to the secretary.

He'd many times hiked this red-rock desert filled with slot canyons so tight the sun never hit the bottom. Towns on the outskirts were populated with Saints, or Mormons as many people liked to call them. Some Saints, himself included, did not particularly care for the label. It came from the mid–19th century when prejudice and hate forced them to gradually flee west, until they found the isolated Salt Lake basin. His ancestors had been with the first wagons that entered on July 24,

1847. Nothing there then but green grass and, if legend was to be believed, a single tree.

A lonely splendor. That's how one Saint had described it.

When their leader Brigham Young entered, ill with fever, lying in the bed of one of the wagons, he supposedly rose up and proclaimed, **This is the place**.

Tens of thousands more settlers followed, avoiding orthodox routes, making the trip along trails blazed by pioneering Saints, replanting crops along the way so later caravans would also have food. On that day, though, in the first wave—143 men, three women, two children, 70 wagons, one cannon, one boat, 93 horses, 52 mules, 66 oxen, 19 cows, 17 dogs, and some chickens—found a home.

"It's just up this ridge," the superintendent said, pointing ahead.

Only the three men had ridden from the helicopter in the Land Rover. Each wore ankle boots, jeans, a long-sleeved shirt, and a hat. At seventy-one years old his body remained strong—his legs ready for the forbidding landscape that spread in all directions.

"What are we," he said, "forty miles inside the park?"

The superintendent nodded. "Closer to fifty. This area is highly restricted. We don't allow hiking or camping here. The slot canyons are too dangerous."

He knew the numbers. Three million people a year visited Zion, making it one of Utah's most popular attractions. Permits were required to do anything and everything, so many that off-roaders, hunters, and anti-conservationists had called for an easing. Privately he agreed, but he'd stayed out of that fight.

The superintendent led the way into a sheer-walled canyon crowded with bigtooth maples. Wild mustard and sturdy creosote bush mixed with tufts of wiry grass. High overhead in the clear sky a soaring condor drifted in and out of view.

"It was because of trespassers," the superintendent said, "that all this came to light. Three people illegally came into this portion of the park last week. One slipped and broke his leg and we had to med-evac him out. That's when we noticed that."

The superintendent pointed at a dark slit in the rock wall. Rowan knew that caves in the sandstone were common, thousands littered southern Utah.

"Back in August," the secretary explained, "there was a flash flood in this area. A good soaking for three days. We think the opening was exposed then. Before that, it had remained sealed."

He gazed at the bureaucrat. "And what is your interest here?"

"To ensure the chairman of the Senate Committee on Appropriations is happy with the services of the Interior Department."

He doubted that, since President Danny Daniels' administration had, for the past seven years, cared little about what the senior senator from Utah thought. They were of different parties, his in control of Congress and Daniels' holding the White House. Usually that kind of split encouraged cooperation and compromise. But lately any amicable spirit had ebbed. **Gridlock** was the popular term. Complicating matters was the fact that Daniels was entering the twilight of his two terms, and a successor was unclear.

Either party had a shot.

But elections did not interest him any longer. He had bigger plans.

They approached the opening and the superintendent dropped his backpack and found three flashlights.

"These'll help."

Rowan accepted the light. "Lead the way."

They squeezed through, entering a spacious cavern, the ceiling twenty feet high. The beam of his light examined the entrance and he saw that it had formerly been much wider and taller.

"That was once a good-sized opening," the superintendent said. "Like an oversized garage door. But it was deliberately covered over."

"How do you know that?"

The man motioned ahead with his light. "I'll show you. But be careful. This is a perfect place for snakes."

That he'd already surmised. Sixty years of exploring rural Utah had taught him respect for both the land and its inhabitants.

Fifty feet farther inside forms rose from the shadows. He counted three wagons. Broad-wheeled. Maybe ten feet long, five wide. And tall, the bows and cylindrical canvas covers long gone. He stepped close and tested one. Solid wood, save for iron rims on the wheels, encrusted with corrosion. Teams of four to six horses would have drawn them, or sometimes mules and oxen.

"Vintage 19th century," the superintendent said. "I know something about them. The desert air, and being sealed inside here, helped with their preservation. They're intact, which is rare."

He approached and saw the beds were empty.

"They would have come in through the opening," the superintendent said. "So it had to be much larger."

"There's more," the secretary said.

He followed a beam of light into the darkness

and spotted rubble. Pieces of more wagons, piled high.

"They destroyed them," the superintendent said. "My guess is there were maybe twenty or more before they started hacking them up."

Twenty-two, actually. But he said nothing. Instead, he followed the superintendent around the debris pile where their lights revealed skeletons. He approached, loose gravel crunching like dry snow beneath his boots, and counted three, noticing immediately how they died.

Bullet holes to the skull.

Scraps of their clothes remained, as did two leather hats.

The superintendent motioned with his light. "This one lived a little longer."

He saw a fourth victim, lying against the cavern wall. No hole to the skull. Instead the rib cage was shattered.

"Shot to the chest," the superintendent said. "But he lived long enough to write this."

The light revealed writing on the wall, like petroglyphs he'd seen in caverns in other parts of Utah.

He bent down and read the broken script.

FJELDSTED HYDE WOODRUFF EGAN
DAMNATION TO THE PROPHET
FORGET US NOT

He instantly realized the significance of the surnames.

But only he, one of the twelve apostles of the Church of Jesus Christ of Latter-day Saints, would know their identity.

"It was the reference to the prophet that caused us to call you," the secretary said.

He gathered himself and stood. "You're right. These men were Saints."

"That was our thought, too."

Throughout human history God had always dealt with His children through prophets. Men like Noah, Abraham, and Moses. In 1830, Joseph Smith had been anointed by heaven as a latter-day prophet to restore a fullness of the gospel in preparation for the second coming of Christ. So Smith founded a new church. Seventeen men since then had each taken the title of prophet and president. Every one of those seventeen had risen from the Quorum of Twelve Apostles, which stood just below the prophet in the church hierarchy.

His plan was to become the eighteenth.

And this discovery might just help.

He gazed around the cavern and imagined what had happened here in 1857.

Everything about this place fit the legend.

Only now it had been proven true.

FOUR

★

Copenhagen, Denmark
8:40 P.M.

MALONE PILOTED THE BOAT WHILE LUKE DANIELS, his clothes soaked from the end of his skydive, kept low to avoid the briskness that raced across the windscreen.

"You a regular jumper?" he asked.

"I've got over a hundred in the logbook, but I haven't landed in the water for a while."

The younger man pointed at Kirk, who sat huddled near the stern, and yelled over the motor's roar, "You're a pain in my ass."

"Care to tell me why?" Malone asked.

"What did Stephanie tell you?"

Good move, answering a question with a question. "Just that an agent is missing and this guy may know where he is."

"That's right. And this one here ran like a scalded dog."

"And why is that?"

"'Cause he's a snitch. And nobody likes a snitch." Luke faced Kirk. "When we get to shore you and I are goin' to have a chat."

Kirk said nothing.

Luke stepped closer but stayed down out of the wind, knees flexed in response to the pitch and pound. "Tell me, Pappy, are you really as good as everyone says you are?"

"I ain't as good as I once was, but I'm as good once as I ever was."

"You know the song. I love Toby Keith. Saw him in concert about five years ago. Didn't take you for a country music man."

"I'm not sure how to take you."

"Just a humble servant of the U.S. government."

"That's my line."

"I know. Stephanie told me to say that."

"You understand," he said, "that plane of yours was about to be sprayed with automatic rifle fire. Charging so low was foolish."

"I saw the rifle. But he was standing on a swaying boat, and it looked like you needed help."

"Are you always that reckless?"

He throttled the engine back as they approached the Copenhagen waterfront.

"You got to admit, that was pretty cool flying. Those wheels weren't, what, six feet off the water."

"I've seen better."

Luke grabbed his chest in mock pain. "Oh, Pappy, you cut me to the core. I know you were once a navy top gun. A fighter jock. But give me a morsel. Somethin'. After all, I saved your hide."

"Really now? Is that what you did?"

In another life Malone had worked as one of Stephanie Nelle's original twelve agents at the Magellan Billet. He was a Georgetown-trained lawyer and a former navy commander. Forty-seven years old now. But he still had his hair, his nerve, and a sharp mind. His sturdy frame bore the scars of being wounded several times in the line of duty, which was one reason why he'd retired early three years ago. Now he owned an old-book shop in Copenhagen, where he was supposed to stay out of trouble.

"Go ahead. Admit it," Luke said. "It was going to be tough to get away from those guys. I saved your ass."

He cut the engine and they eased past the Danish royal residence, then the pier at Nyhavn, swinging starboard into a placid canal. He docked just beyond the Christiansborg Palace near a spate of outdoor cafés where loud patrons were eating, drinking, smoking. The crowded square fifty yards away was Højbro Plads. Home.

The engine quit and he turned, swinging a right uppercut that slammed into Luke's jaw, dropping the agent to the deck. The youngster shook off the blow and sprang to his feet, ready for a fight.

"First off," Malone said. "Don't call me Pappy. Second, I don't like your cocksure attitude, it can get people killed. Third, who were those men trying to kill us? And, finally"—he pointed at Kirk—"who the hell is he snitching on?"

He caught the look in the younger man's eyes, which said, **I so want to jostle with you.**

But there was something else.

Restraint.

Not a single one of his questions had been answered. He was being played and didn't like it. "Is there really a man missing?"

"Damn right. And this guy can show us the way."

"Give me your phone."

"How do you know I have one?"

"It's in your back pocket. I saw it. Magellan Billet issue. One hundred percent waterproof, which they weren't in my day."

Luke found the unit and unlocked it.

"Call Stephanie."

The number was entered.

STEVE BERRY / 48

He gripped the phone and said, "Take Kirk and wait over by that café. I need to speak with her in private."

"I'm not real keen on takin' orders from retired guys."

"Call it repayment for fishing you out of the water. Now go."

He waited for an answer to his call and watched as Luke and Kirk hopped from the boat. He wasn't an idiot. He realized that his ex-boss had schooled this upstart on how to handle him. Probably told him to push, but not push him away. Otherwise a hotshot like Luke Daniels would have been all over him. But that would have been okay. He hadn't had a good fight in a while.

"How long did it take before you punched him?" Stephanie asked after the fifth ring.

"I actually waited a little longer than I should have. And I just killed two bad guys."

He told her what had happened.

"Cotton, I get it. You don't have a dog in this fight. But I really do have a missing man, who has a wife and three kids. I need to find him."

She knew what would work on him.

He spotted Kirk and Luke fifty yards away. He should have waited until they were inside his bookshop to make the call, but he was anxious to know the situation so he kept his voice low, turning back toward the canal away from the cafés.

"Barry Kirk knows things," she said in his ear. "I need him debriefed, then help me out here. You and Luke go find my agent."

"Is this frat boy you sent any good?"

"Actually, he never went to college. But if he had, I assure you he wouldn't have been in any fraternity. Not the type."

He figured Luke was maybe twenty-seven, twenty-eight, probably ex-military, as Stephanie liked to draw from their ranks. But his lack of respect and reckless moves seemed contrary to any form of institutionalized discipline.

And he wasn't a lawyer.

But he knew Stephanie had been gradually relaxing that rule for her agents.

"I imagine he's a handful," he said into the phone.

"To say the least. But he's good. Which is why I tolerate his . . . overconfidence. Kind of like someone else who once worked for me."

"Those men were right there," he said to her. "On the water. Ready for us. That means either they were lucky, Johnny-on-the-spot, or somebody knew you called me. Did your missing man know where Kirk was headed?"

"No. We told Kirk to head to Sweden."

He knew she was asking herself the same question.

How **did** those men know to be there?

"I assume you're only going to tell me what you think I need to know."

"You know the drill. This isn't your operation. Just see about my man, then you're done."

"I'll handle it."

He ended the call, hopped onto shore, and walked toward Luke, saying, "You got yourself a partner for the night."

"Do you have a pad and pen I could borrow so I can take notes on what I learn?"

"You always such a smart-ass?"

"You always so warm and friendly?"

"Somebody's got to see to it the kids don't get hurt."

"You don't have to worry about me, Pappy. I can take care of myself."

"Thought I told you not to call me that."

Luke's back straightened. "Yeah. I heard you. And I gave you, per my orders, one free punch. There won't be any more freebies."

His green eyes threw the kid a challenge.

Which seemed to be accepted.

But not now. Maybe later.

He pointed at Kirk. "Let's hear what this snitch has to say."

FIVE

⭐

STEPHANIE NELLE GLANCED AT HER WATCH. HER day had started at 6:00 A.M.—noon in Denmark—and it was far from over. Of her twelve agents, nine were currently on assignment. The other three were cycled off on downtime. Contrary to spy novels and action movies, agents did not work twenty-four hours a day, seven days a week. Most had spouses and children, lives outside of work. Which was good. The job was stressful enough without compounding it with maniacal obsession.

She'd founded the Magellan Billet sixteen years ago. This was her baby, and she'd nursed it through both adolescence and puberty. Now it was a fully grown intelligence team, credited with some of America's most recent successes.

Right now, though, only one thought filled her mind.

The agent missing in Denmark.

She glanced at the clock on the corner of her desk and realized she'd skipped both breakfast and lunch. Her stomach was growling so she decided to grab a bite in the building's cafeteria, three floors below.

She left her office.

Everything was quiet.

By design, the Magellan Billet was sparsely staffed. Besides her twelve operatives, the division employed five office staff and three aides. She'd insisted it be kept small. Fewer eyes and ears meant fewer leaks. Never had the Billet's security been compromised. None of the original twelve agents remained on the payroll—Malone was the last to leave four years ago. On average she replaced a person a year. But she'd been lucky. All of her recruits had been excellent, her administrative problems few and far between.

She exited through the main door and walked toward the elevators.

The building was located in a quiet north Atlanta office park, home also to divisions of the Departments of the Interior and Health and Human Services. At her insistence the Magellan Billet had been intentionally tucked away, nondescript letters on its door announcing JUSTICE DEPARTMENT TASK FORCE.

She pressed the button and waited for the elevator to arrive.

The doors opened and a thin man, with a long sharp face and bushy silver hair, strolled out.

Edwin Davis.

Like her, he was career civil service, starting two decades ago at the State Department where three secretaries had used him to whip their ailing departments into line. He possessed a doctorate in international relations and was blessed with an uncanny political sense. A folksy, courteous man people tended to underestimate, he'd been working as a deputy national security adviser when President Danny Daniels elevated him to White House chief of staff.

She instantly wondered what was important enough for Davis to fly five hundred miles from Washington, D.C., unannounced. Her boss was the U.S. attorney general, and protocol mandated that he be included in any chain of communication from the White House.

Yet that had not happened.

Was this business? Or a social call? Davis **was** a close friend. They'd endured a lot together.

"Were you going somewhere?" he asked.

"To the cafeteria."

"We'll both go."

"Am I going to regret this?"

"Possibly. But it has to be done."

"You realize the last time you and I stood right here, at this same spot, and had a conversation just like this, we both were almost killed."

"But we won that fight."

She smiled. "That we did."

They descended to the cafeteria and found an empty table. She munched on carrot sticks and sipped cranberry juice while Davis downed a bottled water. Her appetite had vanished.

"How is the president?" she asked.

She and Danny Daniels had not spoken in three months.

"He's looking forward to retirement."

Daniels' second term ended soon. His political career was over. But he'd had quite a ride from a small-town Tennessee councilman to two terms as president of the United States. Along the way, though, he lost both a daughter and a wife.

"He'd like to hear from you," Davis said.

And she'd like to call. But it was better this way. At least until his term was over. "I will. When the time is right."

She and Daniels had discovered that feelings existed between them, an attachment perhaps born from the many battles they'd endured. Neither of them was sure of anything. But he was still the president of the United States. Her boss. And it was better they keep some distance. "You didn't come here just to pass that message along. So get to the point, Edwin."

A crease of amusement touched her friend's face. She knew he was nearly old enough for Social Security, but his youthful physique cast the pose of a much younger man.

"I understand you've drawn some interest from Capitol Hill."

That she had.

Six written requests for classified data from the Senate Committee on Appropriations had arrived last week. Which wasn't uncommon. Congress routinely sought information from the intelligence community. If the particular department or agency was uncooperative, the "requests" were followed by subpoenas, which could not be ignored without a court fight. Public brawls over classified information were rare. Congress had to be placated. After all, they held the purse strings. So usually disputes were privately compromised. These six, though, had not left room for negotiation.

"They want anything and everything to do with my agency," she said. "Top-to-bottom. Financial, field reports, internal analysis, you name it. That's unprecedented, Edwin. Nearly all of that stuff is classified. I passed it on to the attorney general."

"Who passed it to me. I've come to tell you that those requests relate to that favor I asked of you on Josepe Salazar."

Six months ago a call from Davis had started a Billet inquiry into Salazar. The White House wanted a complete dossier, including all financial, business, and political associations. From the cradle to the present. Salazar held both a Danish and a Spanish passport, thanks to his parents who'd hailed from different countries. He lived half of the year in Spain, the other in Denmark. He was an international businessman who'd turned over everyday control of his multibillion-euro ventures to others so he could devote himself solely to his duties as an elder in the Mormon church. By all accounts he was devout, possessed no criminal record, and had lived an exemplary life. That he'd earned the attention of the White House had raised a multitude of questions in her mind. But being the loyal public servant she was, she hadn't asked a single one.

A mistake.

Which she'd finally realized three days ago, when her man sent to Europe to compile the Salazar dossier disappeared.

And even more so after just talking with Malone.

"My agent working on Salazar has disappeared," she said. "I've got people on the ground, right now, tracking him down. What have you gotten me into, Edwin?"

"I had no idea. What happened?"

"The situation escalated. One of Salazar's associates, a guy named Barry Kirk, made contact with my man. He had inside information and even claimed that his boss might have killed someone. We couldn't ignore that. We now have Kirk in custody, though two of Salazar's men were killed in the process. Cotton shot them."

"How'd you manage to get him involved?"

Davis and Malone had worked together before, too.

"He was nearby and doesn't like our men going missing, either."

"There's a connection between Josepe Salazar and Senator Thaddeus Rowan."

"And you're just now telling me this?"

Rowan was chairman of the Senate Committee on Appropriations. All six of the requests for information bore his signature.

"It wasn't my idea to withhold it."

She knew what that meant. Only one person could overrule the White House chief of staff.

"The president should understand that you can't hold back information and expect me to do my job," she said. "This has become a circus. One of our own could be dead."

He nodded. "I realize that."

But there was something else.

True, she had two assets on the ground—Luke and her missing man. Malone had now joined the fray, at least for the night, making for three.

But there was actually a fourth.

One she hadn't mentioned to Malone.

SIX

✦

KALUNDBORG, DENMARK
8:50 P.M.

SALAZAR SMILED AS HE ENTERED THE RESTAURANT and spotted his dinner companion. He was late but had called and asked that his apologies be passed on, along with a glass of whatever his guest might like to enjoy.

"I am so sorry," he said to Cassiopeia Vitt. "Some important matters detained me."

They were childhood friends, he two years her senior, their parents lifelong companions. In their twenties they'd become close, dating five years before Cassiopeia apparently realized that the attraction between them may have been more for their parents' benefit than her own.

Or at least that's what she told him at the time.
But he knew better.

What really drove them apart was more fundamental.

He was born a member of the Church of Jesus
Christ of Latter-day Saints. So was she. That meant
everything to him, but not so much to her.

Eleven years had passed since they were last together. They'd kept in touch, seeing each other on
occasion at social functions. He knew she moved
to France and started constructing a castle, using
only 13th-century materials and technology, which
was slowly rising, stone by stone. He'd seen photographs of it and her country château. Both were
remarkable and picturesque.

Like the woman herself.

"It's all right," she said to him. "I've been enjoying the view."

Kalundborg began as a Viking settlement on
the west coast of Zealand and remained one of
Denmark's oldest towns. Its cobbled square was
anchored by the unique Church of Our Lady, a
12th-century masterpiece comprising five octago-
nal towers. The café sat on one side of the square,
its candlelit tables crowded with diners. Theirs, at
his request, nestled against the front window where
the brick church could be seen lit for the night.

"I've been looking forward to this dinner all

day," he said to her. "I so enjoy it here. I'm glad you could finally come for a visit."

His mother had been an introverted Danish woman totally committed to her husband and their six children, himself the youngest. When church missionaries arrived in the late 19th century, her family had been one of the first in Denmark to become Latter-day Saints. His maternal grandfather helped organize Scandinavia's first ward, and more followed. Those wards eventually were formed into stakes. The same thing happened in Spain, where his father's family had lived. Eventually, both grandfathers headed large stakes. He'd inherited his mother's Danish estate in Kalundborg and spent May to October here each year, escaping Spain's summer heat.

Their waiter appeared, and he ordered a glass of mineral water. Cassiopeia made it two. Menus were produced, and they both scanned the house selections.

"Are you still leaving tomorrow?" she asked.

"Unfortunately, yes. I have some business that requires my attention."

"I hate that. We were just beginning to become reacquainted."

"And you've been so coy, which I've allowed. But it's time you tell me. Why have you returned? Why did you come here?"

She'd first made contact about five months ago with a phone call. Several more calls and emails followed. Another call last week led to an invitation here.

Which she'd accepted.

"I've decided I may have been wrong about things."

Her words intrigued him. He set the menu aside.

"As I've become older," she said, "I've realized that the beliefs of my parents may not have been so wrong."

He knew that, like himself, she'd been schooled from an early age in the Book of Mormon, taught the Doctrine and Covenants and encouraged to read the Pearl of Great Price. Those would have taught her all of the revelations provided to the prophets who'd led the church, along with a full understanding of its history. Every Latter-day Saint was required to study the same.

But he knew she'd rebelled.

And rejected her heritage.

Which, luckily, neither of her parents had lived to see.

"I've waited a long time to hear you say those words," he said. "Your negativity about the church was the source of our estrangement."

"I remember. And look at you. Back then you

were about to lead a ward. Now you're a member of the First Quorum of Seventy, one step away from the Quorum of the Twelve Apostles. Maybe the first man from Spain to achieve such a great honor."

He heard the pride in her voice.

The First Presidency rested at the top of the church leadership, consisting of the prophet and two hand-chosen counselors. Below that were the Twelve Apostles, who served for life and helped establish policy. Then came the various quorums of Seventy, each member a respected elder, charged with aiding organization and administration, holding their apostolic authority as **special witnesses of Christ.** Many apostles came from the Seventies, and every prophet had emerged from the apostles.

"I want to rediscover what I lost," she told him.

The waiter returned with their water.

Salazar reached across and lightly grasped her hand. The gesture seemed not to surprise her. "I would be most happy to help you rediscover your faith. To lead you back would be my honor."

"That's why I contacted you."

He smiled, his hand still atop hers. Dedicated Latter-day Saints did not believe in premarital sex, so their relationship had never been physical.

But it had been real.

So much that it had survived eleven years inside him.

"I'm hungry," he said, his eyes focused on her. "Let's enjoy dinner. Then I'd like to show you something. Back at the estate."

She smiled. "That would be lovely."

SEVEN

⭐

ATLANTA, GEORGIA

STEPHANIE WAS A CAREER LAWYER. SHE'D STARTED at the State Department right out of law school, then moved to Justice and worked her way up through the ranks to deputy attorney general. Eventually she might have garnered the top spot from some president, but the Magellan Billet changed everything. The idea had been to cultivate a special investigative unit, outside the FBI, the CIA, and the military, directly responsive to the executive branch, its agents schooled in both law and espionage.

Independent. Innovative. Discreet.

Those were the ideals.

And the idea had worked.

But she wasn't oblivious to politics. She'd served

presidents and attorneys general from both parties. Though elected and reelected on a pledge of bipartisan cooperation, for the past seven and a half years Danny Daniels had been locked in a fierce political war. There'd been treacherous incidents with his vice president, one attorney general, and a former deputy national security adviser. Even an assassination attempt. She and the Billet had been involved with all of those crises. Now here she was again. Right in the thick of something extraordinary.

"Ever wonder what you'll do when your time here is over?" Davis asked.

They still sat in the cafeteria, empty in the midafternoon.

"I plan to work forever."

"We could both write tell-all books. Or maybe go on TV. CNN or CNBC or Fox. Be their resident expert, spouting zingers. Pointing out how stupid the new administration is. It's so much easier to Monday-morning-quarterback than play the game on Sunday."

She wondered about Davis' fatalism, most likely a case of the last-term blues. She'd seen it before. During Daniels' first term there'd actually been a strong push to replace her, but the effort had fizzled. Maybe because nobody wanted her job. Not much glamour in working out of a quiet Georgia office, away from the D.C. limelight. Careers were woven from much thicker thread. One thing, though, was clear—Edwin Davis was absolutely loyal to his boss. As was she. And one other thing. Usually, no one at Justice or Congress or the White House ever gave her or the Billet much thought. But now she'd materialized on the radar screen of the senior senator from Utah.

"What does Rowan want from me?"

"He's after something that we thought was only a myth."

She caught the tone of his voice, which signaled trouble.

"I need to tell you a story."

On January 1, 1863, Abraham Lincoln issued his Emancipation Proclamation. History notes it as a momentous achievement. The reality, though, is far different. The proclamation was not law. Congress never enacted it, and no state adopted it. Lincoln issued it on his supposed authority as commander in chief of the military. But it freed no one. Its mandate applied only to slaves held in the ten states then in rebellion. It did not outlaw slavery, and granted no citizenship to those freed. In the federally held parts of the South, which included much of Tennessee and Virginia, where blacks could have actually been freed and made citizens, the proclamation had no applicability. Maryland and Kentucky were likewise exempted, as were parts of Louisiana. In short, the Emancipation Proclamation was but a political gimmick. It freed slaves only where Lincoln had no authority. William Seward, Lincoln's secretary of state, said it best. "We show our sympathy with slavery by emancipating slaves where we cannot reach them and holding them in bondage where we can set them free."

Lincoln publicly called the proclamation a "war measure," but privately admitted that it was useless. After all, the Constitution itself sanctioned slavery. Article I, Section 2, specifically designated that slaves would be counted as three-fifths of a person on issues of congressional representation and taxes. Article IV, Section 2, required that fugitive slaves in free states be returned to their masters. Many of the delegates to the Constitutional Convention had owned slaves—so no surprise that not a single word was included that jeopardized those rights.

At the time, the South was winning the Civil War. So the only practical effect the proclamation could have had was to inspire a slave uprising—a rebellion from within that could have crippled the enemy. Revolt was certainly a concern, as most able-bodied Southerners were away fighting in the army, their farms and plantations supervised by the elderly or their wives.

But no uprising occurred.

Instead the effect of the proclamation was felt primarily in the North.

And not in a good way.

Most Northerners were shocked by the stunt. Few connected the war with the abolition of slavery. White Northerners, by and large, despised Africans, their Black Codes offering nothing in the way of equality for the freed slaves already living there. Discrimination was deeply institutionalized. Northern newspapers strongly opposed the end of slavery. And after Lincoln's Emancipation Proclamation, violence toward Northern blacks radically increased.

As did desertions.

Nearly 200,000 fled the Union army. Another 12,000 avoided the draft. 90,000 escaped to Canada. Enlistment rates plummeted. War bonds went unsold.

For the North, the fight was not about slavery.

"What are you saying?" Stephanie asked.

"Abraham Lincoln was no emancipator," Davis said. "He barely spoke of slavery before 1854. Actually, he was publicly opposed to political or social equality for the races. He favored the Fugitive Slave Act, which allowed owners to reclaim their property within free states. Never once, as a lawyer, did he defend a runaway slave. But he did defend a slave owner. He liked colonization, returning freed slaves to Africa, Haiti, British Guiana, the Dutch West Indies. Anywhere but the United States. His administration tried hard to develop a workable plan for the deportation after the war. But there were over four million slaves in America then. Returning them was not a financial or logistical possibility."

She was not unfamiliar with Lincoln. He'd long become the talk of myths, stories, and legends made popular by countless books, movies, and television shows.

"Lincoln made himself clear in his inaugural address," Davis said. "He told the country that he would not interfere with the right to own a slave in the Southern states. Period. End of story. What he opposed was the **spread** of slavery into new territories."

"I never realized you were such a Lincoln authority."

"I'm not. But reality is reality. The Civil War was not fought over slavery. How could it have been? The Constitution itself sanctioned the practice. Which the Supreme Court, in the 1857 **Dred Scott** decision, recognized as legal. No amendment to the Constitution was ever voted on to change that until the Thirteenth Amendment, **after** the war was over. So how could we fight a war to end something that our Constitution specifically allowed?"

A good question.

"But Lincoln, God bless him," Davis said, "did face some tough calls. Ones no other president had ever faced. He was literally looking at the end of the country. Europe was watching, ready to pounce and pick our carcass clean. He had a desperate situation. Which is the reason we're talking right now."

She waited.

"Secession."

"As in a state leaving the Union?"

Davis nodded. "That's what the Civil War was about. The Southern states said they were fed up and had the right to leave the Union. Lincoln said they didn't—the Union was forever and could not be dissolved. Six hundred thousand people died to settle that debate."

She knew a little about this subject, too, as constitutional law was her passion.

"The Supreme court settled that debate in 1869," she said. "**Texas v. White.** The court held that secession was not allowed. The union was unbreakable and forever."

"What else could the court say? The war was over, so many dead, the South in ruins. The country was trying to rebuild. And some black-robed, Northern turkey buzzards were going to rule the whole thing unconstitutional? I don't think so."

"I didn't realize you held judges in such contempt."

He smiled. "Federal judges are a pain in the ass. Appoint anyone for life, and you're going to have a problem. The Supreme Court in 1869 had no choice but to rule that way."

"And we do?"

"Here's the thing, Stephanie. What if Lincoln and the Supreme Court were both wrong?"

EIGHT

✫

MALONE UNLOCKED THE FRONT DOOR TO HIS
bookshop and led Luke Daniels and Barry Kirk
inside. Højbro Plads was busy, but not like in summer when sunset came late and the square stayed
packed until midnight. Then he remained open to
at least 10:00 P.M. This time of year he closed at
6:00.

He switched on the lights and relocked the
door.

"This is cool," Luke said. "Got that Hogwarts
feel to it. And the smell. Seems every old-book
shop has that same aroma."

"It's called the scent of knowledge."

Luke pointed a finger at him. "Is that bookstore

owner humor? I bet you guys get together and trade jokes like that. Right?"

Malone tossed his keys on the front counter and faced Barry Kirk. "I'm told you may know where our missing man is."

Kirk stayed silent.

"I'm only going to ask nice one more time."

"I second that," Luke said. "Tell us what you know, now."

"Salazar has your agent."

"Who's Salazar?" Malone asked.

"He's the center of all this," Luke said. "A Spaniard. Nasty rich. His family's concern is cranes. Like the ones you see at construction sites, up the sides of buildings. His father started the business after World War II."

"I became one of Senor Salazar's personal assistants five years ago. But I came to see that there was a problem with him. My employer is Mormon."

"And how is that a problem?" Malone asked.

"He is an elder, a senior member of the First Quorum of Seventy, perhaps destined to be named an apostle of the church."

"That's real high up on the pole," Luke said.

"I'm familiar with the Latter-day Saints." Malone stared at Kirk. "What's the **problem** with Salazar?"

"He's involved with some nefarious dealings. I

turned a blind eye to them . . . until recently, when I believe he killed someone."

"And how would you know that?"

"I don't, not for sure. But he's been trying to obtain a 19th-century diary. Senor Salazar is an avid collector of Mormon history. The book's owner refused to sell. This was . . . a point of frustration. Then the diary was obtained, and I learned that its owner was found dead."

"And how does that connect to Salazar?" Malone asked.

"Somewhat coincidental, wouldn't you say?"

He glanced at Luke, hoping for more. "Can you fill in the gaps?"

"Wish I could. We were tasked with a simple background check on Salazar. That's all, facts and figures. We had an agent on the ground working that for the past few months. Kirk, here, made contact with him. Then, three days ago, that agent disappeared. I was sent to find him. This afternoon I had a run-in with some of Salazar's men, so I stole one of his planes."

"He has more than one?"

"He's got a friggin' air force. Like I said, **nasty rich.**"

"Your agent talked with me," Kirk said. "He was going to get me to safety. But when I learned Senor Salazar had taken him, I panicked and ran. He gave me a contact number, which I called. I was told to go to Sweden, but Salazar's men followed."

"Your employer has **men**?" Malone asked.

"Danites."

That was a word he hadn't expected, but one he knew.

He stepped over to the aisle marked RELIGION and searched for the book he hoped was still there. He'd bought it a few weeks ago from an odd lady who'd dragged in several cartons.

And yes—it remained on the top shelf.

Kingdom of the Saints.

Published in the mid-20th century.

The term **Danites** had triggered something in his eidetic memory. It didn't take much. **Photographic** was too simplistic a description for the genetic trait, and not altogether right. More a knack for details. A pain in the ass that could, sometimes, be helpful.

He checked the index and found the reference to a sermon delivered June 17, 1838, by Sidney Rigdon, one of Joseph Smith's early converts.

> "Ye are the salt of the earth but if the salt hath lost its savor, wherewith shall the earth be salted? It is henceforth good for nothing but to be cast out and trodden under foot of man. We have provided the world with kindness, we have suffered their abuse without cause, with patience,

and have endured without resentment, until this day, and still their persecution and violence does not cease. But from this day and this hour we will suffer it no more."

Rigdon directed his comments to other apostates who he believed had betrayed the rest, but he also was referring to gentiles who'd repeatedly meted out death and violence toward Latter-day Saints. One new convert, Sampson Avard, a man described as "cunning, resourceful, and extremely ambitious" played upon the feeling aroused by what came to be called the Salt Sermon. He formed a secret military organization within the ranks known as the Sons of Dan, taken from a passage in Genesis, **Dan shall be a serpent by the way, an adder in the path, that biteth the horse's heels so that his rider shall fall backward.** The Danites were to enlist the youngest, the rashest, and the most vigorous as an elite corps, which served secretly. They acted not as a group, but as individuals who could be called upon to effect swift and immediate revenge for any acts of violence practiced against the Saints.

He glanced up from the book. "Danites were fanatics. Radicals within the early Mormon church. But they disappeared long ago."

Kirk shook his head. "Senor Salazar fancies himself living in another time. He is an obsessive believer in Joseph Smith. He follows the old ways."

Malone knew about Smith and his visions of the angel Moroni, who supposedly led him to golden plates, which Smith translated and used to form a new religion—first called the Church of Christ, now known as the Church of Jesus Christ of Latter-day Saints.

"Senor Salazar is intelligent," Kirk said. "Possessed of an advanced degree from the Universidad de Barcelona."

"Yet he follows a man who claims he found golden plates upon which was engraved a foreign language. Nobody, save for Smith and a few witnesses, ever saw those plates. If I recall, some of those witnesses even later repudiated their testimony. But Smith was still able to translate the plates by reading the words on a seer stone dropped in the bottom of a hat."

"Is that similar to the belief that a man was crucified, died, and rose from the dead three days later? Both are matters of faith."

Malone wanted to know, "Are you Mormon?"

"Third generation."

"It means something to you?"

"Since I was a boy."

"And to Salazar?"

"It's his life."

"You took a chance running."

"I prayed upon it, and was told it was the right thing to do."

Personally, he'd never been a fan of blindly placing his life in the hands of faith. But this was not the time to debate religion. "Where is our man?"

"Your agent is being held outside Kalundborg," Kirk said. "On a property owned by Senor Salazar. Not his main estate, but an adjacent tract, directly east. There is a holding cell located in the basement."

"And in the main house," Luke said, "does he keep information there?"

Kirk nodded. "His study is his sanctuary. No one is allowed in there without permission."

Malone stood near the counter, gazing out the front window to the darkened square. Twelve years he'd worked as a field agent for the Justice Department, honing skills that would never leave him. One was to always be aware of what was around him. To this day he never ate in a restaurant with his back to the door. Through the plate glass, a hundred feet beyond his shop, he spotted two men. Both young, dressed in dark jackets and black trousers. They'd been standing in the same spot for the past few minutes, unlike nearly everyone else around them. He'd tried not to stare, but had kept watch.

Luke walked toward the counter, his back to the window. "You see them, too?"

His gaze met the younger man's. "Hard not to notice."

Luke raised his arms and feigned being upset, but his words did not match his actions. "Tell me, Pappy, do you have a rear door into this place?"

He played along, pointing, showing irritation, but nodding his head.

"What's happening?" Kirk asked.

The two men outside moved.

Toward the shop.

Then a new sound could be heard.

Sirens.

Approaching.

NINE

★

Stephanie listened to Davis' explanation.

"The American Revolution was not a revolution at all. At no time was its goal the overthrow of the British government. None of its stated aims included conquering London and replacing the monarchy with a democracy. No. The American Revolution was a war of secession. The Declaration of Independence was a statement of secession. The United States of America was founded by secessionists. Their goal was to leave the British Empire and fashion a government of their own. There have been two wars of secession in American history. The first was fought in 1776, the next in 1861."

The implications fascinated her, but she was more curious as to the information's relevance.

"The South wanted to leave the Union because it no longer agreed with what the federal government was doing," Davis said. "Tariffs were the big revenue raiser. The South imported far more than the North, so it paid over half the tariffs. But with more than half of the population, the North sucked up the majority of federal spending. That was a problem. Northern industrialists owed their existence to high tariffs. Eliminate them, and their businesses would fail. Tariffs had been fought over since 1824, the South resisting, the North continuing to impose them. The newly created Confederate Constitution specifically outlawed tariffs. That meant Southern ports would now have a decisive edge over their Northern counterparts."

"Which Lincoln could not allow."

"How could he? The federal government would have no money. Game over. In essence, the North and South fundamentally disagreed on both revenue and spending decisions. After decades of this, the South decided it just didn't want to be a part of the United States anymore. So those states left."

"What do Josepe Salazar and Senator Rowan have to do with any of this?"

"They're both Mormon."

She waited for more.

By the time the Emancipation Proclamation was issued in January 1863, Lincoln was in a panic. After winning at the Battle of Manassas in July 1861, the Union army had been handed a string of defeats. The decisive Battle of Gettysburg was still six months away, when the tide of the war would turn. So in the winter of 1863 Lincoln faced a crisis. He had to hold both the North and the Far West. Losing the Far West to the Confederacy would mean certain defeat.

To hold the Far West meant making a deal with the Mormons.

They'd occupied the Salt Lake valley since 1847. The area had been known as the Great American Desert before their arrival, and the nearby dead lake had discouraged settlement. But they'd labored sixteen years, building a city, creating the Utah Territory. They'd wanted statehood, but it had been denied, a reaction to their rebellious attitude and unorthodox beliefs, especially polygamy, which they refused to denounce. Their leader, Brigham Young, was both determined and capable. In 1857 he faced off against President James Buchanan when five thousand federal troops were sent west to restore order. Luckily for Young, that invading force was not led by military strategists. Instead politicians called the shots, and they ordered a march across

1,000 miles of harsh wilderness, ending short of Utah just as winter took hold, stuck in the mountains where many died. Young wisely determined it would be futile to fight such an army head-on, so he adapted guerrilla tactics—burning supply trains, stealing pack animals, scorching the earth. Buchanan was eventually backed into a corner and did what any good politician would do—he declared victory and sued for peace. Envoys came with a full pardon for Young and the Mormons. The conflict ended with not a shot fired between the opposing sides and Young once again in total control. By 1862 both the railroad and telegraph lines ran straight through the Utah Territory to the Pacific. If Lincoln did not want them severed, which would cut him off to the far west, he had to reach an accommodation with Brigham Young.

"It's a hell of a tale," Davis said. "Congress had passed the Morrill Anti-Bigamy Act in mid-1862, which targeted polygamy. The Mormons did not like that at all. So in early 1863, Young sent an emissary to meet with Lincoln. The message was clear. **Mess with us and we're going to mess with you.** That meant a break in the railroad and telegraph lines. Mormon troops might even enter the war for the South. Lincoln knew this was serious. So he had a message for Brigham Young."

• • •

"When I was a boy on the farm in Illinois there was a great deal of timber which had to be cleared away. Occasionally, a log was found that had fallen down. It was too hard to split, too wet to burn, and too heavy to move, so we plowed around it. Tell your prophet that I will leave him alone, if he will leave me alone."

"And that's what happened," Davis said. "General Conner, who commanded the federal troops in Utah, was ordered not to confront the Mormons on the issue of polygamy, or any other issue for that matter. He was told to leave them alone. It wasn't until 1882 that the next federal criminal act on polygamy came along. That one was a problem, and thousands were prosecuted. But by then the Civil War was long over and both Lincoln and Young were dead."

"How do you know about this deal?"

"Classified records."

"From 1863?"

Davis sat silent for a moment, and she could see that he was troubled. He was legendary for his poker face, but she knew better. She'd seen him at his most vulnerable, and likewise. Pretense did not exist between them.

"The Mormons didn't trust Lincoln," Davis said. "They had no reason to trust anybody in

Washington. They'd been ignored, put off, and lied to for decades. The government was their worst enemy. But finally here they were in the cat-bird seat. So they made a deal, but they also de-manded collateral."

She was amazed. "What could Lincoln have given them?"

"Here's where we know only bits and pieces. But we know enough. Worse, though, is that Sen-ator Thadeaus Rowan knows some of it, too. He's an apostle in the Mormon Church and, besides us, they're the only other people alive who have any clue about this."

"That's why you wanted Salazar scoped out? His connection to Rowan?"

Davis nodded. "We became aware of some things Rowan was doing about a year ago. We were then told of the connection to Salazar. When we made the request to you for the dossier, we real-ized we had a problem. Now it's grown."

She tried to recall what she could about the Mormons. She was not a religious person, and from what she knew about Edwin Davis, he was similar.

"Rowan is smart," Davis said. "He's plotted this through carefully and waited for the right moment to act. We need our best people on this. What's about to happen could have catastrophic conse-quences."

"All my people are good."

"Can we keep Malone involved?"

"I don't know."

"Pay him. Do whatever. But I want him on this."

"I don't think I've ever seen you this anxious. Is it that bad?"

"I'm sorry that I deceived you. When I asked for the dossier on Salazar, I should have told you what I knew. I held back, hoping we were wrong."

"What's changed?"

"We weren't wrong. I just heard from the secretary of the interior, who's with Rowan in Utah. They found some bodies and wagons from the 19th century in Zion National Park. There's a connection to the Mormons. Rowan flew straight back to Salt Lake City and is meeting with the prophet of the church right now. What they're discussing could change this country."

"I still have a man missing. That's my primary concern at the moment."

Davis stood. "Then deal with it. But I need you in Washington tomorrow morning. We have to handle this quickly and carefully."

She nodded.

Davis shook his head. "Thomas Jefferson once said that a little rebellion now and then is a good thing, as necessary in the political world as storms in the physical, a medicine for the sound health of government. Jefferson didn't live in our world. I'm not sure that would be true anymore."

"What are we talking about here?"

Davis stared at her with ice in his eyes.

"The end of the United States of America."

TEN

★

COPENHAGEN

MALONE WATCHED AS LUKE REACTED TO THE men's advance, protecting Barry Kirk. He moved toward the front window, hand on his gun. He'd never answered Luke's question about a rear door.

"What's going on?" Kirk asked.

"We have visitors."

"Where? Who?"

"Outside."

He saw Kirk's gaze dart past the window to the square beyond. The two men were nearly at the bookshop.

"Look familiar?" Luke asked Kirk.

"Danites. They're Salazar's. I know them. They found me in Sweden. They found me here. You people are useless. You're going to get me killed."

STEVE BERRY / 90

"Pappy, that back door. Where is it?"

"Just follow the aisle in front of you. But you understand, with all those people around out there, these two aren't going to make a scene."

"Okay, I get it. That's why they want us out back. How many you think are waiting there?"

"Enough that one gun between us is not going to solve the problem."

"Call the police," Kirk said.

Luke shook his head. "Useless as teats on a boar hog. But it sounds like somebody already has. Those sirens are getting louder."

"We don't know if those are headed here," Malone said. "But the last thing we need is to be bogged down with the locals. We're going out the front and hope these guys don't want a scene."

"You got a plan after that?"

"Every good agent does."

He'd ragged Luke for his rash decision to flee out the back, but he admired the young man's cool under pressure.

And he'd heard what Kirk had called the men outside.

Danites.

If that group existed at all—and there'd been much historical debate on the issue—it would have been two centuries ago. A reaction to a different time and place. An understandable way to counter the violence Mormons had routinely faced. So what was happening here?

He grabbed his keys off the counter, then opened the front door. Noise from the people enjoying the Danish night grew louder, as did the sirens. He stepped out and waited until Luke and Kirk joined him, then shut and locked the door.

The two men eyed them.

He turned right toward the Café Norden, which anchored the east end of Højbro Plads. The walk was fifty yards across crowded pavement. Between them and the café the lighted Stork Fountain flowed with splashing water. People sat along its edge socializing. Out of the corner of his eye he spotted the two men following. He deliberately slowed to give them a chance to meet up. His pulse quickened, senses alert. He wanted any confrontation to happen here, in public.

The two men adjusted the angle of their approach and ended up in front, blocking the way. The cold weight of the gun beneath his jacket only partially reassured him. Beyond the square, back toward the canal, where the rental boat was moored and the street ended, four city police cars skidded to a stop.

Two officers rushed their way.

Another two headed for the boat.

"That ain't good, Pappy," Luke muttered.

The uniforms rushed into Højbro Plads and turned toward his bookshop. They gazed through the front windows and tested the locked door. Then one of them busted the glass and they entered with guns drawn.

"You killed my people."

Malone turned and faced the two men. "Gee, I'm so sorry. Anything I can do to make it up to you?"

"You think this is a joke?"

"I don't know what **this** is. But your guys came for a fight. All I did was give them one."

"We want him," the man said, pointing at Kirk.

"Can't get everything you want in this world."

"We'll have him, one way or another."

He brushed past, and they kept walking toward the café.

He'd guessed right.

These two did not want a scene.

Around him almost everyone's attention was on the police and what was happening at his shop. Luckily, there were four floors for them to search.

Tables dotted the pavement outside the Café Norden's ground-floor windows, all filled with diners enjoying a late dinner. He was usually one of them, a habit developed after he moved from Georgia to Denmark.

But not tonight.

"How many more you think are lurking?" Luke asked.

"Hard to say. But you can bet they're here."

"Be smart, Barry," one of the men called out.

Kirk stopped and turned.

"You will be shown respect," the younger man said, "if you show the same. You have his word. Otherwise, there will be an atonement."

Fear filled Kirk's face, but Luke led him away.

Malone stepped forward. "Tell Salazar that we'll be seeing each other real soon."

"He'll look forward to it." A pause. "As will I."

The two officers emerged from his bookshop. The search had not taken long. Malone pointed at one of the young men and shouted, **"Jeg ringede til dig. Zdet er Malone. Det er ham, du er efter, og han har en pistol."** I called you. This is Malone. He's the one you're after and he has a gun.

The effect was instant.

The officers bolted toward their target.

Malone retreated into the Café Norden.

"What did you do?" Luke asked.

"Slowed our minders down a little."

He ignored the stairs that led up to the second-floor dining room and wove a path around the crowded tables toward the rear of the ground floor. The restaurant was doing its usual brisk business. Through the outer windows he saw people sauntering back and forth on the cobblestones. He was a regular and knew the staff and owner. So when he entered the kitchen no one paid him any mind. He found the door at the far end and descended a wooden staircase into the basement.

Three exits appeared at the bottom. One for the lift that moved to the building's upper floors, another that opened into an office, and a third that led into a storage room.

He flipped on an incandescent bulb in the storage room. The space was littered with cleaning equipment, empty fruit and vegetable crates, and other restaurant supplies. Cobwebs clouded the corners and a tang of disinfectant floated on the chilly air. On the far side was a metal door. He carefully made his way over and unlocked it. Another room spanned ahead and he flicked on a new bulb. Ten feet above him was a narrow street that ran parallel to the Café Norden on its back side. The cellars beneath the buildings had long ago merged, forming a subterranean level that extended from one block to another, the shopkeepers sharing the space. He'd been down here several times before.

"I assume," Luke said, "we're going to leave where they can't see us."

"That's the plan."

Past the second cellar he found a set of wooden stairs that led up to ground level. He took them two at a time and entered an empty retail space that had once hosted an upscale clothing store. Shadowy islands of boxes, cellophane garbage bags, counters, mannequins, and bare metal racks lay scattered about the dark interior. Through uncovered windows he saw the lighted trees of Nikolaj Plads, which sat a block behind the Café Norden.

"We go out and to the right," he said, "and we should be fine. I have a car parked a few blocks over."

"I don't think so."

He turned.

Barry Kirk stood behind Luke Daniels, a gun nestled at the younger agent's right temple.

"It's about time," Malone said.

ELEVEN

✯

SALT LAKE CITY, UTAH

ROWAN HAD FLOWN DIRECTLY BACK FROM THE southern part of the state via the same government helicopter that had ferried him to Zion National Park. He was accustomed to such perks. They came from being a man with national power. He was careful, though, never to abuse it. He'd seen too many colleagues fall from grace. His fellow senator from Utah was a perfect example. Not a Latter-day Saint, just a gentile who thought little of his office and even less of the people who elected him. He was currently under investigation by the Senate Ethics Committee, and privately the word was that he would be censured for gross misconduct. Luckily, this was an election year and strong opposition had already announced, so the voters should put him out of his misery.

A popular misconception held that Utah was nearly exclusively Latter-day Saints. But that was not the case. Only 62.1% were according to the latest census, dropping every year. He'd started in politics forty years ago as mayor of Provo, then served a short stint as a state representative, and finally moved on to Washington as a U.S. senator. Not a hint of scandal had ever been associated with either his name or anything with which he'd ever been involved. He'd been married to the same woman for fifty-one years. They'd raised six children—two lawyers, a doctor, and three teachers—who were now married with children of their own. All of them had been nurtured in the church and remained faithful, living in various parts of the country, active in their wards. He visited them often, and was close with his eighteen grandchildren.

He lived the Words of Wisdom. He did not drink alcohol, smoke, or consume coffee or tea. The first prophet, Joseph Smith, proclaimed those prohibitions in 1833. A few years back a fourth was added, encouraging a limitation on meat consumption in favor of grains, fruits, and vegetables. He knew of an outside study on members who practiced all four abstentions and the results were not surprising. Rates of lung cancer were low and heart disease even lower. Overall, the health of devout Latter-day Saints was significantly better than the population as a whole. The lyrics to a children's hymn he'd many times heard sung in church rang true.

> That the children may live long
> And be beautiful and strong,
> Tea and coffee and tobacco they despise,
> Drink no liquor, and they eat
> But a very little meat;
> They are seeking to be great and good and wise.

He'd telephoned from the helicopter and made arrangements for a private meeting. Twenty-three years ago he'd been called to serve on the Quorum of the Twelve Apostles. Originally, they'd acted as traveling counselors, in charge of new missions, but they'd evolved into the church's primary governing body. It was a lifetime job. Members were expected to devote their entire energy to their duties, but exceptions had been made.

As with him.

Having an elder as a member of the U.S. Senate came with advantages.

And there was precedent.

Reed Smoot had first served with distinction in both capacities. But it had taken a four-year battle to ensure that, the argument being that his "Mormon" religion disqualified Smoot from office. A congressional eligibility committee eventually recommended that he be removed, but in 1907 the Senate as a whole defeated the proposal and allowed him to serve, which he did, until 1933.

Rowan's tenure had not been as arduous.

Times had changed.

No one today would dare challenge the right of a person to serve in government based on their religion. In fact, to suggest such would be offensive. A Saint had even managed to become the Republican party's presidential nominee.

But that did not mean prejudice had disappeared.

On the contrary, Saints still encountered resistance. Not the beatings, robberies, and killings of 150 years ago.

Prejudice nonetheless, though.

He entered a multistory residential building that stood east of Salt Lake's Temple Square, a modest location that housed a church-owned condominium where the current prophet lived. The lobby was staffed with two security guards, who waved him through.

He stepped into the elevator and entered a digital code.

As not only an elder but president of the Quorum of the Twelve, the man who would almost certainly become the next leader, his access to the current prophet was unfettered.

The church thrived on loyalty.

Seniority was rewarded.

As it should be.

He hadn't changed from his dusty clothes, having driven straight from the airfield. The man waiting had told him formalities were not necessary. Not today. Not with what had been discovered.

"Come in, Thaddeus," the prophet called out as Rowan stepped inside the sunlit residence. "Please, have a seat. I'm anxious to hear."

Charles R. Snow had served as prophet for nineteen years. He was sixty-three then, eighty-two now. He walked only when outside the residence, otherwise he utilized a wheelchair. The apostles had been informed of his various afflictions including chronic anemia, low blood pressure, and progressive kidney failure. Yet the old man's mind remained sharp, as active as forty years ago when he first became an elder.

"I envy you," Snow said. "Dressed in hiking clothes, able to enjoy the desert. I miss those walks through the canyons."

Snow had been born near Zion National Park, a third-generation Saint, descended from one of the pioneer families who'd made the original trek west in 1847. While most immigrants settled in

the Salt Lake basin, Brigham Young had dispatched vanguards to various parts of the new
land. Snow's family had headed south and prospered in the stark, barren environment. He was an
economist, with degrees from Utah State and
Brigham Young University, where he taught for
two decades. He'd served as an assistant stake
clerk, then clerk, bishop, and high councilor before being called for the First Quorum of Seventy,
finally sustained as an apostle. He'd acted for many
years as president of the England mission, a responsibility eventually bestowed by the brethren
on Rowan. His tenure as prophet had been quiet,
with little controversy.

"I've offered to take you into the mountains
anytime," Rowan said as he sat across from the
older man. "Just ask and I'll make the arrangements."

"As if my doctors would allow that. No, Thaddeus, my legs barely work anymore."

Snow's wife had died ten years ago, and his
children, grandchildren, and great-grandchildren
all lived outside of Utah. His life was the church,
and he'd proven to be an active manager, oversee-
ing much of its everyday administration. Yesterday
Rowan had called Snow and briefed him about the
find inside Zion, which raised many questions.
The prophet had asked Rowan to go and see if
there were any answers.

He reported what he'd found, then said, "It's the right wagons. There's no doubt."

Snow nodded. "The names on the wall are proof. I never believed I would hear from those men again."

Fjeldsted. Hyde. Woodruff. Egan.

"**Damnation to the prophet.** They cursed us in death, Thaddeus."

"Maybe they had a right to? They were all murdered."

"I always thought the whole thing a story fabricated at the time. But apparently it's a true one."

One Rowan knew in detail.

By 1856 war seemed inevitable between the United States and the Latter-day Saints. Differences over plural marriage, religion, and political autonomy had festered to the breaking point. Brigham Young ran his isolated community as he saw fit, with no regard for federal law. He minted his own money, passed his own rules, created his own courts, educated the young as he thought best, and worshiped as he believed. Even what to label the newly settled land had been a matter of dispute. Locals referred to it as Deseret. Congress called it the Utah Territory. Finally, word came that a Union army was marching west to subdue the rebels everyone in the east called Mormons.

So Young decided to collect the community's wealth, hiding it until the expected conflict ended.

Every hard asset was converted into gold bullion, church members willingly divesting themselves of almost all their worldly goods. Twenty-two wagons were requisitioned to relocate the gold to California, where other Saints waited to receive it. To avoid detection a circuitous route bypassing populated settlements was chosen.

Little is known of what happened after that.

The official story said the caravan set off with the gold across the uncharted badlands of the south-central part of Deseret. The men soon ran short of water and all efforts to find a source were fruitless. A decision was made to retrace their path back to the last water hole, more than a day's ride behind them. Teamsters were instructed to manage the horses and watch over the gold while forty militiamen set out for the water hole. Upon their return several days later, they found the wagons' charred and blackened hulks, all of the teamsters dead, the horses and gold gone.

Paiutes were blamed for the attack.

The militiamen spent days reconnoitering the region, tracks fading out on rocky scarps or stopping abruptly in dry, meandering riverbeds. Eventually they gave up and returned empty-handed to report their failure to Brigham Young.

More search teams were sent out.

None of the gold was ever found.

Records noted that there was approximately

80,000 ounces being transported, the value at the time nearly $19 an ounce. That same gold now was worth over $150 million.

"You realize that the story we've heard for so long is wrong," he said.

He saw that Snow had already considered the reality.

"Those wagons weren't burned or charred," Rowan went on. "They were deliberately hacked apart inside a cavern. Hidden away. Four men shot. Then the cave sealed up."

And there was one other problem.

"Not a speck of gold was there," he said.

Snow sat silent in his wheelchair, clearly considering something.

"I had hoped that this would not arise during my tenure," the older man whispered.

He stared at the prophet.

"**Forget us not.** It's interesting they chose those words, because we haven't, Thaddeus. Not in the least. There's something you do not know."

He waited.

"We have to cross the street, to the temple. Where I can show you."

TWELVE

★

MALONE ASSESSED THE SITUATION. KIRK HAD clearly come to them armed. But with all the excitement, who would have thought to search the victim for weapons? Still, something had not rung right about the man from the moment they'd met.

And the call with Stephanie had cemented his doubts.

He said, "You work with those two we met in the square."

"More like they work for me."

Luke stood military-straight, his eyes suggesting **We should take this son of a bitch right here, right now.**

But his stare back signaled **No.**

Not yet.

Kirk cocked the hammer of the gun. "I'd like nothing better than to blow his brains out. So you need to do what I say."

"The police came far too quick," Malone said. "Those bodies on the water would have been found, but not that fast. And there's no way the police could have found a trail to us that soon. Your men call them?"

"A good way to flush you out. Keep you moving. We needed you headed out of town."

"Then there were those two on the water. Right place, right time. There was only one way they knew to be there." He pointed at Kirk. "You told them. What's this dog-and-pony show for?"

"We thought we'd learn more by infiltrating the enemy camp. Your agent has been sneaking around for months, asking questions. We've watched with patience, but thought a turncoat might speed the process."

"So you sacrificed two of your men?"

Kirk's face clouded with anger. "That wasn't part of it. They were supposed to make it look good, press you along, reinforce the threat. Unfortunately, you decided to kill them."

"Salazar must have a lot to hide."

"My employer simply wants to be left alone. He does not appreciate your government's interference in his life."

"Is our man dead?" Luke asked.

"If not, he will be. The idea was to draw you to the same place where he's being held and deal with you all at once. But that little ploy back in the square, turning the police on my men, ruined that."

"Sorry to be such a bother," Malone said.

"Better we deal with you here. This empty store seems perfect, as do those rooms beneath. So we're going to wait until my men get here."

"You're tagged?" he asked.

Kirk shrugged. "Cell phones are good for that."

Which meant Malone had to act. "You a Danite?"

"Ordained and sworn. Now I need you to drop your gun to the floor."

Amateur. Only an idiot asked his adversary to toss a weapon away. Smart people just took it.

He reached beneath his jacket and found the Beretta.

But instead of dropping it to the floor he aimed the stubby muzzle at Kirk, who shrank back but kept the gun to Luke's head.

"Don't be stupid," Kirk said. "I'll kill him."

He shrugged. "Go ahead. I don't give a shit. He's a smart-mouthed pain in the ass."

His right eye sighted down the Beretta's short barrel. It had been four years since he'd last been to the range. His skills were a little rusty, but he'd just proven out on the water that he could still shoot. True, it was dark in here, but he pushed all doubt from his mind and took aim.

"Put the gun down," Kirk said, his voice rising.

Luke's gaze was locked on the Beretta, but the younger man's nerve seemed to hold. Malone could sympathize. Caught between two guns was not a good place to be.

"I'm going to count to three," he said. "You better have that gun lowered by the time I finish."

"Don't be an idiot, Malone. My men will be here any second."

"One."

He saw Kirk's trigger finger tighten. The dilemma was clear. He had to either shoot Luke in the head, which meant Malone would shoot him, or swing the gun around and fire across the store. But he'd never make that shot before a bullet from the Beretta left the barrel. The smart play was to lower the gun. Amateurs, however, rarely made the right move.

"Two."

He fired.

The shot rattled the room.

The bullet slammed into Kirk's face and the body spun backward. Hands clawed the air, then Kirk crumbled sideways, finally thudding to the floor.

"Three."

"Are you out of your friggin' mind," Luke screamed. "I felt that bullet whiz by my ear."

"Get his gun."

Luke was already lunging for the weapon. "Malone, you're certifiable. You play awful fast and loose with other people's brains. I could have taken him. We could have used him alive."

"That wasn't an option. He's right. We're going to have company shortly."

He opened the exterior door and searched the cobbled street for any sign of trouble, wondering if the shot had been noticed. Thirty feet to his left a procession of people paraded back and forth on another street, Højbro Plads left of there and back fifty feet. Above him the green dome of the Nikolaj church glowed into the night.

"Get his phone," he told Luke.

"Already got it. I do know a little somethin' about this business."

"Then slide the body over there behind those counters and let's go."

Luke did, then came to the door.

They fled the store, heading down a quiet backstreet toward busy Kongens Nytorv, the city's busiest public square. Roads clogged with night traffic encircled a statue of Christian V. The royal theater was lit brightly, as was the Hotel d'Angleterre. Nyhavn's cafés, on the square's far side abutting the waterfront, were still alive with people. He'd delayed the two Danites back in Højbro Plads, but only for so long. If Kirk was right and they were tracking him, he had to move fast. His eyes raked the crowded scene, settling on the perfect solution.

They crossed the street and trotted for the bus stop.

Copenhagen had a terrific public transportation system and he'd often hopped onto buses from here. They came and went every few minutes all day and one was now easing to a stop, riders streaming on and off.

"The phone," he said to Luke, who produced it.

He casually laid it inside the rear bumper.

The doors closed and the bus lumbered away, heading north toward the royal palace.

"That should keep whoever is coming occupied," he said.

"You think he was tellin' the truth about any of it?"

He nodded. "He took a chance showing his hand. But he thought he was in control and could handle things."

"Yeah. Big mistake. He didn't know he was dealing with a friggin' wild cowboy."

"We have to go see about where he mentioned, even though the whole thing smells like a trap." He pointed south. "I have a car stored a few blocks over. Where is Salazar's estate?"

"Kalundborg."

THIRTEEN

✫

KALUNDBORG, DENMARK
11:00 P.M.

SALAZAR WAS ENJOYING DINNER, THRILLED THAT Cassiopeia had, after all these years, returned to his life. Her calls a few months ago had been as welcome as they were unexpected. He'd missed her. She'd been his first love as a young man, the woman he'd come to believe might be his wife.

But sadly, their relationship ended.

"This is not going to work," she said to him.

"I love you. You know that."

"And I have deep feelings for you, but we have . . . differences."

"Faith should not keep us apart."

"But it does," she said. "You're a true believer. The Book of Mormon is sacred for you. The

Words of Wisdom are a guide for your life. I respect that. But you have to respect that they are not the same for me."

"Our parents believed, as I do."

"And I didn't agree with them, either."

"So you're willing to ignore your heart?"

"Before I grow to resent you, I think it's better that we part friends."

She was right on one count. His faith was important. **No success can compensate for a failure in the home.** That's what David O. McKay taught. Only husbands and wives, acting together, can achieve eternal life in heaven. If either be proven unrighteous, both would be denied salvation. Marriage was an eternal bond—between a man and a woman—the family here a reflection of the family in heaven. Both had to be absolutely committed.

"I was so sorry to hear about your wife," she said to him.

He'd married less than a year after he and Cassiopeia ended their relationship. A lovely woman from Madrid, born to the faith, devout in her following of the prophets. They'd tried to have children, but with no success, the doctors saying that the problem was most likely with her. He'd deemed it God's will and accepted the prohibition. Then, four years ago, she was killed in a car accident. That, too, he'd accepted as God's will. A sign, perhaps, for a change of direction. Now this vibrant, beautiful woman from his past had reappeared. Another sign?

"It had to be awful," she said, and he appreciated her sentiment.

"I try to remember her carefully. The pain of her loss is still there. I can't deny that. I suppose it's why I have not sought another wife." He hesitated a moment. "But I should be asking you this question. Did you ever marry?"

She shook her head. "Kind of sad, wouldn't you say?"

He savored the cod he'd ordered and Cassiopeia seemed to like the Baltic shrimp that filled her plate. He noticed that she hadn't ordered wine, preferring mineral water. Besides the clear religious prohibition, he'd always believed that alcohol made people say and do things they later regretted, so he'd never acquired the taste.

She looked terrific.

Her dark hair, twisted into curls, draped just below her shoulders and framed the same thin brows, brooding cheeks, and blunt nose he remembered. Her swarthy skin remained as smooth and unblemished as a bar of tan soap, her round neck sculpted like a column. The sensuality she projected was so calm and controlled, it might have been choreographed.

A true beauty from heaven.

"Love is that constant, never-failing quality

that has the power to lift us above evil. It is the essence of the gospel. It is the security of the home. It is the safeguard of community life. It is a beacon of hope in a world of distress."

That he knew.

He liked that the angel kept watch over him.

Never failing. Always right.

"What are you thinking?" Cassiopeia asked.

She drew his attention like a magnet.

"Just that it is truly wonderful to be back with you, if only for these few days."

"Does it have to be limited to that?"

"Not at all. But I recall our last conversation from years ago, when you made clear how you felt about our faith. You have to know, nothing has changed for me."

"But as I said earlier, things have changed . . . for me."

He waited for her to explain.

"Recently, I did something I never did as a young girl." She stared into his eyes. "I read the Book of Mormon. Every word. When I was done I realized that everything there was absolutely true."

He stopped eating and listened.

"I then realized that my current lifestyle was not worthy of my birthright. I was born and baptized Mormon, but I've never been one. My father led one of the first stakes in Spain. Both my mother and father were devout believers. While they were alive, I was a good daughter and did as my parents asked."

She paused.

"But I never really believed. So my realizations at reading it now were totally unexpected. Some unseen person kept whispering in my ear that what I was reading was true. Tears poured down my cheeks, as I finally recognized the gift of the Holy Ghost that I first received as a child."

He'd heard similar stories from converts all across Europe. His own Spanish stake comprised nearly five thousand Saints scattered across twelve wards. As a member of the First Quorum of Seventy he oversaw stakes across the Continent. Every day new converts joined with the joy he now saw on Cassiopeia's face.

Which was wonderful.

If it had been there eleven years ago, they would have surely been married. But perhaps heaven was offering them another chance?

"I was struck by the truthfulness of what I read," she said. "I was convinced. I knew that the Holy Ghost had confirmed the truth of every page."

"I recall my first time," he said. "I was fifteen years old. My father read with me. I came to believe that Joseph Smith did see God and His Son in a vision, and was told to join no other religion. Instead, he was to restore the **true** church once again. That testimony has served me well over the years. It keeps me focused, willing to dedicate my-self, with all my heart, to what has to be done."

"I was foolish not to admire that," she said, "all those years ago. I've wanted to tell you this. That's why I'm here, Josepe."

He was so pleased.

They ate in silence for a few moments. His nerves were alive, both from what had happened earlier and with what was happening now. He'd tried to call Elder Rowan and report what he'd learned from the captured agent, but had not been able to connect with him.

His phone vibrated in his pocket.

Normally he'd ignore it, but he was waiting for a return call from Utah and a report from Copen-hagen.

"Excuse me."

He checked the display.

A text message.

FOLLOWING KIRK. ON THE MOVE.

"Problems?" Cassiopeia asked.

"On the contrary. Good news. Another suc-cessful business effort."

"I've noticed that your family's concerns have prospered," she said. "Your father would be proud."

"My brothers and sisters work hard in the com-pany. They do the everyday work, and have for the past five years. They understand that the church now commands my full attention."

"That's not required for a member of the Seventy."

He nodded. "I know. But I, personally, made that choice."

"In preparation for the time when you're sustained as an apostle?"

He smiled. "I have no idea if that will ever happen."

"You seem ideal for the job."

Maybe he was. He hoped so.

"You shall be chosen, Josepe. One day."

"That," he said, "will be a decision for Heavenly Father and the prophet."

FOURTEEN

★

Salt Lake City

Rowan helped Prophet Snow up the stone steps and through the east entrance. Four days after the pioneers first entered the Salt Lake basin Brigham Young had stuck his cane into the ground and proclaimed, **Here we will build a temple to our God**. Construction began in 1853 and continued for forty years, most of the work donated by those first Saints. Only the finest materials had been used, the quartz monzonite for the two-hundred-foot-high walls carted by oxen from quarries twenty miles away. The finished walls were nine feet thick at the base, tapering to six feet at the top. Two hundred and fifty-three thousand square feet lay under the roof. Four stories, all topped by a gold statue of the angel Moroni that, together with its distinctive spires, had become the church's most recognizable image.

Symbolism abounded.

The east side's three towers represented the First Presidency. The twelve pinnacles rising from the towers implied the twelve apostles. The west side's towers reflected the presiding bishops and the church's high council. The east side was purposefully built six feet higher, so to make clear which was superior. Its castle-like battlements illustrated a separation from the world and a protection of the holy ordinances practiced within, a statement in stone that no one would destroy this mighty edifice, as had happened before that time to the temples in both Missouri and Illinois.

Atop each of the center towers were eyes, which represented God's ability to see all things. The earth stones, moonstones, sunstones, cloud stones, and star stones each told a story of the celestial kingdom and the promise of salvation. One of the early elders said it best when he proclaimed, **Every stone is a sermon.**

And Rowan agreed.

The Old Testament taught that temples were the houses of God. The church now owned 130 around the globe. This one anchored ten acres in the center of Salt Lake, the oval-shaped tabernacle building just behind, the old Assembly Hall nearby, two modern visitor centers nestled close. A massive conference center, which could accommodate more than 20,000, stood across the street.

Access inside any temple was restricted to those members who'd achieved "temple recommend." To gain that status a Saint must believe in God the Father and Jesus as Savior. He must support the church and all of its teachings, including the law of chastity that mandates celibacy outside of marriage. He must be honest, never abuse his family, remain morally clean, and pay the required yearly tithe. He must also keep all of his solemn oaths and wear the temple garments, both night and day. Once granted by a bishop and a stake president, the recommend remained valid for two years before being reviewed.

To have a temple recommend was a blessing all Saints desired.

Rowan went through the temple at nineteen, when he served his mission. He'd kept a temple recommend ever since. Now he was the second-highest-ranking official in the church, perhaps only a few months away from becoming the next prophet.

"Where are we going?" he asked Snow.

The old man's legs barely worked, but he made it inside the doors.

"There is something you must see."

With each rise in the hierarchy, Rowan had become aware of more and more secret information. The church had always worked by compartmentalizing, information passed vertically and horizontally on a need-to-know basis. So it made sense that there were matters only the man at the top was privy to.

Two young temple workers waited at the base of a staircase. Usually just the retired served inside, but these two were special.

"Are we to change clothes?" he asked the prophet.

Normally only white garments were worn inside the temple.

"Not today. It's just you and me." Snow crept toward the two men and said, "I appreciate your help. I'm afraid my legs cannot make the climb."

They both nodded, affection and respect in their eyes. No one outside of the apostles was allowed to witness their assistance. Snow settled into their intertwined arms, and they lifted his frail body from the pale blue carpet. Rowan followed them up the Victorian staircase, his hand sliding along on the polished cherry banister.

They ascended to the third floor and entered the council room.

White walls, white carpet, and a white ceiling cast a look of utter purity. Victorian lighting fixtures burned bright. Fifteen low-backed upholstered chairs dotted the carpet. Twelve were arranged in a semi-circle, facing toward the south wall, where three more faced back, lined in a row behind a simple desk.

The center of the three was for the prophet only.

Snow was settled into his chair and the two young men left, closing the door behind them.

"For us," Snow said, "this is the most secure place on this planet. I feel most safe right here."

So had Rowan, for a long time.

"What we are about to discuss none, save the next prophet after you, may know. It will be your duty to pass this on."

They'd never before spoken of succession.

"You assume I will be chosen."

"That has been our way for a long time. You are next in line. I doubt our colleagues will vary from tradition."

The twelve chairs arranged in a semi-circle were for the apostles, Rowan's designated spot at their center, facing the prophet, the desk symbolically between them. On either side of the prophet sat the two councilors of the First Presidency. He'd already been giving thought as to who he would select to flank him when it came his time to lead.

"Look around, Thaddeus," Snow said, voice cracking. "The prophets watch over us. Each is anxious to see how you will react to what you are about to hear."

The white walls were lined with gilt-framed portraits of the sixteen men who'd led the church before Snow.

"My image will soon join them." Snow pointed

to a blank spot. "Hang my portrait there, so you can always see me."

On the desk before the old man sat a plain wooden box, about two feet long, a foot wide, and half a foot tall, its lid shut. He'd noticed it immediately and assumed it was why they were here.

Snow caught his interest.

"I had that brought from the closed archives. It is for prophets only."

"Which I am not."

"But you soon will be, and you have to know what I am about to reveal. It was told to me by my predecessor when I served in your capacity as president of the twelve. Do you recall what happened here, at the temple, in 1993? With the record stone."

The story was legendary. A hole was dug ten feet deep near the temple's southeast corner. The goal was to find a hollowed-out foundation block. In 1867, during the temple's construction, Brigham Young had filled the stone with books, pamphlets, periodicals, and a set of gold coins in denominations of $2.50, $5, $10, and $20, creating a time capsule. The stone was found cracked, which had caused most of the paper inside to rot away. Fragments survived, which had been placed in the church archives, some occasionally on display in the History Library. In 1993 Rowan was beginning his third term in the Senate and had just risen to the level of an apostle. He hadn't been present on August 13, exactly 136 years to the day after the stone had first been sealed.

"I was there," Snow said, "when they climbed from that hole with buckets of mush, like papier-mâché. The gold coins were spectacular, though. Minted right here in Salt Lake. That's the thing about gold—time never affects it. But the paper was another matter. Moisture had done its damage." The prophet paused. "I've always wondered why Brigham Young included coins. They seemed so out of place. But maybe he was saying that there are things on which time has no effect."

"You speak in riddles, Charles."

Only here, inside the temple, behind the closed doors of the council room, would he ever use the prophet's first name.

"Brigham Young was not perfect," Snow said. "He made errors in judgment. He was human, as are we all. On the issue of our lost gold he may have made a grievous error. But with regard to Abraham Lincoln, he might have committed an even bigger mistake."

FIFTEEN

★

DENMARK

MALONE DROVE HIS MAZDA OUT OF COPENHA-
gen, then sixty miles west to Kalundborg and Zealand's northwest coast. Four-laned highway the
entire way made the going quick.

"You suspected Kirk, too, didn't you?" he asked
Luke.

"He was a little too fast with the info in your
shop. What did Stephanie tell you on the phone?"

"Enough for me to know that Kirk wasn't trustworthy."

"When he came up behind me with the gun I
thought it better to give him a little rope and see
where it led. Then I saw you thinking the same.
Of course, I didn't know you were going to go all
William Tell on me."

"Lucky for you my eyes are still good . . . for an old-timer."

Luke's cell phone rang and Malone could guess the caller's identity.

Stephanie.

The younger man listened stone-faced, betraying nothing. Exactly what he was supposed to do. Malone recalled many conversations with his former boss just like that, when she'd told him what he needed to know to get the job the done.

And not an ounce more.

Luke finished the call, then directed him toward Salazar's estate, a tract of expensive real estate north of town, facing the sea. They parked in the woods, off the highway, a quarter mile east from the main drive.

"I know the geography here," Luke said. "Salazar owns a tract that butts up to this property. There are a few buildings there. We should be able to get to them through those woods over there."

He stepped out into the night.

They were both now armed, as Luke carried the gun retrieved from Kirk. Here Malone was again, back in a game that he'd supposedly quit, one that he hadn't wanted to ever play again. Three years ago he decided the rewards were not worth the risks, and the prospects of owning an old-book shop had been too tempting to resist. He was a bibliophile and always had been. So he'd jumped at the chance to move to Europe and start over.

There'd been costs, though.

There always were.

Yet part of being smart was knowing what you wanted.

And he loved his new life.

But there was the matter of an agent in trouble. People had once come to his aid. Now it was his turn to return the favor.

The risks be damned.

They found a pebbled drive that led past a brick gate. A dense canopy of arching trees blocked the blackened sky. He felt a familiar stir of excitement at the unknown. A washed-out yellow glow came from somewhere in the distance, flickering through the trees like a candle in the breeze. A dwelling of some sort.

"The intel on this place," Luke whispered, "is that there are no guards. No cameras. No alarms. Salazar keeps a low profile."

"Trusting soul."

"I'm told Mormons are that way."

"But they're not foolish."

He was still bothered by the Danites. Those two men in Højbro Plads had been real. Were more threats like that lurking in the darkness that surrounded them? Possible. He still believed this a trap. Hopefully, Kirk's reinforcements were still chasing that cell phone on the bus.

They cleared the woods, and he spotted three structures in the dark. A small brick house, two stories with a gabled roof, along with a pair of smaller cottages. Two lights burned in the larger house, both just above ground level, in what was surely a cellar.

They hustled around to the rear, staying in the shadows, and found a short set of steps that dropped down in the ground. Luke descended and Malone was surprised to see that the door at the bottom opened.

Luke stared at him.

Way too easy.

They both readied their guns.

Inside was a dimly lit cellar that stretched the house's entire length. Brick archways provided support to the upper floors. Lots of nooks and crannies raised alarms. Equipment and tools lay about, surely used to maintain the estate.

Over there, Luke mouthed, pointing.

His gaze followed.

Built into one of the archways near a corner were iron bars. Inside, propped against the wall, lay a man with a bullet hole in the forehead, his face beaten into a mottled pattern of blood and bruises. They approached and saw a bucket of water and a ladle just outside the bars to one side. The light was dimmer here, no windows nearby, the cell's floor as hard and dry as a desert. The iron door was locked. No key in sight.

Luke squatted and stared at his comrade. "I knew him. We worked together once. He's got a family."

Malone's gut ached, too. He ran his tongue along the inside of his mouth and swallowed hard, then knelt beside the water bucket with the ladle. "You realize Salazar wanted you to find this. I'm sure we would have had company the moment we did."

Luke stood. "I get it. He thinks we're stupid. Now I'm going to kill the son of a bitch."

"That would accomplish a whole bunch."

"You have a better idea?"

He shrugged. "This is your show, not mine. I'm just here for a limited engagement, which seems to be over."

"Yeah, you keep telling yourself that long enough, Malone, you might start believing it."

"You might have an open-field run now. Those guys are surely still chasing that bus. But there could be more of them around."

Luke shook his head. "Salazar only has five on the payroll. Three are dead. The other two were there in the square."

"Aren't **you** a wealth of information? Would have been nice if you'd shared that before now."

He knew Luke was ready to be rid of him. He'd never liked partners, either, especially difficult ones. And he was ready to be gone. There was still the matter of the Copenhagen police, though, but Stephanie could deal with them.

"I have a job to do," Luke said. "You can wait at the car."

He blocked any retreat and said, "Quit bullshitting me. What did Stephanie brief you on in the car?"

"Look, old man, I don't have time to explain. Get out of my way and go back to your bookshop. Let the A-team handle this one."

He caught the anger and understood. Losing a man affected everyone.

"I told Stephanie I'd see this through. So that's what I'm going to do. Whether you like it or not. I assume you want to take a look at the main house, in that study Kirk so conveniently mentioned?"

"It's my job. I don't have a choice."

They left the cellar and traipsed west through the woods, paralleling the sea, the pound of surf clear in the distance. The lit mansion that awaited them was an excellent example of Dutch Baroque. Three stories, three wings, hip roof. The exterior was sheathed with the trademark thin red brick— Dutch clinkers, Malone had learned to call them.

He counted thirty windows facing their way, only a handful lit, and all on the ground floor.

"Nobody's home," Luke said.

"How do you know that?"

"The man's out for the evening."

Surely more of what Stephanie had told him on the phone.

They stayed toward the mansion's rear, where an expansive terrace faced the blackened sea fifty yards away. A row of French doors and windows opened into the house.

Luke tried the latches. Locked.

A light came on inside.

Which startled them both.

Malone darted left into a shrubbery bed, where darkness and the exterior wall offered protection. Luke found refuge in a similar spot on the terrace's opposite side, the French doors and windows between them. They both peered around the edge into the lit space beyond the glass and saw a red-walled parlor dotted with elegant period furniture, gilt mirrors, and oil paintings.

And two people.

One face—a man's—he did not recognize. But it didn't take a rocket scientist to know his identity.

Josepe Salazar.

The other, though, was a shock. No one had said a word about her involvement.

Not Stephanie. Not Frat Boy.
Nobody.
Yet here she was.
His girlfriend.
Cassiopeia Vitt.

PART
TWO

SIXTEEN

✦

CASSIOPEIA VITT ADMIRED THE MANSION'S INTE-
rior, which reflected the elegance she recalled of
Josepe's mother. She'd been a quiet, refined woman,
always respectful toward her husband and mindful of her family. Cassiopeia's own mother had
been the same, and watching what she took to be
both women's passiveness was one of the reasons
she'd fled both the relationship with Josepe and
the family religion. Those precepts may be good
for some, but dependence and vulnerability simply
were not part of her character.

"I've left the furnishings close to how my mother
arranged them. I always liked her style, so I saw no
need to change. I remember her so clearly when
I'm here."

Josepe remained a striking man. Tall, squarely built, his Spanish ancestry showed in his swarthy complexion and thick black hair. His imposing brown eyes cast the same confidence, the same quiet intensity. Highly educated and with a colloquial command of several languages, he'd enjoyed immense success in business. His family's concerns, like her own, stretched across Europe and Africa. And, like herself, he led a life of wealth and privilege. But unlike her, he'd decided to devote himself to his faith.

"You spend a lot of time here?" she asked.

He nodded. "My brothers and sisters are not fond of the place. So I enjoy summers here. Soon I'll head back to Spain for the winter."

She'd never visited the Salazar family in Denmark. Always in Spain, where they lived only a few kilometers away from her family's estate. She stepped toward a row of French doors that opened to a darkened terrace.

"I imagine there's a lovely view of the ocean from here."

Josepe came close. "A magnificent view, actually."

He walked over and yanked the cantilevered handles down, throwing open the panels and allowing cool air to rush inside.

"Feels wonderful," she said.

She was not proud of herself. She'd just spent an evening lying to a man she'd once cared about. There'd been no reawakening inside her. She'd not recently read the Book of Mormon. The only time she'd ever tried, as a teenager, she stopped ten pages in. She'd always wondered why the philosophies of the lost peoples described in the book were so revered. The Nephites wiped themselves out— no survivors, no trace left of their entire civilization. What was there to emulate?

But she told herself that deceit had been necessary.

Her old love, Josepe Salazar, was involved with something significant enough to have drawn the attention of the U.S. Justice Department. Last week, Stephanie had reported that Josepe may even have been involved with the death of a man. Nothing definitive, but enough to arouse suspicion.

She found it all hard to believe.

"Just a little recon. That's all I need," Stephanie had said six months ago. "Salazar might tell you things he would not tell anyone else."

"Why do you say that?"

"Did you know there's a photograph of you two in his Spanish house? It appears to have been taken years ago. Right there, near his desk, among other family pictures. That's how I knew to approach you. A man doesn't keep a picture like that around without a reason."

No, a man doesn't.

Especially one who'd been married and lost his wife.

Then last week Stephanie asked if she could accelerate her contact.

So she'd arranged for the trip to Denmark.

She'd once thought she loved Josepe. He'd clearly loved her, and seemed to still harbor some feelings. His hand on hers at dinner, which lingered longer than necessary, provided a hint of that. She'd continued the charade to prove to both Stephanie and herself that all of the allegations were wrong. She owed that to Josepe. He seemed utterly at ease with her, and she hoped that she wasn't making a mistake leading him along. When they were younger, he'd been nothing but kind. Their relationship had ended because she refused to accept what he, his parents, and her own all believed to be true. Thankfully, he'd found someone to share his life with. But that person was now gone.

Too late to turn back. She was in.

This had to be played out.

"I sit here, or out on the terrace, most evenings," he said to her. "Maybe we could enjoy the breeze in a little while. But first, I have something to show you."

MALONE ROSE FROM THE GROUND.

At the sight and sound of the man with Cassiopeia—whom he assumed was Salazar—opening the French doors, he'd flattened himself behind a thick hedge. Luke, on the far side, had likewise disappeared downward. Thankfully, no one had stepped outside.

Luke stood.

Malone came close and whispered, "Did you know she was here?"

The younger man nodded.

Stephanie had failed to say a word to him, which surely was intentional. He brushed away damp mulch that covered the bed.

The French doors remained open.

He motioned for them to enter.

SALAZAR LED CASSIOPEIA THROUGH THE GROUND floor to a library that had once been his grandfather's. It was from his mother's father that he'd learned to appreciate the way things had existed in the church's beginning—when heaven ruled absolute—before everything was changed to accommodate **conformity**.

He hated that word.

America professed a freedom of religion, where beliefs were personal and the government stayed out of churches. But nothing could have been farther from the truth. Saints had been persecuted from the beginning. First in New York, where the church was founded, which led to an exodus to Ohio, but the attacks continued. Then the congregation moved to Missouri, and a series of prolonged riots resulted in death and destruction. So they fled to Illinois, but more violence followed, ultimately resulting in a tragedy at the hands of a mob.

Every time he thought of that day his gut churned.

June 27, 1844.

Joseph Smith and his brother were murdered in Carthage, Illinois. The idea had been to destroy the church with the death of its leader. But the opposite had happened. Smith's martyrdom became a rallying point, and Saints flourished. Which he took as nothing short of divine intervention.

He opened the library door and allowed his guest to enter. He'd purposefully left the lights on earlier, hoping he might have an opportunity to bring her here. He could not have done so any sooner since his prisoner had been jailed nearby. That man's soul was surely, by now, on its way to Heavenly Father, the blood atonement assuring admittance. He felt content knowing that he'd bestowed his enemy that favor.

"Do not kill a man unless he be killed to save him," the angel had many times said.

"I brought you here to see a rare artifact," he said. "Since we were last together I have become an acquirer of all things related to Saints' history. I have a large collection, which I keep in Spain. Of late, though, I've been privileged to be a part of a special project."

"For the church?"

He nodded. "I was chosen by one of the elders. A brilliant man. He asked me to work directly with him. I ordinarily would not speak of this, but I think you'll appreciate it."

He approached the desk and pointed to a tattered book that lay open on the leather blotter. "Edwin Rushton was an early Saint. He knew Joseph Smith personally and worked closely with him. He was one of those who buried Prophet Joseph after his martyrdom."

She seemed interested in what he was saying.

"Rushton was a man of God who loved the Lord and was devoted to the restoration. He met many trials in his life and overcame them all. Eventually he settled in Utah and lived there until he died in 1904. Rushton kept a journal. A vital record of the early church that many thought had disappeared." He pointed toward the desk. "But I recently acquired it."

A stiff map of the United States sat displayed on a nearby easel, and he saw Cassiopeia glance toward it. He'd pinned markers at Sharon, Vermont. Palmyra, New York. Independence, Missouri. Nauvoo, Illinois. And Salt Lake City, Utah.

"That traces the Saints' path from where the Prophet Joseph was born, to where the church was formed, then on to Missouri and Illinois where we settled, and finally west. We traversed America and, along the way, became part of its history. More so than anyone even realizes."

He could see that she was definitely intrigued.

"This journal is documentary proof of that fact."

"It seems important to you."

His thoughts were clear. His purpose beyond dispute.

"**Tell her,**" the angel said in his head.

"Do you know the White Horse Prophecy?"

She shook her head.

"Let me read you a passage from the journal. It explains a glorious vision."

MALONE HAD MANAGED TO MANEUVER HIMSELF close to the open door, beyond which he could hear Salazar and Cassiopeia talking. Luke had drifted to other portions of the house, taking advantage of an opportunity to look around. Fine by him. He wanted to know what Cassiopeia was doing with a man who'd killed a U.S. Justice Department agent.

Everything about this rang wrong.

Cassiopeia, a woman he loved, alone with this devil?

He and Cassiopeia had known each other for two years, their beginnings anything but friendly. Only in the past few months had their relationship changed, both of them recognizing that they wanted more from the other, yet neither of them willing to reach too far. He understood that they were not married, nor even engaged, each with their own lives to live as they pleased. But they'd spoken as recently as a few days ago and she'd mentioned nothing about any trip to Denmark. In fact, she told him she was confined to France for the next week, her castle-rebuilding project demanding all of her attention.

A lie.

How many more had she told him?

Outside, he'd caught sight of Salazar. Tall, dark-skinned, hair cut in thick waves. Dressed smartly, too, in a stylish suit. Was he jealous? He certainly hoped not. But he could not deny the strange feeling in the pit of his stomach. One he hadn't felt in a long while. The last time? Nine years ago, when his marriage began to fall apart.

Nothing about that had been good, either.

He'd heard Salazar mention an old journal **recently acquired** and wondered if this was the same artifact Kirk had dangled as bait, the one whose owner was supposedly dead. He also wondered if this was where Kirk had wanted them to end up. After all, the study had specifically been mentioned.

At the moment he possessed too few answers to test any hypothesis.

So he told himself to be patient.

He could not risk a peek past the doorway into the study, his position outside, in the corridor, already precarious. But another open room six feet away offered a retreat.

He stood silent.

Listening.

As Salazar read to Cassiopeia.

SEVENTEEN

✪

ON THE 6TH OF MAY, 1843, A GRAND REVIEW of the Nauvoo Legion was held. The Prophet Joseph Smith complimented the men for their good discipline. The weather being hot, he called for a glass of water. With the glass in hand, he said, "I will drink a toast to the overthrow of the mobocrats. Here's wishing they were in the middle of the sea in a stone canoe, with iron paddles, and that a shark swallowed the canoe and the devil swallowed the shark and himself locked up in the northwest corner of hell, the key lost and a blind man hunting it."

The next morning a man who'd heard the toast returned to visit the house of the prophet and so abused him with bad language that he was ordered out by Smith. My attention was attracted to them, the man speaking in a loud tone of voice. I went towards them, the man finally leaving. Present then was the prophet, Theodore Turley, and myself. The prophet began talking about the mobbings and deridings and persecutions we as a people had endured.

"Our persecutors will have all the mobbings they want. Don't wish them any harm, for when you see their sufferings you will shed bitter tears for them."

While this conversation was going on we stood by the south wicket gate in a triangle. Turning to me, the prophet said, "I want to tell you something of the future. I will speak in a parable like unto John the Revelator. You will go to the Rocky Mountains and you will be a great and mighty people established there, which I will call the White Horse of peace and safety."

"Where will you be at that time?" I asked.

"I shall never go there. Your enemies will continue to follow you with persecutions and they will make obnoxious laws against you in Congress to destroy the White Horse, but you will have a friend or two to defend you and throw out the worst parts of the law so they will not hurt you so much. You must continue to petition Congress all the time, but they will treat you like strangers and aliens and they will not give you your rights, but will govern you with strangers and commissioners. You will see the Constitution of the United States almost destroyed. It will hang like a thread as fine as a silk fiber."

At that time the prophet's countenance became sad.

"I love the Constitution. It was made by the inspiration of God, and it will be preserved and saved by the efforts of the White Horse, and by the Red Horse, who will combine in its defense. The White Horse will find the mountains full of minerals and they will become rich. You will see silver piled up in the streets. You will see the gold shoveled up like sand. A terrible revolution will take place in the land of America, such as has never been seen before, for the land will be left without a supreme government, and every specie of wickedness will be practiced rampantly. Father will be against son and son against father. Mother against daughter and daughter against mother. The most terrible scenes of bloodshed, murder, and rape that have ever been imagined or looked upon will take place. People will be taken from the earth, but there will be peace and love only in the Rocky Mountains."

Here the prophet said that he could not bear to look longer upon the scenes as shown to him in his vision and he asked the Lord to close the scenes.

Continuing, he said, "During this time the Great White Horse will have accumulated strength, sending out elders to gather the honest in heart from among the people of the United States, to stand by the Constitution of the United States as it was given by the inspiration of God. In these days which are yet to come God will set up a Kingdom never to be thrown down, but other Kingdoms to come into it, and those Kingdoms that will not let the Gospel be preached in their lands will be humbled until they will. Peace and safety in the Rocky Mountains will be protected by the Guardians, the White and Red Horses. The coming of the Messiah among his people will be so natural that only those who see him will know that he has come, but he will come and give his laws unto Zion and minister unto his people."

Cassiopeia had heard many tales about the Mormons. The religion thrived on grand stories and elaborate metaphors. But she'd never been told the one Josepe had just read to her.

"The Prophet Joseph predicted the American Civil War eighteen years before it happened. He said that we, as a people, would migrate west to the Rocky Mountains, four years before that occurred. He also knew he would never make that journey. He died less than a year after making the prophecy. He predicted that justice would come to the mobocrats. The ones who tortured and killed Saints in the early days. And it did. In the form of a Civil War that killed hundreds of thousands."

Her father had told her about the persecutions, common prior to 1847. Homes and businesses burned, people robbed and maimed and killed. A pattern of organized violence that forced Saints to flee three states.

But not Utah.

There they dug in. Took a stand. Fought back.

"The prophecy tells us that we, the White Horse, will gather strength, sending out elders to collect the honest in heart from among the people of the United States. That we did. The church grew tremendously in the last half of the 19th century. And we were all **to stand by the Constitution of the United States as it was given by the inspiration of God.**"

She decided it was safe to ask, "What does that mean?"

"That something great is about to happen."

"You seem excited by the possibilities. Is it that inspiring?"

"Indeed, it is. And this journal confirms that what we all suspected is correct. The White Horse Prophecy is real."

She examined the book, carefully turning a few

of its brittle pages. "Can you tell me any more about this?"

"It's a great secret within our church. One that started long ago with Brigham Young. Every religion has its secrets, this is one of ours."

"And you discovered it?"

He shook his head. "More a rediscovery. I found some information in the closed archives. My research drew the attention of Elder Rowan. He called me in and, together, we have been working on this for several years."

She had to press. "And the White Horse Prophecy is part of it?"

He nodded. "Absolutely. But it's more complex than simply the Prophet Joseph's vision. Many events happened after he was murdered. Secret things that only a few are privy to."

She wondered why Josepe was being so forthcoming. Trusting her, after all these years. Or was she being tested?

"It seems fascinating," she said. "And important. I wish you luck with the endeavor."

"I was actually hoping you might offer a little more than that."

SALAZAR HAD CAREFULLY TIMED HIS REQUEST, offering just enough information to impress Cassiopeia with the importance of his mission. He'd searched nearly two years for Edwin Rushton's journal, then labored through three months of pointless negotiations trying to purchase it. Atoning its owner became the simpler method, especially after the man both lied and tried to cheat him.

He watched as she studied the journal.

Rushton was the type of Saint he wanted to be. An early pioneer who magnified his priesthood with good works, accepting the family responsibilities of four wives. He'd endured to the end in righteousness, becoming one of those the Heavenly Father surely accepted as having **kept his second estate,** entitling him to glory forever and ever. Could anyone ever doubt that those early Saints had been chastened, tested, and prepared for their last dispensation?

Of course not.

Those holy ones had established Zion on earth.

And he and every other descendant were the benefactors of their devotion.

"Cassiopeia, I don't want you to leave my life again. Will you help me in my mission?"

"What can I do?"

"First and foremost, be there with me. The glory of its success will be so much sweeter if you are there. Next, there are matters that I could use your help accomplishing. I have followed, over the years, what you have been doing, rebuilding that castle in southern France."

"I didn't know you knew of that."

"Oh, yes. I even donated funds to the effort, anonymously."

"I had no idea."

He'd always admired her. She was smart, with degrees in engineering and medieval history. She'd inherited full ownership of her father's business concerns, a conglomerate currently worth several billion euros. He knew of her competent steward-ship, and of her Dutch foundation that worked closely with the United Nations on world health and famine. Her personal life was not a matter of record, nor had he pried, confining his inquiries to what could be learned from the public record.

But he knew enough to know that he never should have allowed her to leave all those years ago.

"**And she won't. Ever again,**" the angel said in-side his head.

"I meant what I told you at dinner," she told him. "I made a mistake with both my faith **and** you."

He'd been alone a long time.

No one had been able to take his late wife's place.

Then one day he'd found a photograph of him and Cassiopeia, from back when they were together. The simple sight of it brought him joy, so he'd kept it out, on display, where he could see it every day.

Now that image was here.

In the flesh.

Again.

And he was glad.

EIGHTEEN

⭐

Rowan listened as Snow spoke, waiting to learn the significance of the wooden box.

"Brigham Young challenged several American presidents, asserting our religious and political independence. He ignored Congress and all laws he disagreed with, and thumbed his nose at local military commanders. Finally, in 1857, James Buchanan had had enough and took the extraordinary measure of sending troops to subdue us." Snow paused. "Plural marriage was a mistake both Smith and Young made."

Prophets from the Old Testament, like Abraham, had routinely taken many wives. Solomon himself had 700, along with 300 concubines. In 1831 Joseph Smith prayed to the Lord about such practices and was answered with a revelation that plural marriage was indeed part of the true covenant, though the church did not publicly acknowledge the practice until 1852.

Only about 2 percent of members ever participated, and all had to be spiritually selected by the prophet. Most times it was older women incapable of taking care of themselves brought into the nonsexual roles of a plural marriage, and always with the consent of the first wife. But child propagation also lay at its roots, since God had commanded that all **raise up a seed** unto him.

He knew that plural marriage enraged and offended American society. The 1862 Morrill Act allowed the canceling of citizenship for anyone who practiced it. Then the 1887 Edmunds-Tucker Act criminalized it.

"Smith and Young misjudged the effect of plural marriage on both Saints and gentiles," Snow said. "But instead of wisely walking away from something that had clearly become counterproductive, they continued the practice and demanded political autonomy."

Which Rowan admired.

Saints had migrated to Salt Lake to find a refuge. They'd occupied barren land no one had wanted and forged a society where church and state seamlessly meshed together. A provisional government was established in 1849 and statehood applied for. They called it Deseret, a word from the Book of Mormon that referred to a beehive, a symbol of industry and cooperation. Its boundaries would have included present-day Utah and Nevada, most of California, a third of Arizona, and parts of Colorado, Wyoming, Idaho, and Oregon. Statehood was denied. Congress did, though, accept the new land as a territory, shrinking its boundaries and renaming it Utah. Young was appointed its first governor, and did a masterful job keeping the meld of church and state intact.

"On the one hand," Snow said, "we wanted to be part of the greater society. Contribute to the national welfare. Be good citizens. On the other, we demanded the right to do as we please."

"It was a matter of religious belief. A matter of freedom. Plural marriage was part of our religion."

"Come now, Thaddeus. If our religion compelled the murdering of other human beings, would we have the freedom to enjoy that? That argument is weak and indefensible. Plural marriage, in a physical sense, was wrong. We should have recognized that long before 1890, when we finally did the smart thing and abolished it forever."

He did not agree.

"Brigham Young made many wise decisions," Snow said. "He was an effective administrator, a true visionary. We owe him a great deal. But he also made mistakes. Ones he failed to openly acknowledge during his life, but mistakes nonetheless."

He decided against any further argument or rebuttal. He needed information and conflict was not the way to encourage its flow.

"We should discuss the White Horse Prophecy," Snow said.

Had he heard right? He stared at the prophet.

"I'm aware of your explorations in the restricted archives. I know the substance of what Brother Salazar has researched within our closed records. You both have been busy studying that prophecy."

He decided not to be coy. "I want to find our great secret, Charles. We need to find it."

"That secret has been missing a long time."

But the sight of those wagons had provided him hope.

"I made the decision after your call yesterday," Snow said. "Something told me it was the right location." The older man paused, winded, and grabbed his breath.

"The Prophet Brigham hid the great secret away," he said, "intending for us to find it one day."

Snow shook his head. "We don't know that."

Only he and the prophet could have this conversation, as only they were currently privy to the story. Unfortunately, they each knew different parts. His had been learned from hard work and research, both in Utah and D.C., Snow's had been handed to him by his predecessor.

And that's what he needed to know.

"Every prophet since Brigham Young has wrestled with this same dilemma. I was hoping it might pass me by." Snow pointed to the wooden box. "Go ahead."

He opened the lid.

Inside lay an assortment of tattered documents, each tucked safely inside a vacuum-sealed plastic bag. Mainly books and old newspapers, badly damaged from rot and mildew.

"That's what we could salvage from the record stone in 1993," Snow said. "Unimportant writings from long ago, save for the two packets on top."

He'd already noticed both. Single sheets lay inside, their outer edges stained, as if burned. But their writing had survived.

"Examine both," the prophet told him.

He lifted out the first plastic protector.

The script was tight and small, the ink barely readable.

I fear there has been too much mixing
of the hairs with the butter for the good of
the butter. The workers of wickedness would
really like, now that the great Civil War
is but a memory, to have attention again
drawn to us and troops sent again to break

us up. They openly avow their intention
to break the power of the priesthood and
destroy our sacred organization. I once
thought that we could co-exist. That
agreements could be honored. But it will
not do for us to mix with the world and hope
thereby to gain favor and friendship. I so
tried to do what seemed correct and decent.
During my life I spoke of this to no one.
Instead, I leave this message for the faithful
who come after me. Know that we carry
a burden, one thrust upon us by Lincoln
himself, but one we voluntarily accepted.
When the great Civil War broke out I saw
that fight as the White Horse Prophecy
come true. Prophet Joseph predicted all
that eventually happened, including our
journey into the Rocky Mountains and his
own demise. By 1863 the Constitution did
in fact hang by a thread and, just as the
prophecy stated would happen, Congress
passed a law aimed at ruining us. So I sent
an emissary to Mr. Lincoln. He received
him with kindness and without formality.
His stated mission was to inquire about
statehood, which Mr. Lincoln avoided.
Instead, a message was sent to me. Lincoln
said he would leave us be, if I would leave
him be. This was precisely what we had

waited so many years to hear. All we have
ever sought was the freedom to live in our
own way. Lincoln knew us from Illinois. He
told my emissary that he had read the Book
of Mormon, which was encouraging to hear.
But it would have been ill advised to make
an agreement with any president without
some sort of assurance that its terms would
be honored. This was told to Lincoln, who
offered something of a sufficient magnitude
that we would know he intended to keep
his word. He, in turn, demanded the
same from us, which I provided. We each
accepted the other's offering and both sides
honored the agreement. Unfortunately,
Mr. Lincoln died before either one of our
collaterals could be returned. No one from
the government ever asked about what
we held of theirs, nor of what they held
of ours, which led me to conclude that no
one other than myself knew either existed.
So I kept silent. In doing so I fulfilled the
rest of the prophecy, which said that we
would act as the white horse savior of the
nation. But Prophet Joseph also told us
to stand by the Constitution of the United
States, as it was given by the inspiration
of God. That has never been done, at least
not in my lifetime. What I gave Mr. Lincoln

was the secret location of our wealth. Ever since the federal troops came in '57 Saints have talked of our lost gold. I tell you now that none of that gold was lost. Instead, all was put to good use. I provided a map of its hiding place, where I also hid what Mr. Lincoln entrusted to us. Two months after our bargain was sealed Lincoln sent me a telegram that said Samuel, the Lamanite, stood guard over our secret in Washington, among the Word, which gave me great comfort. He also said that he keeps the most important part of the secret close to him every day. I told him that providence and nature guard his half of the bargain. He seemed to enjoy the great mystery he and I created. Prophet Joseph was right in all that he foretold. May you be equally correct too.

"Brigham Young wrote this?" Rowan asked.
"It is his script."
"The lost gold and our great secret are linked?"
Snow nodded. "From the beginning. Solve one and you solve the other."
"What did the prophet mean by the reference to Samuel and the telegram?"
"That's where Lincoln was quite clever. In mid-1863, to ensure the lines still operated, the president sent a telegram to Brigham Young. He told

the prophet that what he'd read about Samuel in our good book rings true, so what better sentinel than a Lamanite."

Cryptic, for sure. But all new information. "This telegram still exists?"

"Sealed away, for the eyes of a prophet only. Its wording is actually quite meaningless unless you've read what you're holding. But now you and I both know the truth. Tell me, Thaddeus, how do you know of this secret? This was supposedly only for prophets."

The time for pretense was over. "As Prophet Brigham said, there were two sides to that bargain. Ours and Lincoln's. References to America's involvement with Brigham Young still exist in the national archives."

"I have known for some time that you were searching. Your accomplice, Senor Salazar, has made a nuisance of himself."

"You have a problem with Josepe?"

"He's a fanatic, and they are always dangerous, no matter how sincere they profess to be. He follows blindly the teachings of Joseph Smith, ignoring the continuing revelations prophets have received through the years."

"That sounds like blasphemy."

"Because I question what I know to be wrong? How could that be anything other than smart and practical?"

"Strange talk from our prophet."

"But that's the point, Thaddeus. I **am** the prophet. So my words carry the same significance as the ones spoken by those who came before me."

He motioned with Young's message. "Why are you showing me this?"

"Because I, too, now want to know the great secret. The White Horse Prophecy was always thought by us to be false, written years after the fact, incorporating what its drafters already knew to be reality, making Prophet Joseph sound more accurate than he deserved."

"It's real, Charles. Brother Salazar has proven that."

"I'll be interested in seeing that proof."

"We have an opportunity to fulfill the prophecy. We can stand by the Constitution of the United States, **as it was given by the inspiration of God.**"

"And if that destroys all that He created?"

"Then so be it."

"Study the second page."

He stared through the next stiff plastic protector and saw a map.

"That's where both the secret and the gold are hidden," Snow said.

"But it tells us nothing."

"Young apparently made the quest a challenge. I assume there's a good reason for that. It seems

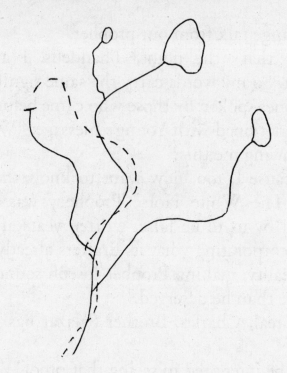

you must find what Mr. Lincoln hid away to solve this puzzle."

And he already knew exactly where to look.

"May I have these?"

Snow shook his head. "Not those. But I'll provide copies."

"You want me to go after it, don't you?"

"I want you to pray on the proper course. Whatever answer Heaven provides, act upon it. That's what I've done."

NINETEEN

★

STEPHANIE HAD FOUND ONLINE THE U.S. Supreme Court decision of **Texas v. White,** issued April 12, 1869.

The issue was simple.

Were $10 million of treasury bonds, transferred by Texas to private individuals after Texas seceded from the Union, valid? Everyone agreed that the transfer violated federal law, and happened at a time when Texas had declared itself no longer part of the Union, the former state setting up its own rules governing the transfer. So if Texas' secession from the Union was legal, then the bonds were valid and worth their face value. If not, they were worthless. An elementary dispute that, at its heart, raised a monumental question.

Was secession allowed by the Constitution?

She again scanned the opinion, just as she and Edwin had done two hours ago. He was gone, due back in Washington for an evening engagement. They would meet again tomorrow. The relevant portion came about halfway through.

The union of the States never was a purely artificial and arbitrary relation. It began among the colonies, and grew out of common origin, mutual sympathies, kindred principles, similar interests, and geographical relations. It was confirmed and strengthened by the necessities of war, and received definite form, and character, and sanction from the Articles of Confederation. By these the union was solemnly declared to "be perpetual." And when these Articles were found to be inadequate to the exigencies of the country, the Constitution was ordained "to form a more perfect Union." It is difficult to convey the idea of indissoluble unity more clearly than by these words. What can be indissoluble if a perpetual union, made more perfect, is not?

When, therefore, Texas became one of the United States, she entered into an indissoluble relation. All the obligations of perpetual union, and all the guaranties of republican government in the Union, attached at once to the State. The act which consummated her admission into the Union was something more than a compact; it was the incorporation of a new member into the political body. And it was final. The union between Texas and the other States was as complete, as perpetual, and as indissoluble as the union between the original States. There was no place for reconsideration, or revocation, except through revolution, or through consent of the States.

The ordinance of secession, adopted by the convention and ratified by a majority of the citizens of Texas, and all the acts of her legislature intended to give effect to that ordinance, were absolutely null. They were utterly without operation in law. The obligations of the State, as a member of the Union, and of every citizen of the State, as a citizen of the United States, remained perfect and unimpaired. It certainly follows that the State did not cease to be a State, nor her citizens to be citizens of the Union. If this were otherwise, the State must have become foreign, and her citizens foreigners. The war must have ceased to be a war for the suppression of rebellion, and must have become a war for conquest and subjugation.

Which was precisely how the South viewed the conflict.

Not the War Between the States. Or the Civil War.

But the War of Northern Aggression.

Conquest and subjugation. Absolutely.

Southerners felt that then, and many still did today. Go southeast of Atlanta into central Georgia, as she'd done many times, and mention the name General William Tecumseh Sherman in the right places, to the right people, and they'd spit on the ground.

She'd never really given secession serious thought. After Lincoln's time the issue was thought resolved. True, occasionally, there were rumblings in the press about some city, or county, or fringe faction who wanted out. Key West was famous for its Conch Republic. But nothing ever came of any of it.

Then she'd listened to Edwin. He wasn't some lunatic trying to avoid taxes, or ignore a law he didn't like, or just wanting to do as he pleased. He was the White House chief of staff.

And he was scared.

"This could become a real problem," Davis said. "We were hoping that time had taken care of things. But we've received information indicating that this is not the case."

"What could be so frightening?"

"Stephanie, we watch twenty-four-hour news, listen to talk radio, read editorials. Information comes at us all day long. Everybody has an opinion on everything. Bloggers, journalists. Twitter feeds and Facebook posts have become authoritative sources. No one really pays attention anymore. We only scratch the surface, and that's deemed enough."

He pointed at a paragraph on the screen. From Texas v. White.

Which she read again.

> Our conclusion therefore is, that Texas continued to be a State, and a State of the Union, notwithstanding the transactions to which we have referred. And this conclusion, in our judgment, is not in conflict with any act or declaration of any department of the National government, but entirely in accordance with the whole series of such acts and declarations since the first outbreak of the rebellion.

"The damn Supreme Court only scratched the surface," Davis said. "They issued a political opinion, not a legal one. Its author, Chief Justice Salmon Chase, served in Lincoln's cabinet. What was he going to say? The whole Civil War was unconstitutional? That secession was legal? And, by the way, 620,000 men died for nothing."

"Isn't that a bit melodramatic?"

"Not in the least. Texas v. White remains the definitive statement by the Supreme Court on the issue of secession. If a state tried to secede, any judge in the country would immediately hold that it's unconstitutional based on Texas v. White."

She knew that to be true.

"That opinion, though, was far from unanimous," Davis said. "Three justices dissented."

She stared again at the words on the screen.

And this conclusion, in our judgment, is not in conflict with any act or declaration of any department of the National government.

She heard again what Edwin had told her, ending with "What if we know something the Supreme Court in 1869 didn't?"

What if, indeed.

TWENTY

★

Denmark

Malone did not like anything Cassiopeia
had said.

Luke had returned in time to catch the tail end
of the conversation. **Stay cool**, the young man's
eyes signaled. This Frat Boy obviously knew of his
connection with Cassiopeia.

"Let me get you back to your hotel," Salazar
said from the study.

Malone pointed to the open doorway six feet
away, and they both slipped inside a darkened
media room. Soft chairs faced a huge video screen,
an obvious addition to such an old house.

They flattened themselves against the wall.

He heard movement from the study, then steps
in the corridor outside. Both Salazar and Cassio-

peia came into view outside the half-open door. He peered out and watched as Salazar grabbed Cassiopeia by the arm, drawing her close and kissing her.

Her arms embraced him, caressing his shoulders.

The sight was at once unnerving and disturbing.

"I have wanted to do that for a long time," Salazar said to her. "I never forgot you."

"I know."

"What do we do from here?"

"Enjoy our time together. I've missed you, Josepe."

"Surely you have loved and been loved."

"I have. But what we had was special, and we both know it."

Salazar kissed her again. Tender. Sweet.

Malone's gut churned.

"I could stay here tonight," she told him.

"That would not be wise," Salazar said. "For either of us."

"I understand. But know that I wanted to."

"I do, and it means more than you can imagine. Tomorrow, I'll come for you around ten. Be packed and ready to leave."

"Where are we going?"

"Salzburg."

They disappeared down the corridor. A door

opened, then closed. A few moments later a car engine growled, then faded into the distance.

He stood still, his heart pounding.

"You okay?" Luke asked.

His mind snapped back to the situation at hand. "Why wouldn't I be?"

"That's your girl and—"

"I'm not some high schooler. And how do you know she's my girl?"

"Three guesses. Look, that would have hurt, if it were me."

"You're not me."

"Okay. I get it. The subject is off limits."

"Stephanie tell you to keep her involvement from me?"

"She and Salazar were not supposed to be here. Vitt's job was to keep him away for the evening."

"Her **job**?"

"She's helping Stephanie. A favor. We discovered that she and Salazar once knew each other. They were . . . close. Obviously. We just saw that. Stephanie asked her to make contact and see what she could learn. She's just working him."

But he wondered. Was she playing a part? Simply trying to gain Salazar's confidence? If so, she was an excellent actress. Every word had sounded believable. Now Salazar himself was enlisting **her** help.

"I need to take a look inside that study."

He grabbed Luke's arm. "Is that all you've held back?"

"You said back at your bookshop you knew about Mormons. Did you know Cassiopeia Vitt was born one?"

He glared at Luke.

"I didn't think so. Part of the connection here is that she and Salazar were childhood friends. Their families close. Same religion, too."

Seemed like a night of surprises.

"Could you let go of my arm?"

He released his grip.

Luke brushed past and fled the media room.

He followed.

They entered the study, a warm space with paneled walls painted a sage green. The lights remained on, curtains drawn on the windows.

He focused on the task. "He doesn't have any staff in this house?"

"Reports say there are a few, but they don't stay overnight. Salazar likes his privacy."

But the remaining Danites could appear at any time. "Those two may have discovered the ruse with the bus by now. Do what you have to do. He was reading to her from something. That old journal, there."

Luke moved toward the desk and, with his Billet phone, snapped pictures of the tattered pages, especially the ones marked with slips of paper.

While Luke searched the desk drawers, Malone was drawn to the map displayed on an easel. He'd heard earlier when Salazar rattled off the places where Mormons had settled on their way west to the Salt Lake valley. He'd actually once visited Nauvoo, in central Illinois, where they headquartered for seven years. The temple that stood there now was a reconstruction, the original 19th-century version destroyed by mobs.

Hate.

What a powerful emotion.

So was jealousy.

And he was feeling both right now.

He needed to listen to himself—he **wasn't** some high schooler—he **was** a man who cared for a woman. He'd been divorced three years, separated from his ex-wife going on ten years. He'd lived alone a long time. Cassiopeia's entrance into his life had changed things. For the better. Or at least that's what he'd thought.

"Take a look at this," Luke said.

He stepped to the desk—huge, inlaid with ivory and decorated with an ornate onyx inkwell. Luke handed him a catalog for Dorotheum, one of the world's oldest auction houses, headquartered in Austria. He'd dealt with them while on Billet assignments and with his bookshop.

"Seems there's an event tomorrow night," Luke said. "In Salzburg."

He noted the date, time, and place from the catalog. Thumbing through, he discovered it was an estate sale. Furniture, porcelain, china, books. One page was dog-eared. An offering for a Book of Mormon. From March 1830. An original printing. Published by E. B. Grandin. Palmyra, New York.

He knew that volume.

There'd been many editions printed since 1830, but only a few of the original lot still existed. He recalled reading a few months ago how one had sold for nearly $200,000.

"Apparently Salazar wants to buy a book," he said.

And not just any book. One of the rarest in the world.

He stepped from the desk and again studied the map. Someone had taken a pink highlighter to Texas, Hawaii, Alaska, Vermont, and Montana.

"Why are those states colored? And don't tell me you don't know."

Luke stayed silent.

He placed his finger on Utah, which had been highlighted in yellow. "And this?"

"It's the center of the whole damn thing."

Utah was the home of the Church of Jesus Christ of Latter-day Saints. Several splinter groups of that religion existed, but its main body was headquartered there.

177 / THE LINCOLN MYTH

"The center of what?" he asked.

"Hard to believe, actually. But Stephanie told me on the phone there's a connection between Joseph Smith, Brigham Young, James Madison, and Abraham Lincoln. One that she's just been briefed on. It stretches straight back to the Founding Fathers."

"Involving?"

"The U.S. Constitution."

"Leading to what?"

"A whole bunch of really bad trouble."

TWENTY-ONE

★

Denmark
Thursday, October 9
9:20 a.m.

Salazar spoke into the phone but studied the map. He was in his study, finally connecting with Elder Rowan, explaining some of what had happened yesterday in Denmark. Their fears were now confirmed. The U.S. government was focused on him.

"They found you through me," Rowan said. "There are people in Washington who do not want us to succeed."

That he believed.

There'd always been animosity.

"From the beginning, Josepe," the angel said in his brain.

Every Saint knew how Joseph Smith, in 1839, knocked on the door of the White House—which he described as a **palace, large and splendid, decorated with all the fineries and elegance of this world**—and requested to see President Martin Van Buren. When Smith asked to be introduced as a Latter-day Saint, the request was viewed as nonsense. When he insisted, Van Buren merely smiled at the label.

"**With his arrogance, Josepe.**"

Smith had brought a letter that outlined all of the violent atrocities Saints had faced in Missouri, detailing the shocking loss of life and property. He described the infamous Executive Order 44, issued by the Missouri governor, which called for the extermination of all Saints. He respectfully asked the federal government to intervene, but Van Buren did nothing.

"**He said that to take up their cause would cost him the vote of Missouri,**" the angel reminded him. "**He judged us before he even knew us.**"

Many presidents thereafter shared Van Buren's apathy.

"**The government has always been controlled by ignorance, folly, and weakness.**"

The angel was right.

"**What is the government's strength? It is like a rope of sand, weak as water. There is little re-**

gard for truth or right. Shame on the rulers of the American nation."

Just as prophets had been with presidents, he was careful with Elder Rowan. But not out of mistrust. Rowan had made clear from the beginning that he did not want details. So he omitted what happened to the American agent, the deaths of two of his own men, and the disappearance of Barry Kirk. He understood the line of demarcation between the Quorum of Twelve and the remainder of the church. Joseph Smith, and his successor Brigham Young, had utilized men just like him who likewise safeguarded the collective interest.

"Is the situation in hand?" Rowan asked.

"Totally."

"It's important that it stay that way. The government will try with all its might to stop us. It's inevitable. We could only keep this secret for so long. Luckily, we're approaching the goal."

"Would it not be helpful to know the extent of their knowledge?" he asked.

"I plan to make inquiries on this end. Perhaps you could see what could be learned there?"

"My thoughts exactly."

"But rest assured, Josepe, neither of us has broken any laws. Their inquiries are simply investigatory."

He again said nothing.

Danites had always worked in secrecy. Recruitment 150 years ago, as now, was by personal contact only. Meetings were carefully guarded. Teachings were not openly discussed, even with fellow Danites, outside those gatherings. Members were taught to obey their leader's instructions without question or hesitation, admonished to prove faithful in all things committed to their trust, come life or death. Each recruit took a solemn covenant not to reveal anything. Punishment for violations of the code was carried out in secret.

"We live in a new and different dispensation," the angel said. "One in which the Kingdom of God will break into pieces and consume all earthly kingdoms. The duty of all noble and loyal Danites is to waste away the gentiles and consecrate them to the Kingdom of God. The earth is the Lord's, Josepe, not man's. And the laws of the land do not apply when one commits himself to God."

"My fear," he said to Rowan, "is that their investigative efforts could escalate."

"And they will. So conduct yourself accordingly."

He understood the instruction. Nothing the Danites did could ever become public. Josepe knew his role. He was the hammer and the sword. His reward was an inner satisfaction, not one to be flaunted for the benefit of others.

"It is not your business or place to know what is required by God," the angel said inside his head. "He will inform you by means of the prophet, and you must perform."

Amen, he mouthed. "I have matters in hand."

"As I knew you would. I may need you here soon, so be prepared to travel. I'm on the way back to Washington. Contact me when you have more to report."

He stared at the map and the states highlighted.

Texas, Hawaii, Alaska, Vermont, and Montana. And Utah.

He checked his watch.

"May Heavenly Father watch over you," Rowan said.

"Same to you, sir."

TWENTY-TWO

✶

COPENHAGEN

MALONE FELT LIKE THE OLD DAYS, TOSSING ONLY the essentials into a travel bag, then grabbing the knapsack from beneath his bed and retrieving the few hundred euros he always kept on hand, along with his passport. Years ago passports were the least of his concerns. As a Magellan Billet agent he'd moved about the world at will, sometimes legally, most times not. What a life. Occasionally he missed it, no matter how much he might say otherwise. He'd once been involved with some important assignments, a few that even changed history. But that was not his life anymore. Or at least that's what he'd told himself for the past few years, ever since he walked away. Yet he'd also been part of some astounding stuff since retiring.

Which seemed the case here, too.

What had Luke Daniels said last night? **There's a connection between Joseph Smith, Brigham Young, James Madison, and Abraham Lincoln. One that stretches straight back to the Founding Fathers.**

He'd parted ways with Luke after they returned to Copenhagen, and the younger agent had seemed glad to be rid of him. He'd once viewed Magellan Billet business through fresh eyes, too. Straight from the navy JAG, where Stephanie had recruited him for what became a permanent reassignment to the Justice Department. When he quit the government he'd also resigned his navy commission as Commander Harold Earl "Cotton" Malone, son of Forrest Malone—also a commander, United States Navy, lost at sea. His gaze darted to the frame on the wall and the handwritten note, dated November 17, 1971. His father's last 640 words. Written especially for his family. He'd savored every one. Especially the final sentence.

I love you, Cotton.

Not something he'd ever heard much while his dad had lived.

He'd tried not to make the same mistake with his own son, Gary, now sixteen. He certainly hoped the boy knew how he felt. God knows they'd been through enough together.

He grabbed hold of the Beretta. It had served

him well yesterday. How many people had he killed with it over the years? Ten? Twelve? Fifteen?

Hard to remember.

Which bothered him.

As did what he'd witnessed last night with Cassiopeia. Her kiss with Salazar hurt, no matter how much of a role she may have been playing. He was jealous, there was no other way to view it. She'd readily offered to stay the night. What would have happened if Salazar had said yes? He didn't want to think about it. Of course, he had no idea what happened after they'd left the estate. Salazar could have stayed over at her hotel.

Stop.

Quit this.

He hated the doubts that swirled through him, wishing he'd never seen nor heard any of it. He was better off not knowing.

Or was he?

His marriage had disintegrated thanks to lies and mistrust. He'd many times wondered what honesty would have added to that equation. Could it have saved the relationship?

His cell phone rang.

He'd been expecting the call and was not disappointed to see Stephanie Nelle appear on the screen.

"I heard you had a rough night," she said.

"You worked me."

"I needed your help. This started off as a simple background investigation on a foreign national. But it's turned into something else entirely. A U.S. senator is involved. A man named Rowan from Utah. I also had no idea Barry Kirk was a plant. Obviously, Salazar is way ahead of us."

"Get to the important part."

"Cassiopeia is there to expedite things and learn what she can. She's the closest person to the problem. But I'm not sure that's a good thing anymore."

"You kept that from me."

"You weren't supposed to get that close."

"So you just used me?"

"To find my missing man? You're damn right."

"Frat Boy tell you he's dead?"

"He did. My first inclination is to take Salazar down. But I've been ordered not to do that. Luke also said you were upset by what you saw. Cassiopeia is doing me a favor, Cotton. That's all."

"So she's lying to Salazar?"

"That's right. And she's not happy about it, but agreed to play it out a little longer."

"She didn't look like she was suffering."

"I know this hurts—"

"Does she know I was there?"

"I've told her nothing about your involvement."

"Keep it that way."

"She and Salazar were not even supposed to be in the house."

"The whole thing seemed a setup."

"I agree," she said. "But it worked out. We learned some valuable intel."

"That's what Frat Boy said?"

"He's not an idiot, Cotton. In fact, he's quite good. Just a bit impetuous. Maybe a symptom of his last name."

He hadn't made the connection before this moment. Daniels. "He's related to the president?"

"He's Danny Daniels' nephew. One of his brother's four sons."

"That how you ended up with him?"

"It's not what you think. Luke's a southern boy, like you, born and raised in Tennessee. After high school he enlisted and became an Army Ranger. A good one. His personnel jacket is loaded with commendations. He served all over the Middle East, including three tours in Iraq. He wanted to work for the CIA, but the president asked if I'd take him. No conditions, no special treatment. If he couldn't cut it, I was free to fire him."

"If he didn't get killed first."

"I remember, fifteen years ago, thinking the same thing about you. But that turned out all right."

"You held back on me, Stephanie. I hated that when I worked for you and I really hate it now."

"I never mentioned anything about Cassiopeia because I didn't think you'd be around long enough to find out. She's helping me out, and wanted it kept between us."

"And that's supposed to make me feel better?"

"You're not married to her, Cotton. She has her own life to live as she pleases, just like you do."

"Common courtesy would say otherwise."

"So I assume you tell her everything?"

"What exactly is she doing for you?"

"I can't go into that on this phone."

"Luke said there's something going on that involves the Founding Fathers."

"It's my mess, not yours."

He hesitated a second before saying, "I agree. I also agree that Cassiopeia is a big girl. She can handle herself."

"I'm sure she can. The question of the day is, can you?"

He could not bullshit Stephanie. She knew him, as he knew her.

"You love her, Cotton. Whether you want to admit it or not."

"She didn't involve me here. So it's not my business. Like you say, we're not married."

"I've recalled Luke. He should be back here in the States shortly. Salazar's men saw him and you, so his effectiveness there has been compromised."

"Do Frat Boy and the president get along?"

"Luke has no idea that his uncle intervened on

his behalf. That was another presidential condition."

He was impressed Stephanie had done the favor. Not necessarily her style. But he'd learned from Cassiopeia that feelings existed between his former boss and the current president. Which had surprised him. But never had he and Stephanie spoken on the matter. Neither one of them liked to talk about those kinds of things.

"Hard to fault a boy who calls his mother every Sunday," she said.

His own mother still lived in middle Georgia, on the sweet onion farm her family had owned for over a century. But unlike Luke Daniels, he did not call every week. Major holidays, birthdays, Mother's Day. That was the extent of his contact. She never complained, but that was her way. A negative word never came from her mouth. How old was she now? Seventy? Seventy-five? He wasn't sure. Why didn't he know his mother's age?

"And I made a call to Copenhagen," she said. "The locals won't be bothering you."

He'd wondered why the bookshop had not been overrun with police.

"They broke my front door glass."

"Send me the bill."

"I just might."

"I know you're pissed," she said. "I can't blame

you. But, Cotton, you're going to leave Cassiopeia alone, right? We can't risk her. Leave her be, until this is over. Like you say, she's a big girl. There are no more agents backing her up. She's on her own."

"Whatever you say."

He ended the call and stared down at the travel bag.

He was being played again.

No question.

He slipped the Beretta back into the knapsack and slid the bag beneath his bed. Unfortunately, he could not tote the weapon with him. Not allowed on planes, and checking it raised questions he preferred not answering. That was another perk that had come from carrying government credentials.

No matter. He'd adapt.

The U.S. government employed thousands of agents whose job it was to guard the national interests. He once worked as one. His job now was more personal. What had Stephanie just said about Cassiopeia? **No more agents backing her up. She's on her own.**

Not exactly.

And Stephanie knew it.

He needed to hurry.

His flight to Salzburg left in two hours.

TWENTY-THREE

★

KALUNDBORG

CASSIOPEIA FINISHED PACKING HER BAG. SHE'D
brought precious little, just a few outfits, the en-
sembles interchangeable for a variety of looks.
She'd expected to be gone only a few days. Now
her trip had been extended. The French doors were
swung open, offering a spectacular view of the
fjord and the Great Belt Strait, the gray-brown waters stirred by a stiff easterly breeze. Josepe had arranged her accommodations at the seaside inn,
purposefully not allowing her to stay at his estate.
That could be because he preferred to keep their
relationship on a proper level, or it could be because he did not want her there. She'd been in
Denmark three days and last night was the first
time he'd taken her for a visit.

Everything that happened last night disturbed her.

Kissing Josepe again, after so many years, had brought back memories she'd thought were gone. He'd been her first love, and she his. He'd always been a perfect gentleman toward her, their relationship loving but never passionate. Church doctrine forbade premarital sex. So her offer to stay the night with him had been risky, but not overly so. If nothing else, the gesture had further ingratiated her.

She still felt awful deceiving him, regretting more by the minute her participation in this charade. When she'd agreed to help she hadn't known that he still harbored such deep feelings. Sure, Stephanie had told her of the photograph, but that could have been explained in many ways. Instead the actual explanation had become abundantly clear.

Josepe cared for her.

She arranged the last of her clothes in the bag and zipped it shut.

She should stop this farce. That was the right thing to do. But the allegation of murder counseled otherwise. Mormonism abhorred violence. Sure, once, long ago, things had been different and Saints had dished out their share. But that had been a matter of survival. An issue of self-defense, a sign of those times. Josepe was a devout believer in church doctrine, which forbade harm to others, so why would he venture away from principles so fundamental? There had to be another explanation. One that did not link him with murder.

She checked her watch: 9:30 A.M.

He would be here soon.

She walked to the open doors and listened to the rhythmic beat of the surf and the cries of birds.

Her cell phone chimed.

"We had an incident last night," Stephanie said when she answered.

She listened to what had happened on the Øresund and in Copenhagen with one of Josepe's associates.

"I had to involve Cotton," Stephanie said. "He was all I had at the moment. He handled it, but he killed three men."

"Is he okay?"

"He's fine."

"Anything on your missing man?"

"Still missing. The men who came after Cotton were Danites in Salazar's employ."

Danites? She recalled reading about them as a teenager, but they no longer existed, extinct since the 19th century. "I've seen no evidence of that here." Then she reported what had happened between her and Josepe. "He cares for me a great deal. I feel like a cheat. I should get out of this."

"I need you to hang with it a little longer. Things

have escalated on this end, and I'll be learning more today. Go to Salzburg with him and see what you might pick up. After that, you can leave. He'll never know the difference."

"But I will. I lied to Cotton, too. He would not be happy with what I'm doing."

"You're assisting a U.S. intelligence operation. That's all. The Elder Rowan, Salazar mentioned, is Senator Thaddeus Rowan of Utah."

She explained about the map in Josepe's study. "Utah was highlighted in yellow. The other five states in pink."

"Which ones?"

She told her.

"At the moment, Senator Rowan has me in his congressional sights. That great mission Salazar mentioned? That's what we need to find out about. It's important, Cassiopeia. And you're our fastest way in."

"I need to call Cotton."

"Let's not do that. He seems okay. He helped me out last night and now he's back to work at his bookshop."

But **she** wasn't okay.

She felt alone.

And that bothered her.

She'd been thinking about Cotton all morning. Technically, what she'd done with Josepe wasn't cheating. More a deception. Interesting the differences between the two men. Where Cotton was unassuming, reserved, and stingy with his emotions, Josepe was flamboyant, warm, and loving. His deep religious beliefs were both an asset and a curse. Both were strikingly handsome, alpha males, sure and confident. Both possessed flaws. She wasn't sure why comparisons had become relevant, only that, ever since last night, she'd been making them.

"Play this out a little longer," Stephanie said.

"I'm not okay with this anymore."

"I hear that, but there's a lot at stake. And, Cassiopeia, no matter what you want to believe, Salazar is not an innocent."

STEPHANIE ENDED THE CALL.

She hadn't liked lying to Cassiopeia, but it had been necessary. Cotton was not fine. That was clear from the call earlier. Luke, too, had confirmed that Cotton was upset.

And her dead agent.

She'd withheld that also.

If she'd told Cassiopeia the truth on both counts, there was no telling what the reaction might be. She could try to confront Salazar. Or she might leave. Better to keep that information close for a little while longer.

She sat up in her bed and glanced at the clock on the nightstand. 3:50 A.M.

Her flight to Washington left in four hours. Edwin Davis had said he'd meet her at Reagan National. She was anxious to find out more. The little she knew so far was troubling enough. Thirty years she'd worked for the government, starting during the Reagan administration with the State Department, then moving to Justice. She'd seen a lot of crises. Through it all she'd developed a sixth sense. If that sense was right this time, Malone was on his way to Salzburg. He'd been coy on the phone, but she knew better. Especially after she told him Cassiopeia was on her own. No way was he going to allow her to fly solo. Nothing would keep him away.

Sleep had fled her. She was wide awake.

And not just from the two phone calls.

Apprehension gnawed at her brain.

What was it she did not know?

TWENTY-FOUR

✦

KALUNDBORG

SALAZAR COMPLETED ALL OF THE ARRANGEMENTS for his trip to Salzburg. His latest toy, a Learjet 75, was waiting. A car was outside, ready to take him into town for Cassiopeia, then to the airfield. He'd altered the hotel reservations and the Goldener Hirsch had been accommodating, assuring him that two suites would be ready. The flight would take less than two hours, and he was looking forward to being back in the Austrian mountains. The weather should be lovely. He loved Salzburg. It was one of his favorite cities—and now the trip would be that much more enjoyable, thanks to Cassiopeia coming along.

The doors to his study opened. One of his two

remaining men, a loyal Danite who'd been in Copenhagen, entered.

"Cotton Malone," his man said, "is a bookseller in Copenhagen."

"Yet he managed to kill two of our own." Those deaths bothered him. He'd never lost a man before. "And Barry? Any sign of him?"

"We found the cell phone on a public bus, put there to lead us off the trail. Brother Kirk has made no contact since last night outside the bookstore."

He knew what that meant.

Three men gone.

"Did you handle things?"

His acolyte nodded. "I personally disposed of the American agent's body."

"Any link to us with the two who will be found in the Øresund?"

"There should not be."

He'd already been briefed on what had happened yesterday when another American agent had been cornered outside Kalundborg, then fled, stealing one of his prop planes—which, by now, from the reports he'd received, was at the bottom of the North Sea.

"Your assessment?" he asked.

He valued his men's opinions. Good advisers made for good decisions. That was something all of the prophets had in common, counting on smart and obedient men to provide wisdom and guidance. He and his Danites served that function for Elder Rowan.

"Brother Kirk briefed me before he left for Sweden. He said the Americans' interest piqued when he mentioned the death. They seem intent on finding whatever negatives they can."

They'd used the possibility of a murder relative to the Rushton journal as a way to excite their enemy into making a mistake. And though the owner of the journal, which still lay on his desk, was indeed dead, nothing linked that to him—other than a wild assertion.

"Do you think they have Barry?" he asked.

Kirk's task had been to learn what he could from the inside, then divert his saviors here. But something had gone wrong.

"It's unlikely. How would they have known to plant the phone on the bus? Brother Kirk never would have told them anything voluntarily. In the square, just before Malone diverted the police our way, Brother Kirk signaled to me to stand ready. We were to follow using the phone tracker. I was the one who reported the killings on the water to the police. I gave them Malone's location. It was meant to flush them out, keep things moving. But it backfired."

That it had.

He recalled his conversation earlier with Elder Rowan. Things were happening across the Atlantic and he would soon be needed there. In the meantime Rowan had told him to learn what he could on this end.

And that was what he planned to do.

He reached for a remote control and pointed the device at a flat screen mounted on the far wall. The image that appeared was of the study, from last night, two men rummaging through the desk and examining the map on the easel, which had been left on display for a reason.

"Barry seems to have told them to come here, though, as we planned," he said.

He and Kirk had agreed to lead the Americans so that, before killing them, they could see what might be learned when their enemy thought no one was listening. They would first find the body then, enraged, head for the main house. After saying what they might not otherwise say, they were to join their compatriot in eternity.

But that had not happened.

And from the time indicators on the video, he realized that the enemy had been inside the house as he and Cassiopeia had left.

Which was never part of the plan.

Of course, as things unfolded last night he'd been unaware of any problems. From the text received at dinner, he'd believed all was proceeding smoothly.

"The younger man is the one who stole the

plane and was in Copenhagen last night," his man said. "That's Malone studying the map."

"Why are those states colored?" Malone asked. "And don't tell me you don't know. That call from Stephanie, in the car, was a briefing. I used to get them, too."

"Those states are the problem."

He watched as Malone pointed to Utah.

"And this?"

The answer to that question surprised him.

"It's a complicated thing. Hard to believe, actually. But there's a connection between Joseph Smith, Brigham Young, James Madison, and Abraham Lincoln. One that stretches straight back to the Founding Fathers."

"Involving?"

"The U.S. Constitution."

They watched as the two Americans found the auction brochure on the desk, the marked reference to the Book of Mormon being offered for sale. He clicked off the video, pleased that the micro-camera installed in the ceiling had worked perfectly. They had, indeed, learned from their enemy.

"I'm leaving for Salzburg in a few minutes."

"Will you be alone?"

"No. Miss Vitt will be joining me."

"Is that wise?"

He recognized that this man's job was to look

after him, especially considering what had happened over the past twenty-four hours.

"She is a trusted old friend."

"I didn't meant to offend. It's just that it might be better if this was handled by us alone."

"I want her there."

He wasn't going to listen to any negativity toward Cassiopeia. He could still feel her lips on his skin and the exhilarating electricity that had swept through him. She'd given him no reason to doubt her in any way.

"It's not a matter for debate."

His man nodded.

"We owe Malone for our dead brothers," he said, shifting the subject.

"I watched from shore as he killed them, powerless to do anything."

"**We must stand by one another and defend one another in all things**," the angel said in his head. "**If our enemies swear against us, we can swear also. In this way we will consecrate much unto the Lord and build up His kingdom. Who can stand against us?**"

No one.

"Be ready to leave shortly."

His man left.

He thought about the coming few hours and wondered if they might have been too bold, too clever, providing their enemy too much latitude.

The idea of sending Kirk into their midst had made sense.

But it could have cost his friend's life.

Perhaps one or both of the two Americans from yesterday would travel to Austria.

If so, he would learn Kirk's fate and deal with them.

Heavenly Father might even smile upon him and send Cotton Malone.

TWENTY-FIVE

⭐

Stephanie rode in the limousine, Edwin Davis beside her. True to his word, after her Delta shuttle from Atlanta landed he'd met her at Reagan National. He'd told her to pack a bag, as she might be here for a few days. Beyond that, she had no idea what to expect.

Morning traffic puttered along, stop and go, the syrupy congestion continuing even after they exited the expressway. Davis had been cordial with his greeting but beyond that he'd been quiet, staring out the window. She, too, had watched as the Lincoln Memorial, the Washington Monument, and the Capitol passed by. Though she'd lived and worked here off and on for over thirty years, the sights never failed to impress her.

"It's interesting," Davis said, his voice nearly a whisper. "All of this was started by a group of men holed up behind closed doors in the brutal heat of a Philadelphia summer."

She agreed about the accomplishment. Fifty-five delegates from twelve states arrived in May and stayed until September 1787. Rhode Island never sent any representatives, refusing to participate, and two of the three New York delegates left early. But the men who remained managed a political miracle. Sixty percent of them had participated in the Revolution. Most had served in both the Confederation and Continental Congresses. Several had been governors. Over half were trained as lawyers, the rest a varied lot—merchants, manufacturers, shippers, bankers, doctors, a minister, and several farmers. Twenty-five owned slaves. Two, George Washington and Gouverneur Morris, were among the wealthiest men in the country.

"You know what happened at the convention's end?" Davis asked. "When it came time to sign."

She nodded. "Only 42 were there that day, and just 39 signed."

"Washington went first, then the representatives marched up, north to south, one state at a time. Nobody was really happy. Nathaniel Gorham, from Massachusetts, said he doubted the new nation would last 150 years. Yet here we are. Still going."

She wondered about the cynicism.

"What happened during those few months in Philadelphia," he said, "has become more legend than fact. Watch some of the cable news shows and you'd think those men could do no wrong." He finally faced her. "Nothing could be further from the truth."

"Edwin, I know the founders were flawed. I've read Madison's notes."

The definitive record of what happened in Philadelphia was James Madison's **Notes of Debates in the Federal Convention of 1787**. Though not the convention's official secretary, Madison kept a meticulous record, which he faithfully transcribed each evening. The delegates had first assembled to amend the impractical Articles of Confederation, but quickly decided to discard those articles entirely and draft a new constitution. Most states, if informed of that intent, would have recalled their delegates, ending the convention. So the proceedings were held in secret and, afterward, the working papers kept by the official secretary were destroyed. Only a tally of resolutions and votes survived. Other delegates kept notes, but Madison's became the most authoritative account of day-to-day deliberations.

"The problem," he said, "is that his record is not reliable."

She knew that, too. "He didn't publish them until 1840."

And during those ensuing 53 years Madison admitted embellishing his remembrances, making countless emendations, deletions, and insertions. So many that it was now impossible to know what actually took place. Compounding things was Madison's refusal to allow his record to be published until all of the convention members, including himself, were dead.

Which meant nobody was left alive to contradict his account.

"Those notes," Davis said, "have formed the basis for many a landmark constitutional decision. They are cited by federal and state courts every day as the founders' supposed intent. Our entire constitutional jurisprudence is, literally, based on them."

She wondered if this related to what he'd said yesterday about the Supreme Court being wrong in **Texas** v. **White**, but knew Davis would tell her only when he was ready.

She noticed their route.

Toward the northwest, past the university at Georgetown, along a picturesque tree-lined boulevard. She knew these neighborhoods, many of the foreign embassies located nearby. Finally, the car motored to an iron gate, staffed by uniformed guards, which was immediately opened.

She knew where they were.

The Naval Observatory.

Seventy-two wooded acres perched on a hill, thirteen of which formed the compound where the vice president of the United States resided.

They turned onto a street marked OBSERVATORY CIRCLE and she caught sight of the white-bricked, three-story Queen Anne–style house. Sage-green shutters adorned its many windows.

The car stopped and Davis exited.

She followed.

They climbed the steps to a veranda adorned with white wicker furniture. Fall roses bloomed in beds at its base.

"What business do we have with the vice president?" she asked.

"None," Davis said as he kept walking toward the front door.

They entered a spacious foyer, the floor covered in a thick green-and-beige Oriental carpet. True to its Queen Anne architecture, the rooms opened into one another without adjoining corridors. A palette of celadon, lime, and light blue dominated the décor.

Davis pointed to the right and led the way.

They entered the dining room.

Sitting at the table was President Robert Edward "Danny" Daniels Jr. He wore a suit and tie but had removed the jacket, which hung on the back of his chair. His shirtsleeves were rolled up.

She stopped herself from smiling.

"Have a seat," the president said to her. "We have a lot to discuss."

"About what?"

"Your problem."

"I have quite a few of those," she said.

"But only one," he said, "that involves Thaddeus Rowan, the distinguished senator from Utah."

TWENTY-SIX

✦

Salt Lake City
9:00 A.M

Rowan entered the Hotel Monaco, located
in the heart of downtown, a couple of blocks south
of Temple Square. Salt Lake had been laid out on
a grid, its major streets running in a crisscross pattern, all emanating from Temple Square. Brigham
Young had demanded that each street be wide
enough that a wagon team could turn about **without resorting to profanity**. His plan was followed
and remained today, and was incorporated into
many later settlements.

The Hotel Utah, owned by the church near
Temple Square, had once been the city's premier
establishment. But it closed in 1987, the site refur-
bished into a church administrative center. Now

the Monaco had acquired that label, the building itself a former bank and city landmark. He'd suggested the accommodations to the occupants of the upper floor's Majestic Suite—called that, he knew, because of the sweeping views offered of downtown and the steep Wasatch and Oquirrh Mountains ringing the Salt Lake basin.

Waiting for him were three men.

His command team. Assembled more than three years ago, ready for the coming fight.

He entered the suite and they all shook hands.

This gathering had been planned for several weeks. But now, with the finding of the wagons and the revelations from the wooden box, their talk had taken on a new sense of urgency.

All three were highly trained appellate litigators. Two were equity partners in major firms, one in New York, the other in Dallas. The third was a professor at Columbia Law School. Each had argued and won cases before the U.S. Supreme Court. They were respected, brilliant, and expensive, recruited by Rowan after it was determined that they all shared the same political philosophy.

He noticed that a silver serving cart had been ordered with juice, fruit, and croissants. They each filled a plate and sat around a walnut dining table that dominated one corner of the spacious suite. Far below, the streets of Salt Lake City pulsed with morning traffic. A steady string of headlights in the distance delineated Interstate 15, which cut a north–south path through the state.

"Tell me how we are across the country?" he asked.

"We have good people on the ground, ready to go, in every state," one of the lawyers said. "They'll be assets when the time comes. They range from PR specialists to lawyers to clerks to academics. Everything we'll need."

"Secrecy?"

"So far, no problems in that area, but we're stingy with information and liberal with money."

"And the main thrust?"

"That will come in Texas, Hawaii, Alaska, Vermont, and Montana, as agreed. Sentiments are highest in the legislatures of those states. Polling indicates that the people there are not opposed. So we have legislative measures ready to go."

Which will give the movement a stamp of nationalism, though Utah would lead the way.

"You saw the petition from Texas?" the other lawyer asked him.

He had. Two weeks ago. More than 125,000 had signed, stating that they no longer wanted to be part of the United States.

"We didn't spearhead that, but we didn't discourage it, either. It came from a fringe group. Take a look at its preamble."

He accepted an iPad and read from the screen.

> Given that the state of Texas maintains a balanced budget and is the 15th largest economy in the world, it is practically feasible for Texas to withdraw from the union, and to do so would protect its citizens' standard of living and re-secure their rights and liberties in accordance with the original ideas and beliefs of our founding fathers which are no longer being reflected by the federal government.

He liked the wording but had not liked the comments made in the press by its creators. Too radical. Too fanatical. They'd sounded absurd. What the petition had done, though, was draw attention to the issue, which the news channels had salivated over for several days.

"Georgia, Florida, Alabama, and Tennessee now have started similar petitions. But none of them comes close to the 125,000 signers from Texas. These are just publicity stunts, but they don't hurt a thing."

He laid the iPad on the table. "We have to bring this discussion out of the South."

One of the others said, "We know. A recent Zogby poll shows that, nationwide, 18% favored secession of their state from the Union. Another poll, from **The Huffington Post,** found that 29% said their state should be allowed to secede, if a majority of the residents so wanted. But here's the interesting part. Another 33% in that study were unsure."

Which meant a potential 62% could be in favor of a state's right to leave the Union.

No surprise, really.

"Which is why we have to change the tone," he said. "Luckily, to quote John Paul Jones, **We have not yet begun to fight**. Where are we legally?"

"I've had my students working on that," the professor said. "A hypothetical exercise in legal reasoning, I called it. They're all bright people and they've developed a solid treatise."

He listened as the academician explained their premise.

The Declaration of Independence contained the clear statement **that whenever any form of government becomes destructive, it is the right of the people to alter or to abolish it, and to institute new government, laying its foundation on such principles and organizing its powers in such form, as to them shall seem most likely to effect their safety and happiness.** It went on to pronounce, in no uncertain terms, **when a long train of abuses and usurpations evinces a design to reduce the people under absolute despotism, it is their right, it is their duty, to throw off such government, and to provide new guards for their future security.**

Each of the original thirteen colonies had declared its own independence from Great Britain. After the war, England recognized each state as sovereign. The states eventually formed the Articles of Confederation and Perpetual Union, which created a federal government as their collective agent. But in 1787 the states seceded from that perpetual union and adopted a new constitution. Nowhere were the words **perpetual union** included in that new constitution, and no state had agreed to such permanency when ratifying. In fact, Virginia, Rhode Island, and New York, in their ratification votes, specifically reserved the right to secede, which was not opposed by the other states.

He liked what he was hearing.

Since the Civil War any talk of secession had been muted by the fact that the South lost and the Supreme Court of the United States proclaimed in 1869 that the act was unconstitutional.

The professor produced a bound document, two inches thick.

"This is their analysis of every judicial decision in the country that ever considered the issue of secession. Mainly federal cases from the mid-19th century and a few state decisions. All, though, are uniform in holding the concept of secession illegal."

He waited to hear what he needed to know.

"Nearly all of those decisions, though, use **Texas v. White** as their basis," the professor said. "Knock that out, and there's no precedent. We'd be in virgin territory. I had them analyze that aspect quite carefully. The conclusion is inescapable." The professor laid the bound pages before him. "It's a house of cards. Removing just that one will cause the whole thing to collapse."

He realized his ally was referring to the legal precedents, but the same metaphor applied to the assemblage of fifty states.

Secession was an issue he'd long considered, ever since he decided that the federal government was broken beyond repair. It had become too big, too arrogant, too foolish. The Founding Fathers fought a long and bloody war against a centralized authority—England and its king—so they never would have created a new autocracy. It was self-evident in 1787 that no state could be forced to either join or stay in the Union. Both decisions were up to the people of each state. In fact, a specific proposal to allow the federal government to suppress a seceding state failed at the Constitutional Convention.

So when had the notion of a **perpetual union** taken hold?

He knew exactly when.

Lincoln.

And only a handful of historians had ever

grasped the truth that Lincoln fought the Civil War not to **preserve** an indivisible union. Instead, he fought that war to **create** one, coining the notion that the Union was somehow **perpetual**.

But Lincoln was wrong.

The Declaration of Independence was an act of secession, executed in direct conflict with British law. The ratification of the new Constitution was a secession from the Articles of Confederation, even though those articles, as first drafted and approved in 1781, expressly stated that **the union shall be perpetual**.

The issue was crystal clear.

States had never lost their right to secede.

And history supported that belief.

The Union of Soviet Socialist Republics dissolved in 1991 when fifteen of its states seceded. Maine formed when it seceded from Massachusetts. The same thing happened when Tennessee left North Carolina and West Virginia emerged from Kentucky and Virginia. And in 1863, when Lincoln created West Virginia, he did so without the consent of its people. International law proclaimed that sovereignty cannot be surrendered by implication, only expressly, which means the Constitution's silence on the issue of secession is significant. The Tenth Amendment itself stated that **the powers not delegated to the United States by the Constitution, nor prohibited by it to the**

States, are reserved to the States respectively, or to the people.

Nowhere in the Constitution were states prohibited from seceding.

"I like where we are," he said. "You've done a great job. But keep prepping."

"Are things progressing on your end?" one of the lawyers asked.

He knew what he'd promised to deliver.

The most important ingredient.

"We're closer every day. It could happen anytime. I'm heading back to Washington when I leave here to follow up on a new lead, which could be significant."

He felt a surge of excitement.

A civil war was coming.

But not like 1861.

This time there would be no troops on the battlefield. Hundreds of thousands would not lose their lives. No bloodshed at all, in fact. The only weapons would be words and money.

The words seemed to be coming together. Perhaps the final piece of the puzzle awaited him in Washington. And he had access to plenty of money. Soon he might even have the entire Church of Jesus Christ of Latter-day Saints—with its billions—at his disposal.

If Charles R. Snow would just go and meet Heavenly Father.

All was right.

He stood from the table and faced his associates, like a general with his colonels.

"Gentlemen, just remember one thing. Unlike
the first attempt at secession and the failed Confederacy, we're going to win our war."

TWENTY-SEVEN

★

Salzburg, Austria
5:20 p.m.

Malone had visited Salzburg before. Guarded on its flanks and rear by the towering Mönchsberg cliffs, the ancient town occupied both sides of the swift-moving Salzach River. A forest of church spires pierced the evening sky, gathered about cobbled squares and a maze of streets that, four hundred years ago, had formed a religious mecca. First a Roman trading center then a Christian outpost, it became a bishopric in the 8th century. Called the German Rome, its cathedrals and palaces were built to satisfy the lavish tastes that princes of the church had then demanded. Salt gave the province, the town, and the river its identity—culture, music, and art had provided its heritage.

He'd arrived on a flight from Copenhagen and taken a taxi into town. He chose a hotel near the Mozartplaz, a small establishment away from where he thought Salazar and Cassiopeia would be staying. He knew little about his adversary but enough to conclude that the Spaniard was at either the Hotel Sacher or the Goldener Hirsch. The Sacher sat across the river, near the Mirabell Palace, in what many called new town. The Goldener Hirsch occupied a more central locale in old town on Getreidegasse, one of the most famous shopping streets in the world. He decided that the Goldener Hirsch was the best bet and walked there, following the pedestrian-only routes. Narrow houses rose on both sides, the fronts washed with green, tawny, or a rusty pink. Each was a backdrop for a canopy of black ironwork filigree, cantilevered signs announcing each business with an image depicting the appropriate guild. The one for the Goldener Hirsch was particularly fitting—a lacy grillwork supporting a leaping golden stag.

He entered through dark green wooden doors into a lobby filled with rural Bavarian furniture. A long mahogany desk ran its length toward a staircase and elevator. He decided the best way to handle matters was to act like he knew what he was doing.

"I'm here to see Senor Salazar," he told the young woman behind the counter. She had a broad face and unblinking eyes and was dressed in a staff uniform, like the other two attendants standing nearby. He kept his gaze focused on her, as if expecting action on his request.

"He has only recently arrived," the woman said. "And did not mention any guests were expected."

He feigned annoyance. "I was told to be here now."

"He's in the restaurant," one of the young men in uniform said.

He smiled at the attendant, then found a wad of cash he'd purposefully stuffed into his pant pocket and handed over twenty euros.

"**Danke**," he said, as the offering was accepted.

The woman threw him a look, as she realized her lost opportunity. He nearly smiled. Even in supposed highbrow accommodations with centuries-old traditions, money talked.

He'd stayed at the Goldener Hirsch before and knew that its restaurant was on the ground floor, on the opposite side of the building. He followed a narrow corridor through arches, past the bar, to its entrance. Once a blacksmith's shop, it was now regarded as Salzburg's swankiest place to eat, though he imagined there were other establishments that might challenge the assertion. Austrians tended to dine after seven o'clock, so the clothed tables with sparkling china and crystal were empty.

Except for one, near the center.

Where Salazar sat facing toward him and Cassiopeia away.

He stayed short of the doorway, concealing himself, and studied the Spaniard.

Whatever he chose to do next came with risk.

But he'd come this far.

★ ★ ★

SALAZAR WAS PLEASED.

He and Cassiopeia had flown by private jet from Denmark to Salzburg, then checked into their suites. The auction was set to begin at 7:00 P.M., so they'd decided to have an early dinner. The event was to be held within the Hohensalzburg, a grim hulk of a fortress resting 120 meters above the city on a pine-clad granite mound. The castle was first built in the 11th century, but another six hundred years had been needed for its completion. Today it was a museum and tourist attraction that offered lovely panoramas. He thought a walk along its parapets before the auction would be perfect, especially considering the evening's clear skies and seasonable air.

Cassiopeia looked lovely. She'd chosen a black silk pantsuit, low heels, moderate jewelry, and a gold belt that wrapped loosely around her trim waist. He had to catch himself from noticing her décolletage, framed by a low-cut blouse. Her dark hair hung in curled layers past her shoulders, her face cast in muted tones from only a touch of color. Some of the auctions he attended were formal affairs. This one tonight not so much, but he was glad that she'd nonetheless dressed for the occasion.

"Would it be inappropriate to say that you look stunning?"

She smiled. "I'd be disappointed if you didn't."

He'd asked the waiter to give them a few moments before offering anything to drink.

"We have time for a leisurely dinner," he said. "Then I thought we'd take the funicular up the mountainside to the castle. It's the easiest way to get there."

"That sounds perfect. Is the book the only thing you're after at the auction?"

They'd discussed the sale on the plane. The greatest acquisition any collector of Saints' artifacts could hope for was an original Book of Mormon. An 1830 American edition had been found among the personal effects of an Austrian who'd recently died. Auctions and private sales had been how most of his collection had been acquired, only a few items gifts or heirlooms. He'd known of this sale for some time, wanting to come, then the appearance of the Americans had added a new purpose.

The first agent in the cell had proven tight-lipped.

The second stole his plane and escaped.

The third was some sort of bookseller, working with his enemy, who killed at least two of his men.

And just now entered the restaurant.

Thank you.

"You're welcome," the angel said.

MALONE CAUGHT JOSEPE SALAZAR'S INTENSE scrutiny. But if the Spaniard recognized him, nothing in the man's countenance betrayed the fact. The brown eyes remained expressionless. The Danites had surely reported his involvement, but that did not mean Salazar knew his face.

He approached and Salazar said, "May I help you?"

He slid a wooden chair from the adjacent table and, not waiting for an invitation, sat at their table.

"Name's Cotton Malone."

CASSIOPEIA HAD BEEN IN TIGHT SPOTS, A FEW EVEN life threatening, but she could not recall one more uncomfortable than this. Her first thought was wondering how Cotton had managed to be here, in Austria, at the Goldener Hirsch. The second was if Stephanie knew. Surely not. Or she would have warned her of the possibility, especially considering the consequences. The third was guilt. Had she betrayed Cotton? Did he think she had? What **did** he know?

"Is your name supposed to mean something to me?" Josepe asked.

"It should."

"I've never met anyone with the name Cotton. I'm sure there's a story there. Am I right?"

"A long one."

She noticed that Cotton had not offered his hand to shake, and she did not like the hard look in his green eyes.

"And who are you?" he asked her.

"I'm not sure that matters, considering that neither one of us seems to know who you are."

She kept her voice curt.

Face cold.

"I'm an agent for the U.S. Justice Department," Malone said.

He hadn't said those words in four years, not since he tendered his resignation and moved to Denmark.

"Is that said to frighten me?" Cassiopeia asked.

"Ma'am, you'll have to excuse us. I'm here to talk with Mr. Salazar."

"Are you telling me to mind my own business?"

"That's exactly what I'm saying. It might be better if you waited outside."

"She's not going anywhere," Salazar said, a definite edge to his voice.

Keeping her here was fine by him. He'd missed seeing her. Hearing her voice. But, like her, he had to stay in character, so he asked, "Are you the lady's protector?"

"What is your business with me?" Salazar asked.

He considered the question a moment, shrugged, and said, "Okay. If you want her here, then we'll do this your way. Things have changed. Our investigation of you is no longer covert. It's wide open, in your face. And I'm here to get the job done."

"That means nothing to me."

"Should I have the hotel call the police?" Cassiopeia asked Salazar.

"No, I can handle this." Salazar faced him. "Mr. Malone, I have no idea what you are talking about. Are you saying the U.S. Justice Department is investigating me? If so, that is news. But if that is true, I have lawyers who look after my interests. If you'll leave your card, I'll have them contact you."

"I don't like lawyers or Mormons," he said. "I especially don't like hypocritical Mormons."

"We are accustomed to both ignorance and bigotry."

He chuckled. "That's a good one. If the person is stupid, they won't even get that you insulted them. If smart, they'll get angry. Either way, you win. They teach you that in cult school?"

This time, no reply.

"Isn't that where all Mormons go to learn the party line? Out in Temple Land. Salt Lake City. What are you taught? Just smile, be cool, and tell everyone Jesus loves them. Of course, Jesus will love you even more if you become a Mormon. Read the Book of Mormon and all will be right. Otherwise, you might just freeze to death in the outer darkness. Isn't that what you call it?"

"There must be an exile for those who choose to follow Satan, in defiance of Heavenly Father's plan," Salazar said. "A place for tortured souls, like yourself."

The mocking tone of the speech annoyed him. "How about blood atonement? Is that part of the grand plan?"

"You obviously read about my church's history, matters that happened long ago, in another time. We no longer practice blood atonements."

He pointed to Cassiopeia, who looked great. "Is she wife number one? Three? Eight?"

"We no longer practice plural marriage, either."

He was pushing buttons, searching for the right one, but Salazar was maintaining a calm, self-confident demeanor. So he tried another tack and asked Cassiopeia, "You do realize that you're having dinner with a murderer?"

Salazar sprang to his feet. "That's enough."

Finally. The right stimulus.

"Leave," Salazar demanded.

He glanced up. Hate filled the eyes that stared back. But the Spaniard was smart enough to keep his mouth shut.

"I saw the body," he said, his voice low and soft.

Salazar said nothing.

"He was an American agent. With a wife and kids."

He threw a final glance at Cassiopeia. Her features had gained a brittle look. Her eyes said, **Go.**

He slid back the chair and stood. "I took down two of your men and Barry Kirk. Now I'm coming for you."

Salazar stared back, still saying nothing. Something he learned long ago came to mind. Stir a person up and they could be made to think. Add in anger and they'll screw up, sure as hell.

He pointed his finger. "You're mine."

Then he stepped for the exit.

"Mr. Malone."

He stopped and turned.

"You owe this lady an apology for your insults."

He threw them both a look of contempt, then focused on Cassiopeia. "I'm sorry."

He hesitated.

"If I offended you."

TWENTY-EIGHT

★

WASHINGTON, D.C.

STEPHANIE FELT AWKWARD BEING ALONE WITH Danny Daniels. They'd neither seen nor spoken to each other in several months.

"How is the First Lady?" she asked.

"Anxious to leave the White House. As am I. Politics ain't what it used to be. Time for a new life."

The Twenty-Second Amendment allowed a person to serve only two terms. Nearly every president had wanted a second term, despite the fact that history clearly taught the last four years would be nothing like the first. Either the president became overly aggressive, knowing he had nothing to lose, which alienated both supporters and detractors. Or he became cautious, placid, and docile, not wanting to do anything that might affect his legacy. Either way, nothing could be accomplished. Bucking the trend, Daniels' second term had been active, dealing with some explosive issues, many of which she and the Magellan Billet had been involved with solving.

"This table," Daniels said. "It's really beautiful. I asked. It's on loan from the State Department. These chairs were made for the Quayles, during the first Bush's term."

She could see he was unusually nervous, his booming baritone voice down many decibels, his look distracted.

"I had breakfast prepared. Are you hungry?"

Arranged on the table before them was a place setting each of white Lenox china adorned with the vice president's seal. Tulip-shaped stemware stood empty, sparkling in bright morning sun that rained through the windows.

"Chitchat is not your specialty," she said.

He chuckled. "No, it's not."

"I'd like to know what this is about."

She'd already noticed the file on the table.

Daniels opened the folder and lifted out one sheet, which he handed to her. It was a photocopy of a handwritten letter, the script distinctly feminine, the words difficult to read.

"That was sent to president Ulysses S. Grant on August 9, 1876."

The signature she could read.

Mrs. Abraham Lincoln.

"Mary Todd was a funny bird," Daniels said. "Lived a tough life. Lost three sons and a husband. Then she had to fight Congress to award her a pension. It was an uphill battle since, while in the White House, she managed to alienate most of them. Just to shut her up, they finally gave her the money."

"She was no different than any of the hundreds of thousands of other veterans' widows who were granted a pension. She deserved it."

"Not true. She **was** different. She was Mrs. Abraham Lincoln and, by the time Grant was elected president, no one wanted to hear Lincoln's name. We worship him today like a god. But in the decades after the Civil War, Lincoln was not the legend he ultimately became. He was hated. Reviled."

"Did they know something we don't?"

He handed her another sheet, typewritten.

"It's the text from the copy you're holding. Read it."

```
I have led a life of most
rigid seclusion since I left
Washington. If my darling
husband had lived out his four
years, we would have passed our
remaining years in a home we
```

both should have enjoyed. How
dearly I loved the Soldier's
Home where we spent so much
time while in Washington, and I
loathe that I should be so far
removed from it, broken hearted,
praying death to remove me from
a life so full of agony. Each
morning, on awakening from my
troubled slumbers, the utter
responsibility of living another
day so wretched appears to me
as an impossibility. Without my
beloved, life is only a heavy
burden and the thought that I
should soon be removed from this
world is a supreme happiness
to me. I wonder each day if I
should ever regain my health and
my strength of mind. Before they
leave me entirely, there is a
matter of which you must know.
With all of the bereavement I
have endured my mind had purged
the thought, yet it reoccurred
the other night as I lay waiting
for sleep. Two years into his
first term my beloved was given
a message from his predecessor,

Mr. Buchanan, one that had
been passed from leader to
leader since the days of Mr.
Washington. Those words greatly
upset my beloved. He told me
that he wished the message had
never been delivered. Three more
times we discussed the matter
and on each occasion he repeated
his lament. His anguish during
the war was deep and profound. I
always thought it a consequence
of being the commander in chief,
but once he told me that it was
because of the message. In the
days before he was murdered,
when the war was won and the
fight over, my beloved said that
those disturbing words still
existed. He'd first thought to
destroy them but had instead
sent them west to the Mormons,
part of a bargain made with
their leader. The Mormons kept
their end, as had he, so it was
time to retrieve what he had
sent them. What to do with it
then he did not know. But my
beloved never lived to make that

```
decision and nothing was ever
retrieved. I thought you might
want to know this. Do with the
knowledge as you please. None of
this matters to me any longer.
```

She glanced up from the sheet.

"The Mormons still have that information," Daniels said. "They've had it since 1863, when Lincoln made the deal with Brigham Young."

"Edwin told me about that."

"Pretty smart move, actually. Lincoln never enforced the anti-polygamy act against the Mormons, and Young kept the telegraph lines and the railroads heading west. He also never sent men to fight for the South."

"This message passed between the early presidents. Is it real?"

"Apparently so. Something akin to it is mentioned in other classified documents. Ones only presidents can see. I read them seven years ago. The references are fleeting, but there. George Washington definitely passed something down that eventually made its way to Lincoln. Unfortunately, the sixteenth president was killed before he had a chance to pass it to the seventeenth. So it was forgotten. Except by Mary Todd."

She sensed something else. "What aren't you saying?"

He opened the file and handed her another sheet of more typed text.

"That's a clean version of a note included in the classified papers. It's from James Madison, written at the end of his second term in 1817. Presumably for his successor, James Monroe."

```
As to the message sent forward
by our first president, I,
being the fourth man to hold
this honored post do add
this addendum, which should
likewise be passed forward.
Mr. Washington was present
that Saturday evening of the
great convention. He chaired
the extraordinary session and
has personal knowledge of all
that transpired. Until assuming
this office, I was unaware
as to what, if anything, had
occurred with the result of
that gathering. I was pleased
to discover that Mr. Washington
had ensured that it be passed
from president to president.
Having never missed a day of
the Constitutional Convention,
nor at most a casual fraction of
```

an hour in any day, I assumed a
seat in front of the presiding
member, with the other members
on my right and left hands. In
this favorable position for
hearing all that passed, I noted
what was read from the chair
or spoken by the members. My
notes of the great convention
were motivated by an earnest
desire for completeness and
accuracy and, past my death,
which hopefully will not occur
for a number of years, they
shall be published. But all
later presidents must know that
those notes are not complete.
Hidden beneath my summer study
is what is needed for a total
understanding. If any subsequent
holder of this office deems
it prudent to act upon what
Mr. Washington has allowed to
survive, that bounty could prove
most useful.

"We've had a lot of presidents," she said, "since
Madison. Don't you think one of them went for a
look?"

"This note was never attached to anything, nor passed on. It was apparently secreted away, then found a year ago in some of Madison's private papers stored at the Library of Congress. No president, except me, has ever seen it. Luckily, the person who found it works for me." He handed her another item from the file encased with a plastic sheet protector. "That's Madison's original note, as handwritten. Notice anything?"

She did. At the bottom.

Two letters.

IV.

"Roman numerals?" she asked.

He shrugged. "We don't know."

Daniels was clearly not his usual gregarious self. None of the brash stories or loud voice. Instead, he sat rigid in the chair, his face as stiff as a mask. Was he afraid? She never had seen this man flinch in the face of anything.

"James Buchanan is quoted, just prior to the Civil War, saying he might be the last president of the United States. I never understood what he truly meant by that comment, until recently."

"Buchanan was wrong. The South lost the war."

"That's the problem, Stephanie. He may not have been wrong. But Lincoln came along and bluffed a pair of twos in a poker game where everyone else was holding a much better hand. And he won. Only to have his brains blown out at the end. I'm not going to be the last president of the United States."

She had to learn more, so she tried a safer subject. "What did Madison mean by his **summer study?**"

"It's at Montpelier, his home in Virginia, where he built himself a temple."

She'd visited there twice and had seen the columned structure. Madison loved Roman classicism, so he'd based the structure on the **tempietto** of Bramante in Rome. It sat on a knoll, among old-growth cedar and fir trees, in the garden adjacent to the house.

"Madison had style," Daniels said. "Beneath his temple he dug a pit, which became the icehouse. The original flooring above was wood, so it would have been cool in summer to stand out there. Like air-conditioning. That wood floor is gone, replaced by a concrete slab with a hatch in the middle."

"And why do I need to know this?"

"Madison called the temple his summer study. I need you to find what he hid beneath it."

"Why me?"

"Because, thanks to Senator Rowan, you're the only one who can."

TWENTY-NINE

✦

SALZBURG

MALONE FLED THE GOLDENER HIRSCH AND
walked down a crowded Getreidegasse toward his
hotel. He'd gone to rattle Josepe Salazar and he
supposed that mission had been accomplished.
But he'd also wanted to send a three-pronged message to Cassiopeia. First, she was not alone. Second, he knew she was there. And third, Salazar
was dangerous. When he'd insulted Cassiopeia
he'd caught the contempt in Salazar's eyes—how
he'd been personally offended by the attack on her
honor. He understood that Cassiopeia would have
stayed in character, playing her part, but he still
wasn't sure it was a part. He didn't like anything
about this. The fact that they were both staying at
the Goldener Hirsch, having dinner, about to at-

tend an auction together, then head back to the hotel for—

Stop it.

He needed to think straight.

He turned and headed for the Residenzplatz, an open cobbled square bordered by the city's cathedral and its former archbishop's residence, centered by a white marble Baroque fountain. His hotel was just to the northeast, past the state museum. Daylight still shone, but evening was taking hold, the sun rapidly fading in the west.

He stopped at the flowing water.

Time to start acting like an agent.

So he found his phone, and did the sensible thing.

STEPHANIE'S PHONE VIBRATED IN HER JACKET pocket.

"You going to get that?" Daniels asked.

The pulse of the hum could be heard in the quiet of the dining room.

"It can wait."

"Maybe not."

She found the phone and read the caller ID. "It's Cotton."

"Answer it. On speaker."

She did, laying the unit on the table.

"I'm in Salzburg," Malone said.

"Like I'm surprised."

"It's a bitch being predictable. But I have a problem. I've rattled Salazar and he now knows we're all over him."

"Hopefully not at Cassiopeia's expense."

"No danger of that. This guy thinks he's her knight in shining armor. It's touching to watch."

She saw Daniels smile at the sarcasm and wondered just how much the president knew. He definitely seemed like a man informed.

"There's an auction happening here. I want to buy a book."

"You're the expert on that."

"I need money." He told her the amount.

Daniels mouthed, **Do it.**

"Where do you want it deposited?" she asked.

"I'll email my account info. Wire it immediately."

The president reached over and drew the phone closer. "Cotton, this is Danny Daniels."

"I didn't know I was interrupting a presidential conference."

"I'm glad you did. It's important you keep Salazar busy for the next day or so. Can you manage that?"

"Shouldn't be too much of a problem. If I can buy that book, I'll be tops on his list of things to do."

"Then buy it. I don't care what it costs."

"You know he needs a bullet in his brain."

"He'll pay for what he did to our man. But not yet. Be patient."

"I specialize in that."

The call ended.

She stared at Daniels.

"Stephanie," he said. "If we lose this one, it's all over."

CASSIOPEIA TRIED TO ENJOY HER DINNER, BUT Cotton's appearance was troublesome. Josepe, too, seemed distracted. He'd apologized to her, expressing concern that the man named Malone was deranged. She'd again suggested the police, but he'd vetoed the move. Ten minutes after Cotton left another man appeared in the restaurant—young, muscular, short hair—obviously someone who worked for Josepe, and they stepped outside.

A Danite?

She'd watched them through the windows, sipping her water, trying to seem disinterested. Cotton had come to deliberately announce his presence to both Josepe **and** her.

Of that there was no doubt.

But he wanted her to know about the dead agent, too.

Was it possible Josepe was involved?

"Are you enjoying the food?" he asked her, returning to the table.

"It's delicious."

"The hotel chef is renowned. I always enjoy visiting here."

"You come often?"

"There's an active stake in Salzburg, started in 1997, now with over a thousand members. I've visited several times, as part of my European duties."

"The church has truly become worldwide."

He nodded. "More than fourteen million members. Over half live outside the United States."

She was trying to calm him down, help him forget about the intrusion. But she could see that he was still bothered.

"What Malone mentioned," she said. "About the U.S. government investigating you. Is that true?"

"There have been rumors. I've been told that it involves the church and some vendetta the government has against us. But I know nothing for sure."

"And the allegation of you being a murderer."

"That was outrageous, as was his personal attack on you."

"Who is Barry Kirk?"

"He works for me and **has** been missing for a few days now. I have to confess, that part of what he said is of concern."

"Then we should call the police."

Josepe seemed troubled. "Not yet. I have my associate investigating. It could be that Barry simply quit without notice. I need to be sure before involving the authorities."

"I appreciate you coming to my defense."

"My pleasure, but I want you to know that there is nothing here to be concerned about. I just told my associate to telephone Salt Lake City and report what happened. Hopefully, church officials can contact the right people in the government and make sure that we've seen the last of Mr. Malone."

"He made some wild accusations."

Josepe nodded. "Designed, I'm sure, to provoke a response."

"If I can help in any way, you know I'm here for you."

He seemed to appreciate her concern. "That means a lot." He glanced at his watch. "Shall we prepare ourselves for the auction? We can meet in the lobby in, say, fifteen minutes."

They rose from the table and walked from the restaurant, back into the hotel. Her apprehensions had now turned to outright fear.

Unfortunately Josepe was wrong.

Neither one of them had heard the last of Cotton.

THIRTY

★

MALONE SHOWERED AND CHANGED, DONNING A
pair of dress slacks, a buttondown Paul & Shack
shirt, and a blazer. He'd brought the clothes especially for the auction, unsure whether to attend.
But after his visit with Salazar, he knew he had
to go.

The brochure he'd found in Salazar's study had
indicated that the sale would happen in the Golden
Hall of Festung Hohensalzburg, the High Salzburg Fortress, which sat four hundred feet above
the city. Two great bastions rose, the lower one
hewn straight from the rock, both bristling with
the battlements and towers expected of a medieval
fortress. He'd visited once, following its twisted

corridors into great halls and gilded chambers, past glistening tile stoves and down to a dungeon.

He avoided the funicular, thinking that might be the way Salazar and Cassiopeia would ascend. Instead he walked the footpath, a steep thirty-minute stroll beneath trees shedding their summer foliage. Visitors from the castle, leaving for the day, passed him on their way back down to town. Dusk fell along the way, the moon and stars emerging overhead, the air chilly but with a benign bite.

The climb provided him an opportunity to think.

Danny Daniels being on the phone with Stephanie had surprised him, and he wondered what was happening across the Atlantic. The president knew of Salazar, so whatever was happening reached all the way to the Oval Office. That meant the stakes were at their highest.

Fine by him.

Nothing kept the senses sharper.

And he needed to stay focused.

He entered the castle across a stone bridge that traversed what was once a moat. Above the archway he spotted a circular loophole, above that a bay from where projectiles could be hurled down onto intruders. He'd timed his appearance to just after the auction's beginning. He noticed from a placard that the castle closed at 6:30, its Golden Hall presumably leased out in the evenings for special events. An older woman guarded the stairs that led inside. He explained he was here for the sale and she waved him ahead.

He was familiar with Dorotheum. They ran a professional, no-nonsense sale. Upstairs, in a spacious hallway, another woman handed him a catalog and registered him. His gaze settled across the space on a towering statue of Charlemagne that guarded the entrance to the Golden Hall. Another of the castle's claims to fame was that the first Holy Roman Emperor once visited. Beyond the open doorway he could hear the auctioneer going about his business.

"Sales are all final," she said to him, "and require immediate payment of certified funds."

He knew the drill, so he displayed his phone and told her, "I have money ready and waiting."

"Enjoy yourself."

That he would.

CASSIOPEIA SAT BESIDE JOSEPE.

They'd journeyed up to the castle by way of the funicular railway, a one-minute steep-angled haul through a tunnel in the lower bastion. Twilight had firmly taken hold, the city lights springing to life, an orange sun disappearing into the western horizon.

Arm in arm, they'd wandered the ramparts and taken in the labyrinth of spires, towers, and domes in the streets below. Beyond Salzburg, in the gray dusk, lay undulating hills and green meadows dotted with farmhouses. A placid, rural scene, much like where she lived in southern France. She missed her house and her castle. Being here, inside this ancient fortress, appreciating what it had taken to build it so long ago, had made her think of her own building project. The reconstruction was progressing, three of the outer walls now standing. Her engineers had told her that another decade would be required to finish the 13th-century structure.

She'd thumbed through the catalog for the estate sale, the offered items impressive. Apparently the deceased was a person of means. Porcelain, china, silverware, three paintings, and several books, one an original edition of the Book of Mormon. Josepe had seemed excited about the prospect of owning that treasure. The local ward had alerted him to the sale, and he'd voiced a hope that not many serious collectors would come. Normally telephone bids were allowed at a Dorotheum sale, but this one had specifically omitted that possibility, which meant bidders had to be in the hall, with money, to claim their prize. She was still troubled by what had happened in the restaurant. She'd caught the look in Cotton's eyes. Half wary, half pleading, angry.

No. More hurt.

Waves of doubt flowed through her.

So she told herself to stay alert.

No telling what was about to happen.

★ ★ ★

MALONE STOOD OUTSIDE THE HALL, LISTENING to the bidding on other items, taking inventory. About fifty people filled the chairs that faced a small stage. The room was aglow from gold carvings, gilded walls, and the enormous tile stove that filled one corner. Red marble dominated the twisted columns. A rich coffered ceiling was adorned with gold buttons that twinkled like stars. Princes had once entertained here, and now it was a tourist attraction and rental space.

He'd spotted Salazar and Cassiopeia, sitting near the front, both focused on the auctioneer, who was accepting bids on a porcelain vase. He studied the catalog. The Book of Mormon was three items away.

He checked his phone.

A message from Stephanie indicated that the money had been transferred and more would be added, if needed.

He smiled.

Never a bad thing to have the president of the United States as your banker.

SALAZAR WAS BECOMING ANXIOUS. ALL OF HIS LIFE he'd dreamed of holding something that perhaps the Prophet Joseph himself may have touched. He knew the drama involved when the first 5,000 copies of the Book of Mormon were printed. For a small shop in upstate New York, the task had been enormous. It had required eight months to produce the nearly three million pages needed for the complete first edition. On March 26, 1830, the books finally went on sale. Initially they sold for $1.75 but because of poor response the price was dropped to $1.25. An early Saint, Martin Harris, eventually sold 150 acres of his farm and raised the $3,000 owed the printer.

"Thou shalt not covet thine own property, but impart it freely to the printing. That is what Elder Harris was told," the angel said inside his head. **"His sacrifice made it all possible."**

Eleven days after the book was available for sale, believers in the word met in Fayette, New York, and legally organized what eight years later was renamed the Church of Jesus Christ of Latter-day Saints.

"This is your moment, Josepe. The prophets are watching. You are their Danite, the one who understands what is at stake."

He'd come to claim his prize.

And not just one.

He desired the book **and** Cassiopeia. The more he was around her, the more he wanted her.

He could not deny it.

Nor did he want to.

THIRTY-ONE

✦

WASHINGTON, D.C.

STEPHANIE NIBBLED AT THE BREAKFAST THE STAFF
had served her and the president. She wasn't particularly hungry, but the food offered her time to
think. She'd been around long enough to know
the lay of the land. Some of the games she was
forced to play were silly. A few nonsensical. Others
bothersome or a nuisance. Then there was the real
thing.

"Edwin and I have been working this for over a
year," Daniels said. "Just the two of us, with a little
help from the Secret Service. But things are esca-
lating. When Rowan moved on you, we knew
what he wanted."

She laid down her fork.

"You don't like the eggs?"

"Actually, I hate eggs."

"It's not that bad, Stephanie."

"You're not the one facing a congressional inquiry—which, apparently, you knew was coming."

Daniels shook his head. "I was only hoping it would, but I didn't know."

"Hoping?"

Daniels shoved his plate aside. "Actually, I'm not all that fond of eggs, either."

"Then why are we eating them?"

He shrugged. "I don't know. I just told them to fix some food. This isn't easy."

"And why are we here, as opposed to your office?"

"Too many eyes and ears there."

A strange response, but she let it go.

"You realize," he said, "that Mary Todd Lincoln was probably a manic depressive."

"She was a sad woman who lost nearly everything dear to her. It's amazing she didn't lose her mind completely."

"Her surviving son, Robert, thought she had. He committed her."

"And she managed to legally reverse that decision."

"That she did. Then, not long after that, she sent Ulysses Grant a letter. Why in the world would she do that?"

"Apparently she wasn't as crazy as history wants her to be. Grant not only kept what she sent, he classified it. There have been a lot of presidents since 1876. Why are you the first one to be concerned about this?"

"I'm not."

Now she was interested.

"There are indications that both Roosevelts looked into it, along with Nixon."

"Why am I not surprised."

Daniels chuckled. "I thought the same thing. Nixon had two Mormons in his cabinet. He liked the church and the way it thought. He courted them in 1960, '68, and '72. In July 1970 he visited Salt Lake City and met with the prophet and twelve apostles. A thirty-minute, off-the-record discussion, behind closed doors. A bit unprecedented for a president, don't you think?"

"So why did he do it?"

"'Cause I imagine ol' Tricky Dick wanted to know if what Mary Todd Lincoln wrote was right. Did the Mormons still have what Abraham Lincoln gave them?"

"And what did he find out?"

"We'll never know. Everybody there that day, save one, is dead."

"Seems like you need to talk to that one."

"I intend to do just that." He pointed at Madison's message. "Thank goodness we found that, or we wouldn't even know to ask or look."

Her gaze wandered the room and settled on a portrait of John Adams, the first person to serve as vice president. "You need to get to the point, Danny."

The use of his first name signaled how irritated she truly was with him.

"I like it when you say my name."

"I like it when you're straightforward." She paused. "Which is a rarity, by the way."

"I just wanted to finish out my eight years," he quietly said. "The last few months should have been peaceful. God knows we've had enough excitement. But Thaddeus Rowan had other ideas."

She waited for more.

"He's been trying for over a year to access certain classified files. Things his security clearance doesn't even get close to allowing. He's pressured the CIA, FBI, NSA, even a couple of White House staffers. The man's been around and knows how to throw his weight. So far, he's been moderately successful. Now he's focused on you."

She understood. "So I'm to be the bait?"

"Why not? You and I understand each other. Together, we can solve this."

"Looks like **we** don't have a choice."

"That's the thing I'm going to miss most about

this job. People are once again going to have choices when it comes to me."

She smiled. He was impossible.

"I actually wanted to bring you in earlier, but I'm glad I didn't. Now that Rowan himself has focused on you, it's perfect. He'll never see it coming and, if he does, he wants this so bad he'll take a chance."

"What exactly do you want me to do?"

He pointed again at Madison's note. "First, find whatever it is Madison left at Montpelier. I don't want you to do it personally, though. Do you have an agent you can trust?"

"I do. He should be back here, in Washington, right now."

She stared at him long enough that he understood.

"Can Luke handle this?" he asked.

"He's good, Danny."

"Okay, let him handle it. But God help him if he screws this up. I'm bettin' the farm on that wild boy."

"Seems like Luke's not the only one in the firing line."

"You're a pro, Stephanie. You can handle this. I **need** you to handle this. I'm also going to want you to meet with Rowan and gain his trust."

"And why in the world would he ever trust me?"

"Tell him you can't respond to his subpoena.

To do so would end your career. But you get why you were served. No one would ever respond to such a sweeping request without a fight or a compromise. Obviously, he wants something. So ask him what it is, then make a deal."

"Again, there's no way he's going to buy that."

"Actually, he will. Last evening we leaked through secured channels that your job is on the line."

She was civil service, not a political appointee, and worked for the attorney general. Once Daniels' term ended and a new AG was appointed by the next president, though she would not be fired, she could be reassigned. So far, she'd survived several changes in administrations and had many times wondered when her luck would run out.

"And why is my job in jeopardy?"

"You've been stealing."

Had she heard right?

"From your discretionary account, the money used for your covert operations. I'm told, on any given day, there's several million dollars at your personal disposal, not subject to any regular GAO audit. Unfortunately, information has come to us that that around $500,000 is unaccounted for."

"And how did this information come your way?"

"That would be classified," Daniels said. "But you're going to tell Rowan that you have a problem, one his subpoena may draw attention to. Ask him what you can do to make it go away."

"Why would he believe me?"

"Because you actually have been stealing, and I have the records to prove it."

THIRTY-TWO

✦

SALAZAR WAS READY.

He told himself to calm down, be patient.

"Our next item," the auctioneer said, "is an original Book of Mormon, bearing the Palmyra, New York, identification and the statement, **printed by E. B. Grandin, for the author, 1830.** Its provenance is detailed in the catalog, verified by experts. A rare find."

Fair market value was 150,000 euros, give or take a few thousand. He doubted anyone here possessed the resources to outbid him as, so far, items had sold for only modest amounts. But he'd learned not to underestimate the zeal of collectors.

"The opening bid is one hundred thousand

euros," the auctioneer said. "We will work off increments of one thousand euros."

That was common for a Dorotheum sale. The house generally started things rolling. If no one bid that amount, the item was returned to its owner. If no house floor was proffered, that meant the highest bid won, no matter what that might be.

He flicked his right hand, signaling that he opened with one hundred thousand. He'd already informed the auctioneer that he would be bidding on this item.

"We have one hundred thousand."

"One hundred twenty thousand," a man said from across the aisle.

"One fifty," Salazar stated.

"The bid is 150,000 euros. Is there more?"

No one replied. He was pleased.

"One hundred sixty," a new voice said.

He turned and saw Cotton Malone standing at the rear of the hall.

"It's the man from earlier," Cassiopeia said.

"That it is," he whispered.

Malone stepped toward the chairs and sat in an empty one.

"We have a bid of 160,000 euros," the auctioneer announced.

"One hundred seventy," Salazar said.

"Two hundred thousand," Malone called out.

The auctioneer seemed surprised.

So was Salazar. "I request to know if the gentleman is certified."

That was allowed, particularly when bids exceeded market value. Otherwise, owners and speculators could run up the price through nonsensical amounts that they were not prepared to honor.

"Herr Salazar wishes to know your credentials," the auctioneer asked.

MALONE STOOD FROM HIS CHAIR. HE'D AT-tended enough auctions to know this might happen, which was why he'd removed from the knapsack beneath his bed back in Copenhagen his Justice Department credentials, which Stephanie had allowed him to keep. Rarely in his former occupation had he ever carried them. He fished the leather wallet from his pocket and flashed the gold badge and photo identification to the auctioneer.

"Cotton Malone. United States Justice Department. Good enough?"

The auctioneer never flinched. "So long as you can honor your bid."

"I assure you I can."

"Then, let us proceed. The bid is two hundred thousand euros. Herr Salazar?"

"Two fifty."

Cassiopeia grabbed Salazar's arm and whispered, "You told me the value of this book, which is far less than you just bid."

"Things have changed."

"Three hundred thousand," Cotton said.

Salazar turned and faced his adversary. True, he'd wanted the Americans to come, even hoped that Malone himself would appear. But he'd not expected this type of challenge.

"Four hundred thousand," he said, his eyes on his opponent.

"Four hundred fifty," Malone quickly replied.

"Five hundred thousand."

Silence filled the room.

He waited.

"One million euros," Malone said.

He kept his gaze locked on his enemy.

"Satan is here. See him, Josepe. There he sits. He is an agent of the U.S. government. Wherever there is any dominion that is beneath that of the celestial world, we are to be free of it. The American continent was not designed for such a corrupt government as the United States to prosper long upon it. Let him win. Then make him pay."

He'd never questioned the angel before and was not going to start now.

He turned toward the auctioneer and shook his head.

Ending the sale.

He watched as Malone paid the cashier an amount seven times what any other original edition would command. The Book of Mormon lay on the table, sealed in plastic, inside a stylish wooden box.

Malone lifted the prize out for a quick inspection.

Cassiopeia marched over and said, "Was it worth it?"

Malone smiled. "Every euro."

"You are a despicable man."

The American shrugged. "I've been called worse."

"You'll regret what you just did," she said to him.

Malone threw her a quizzical look. "Is that a threat, ma'am?"

"Take it as a promise."

Malone chuckled as he laid the book back inside the box and sealed the lid. "I'll do that. Now, if you'll excuse me, I have to go."

"Know that there are more treasures than one for you in this world," the angel told Salazar. "Worry not over the loss of this one. But neither allow the enemy to walk easy."

The auction house was holding a reception after the sale, one he'd originally planned to attend.

Not anymore.

He and Cassiopeia descended to the castle's lower level and made their way to the funicular station. The route took them across another of the castle's open terraces, past a restaurant busy with evening diners. He pointed beyond the parapets, eastward, where she could see the streets and building lights of Salzburg's antiseptic suburbs.

"The local ward is headquartered down there. I should call and schedule a visit before we leave town."

"We can do that tomorrow," Cassiopeia said.

They entered the station and found the railcar. Inside stood Cotton Malone. The interior was claustrophobic, the car nearly full. A few more people trickled inside, then the doors shut and the steep descent began. He kept his attention out the forward windows for the entire minute of the journey.

At ground level, they exited and found the street.

Malone passed them and kept walking.

His two Danites were waiting where he'd directed them to be earlier.

"I thought we'd take a stroll through the streets of old town," he said to Cassiopeia. "Before heading back to the hotel. It's a lovely night."

"I'd like that."

"Let me speak a moment with my associates. I had asked them to be here so they might take charge of my purchase. Of course, I don't have one now."

He left her and walked to his men. With his back to Cassiopeia he stared at them both and said, "I assume you saw Malone?"

They nodded.

"Seize him. Call me when you have him. And retrieve that wooden box he's holding."

PART
THREE

THIRTY-THREE

✦

Luke had not been home in several weeks. He leased an apartment near Georgetown in an ivy-veined brick building brimming with tenants in their seventies. He liked the quiet and appreciated the fact that everyone seemed to mind their own business. He spent only a few days here each month, between assignments, on the downtime Stephanie Nelle required all her Magellan Billet agents to take.

He'd been born and raised in a small Tennessee town where his father and uncle were both known, particularly his uncle, who served in various local political offices, then as governor before becoming president. His father died when he was seventeen.

Cancer. Fatal eighteen days after diagnosis. What a shock. He and his three brothers had been there for every moment of those final days. His mother took the loss hard. They'd been married a long time. Her husband was everything to her, and then, suddenly, he was gone.

That's why he called her every Sunday.

Never missed.

Even when on assignment.

It might be late at night her time when he had the chance, but he called. His father always said that the smartest thing he ever did was marry her, proclaiming that **even the blind-eyed biscuit thrower occasionally hits the target.**

Both his parents were devoutly religious—Southern Baptists—so they'd named their sons to correspond with the books of the New Testament. His two older brothers were Matthew and Mark. His younger, John. He was the third in line and acquired the name Luke.

He would never forget his last conversation with his father.

"I'm going to die later today or tomorrow. I'm done. I can feel it. But I have to say this to you. I want you to make something of your life. Okay? Something good. You choose what works. Doesn't matter. But, whatever it is, make the most of it."

He could still feel the gentle grip of his father's

sweaty palm as they shook hands for the last time. All of the sons had been close to their father. And he'd known exactly what his dad had meant. School had never interested him, his grades barely passing. College was not in his future. So he'd enlisted right out of high school and was accepted for Army Ranger training. Sixty-one of the hardest days of his life. **Not for the weak or fainthearted—** that's what it said right in the Ranger handbook. Kind of an understatement, considering the failure rate was way over 50 percent. But he'd made it, earning his lieutenant bars. Eventually he'd been deployed to some of the hottest spots on the planet, wounded twice, and received multiple commendations.

His father would have been proud.

Then he was chosen to work for the Magellan Billet, where he'd been involved in more high-stakes action.

He was now thirty years old, and the loss of his dad still hurt. What was the saying? **Real men don't cry.** Bullshit. Real men bawl their eyes out, as he and his brothers had thirteen years ago when they watched the man they idolized take his last breath.

A knock at the door disturbed his thoughts.

He'd been sitting in the quiet for half an hour, shaking off jet lag, trying to re-acclimate himself to Eastern Daylight Time. He opened the door to find Stephanie Nelle. He was not aware that she knew where he lived.

"We have to talk," she said. "May I come in?"

She stepped inside and he caught her taking in the décor.

"Not what I expected," she said.

He prided himself on the warm look, most of which came with the unit but some of which he'd selected. Masculine, but not overly so. Wood furniture. Muted fabrics. Lots of greenery, all fake but looking real. Contrary to what people thought, he liked order.

"You were expecting a college dorm room?"

"I'm not sure. But this is lovely."

"I like it here—the few days a month I get to enjoy it."

She stood, arms at her sides. "You and Cotton part okay?"

"He nearly killed me. He shot Kirk right over my shoulder."

"I doubt you were in any danger. Cotton knows how to handle a weapon."

"Maybe so. But I was glad to be rid of the old-timer. He has a piss-poor attitude."

"That old-timer was awarded every commendation we have, every one of which he refused."

"**Was.** That's the key word. He walked away. His time is done. And let me tell you, he didn't like watching his girl kiss Salazar one bit. It messed him up, though he tried to hide it. But on that I can't blame him. I did what you said, though. I aggravated him. Tried to keep him interested. Then I fed him the information about the Founding Fathers and the Constitution. Unfortunately, he didn't take the bait and hang around."

"He's in Salzburg."

That surprised him. "And you're thinking that's a good thing?"

"Cotton's a pro. He'll handle things right."

"If you say so. I say his head isn't screwed on for this one."

"I just came from your uncle."

"And how is dear Danny? I don't think I've heard from him since my dad died."

"He's concerned." She paused. "And I'm about to be fired."

"Really now? What did you do?"

"Seems I'm a thief. A situation fabricated for the benefit of Thaddeus Rowan. It's time for you to know some additional information, so listen up."

STEPHANIE LIKED LUKE, THOUGH HE WAS A WILD spirit. She envied that freedom. How liberating it must be to have so much life ahead of you. She'd been there once, intent on making the most of every opportunity. Some she maximized, others eluded her. She'd sat at the dining room table in the vice president's mansion for over an hour and listened as Danny Daniels told her more of what was going on.

Thaddeus Rowan was planning a secession.

He wanted to dissolve the Union and end the United States of America.

Ordinarily, that would be treated as nonsense, but Rowan had a specific plan with specific objectives, all of which—thanks to James Madison, Abraham Lincoln, and Brigham Young—might be achievable. She could not, and would not, reveal all that she knew to Luke, but she told him enough so that he could do his job.

"You're going to Montpelier and into that ice pit," she said. "I want to know what, if anything, is there."

Luke stepped over to his Magellan Billet–issued laptop and she watched as he pecked at the keyboard. His fingertips then maneuvered the cursor and a couple of clicks led to Montpelier.org.

"That pit was dug in the early 1800s," he said. "Twenty-three feet deep, brick-lined. Madison built the temple over it around 1810. How could there be anything secret down there? It's surely been picked over for years."

"Maybe not. I also checked. There's not a single photograph of what the inside looks like posted anywhere on the Web. Kind of strange, wouldn't you say? We don't have a clue what's down there."

"How do you suggest I get in?"

"Break and enter."

"Can't we just ask to see it?"

She shook her head. "We can't involve anyone. It's just you and me. Not even Atlanta knows what we're doing. Get in, find out if Madison left anything, and get out. But don't. Get. Caught."

"I can handle that."

"I knew you could. I'll be available by cell. Let me know the minute you're done."

"How did you know Malone would go to Salzburg?"

"Because he cares for Cassiopeia. He wasn't going to allow her to fly blind, now that he knows she's there and Salazar killed our man. He's probably even a little jealous, which is good for him. He'll give Salazar just what the bastard deserves."

"Salazar needs taking down."

"I agree. And we'll get our shot. But not just yet."

"Does my loving uncle know I'm working this?"

She nodded. "He approves."

Luke chuckled. "I bet he does. He'd sooner bust my chops than look at me."

"How about you don't worry about the president of the United States. And that's what he is.

He's the commander in chief. Our boss. He's ordered us to do a job, and that's what we're going to do."

Luke saluted. "Yes, ma'am."

He was impossible, just like Cotton once was.

"And you know I meant no disrespect," he said. "But you're not a Daniels, so you don't know what I know."

"Don't be so sure about that."

Never would she mention the turmoil that she and Danny Daniels had been through together. That was not this youngster's business. A part of her understood Luke's bitterness. The president could be a hard man. She'd seen that firsthand. But he was not made of stone, and she'd seen that, too. Right now, though, she was the one in the crosshairs. She'd told Luke to not get caught, but the same advice applied to her.

She turned to leave. "I've emailed you particulars on the security at Montpelier, which isn't all that much. It'll be a nearly moonless night, so you should be able to get in and out with no problem."

"Where will you be?"

She grabbed the front doorknob. "No place good."

THIRTY-FOUR

★

SALZBURG

MALONE KNEW THEY WERE COMING. HE'D ACTU-
ally be disappointed if they didn't. He'd purposefully chosen to descend from the castle with Salazar
and Cassiopeia, and immediately spotted the two
young men waiting for their boss. Cassiopeia's little
show at the cashier's desk had—he hoped—been
for Salazar's benefit. Nice touch, actually. Her anger
had appeared genuine, her defense of Salazar entirely reasonable under the circumstances.

He walked at a leisurely pace down the inclined
cobbled street, into an open square behind the cathedral, risking no surreptitious glances over his
shoulder. The night was chilly, the sky cloudy and
devoid of celestial glory. The shops were all closed,
their fronts tightly shuttered with iron grilles. He

picked once more through his many threads of recollection about these narrow streets. Most were pedestrian-only, connected by winding paths built under the close-packed houses that served as short-cuts from one block to another. He spotted one of the passageways ahead and decided to avoid it.

He passed the cathedral and crossed the **domplatz**. He'd once visited the Christmas market held here every year. How long ago was that? Eight years? Nine? No, more like ten. His life had changed immeasurably since then. Never had he dreamed of being divorced, living in Europe, and owning an old-book shop.

And being in love?

He hated even admitting that to himself.

He glanced up at the cathedral, parts of it reminiscent of St. Peter's in Rome. The archbishop's former residence, its 17th-century façade tinted green and white and gold, blocked the path ahead. The Residenzplatz, from which he'd called Stephanie earlier, spread out before the building, the lighted fountain still splashing water.

He needed privacy.

And darkness.

A location occurred to him.

He turned left and kept walking.

★ ★ ★

SALAZAR TRIED TO CONCENTRATE ON CASSIOPEIA, but his thoughts kept returning to Cotton Malone.

The insolent gentile.

Malone reminded him of other arrogant foes who, in the 1840s, terrorized Saints with unchecked vengeance. And the government? Both state and federal had sat by and allowed the mayhem to happen, eventually joining the fray on the side of the mobocrats.

"What did you mean," he asked Cassiopeia, "when you told Malone he'd be sorry for what he did?"

"I'm not without abilities, Josepe. I can cause that man many problems."

"He works for the American government."

She shrugged. "I have reach there, too."

"I didn't realize you had such wrath inside you."

"Everyone does, when challenged. And that's what that man has done. He challenged you, which means he's challenged me."

"**Dissenters,**" the angel said in his head, "**must be trodden underfoot, until their bowels gush out.**"

That they must.

"I'm so glad to have you here with me," he said to Cassiopeia.

They continued to walk beside each other, finding Getreidegasse and turning back toward the Goldener Hirsch, which sat at the far end. He'd come a long way in the eleven years since he and Cassiopeia had last been together. Both personally and professionally. Thankfully he'd met Elder Rowan, who'd encouraged the re-creation of the Danites. Rowan had told him that Charles R. Snow himself had sanctioned the move but, as in the beginning, there could be no direct link. His job was to safeguard the church, even at the expense of himself. A difficult task, for sure, but a necessary one.

"It is the will of God that those things be so."

The angel had just repeated what Joseph Smith had said when he first visited a Danite meeting. Intentionally, the prophet had not been told the extent of the group's mission, only that they were organized to protect the Saints. From the beginning there were those who spoke with Heavenly Father, as Prophet Charles now did. Those who administered and implemented the revelations, as Elder Rowan and his eleven brethren did. And those who protected and defended all that they held dear, as he and his Danites did.

Cotton Malone threatened that.

This gentile had come for a fight? Okay. That he would receive.

He and Cassiopeia arrived at the hotel.

"I will leave you here," he said to her. "I have some church business that must be handled before we leave. But I will see you in the morning, at breakfast."

"All right. Have a good evening."

He walked away.

"Josepe," she said to him.

He turned back.

"I meant what I said. Malone now has **two** enemies."

MALONE ENTERED ST. PETER'S GRAVEYARD, A Christian burial site founded only a few years after Christ's crucifixion. The oldest parts were the caves hewn into the rock face, and a hundred feet above them were strangely labeled catacombs. Centuries ago the monks of St. Peter's lived there, in seclusion, the isolated perch their hermitage. The ancient Benedictine monastery remained—towers, offices, storehouses, a church and refectory, all grouped behind a fortified wall encasing both the cemetery and the Gothic St. Margaret's Chapel.

The scene was a bit surreal, more like a garden than a cemetery, the colorful flowers adorning the elaborate graves muted in the darkness. He'd visited before and always thought of the von Trapps as they fled to freedom through here in **The Sound of Music**, though their escapades all happened on a sound stage. Many of Salzburg's wealthiest families lay buried in the outer Baroque porticoes. What made the place unique was that the graves were not owned but rented. Fail to pay the yearly fee and the body is moved. He'd always wondered how many evictions had actually occurred, since each plot was always lovingly tended, decorated with candles, fir branches, and fresh blooms.

His minders had stayed back and unsuccessfully tried to be inconspicuous. Maybe they wanted him to know they were coming. If so, they were clearly amateurs. Never give yourself away by signaling your intentions.

He needed both hands free, so he laid the wooden box at the base of one of the markers, among a cluster of pansies. Then he hustled ahead, toward St. Margaret's Chapel, its entrance doors closed and iron-barred. He rounded a corner and pressed himself against the rough stone, spying back toward the entrance. There were two ways into the cemetery. The one he'd just utilized and another a couple of hundred feet ahead of him, down a paved path that paralleled the rock face. All of the monastery buildings were pitch dark, only a few incandescent fixtures attached to the outer porticoes breaking the blackness.

One of the men entered through the gate to his right.

He smiled.

A little dividing and conquering? One at a time? Okay.

To draw the man his way, he bent down, retrieved a few pebbles, and tossed them toward one of the iron grilles that protected the porticoes.

He saw the shadow react and head his way.

Another tossed pebble ensured the decision.

The Danite would have to come right past the edge of the chapel, where he waited, darkness making any danger invisible.

He heard footsteps.

Approaching.

The shadow cleared the chapel wall, staring ahead, toward the porticoes, surely wondering where his target could be. He lunged, wrapped an arm around the man's neck, and tightened, cutting off air. A few seconds of pressure, then he released his grip, spun the man around, and slammed his elbow up and into the chin. The combination of blows staggered the Danite. A kick to the face sent the body sprawling to the ground.

He searched the man's clothes and found a pistol.

The other threat would not be far behind so he doubled around the chapel, rounding its rear and heading for the porticoes that lined the outer wall. A tiled pavement fronted them that kept his steps silent. He came to the end and picked his way through the hard-packed earth, back toward the entrance that both he and the first Danite had used, keeping down, using the tall markers as cover. The terrain inside the compact cemetery was inclined, rising to the chapel at the center.

He spotted the second pursuer.

On the pavement, heading up the incline, through the graves.

He kept his steps light and closed the gap.

Forty feet.

He passed where he'd left the wooden box and reached down and retrieved it.

Twenty feet.

Ten.

He pressed the barrel of his pistol into the nape of the man's neck. "Nice and still, or I'll shoot you."

The man froze.

"Is Salazar waiting to hear that you have me?"

No answer.

He cocked the hammer. "You mean nothing to me. Nothing at all. You understand?"

"He's waiting on my call."

"Nice and slow, find your phone and tell him you have me."

THIRTY-FIVE

★

ORANGE, VIRGINIA
4:15 P.M.

LUKE ARRIVED AT MONTPELIER JUST IN TIME
for the last tour of the day. The group was small,
led by an attractive young lady identified by a
badge as Katie and wearing some impressive tight-
fitting jeans. He'd driven straight from Washington in his Mustang, a wonderfully restored 1967
first-generation model that he'd bought as a gift
to himself while in the army. Silver with black
stripes—not a scratch on it—it was stored in a
garage adjacent to his apartment building. He
didn't own a lot of things, but his car was special.

Stephanie's sullenness had troubled him. All
she seemed interested in knowing was what, if

anything, awaited at James Madison's home. He was no student of history. God knows he'd barely made it out of high school. But he knew the value of information.

So he'd managed some quick browsing.

Madison was born and raised in Orange County. His grandfather first settled the land where Montpelier stood in 1723. The house itself was built by Madison's father in 1760 but, after inheriting the estate, Madison made many changes. He was an ardent Federalist, a believer in a strong central government, and had been instrumental in drafting the Constitution. He served in the first Congress, fought to have the Bill of Rights adopted, helped form the Democratic party, was secretary of state for eight years, then a two-term president.

"Mr. Madison retired here in 1817, when his last term as president ended," Katie told the group. "He and his wife, Dolley, lived in this house until he died in 1836. After that, Dolley sold the estate and nearly all of their belongings. The estate was reacquired by the National Trust for Historic Preservation in 1984."

The house was nestled on 2,700 acres of farmland and old-growth forest in the green foothills of the Blue Ridge Mountains. A $25 million project had restored the house to the size and shape it had boasted when Madison had lived here, its columned portico, brick walls, and green shutters now reminiscent of colonial times.

He was following Katie from room to room, more watching her jeans than the décor, but definitely absorbing the geography, his gaze occasionally drifting out the windows to the grounds.

"There were once tobacco fields, farms, slave quarters, a blacksmith's shop, and barns out there."

He turned and saw that Katie had noticed his interest outside. He threw her a smile and said, "Everything a 19th-century country gentleman needed."

She was cute and wore no wedding ring. He never touched the married ones, at least not if he knew they were hitched. There'd been a few who'd lied, which he wasn't responsible for, but a couple of their husbands had not seen it that way. One broke his nose. Another tried, but had come to regret the challenge and spent a few days in the hospital.

Women.

Nothing but trouble.

"Tell me, darlin', what's that thing out in the field? It looks like a Greek temple."

She stepped to the window and gestured for the others to join her. He caught a whiff of her perfume. Not much. Just a tad, the way he liked it. She stood close, inside his space, and seemed not to mind.

Neither did he.

"That was built by Madison. Below is a thirty-foot-deep pit where he kept ice year-round. We'd call it a gazebo today, albeit an elaborate one. He intended it to become his summer study, where he could work and think in peace, with the cool from the ice below refreshing him, but it never happened."

"Anybody ever been into the pit?" he asked.

"Not since I've been around. It's sealed up."

She moved away from the window and led the group through the dining room and into Madison's library. The escorted tour only extended to the ground floor, the upper floor self-guided. He checked his watch. Maybe another three hours of daylight left. But he'd have to wait until much later to return. He decided to bypass the rest of the house and left out the front door, following a graveled path to the garden entrance. He passed through a portal in a long brick wall, guarded by hydrangeas, and walked toward a low knoll among the trees in the north yard.

Eight white columns held up the temple's domed roof. No walls, the fifteen-foot circle open to the elements. Katie had been right. Just a fancy gazebo. He stepped onto the concrete floor and tested one of the columns. Solid. He stared down at the flooring and stamped his foot. Rock-hard. The concrete was gray-aged but at its center lay a separate square-shaped piece, outlined by a one-inch grout line. Surely a way to get below, if need be.

He glanced back out at the grounds.

Black walnut, cedar, fir, redwood, and evergreens dominated, all old growth. A few appeared as if they could have even been around when Madison himself lived. He noticed little to no security, though the house interior was equipped with motion sensors. No problem. He wasn't going anywhere near there. No fence encased the property. But with 2,700 acres he could understand why not. He'd already checked Google Earth and learned that a road cut close to the temple, through the woods to his left. Maybe three hundred yards, he estimated. An easy way in and out. He'd brought some rope and a flashlight.

But what the hell was he looking for?

Like he'd told Stephanie, during the last two hundred years, that pit had surely been picked through.

But she'd also been right.

Not a single image of the inside existed anywhere online. Before entering the house, after buying his ticket, he'd thumbed through every book in the visitor center. Not a photo there, either.

So what was down there?

Probably not a damn thing. But he had his orders.

"You enjoying the view?"

He turned to see Katie standing beyond the columns.

"You need a bell on or somethin'," he said. "You can creep up on a guy."

"I saw you leave."

"I wanted to check this out," he said. "It's a beautiful spot. Real peaceful."

She stepped beneath the dome. "You don't look like a history buff."

"Really? What do I look like?"

She apprized him with a soft glare, through eyes that were a lovely shade of blue. A crop of short strawberry-blond hair hung in sexy, layered bangs that flattered her freckled face.

"I think you're military. Home on leave."

He rubbed his jaw, which like his neck was dusted with a two-day stubble. "Guilty. Just back from two tours overseas. Had some time, so I thought I'd visit a few presidents' houses and see what I was fighting for."

"You got a name?"

"Luke."

"As in the evangelist?"

He chuckled. "That was the idea."

Confidence fueled her forwardness and he liked it. He'd never cared for the Melanie Wilkeses of the world. Give him the Scarlett O'Haras. The tougher the better. Nothing excited him more than a challenge. Besides, he needed to learn about this place, and what better way than from an employee.

"Tell me, Katie, where do you get somethin' good to eat around here?"

She smiled. "Depends. You eat alone?"

"Wasn't plannin' on it."

"I'm off in twenty minutes. I'll show you."

THIRTY-SIX

★

SALZBURG

CASSIOPEIA NEVER ENTERED THE GOLDENER Hirsch. Instead she'd waited until Josepe had turned a corner fifty meters away, then rushed after him, following, hoping not to be noticed. Thankfully, she'd worn low-heeled shoes to the auction, which helped on the street's uneven stones. Dusk had deepened to night. Josepe remained fifty meters ahead, darkness providing plenty of cover.

He stopped.

So did she, retreating into a doorway, glimpsing a neat list of names posted to one side that signaled apartments overhead.

The angle of his shadowed right arm confirmed that he was talking on the phone. A short call. Just a few seconds. He then replaced the unit inside his jacket and kept walking. He was headed down a street identified as Sigmund-Haffner-Gasse. They were a block or so over from the cathedral and the Residenzplaz, heading toward the rock face that rose north of the city and supported the castle. Shadows from the streetlights near him danced a strange jig on the pavement. If caught, she could use the excuse that she'd risen to his defense at the auction and had not wanted to sit idly by while he might need her. Sounded good. She was still angry with Cotton, and wondered why he was so involved. Buying that book for a million euros had made a loud statement. She needed to speak with him.

But not right now.

Josepe came to the end of the street and turned left.

She hustled to the intersection, arriving just as he disappeared around another corner. Above she saw the dark outline of St. Peter's church, its onion-shaped roof distinctive. She entered the abbey's courtyard, which spread out before the church's main entrance, buildings encasing all sides. Another fountain splashed at its center.

No sign of Josepe.

All of the buildings were dark, no way out of the courtyard.

Except.

An open passageway, to the right of the church.

✯ ✯ ✯

SALAZAR FOUND THE CEMETERY.

His man had called and said that Malone was in custody and that they had retrieved the book. His Danites were good. Not as highly trained as an American intelligence agent, but competent. Thanks to three deaths he was down to two men, but he had an ample reserve of candidates from which to replenish the ranks.

St. Peter's graveyard was a familiar place. He'd visited several times, always amazed at how gentiles adorned their tombs as shrines.

Here was a perfect example of that excess.

Graves intentionally decorated with flowers and ironworks, open all day for people to gawk at as a tourist attraction. No Saint would ever be treated that way. True, there were places of pilgrimage. He'd witnessed where Joseph Smith, his brother, and his wife lay buried in Illinois. And Brigham Young's final resting place in Salt Lake. A Saint might also pay homage to an individual pioneer's grave if they were a descendant. But on the whole, Saints were not honored with great memorials. The body was a sacred entity, formed in the image of Heavenly Father. A temple of the Holy Spirit. The flesh was to be treated with great respect, both in life and death. During life it must be kept clean and free from evil contamination. When the spirit left the body to return to its heavenly home, mortal remains were laid to rest with reverence and dedication. His eternal reward should be great, as he'd led an exemplary life, directed by the prophets, guided by the angel, all in furtherance of his church.

His man had told him that they were holding Malone near the entrance to the catacombs, which were actually caves high overhead. The darkness here was nearly absolute, the cemetery framed in jagged shadows. No one else was around, the silence broken only by the sudden scurry of a startled animal. High overhead, lights still burned in the castle where the auction reception was surely in progress.

"Here, sir."

He scanned the shadows in the direction of the voice.

Two men stood at the top of a short incline, one holding the other from behind. The body in front seemed limp, with its head down and arms drooping at the sides.

He approached.

The man holding the body released his grip, allowing the shadow to fold to the ground. The gun came up, level to his face, and the form said, "It's time for you and me to have a chat."

New voice.

Malone.

A twinge of alarm jarred his nerves, but he quickly regained control. "Perhaps we should."

Malone motioned with the gun. "Inside."

He saw that the iron grille gate that restricted access to the caves above was open. "You would think they lock that at night."

"They do. Up the stairs. We'll talk there."

CASSIOPEIA WATCHED AS JOSEPE STOPPED AT THE top of the inclined path, then turned and disappeared to her right. She was unsure of her location, as Salzburg was only partially familiar to her, but it appeared that she'd entered St. Peter's cemetery. Graves lined the path on both sides. Her position was exposed so she kept to the sides, utilizing the stone markers for cover. She'd heard the sound of voices. Not loud but there, to the right. Unfortunately, she'd not been able to hear the words.

At the top of the incline she hesitated, using shrubbery to shield her body. She peered right and saw nothing. To her left, twenty meters away, she caught sight of a black mass with form and definition. A man. Staggering to his feet. She rushed over and saw it was one of the men from earlier, who'd been waiting for Josepe when they returned from the auction.

"You okay?" she asked him.

He nodded. "Got pounded hard."

And she knew by whom.

"Where is Senor Salazar?" he asked.

"This way."

She led him back to where Josepe had gone, and they carefully approached a portal blocked by an iron grille.

Another body lay just before it.

They helped the second man to his feet. He was also dazed from a blow to the head.

Both seemed okay.

She stepped to the gate and saw that its wooden jamb had been kicked open.

That meant Cotton had Josepe.

She motioned for quiet and led them away.

"Does either of you still have a weapon?" she whispered.

The second man shook his head and said that his attacker most likely took his. The first man she'd encountered produced a pistol. Cotton must have been in a hurry to leave it behind.

She gripped the gun. "Stay here."

"It's our duty to look after Senor Salazar."

"You know who I am."

Their silence confirmed that they did.

"Do as I say. Stay here."

"You should not be the one to go in there."

She was grateful for the darkness, which concealed the deep concern on her face. Any other time this man would be right.

"Unfortunately, I'm the only one who can."

THIRTY-SEVEN

✦

MALONE FOLLOWED AS SALAZAR LED THE WAY UP steps chiseled from the rock that encased them, smooth and concave from centuries of wear. At the top they entered a small chamber, the sagging form of its ceiling and rough walls evidence that it had once been a cave. He found a switch and lit a series of dim incandescent candle bulbs, whose pinpricks of light spread out into a rich glow. Six flat, arched niches lined the wall opposite the entrance. He knew what they were—seats for the priests during liturgy. This was the Gertraude Chapel, conse-crated in the 12th century and still used for ser-vices. In the center rose a Romanesque Gothic pillar, an altar of clay plates to its left, reminiscent of something seen in an actual subterranean catacomb. The contours of an anchor, cross, and fire adorned the altar, representing the divine virtues of hope, faith, and love. A line of five oak benches faced the altar.

"Over there," he told Salazar, motioning with the gun toward the benches.

He positioned himself between Salazar and the exit. The light barely pushed at the gloom, a washed-out yellow flickering like candles in a breeze. He laid the wooden box on the altar. "I was surprised you let me buy this. A million euros isn't all that much to a man like you."

"May I ask why the U.S. government is so interested in my purchases?"

"We're interested in you."

"You made that clear."

He was flying blind. He knew only the tiny bit garnered last night in Salazar's study. "Tell me about Texas, Hawaii, Alaska, Vermont, and Montana."

"I see you've been inside my residence. Wasn't that illegal?"

"And Utah. Add that to the mix. What does a citizen of Spain and Denmark care about six American states?"

"Have you ever heard of the White Horse Prophecy?"

He shrugged. "Can't say that I have."

"It's part of my religion. It foretells a great change for America. One that Latter-day Saints will be participants in accomplishing."

"You're not serious with 'the Mormons are going to take over,' are you? That **is** insulting to your religion."

"On that we agree. And no. That is not what I mean. The Constitution of the United States is sacred to us. Our Doctrine and Covenants declare that the Constitution is an inspired document, established by the hands of wise men, whom God raised up onto that purpose to free them from bondage. It is a golden mean between anarchy and tyranny. For whatsoever is more or less than the Constitution, cometh of evil. Our founder, Prophet Joseph Smith, believed in those precepts. But we revere the document in its entire form, as it was meant to be understood."

"What the hell are you talking about?"

Salazar smiled like a man at ease. No concern filled his face. "I have no intention of explaining myself to you. I need you, though, to answer me a question. What laws have I broken?"

"Murder, for one."

"Who did I kill?"

"Barry Kirk said you killed a man for a book."

"And you believed him?"

"Not really. You sent him to see what he could

learn. So he dangled enough bait to get us interested. Smart. Unfortunately, for you, Kirk pushed too far and I killed him."

"And the two men on the boat?"

"They got what they asked for."

"Then I'd say I owe you two deaths."

A clever admission about the dead agent. Indirect. But nonetheless clear. Which meant Salazar was confident he would be the one leaving here. He'd taken out two Danites below. But how many more were there?

"At least we've dropped the pretense. Can we get down to business?"

"The only business I have with you, Mr. Malone, is seeing to your salvation."

"You don't think I'm here alone, do you?"

"I could ask you the same thing."

He said, "At the moment it seems we have a standoff. Just you and me. Why don't we make the most of it?"

CASSIOPEIA STEPPED THROUGH THE GATE AND carefully shut the iron grille. Josepe's two men waited outside, out of view. Though they were clearly ready to help, this she had to do alone.

The crypt surrounding her was small, only a few graves visible in the darkness. A soft orange glow, which acted as a night-light, illuminated a Baroque crucifix. To its right and left, painted on six wooden panels, she saw a danse macabre of medieval paintings. Above one, where it appeared Death toted a basket of bones, was written **huc fessa reponite membra**.

She translated.

Here are buried the tired limbs.

Below was another painted inscription, in German, which she also translated.

After a holy life and good works
Just remember,
You will gently rest.

Really? She wasn't so sure about that.

She tried to live a good life, but it seemed little reward ever came her way. Instead, it was one problem after another. She was actually tired of the battles, longing for some peace and stability. She thought that falling in love might be a step in the right direction. Unfortunately she fell for another wayward soul, Cotton's spirit seemingly as free as her own.

Which had probably been part of the attraction.

On both sides.

But that was also a liability.

A set of risers cut a path straight up into the rock. Worry was not improving her ill-temper.

A cold draft of night air brushed the floor and touched her ankles. A few deep breaths calmed her. The darkness offered courage, but no wisdom.

She carefully began the ascent.

✳ ✳ ✳

SALAZAR STAYED CALM. NO MATTER HOW MUCH bravado Cotton Malone showed, he doubted he was in physical danger. He was merely one of a thousand secondary officials in the Church of Jesus Christ of Latter-day Saints. Unlikely the U.S. government was here to assassinate him. But that didn't mean the situation wasn't perilous. He'd already noticed that Malone had relieved one of the Danites of his weapon, as he recognized the pistol aimed at him. All of his men carried the same make and model. Guns were a passion. He loved them, and had all of his life. His father taught him about weapons and how to respect them. On his own, though, he'd mastered how to use them for the good of the church.

"It's interesting," he said, "that your superiors sent you here to confront me with so little information. Seems you would know the connection among those six American states."

"You'd be surprised how much I know."

And he did not like the look of confidence on his captor's face.

"My guess," Malone said, "is you're the one who's curious. You want to know how and why we're so interested in you. Get ready. You're going to find out the answer to that real soon."

"I look forward to it."

"I wonder," Malone said. "Does the current prophet know about your merry little band of Danites? I can't imagine he would sanction that. The Mormon Church has come a long way since its beginnings. The need for such extremes has long passed."

"I'm not so sure about that. My church has been the subject of much abuse and persecution. We have suffered through insults, like the ones you delivered earlier, violence, even death. And we've survived all of that by not being weak."

He was stalling, giving his men time to act— which, he hoped, they were doing. "I twice under-estimated you, Mr. Malone."

"I get that a lot."

"I won't a third time."

CASSIOPEIA STEPPED FROM THE SHADOWS, JUST outside the doorway leading into what appeared to be a chapel.

Four steps and she was directly behind Cot-ton.

She pressed her weapon into his spine and said, "Drop the gun."

✬ ✬ ✬

MALONE FROZE.

"I'm not going to repeat myself," Cassiopeia made clear.

He decided that he had no choice.

The gun clattered on the floor.

Salazar retrieved the weapon, finger on the trigger, and immediately raised it to Malone's forehead. "I should shoot you here and now. You killed three of my employees. Kidnapped me, demanding answers to your questions. The U.S. government has no right to be doing any of this."

Rage filled Salazar's eyes.

"You killed an American agent," Malone said.

"Liar," Salazar screamed. "I killed no one."

The black dot of the gun barrel remained in his face.

But he'd faced one before and did not flinch.

"No, Josepe," Cassiopeia said, coming around to where Malone could see her. "No violence. I came to end this."

"He is evil," Salazar said.

"But killing him would be equally as bad."

Salazar lowered the weapon, his expression one

of disgust. "Of course. You're correct. I have done nothing wrong. Nothing at all."

Malone wondered how long Cassiopeia had been outside the chapel. Had she heard Salazar's tacit confession? Perhaps Salazar was wondering the same thing. Which would explain his show.

Cassiopeia stepped to the altar and retrieved the book. "This belongs to us."

She handed the box to Salazar, who said, "Tell your superiors, Mr. Malone, that I thank them for the purchase."

"So stealing is okay?"

Salazar threw him a smile. "Under the circumstances, I would say no. We'll call it partial compensation for what I owe you."

He caught the meaning.

They headed for the doorway.

Cassiopeia backed away, her gun aimed on him.

His eyes never wavered from her, either. "You going to shoot me?"

"If you don't stay here, until we're gone, I'll do just that. I haven't forgotten your insults. To me. To him. To **our** religion. I believe in restraint. But if pushed, I **will** shoot you."

And she left.

MALONE STOOD IN THE SILENCE. HE HAD NO INtention of following. Cassiopeia had ended the confrontation her way.

And that was as far as it could go.

He stepped from the chapel into a small foyer hewn from the rock, and approached a rectangular opening in the outer wall. No glass filled the window. A gray-yellow amorphous quarter moon hid behind scattered cloud cover. Below, he saw the silent forms of Cassiopeia, Salazar, and the two Danites as they retreated from the graveyard, heading back into town. He felt angry, betrayed, disillusioned, bitter, and, more than anything else, foolish. He'd confronted Salazar with no real purpose, other than to pick a fight.

Not his style.

He usually never made a threat he could not back up. But this time had been different. The president of the United States had wanted Salazar hassled. What just happened certainly qualified.

The four shadows disappeared into the night.

One of whom he loved.

Now what?

Hell if he knew.

CASSIOPEIA ENTERED THE GOLDENER HIRSCH, the gun back in the possession of the younger man.

She'd learned that both were staying on the third floor in a room down the hall from Josepe's. She was one floor below them in a spacious suite. Josepe handed over the book to his associates then excused them, escorting her to her door. She inserted the key. He gently grasped her arm and drew her close.

"I want you to know that I have hurt no one. That allegation was false and malicious."

"I know, Josepe. That's not you."

"Did you mean what you said? About **our** religion and that he insulted **us**?"

"Every word."

Lying was becoming far too easy for her.

"Why did you follow me?"

"I have skills, Josepe, that may be of assistance to you."

"That I can see."

"I've been involved with several high-profile investigations. I can handle myself in . . . difficult situations."

"I saw that, too."

"The important thing is that you now have the book and he did not win. Whatever else exists between you and Malone and the Americans, I'm here if you want my help."

He appraised her with careful eyes. She could almost hear his thoughts as he considered the reasons why he should not trust her.

"I could use your help," he finally said.

"Then you have it."

"We'll discuss it more tomorrow." He gently kissed her. "Good night."

And he walked away, climbing to the third floor.

She listened as his footfalls receded.

Cotton had sent her another message with his accusation.

One she'd received, loud and clear.

And something had become abundantly clear.

This Josepe Salazar was not the man she once knew.

THIRTY-EIGHT

★

STEPHANIE HAD BEEN PROVIDED THE ADDRESS BY
Danny Daniels. Then she'd listened as Daniels explained how her discretionary account was short
some $500,000 thanks to an adjustment made to
confidential audits conducted by the Justice Department. The attorney general's assistance had
been recruited, though he hadn't been told the reason why, only that it was necessary that her job be
in jeopardy. She thought, perhaps, the AG might
actually like that, since the two of them had been
known to clash. The appropriate leaks of the White
House's suspicions were made yesterday evening,
after Edwin returned to Washington, to ensure

that the rumor quickly made its way to Senator Thaddeus Rowan.

"I hate that righteous SOB," the president said. "And I don't say that about many people."

"I never realized you and Rowan were enemies."

"And nobody ever will. When I assemble a firing squad, we don't line up in a circle."

She smiled. Finally, a little levity. She'd been worried about him.

"Don't get me wrong," the president said. "I have the utmost respect for the Mormon religion. Charles Snow has always been straightforward with me. But every religion has its share of fanatics and nutcases. Unfortunately for us, one of theirs serves as head of the Senate Appropriations Committee."

She'd left the president sitting alone at the dining room table. Edwin had escorted her to the Mandarin Oriental, the hotel where she stayed when in Washington. She'd freshened up, checked in with Atlanta, and spoken with Cassiopeia Vitt on the phone, learning what happened in Salzburg at the auction.

"You knew Cotton was coming here," Cassiopeia said. "And said nothing?"

"I merely suspected it. And yes, I kept my fears to myself."

"I should walk away from this right now."

"But you won't."

"Cotton said that your agent is dead. He accused Josepe of his murder."

"He's right, on both counts."

"I need to prove that to myself."

"You do that. And while you're at it, get your head screwed on right."

"I'm not one of your people, Stephanie. I don't take orders from you."

"Then leave. Now."

"If I leave, Cotton will still be here."

"That's right. And we'll deal with Salazar our way."

A taxi deposited her at the curb.

She was back in Georgetown, not far from where Wisconsin Avenue and M Street crossed. Three hundred years ago it was the farthest point upstream that oceangoing ships could navigate the Potomac River, so the spot became a trading post. Now it was a trendy suburb of the nation's capital, home to high-end fashion shops, outdoor bars, and renowned restaurants. Parkland and green space buffered exclusive neighborhoods from urban sprawl. The homes and town houses were some of the priciest in the city, Rowan's a lovely Federal-style building nestled among a cheerful cluster of Colonial and Victorian architecture. A towering canopy of live oaks shadowed the two-story white brick home. Flowers lined a brick walk and sprouted from planters dot-

STEVE BERRY / 316

ting the porch railing. She climbed the stairs, crossing wooden planks, and rang the bell. Daniels had said that the senator should be arriving home from Utah around four thirty.

Rowan himself answered.

He was one of those people who made no attempt to reduce their stature, maintaining a perfect military bearing. His thick pale hair and weathered face cast the look of an aging sportsman. The eyes were like chips of coal, and their gaze appraised her with a palpable wariness. Her being here was a serious breach of protocol, a violation of the unwritten rule that proclaimed a person's home sacrosanct, never to be breached.

"I need to speak with you," she said.

"That would be wholly inappropriate. Call my office. Set up an appointment, with a Justice Department lawyer present. That's the only way we're going to talk."

He moved to shut the door.

"Then you're never going to see what it is you're after."

The door stopped just before closing.

"And what is that?" he coolly asked.

"What Mary Todd Lincoln wrote to U. S. Grant."

She glanced around and admired the two Regency chairs and an antique settee, their burnished-gold upholstery held in place by dull brass tacks.

Wooden pedestal tables supported an assortment of family photographs. Two crystal lamps with oversized tassels dangling from their shades burned softly. The parlor was like stepping back to the 19th century. Memories flooded through her mind of her grandmother's house, where many of the same things could once be found.

"I'm listening," Rowan said.

He sat across from her in one of the chairs, his spine rigid, posture perfect.

"I can't respond to your subpoena. And not just for the obvious reason that it's overbroad."

"Why did you mention Mrs. Lincoln?"

"I know about your efforts to access some of the classified archives. I've been around a long time, Senator. Just like you. You sent your subpoena as a way to grab my attention. You tried pressuring, bullying, and threatening some of my colleagues in other intelligence branches and came up short. So you decided to give me a try and thought some carefully applied legal pressure might work. What you didn't know was that I have a problem."

"As I've been told. My chief of staff says the White House is looking at you."

"To put it mildly. And your subpoena is shining a bright spotlight right in my direction."

"What have you done?"

She chuckled. "Not yet. No admissions until we have a deal."

"And why would I trust you?"

She reached into her jacket pocket and removed the copy of Mary Todd's original letter, along with the typed version. Rowan accepted both and read. Though he tried hard to contain himself she could see the excitement.

"Is that some of what you're after?" she asked.

He shrugged, as though the answer was obvious. "You seem quite knowledgeable about my activities."

"I'm in the intelligence business. It's my job. But those requests of yours have screwed me up good."

"In what way?"

"Let's just say that I have an accounting problem. One I was about to quietly resolve, until you came along. Now the White House is asking questions I don't want to answer."

He appeared surprised. "I never took you for a thief."

"Then let's call me an underpaid public servant who wants to enjoy her retirement years. Once the current administration is gone, I'll be gone, too. It's the perfect time for me to fade away. I just needed a few more months, without any undue attention."

"Sorry to interfere with your plans."

"It might not be so bad, after all," she said,

keeping her voice matter-of-fact. "There's something else I think you might want to see. Something I doubt you know exists."

She found the copies of Madison's original note and the typed rendition.

Rowan read them.

"You're correct. I did not know this existed."

She glanced at her watch. "And by morning I'll have whatever it is Madison hid in his summer study."

She could see he was impressed.

"Which you want to use to bargain with?"

She shrugged. "I have what you want and you have what I want."

Her stomach turned. Voicing those words was disgusting enough, but the man sitting across from her made things worse. His public image was one of staunch conservatism. No nonsense. Straight shooter. Zero scandal. But he had no problem turning a blind eye to a corrupt public employee in order to get what he wanted. Even worse, he'd apparently bought into her story, which meant he had little to no opinion of her.

"You're correct," he said. "There are certain documents I would like to see. They are important . . . on a personal level. Unfortunately, I've been unable to access them. This letter from Mrs. Lincoln was one that I believed existed. You see, she sent a similar letter to the head of my church. We have that in our archives. But this note from Mr. Madison is something entirely new."

"I don't know what you're doing, nor do I care. I just want all this attention on me to go away. I want to serve out my time till Daniels is out, then I'm gone." She added a bitter edge to her voice. "I came here to make a deal. If I can get you off my back, I can handle the White House. But I can't fight them **and** Congress. I brought two offerings to show my good faith. By morning, I'll have a third."

"I, too, am in my final years in office. I will not be running again."

That was news.

"Retiring back to Utah?"

"Back to Utah. But no retirement."

She felt like an accused walking to the scaffold after tying the noose around her own neck. But she decided to embrace her new persona. It wasn't often that one was given a free pass to break the law.

"Then your subpoena will be withdrawn?" she asked.

"Not exactly."

Why had she known this wasn't going to be that easy?

"While I appreciate your two immediate offers, and the one coming tomorrow, there is another item I require. And I'd like to see it tonight."

THIRTY-NINE

✪

SALZBURG
11:50 P.M.

MALONE LAY ON THE BED IN HIS HOTEL ROOM,
legs crossed, hands laced together behind his head.
Fatigue had hit him like a wave, but sleep was elusive. He chided himself for his fears and worries.
Hated the nagging ache of doubt in his gut. He
could not remember being in a stranger situation.
But he hadn't allowed a woman into his life for
some time. The final five years of his marriage to
Pam had been anything but intimate. They were
more like strangers living together, both realizing
that the relationship was over, neither one of them
wanting to do anything about it. Finally Pam had
forced the issue by moving out. Eventually he
ended the estrangement by divorcing her, retiring

from the government, quitting his job, and leaving Georgia for Denmark.

He could work a mission with Swiss precision— plotting, planning, and executing exactly what needed to be done. Yet he faltered like an amateur when it came to emotions. He simply could not make the right call at the right time. He'd messed up with Pam. Now he wondered if he was repeating the mistake with Cassiopeia.

A light rap disturbed the silence.

He'd been hoping she'd visit.

He opened the door and Cassiopeia walked inside.

"Stephanie told me where you were," she said. "I'm not happy with her or you right now."

"Nice to see you, too."

"What are you doing here?"

He shrugged. "Ran out of stuff to do. Thought I'd come and see what you were up to." He could see she was not in the mood for sarcasm. Neither was he, actually. "You're a long way from your castle."

"I realize I lied to you. It was necessary."

"Apparently so."

"What's that supposed to mean?"

"You can let it mean whatever you want it to."

"I took a chance coming here," she said. "But I thought we should talk."

He sat on the edge of the bed.

She remained standing.

"Why did you buy that book?" she asked.

"The president of the United States told me to." He could see she was unaware of Daniels' involvement. "Stephanie left that tidbit out? Get used to it. You're going to be told only what they want you to know."

She wasn't her usual self. Her eyes were elusive, her voice flat.

"Why are **you** here?" he asked her.

"I thought I was helping clear the name of an old friend. Now I'm not so sure."

Time they lay all the cards on the table. "He's more than an old friend."

"He was my first love. We were supposed to marry. Our parents wanted that so much. But I ended it."

"You never mentioned him. Or that you were Mormon."

"Neither seemed relevant to anything between us. My parents were Mormon, and I was born one. Once they died, I left the religion. And Josepe."

He wondered again how much she'd heard in the catacombs. "How long were you outside the chapel?"

Her eyes stayed cold. "Not long."

"You didn't hear him admit he killed our agent?"

"No, I didn't. And it's a lie. Stephanie said the same thing."

Her denial sent through his mind the sight of her kissing Salazar. "Why are you so quick to think it's not true?"

"Because you're jealous. I saw it in the restaurant."

"I'm not a kid, Cassiopeia. I'm working a case. Doing my job. Wake up and do the same thing."

"Go to hell."

His anger rose. "You understand Salazar has fanatics who do his dirty work. Danites. That's what those two from the cemetery are."

"Cotton, you're going to have to let me handle this. Alone."

"Tell that to Stephanie."

"What you did tonight, taking Josepe, was foolish. Luckily it turned in my favor. I was able to capitalize on the situation. He's beginning to trust me."

Now he was pissed. "**Josepe** is a murderer."

Her eyes flashed hot. "And what proof do we have of that?"

"I saw the body."

That seemed to register, but then she said, "I have to find out what's going on. In my own way."

"I was there," he said. "Last night. That kiss between you two was no act." He could see that the revelation surprised her. "More info that wasn't passed on by Stephanie?"

"You don't know what it was you saw. I don't even know what it was."

"Which is my point exactly."

He'd come a long way with this woman. From enemies to lovers. They'd endured a lot, formed a bond, a trust—or at least he'd thought so. At the moment she seemed a universe away. A stranger.

And he hated that.

"Look, you've done a good job. Why not get out and let me finish this?"

"I can handle it. Without you."

He kept his emotions in check and risked one more attempt at reason. "This old friend is into something big enough that it involves the president of the United States personally. One agent is dead, whether you want to believe it or not. Three of his men are dead. I killed them. You gotta get with the program, Cassiopeia." He paused. "Or get out."

"You really can be an ass."

"I'm not trying to be."

"You need to go home."

She turned for the door.

He did not move.

Not once had she offered anything in the form of affection. No smile. No joy. Nothing. She was as expressionless as a piece of stone. He regretted pressing her. But somebody had to.

She reached the exit.

He didn't want her to leave.

"Would you have shot me?" he asked.

A rhetorical question, for sure, asked more as a matter of hope than for an answer.

She turned back and stared at him.

Uncertainty filled the air between them. Her eyes were as hard and brilliant as granite, her face a death mask of emotions.

Then she left.

SALAZAR KNELT ON THE WOOD FLOOR OF HIS suite. The intense pressure to his knees reminded him of the hardness the pioneers endured to make their journey west, escaping persecution, seeking safety and freedom in Salt Lake. It was important that Saints never forgot that sacrifice. They existed today thanks to what all of those brave men and women endured, many thousands dying along the way.

"We were not compatible with the social, religious, and ethical mores of our neighbors," the angel said to him.

The apparition floated on the far side of the room inside a brilliant halo. He'd been praying before sleep when the messenger appeared, worried that Malone might be right. Cassiopeia's theft of the book, and his retention of it, might be sinful.

"Know this be the truth, Josepe. A certain nobleman had a spot of land, and the enemy came by night, broke down his hedge, felled his olive trees, and destroyed his works. His servants, affrighted, fled. The lord of the vineyard said unto the servants, Go and gather your residue and take all my strength of my house, which are my warriors, my young men, and go straightaway and redeem my vineyard, for it is mine. Throw down their tower and scatter their watchmen. And inasmuch as they gather against you, avenge me of mine enemies that by and by I may come with the residue of my house and possess the land."

He absorbed the parable and understood its meaning.

"What was done was necessary. The redemption of Zion will come only by power. That is why Heavenly Father raised unto his people a man to lead them, as Moses led the children of Israel. For ye are the children of Israel, and of the seed of Abraham, and ye must be led out of bondage by power with a stretched-out arm."

"My servants have been amassed and they are ready for battle."

"All victory and glory is brought to pass through diligence, faithfulness, and prayers of faith."

So he prayed harder, then said to the angel, "I allowed my anger to take over with Malone. He taunted me with the deaths of my men and I became boastful and said more than was necessary."

"Do not lament. That man shall dwell in darkness, while you enjoy eternal light. The book is ours now. The gentile had no right to possess it. He did so to cause you harm."

He should have atoned Malone, but Cassiopeia's appearance made that impossible. But he wondered, had she heard all that he and Malone had discussed?

"It matters not," the angel said. "She is of Zion and her purpose is your purpose. If she be repulsed by what had to be done, then she would not have interfered."

Which made sense.

"She is your ally. Treat her as such."

He stared at the vision and asked what he'd never before possessed the courage to say. "Are you Moroni?"

Nothing would exist but for Moroni. He'd lived on earth around A.D. 400 and became the prophet who buried a record of his people on golden plates. Centuries later, he appeared to Joseph Smith and led him to the spot where the plates rested. Under the divine inspiration of Heavenly Father, with Moroni's help, Prophet Joseph had translated the plates and published them as the Book of Mormon.

"I am not Moroni," the angel said.

He was shocked. He'd always assumed that to be the case. "Then who are you?"

"Have you ever wondered about your name?"

An odd question.

"I am Josepe Salazar."

"Your first name is one of long standing in Hebrew. Your last from the Basque heritage of your father."

He knew that, the surname originating from a medieval town in Castile where a noble family adopted the identity as their own.

"You are Josepe. Joseph in English. Joseph Salazar. As with the prophet, Joseph Smith, whose initials you share. J. S."

He'd long noticed that coincidence, but thought little of it. His father had intentionally chosen his first name to honor the prophet.

"I am Joseph Smith."

He did not know what to say.

"I am here to aid you in the battle ahead. Together, we shall reclaim the freedom that belongs to Zion. Know this, Josepe. Heavenly Father has promised that, before the generation living has passed, we shall defeat the gentiles and fulfill all His promises. It will come to pass. Elder Rowan will soon lead the church, and you shall be at his side."

He felt so unworthy. Tears welled in his eyes. He fought the urge to cry, but then succumbed, allowing his emotions to spew forth. He hinged his spine forward and extended his arms to the floor.

"Cry, Josepe. Cry for all who have died for our cause, myself included."

He looked up at the apparition.

Smith had been thirty-eight years old that day in June 1844, jailed in Illinois on trumped-up charges. A mob had attacked, and Joseph and his brother Hyrum were shot dead.

"I went like a lamb to the slaughter, but I was calm as a summer's morning. My conscience was void of offense toward God and toward all men. They took my life, but I died an innocent man. It has forever since been said of me that I was murdered in cold blood."

That it had, and it was true.

But the eyes that stared down at him were, for the first time, full of power.

"My blood cries from the ground for vengeance."

He knew exactly what to say.

"And you shall have it."

FORTY

✦

LUKE WAS BACK AT MONTPELIER. HIS DINNER with Katie had lasted three hours. She'd taken him to a cozy roadside diner north of town where they'd drunk beer and nibbled on some not-half-bad fried chicken. She was a doll baby and he wished he had the time to spend the night. She seemed to like military guys. They'd taken separate cars to the diner, so she'd driven herself home while he headed back to the estate, her phone number and email address tucked in his pocket.

Three more hours he'd sat in his Mustang, parked among the trees off the road behind the main house. The temple stood a few hundred yards away. Not a light burned anywhere, save for a smattering on the exterior of the mansion, which he could see in the distance through the trees. No patrols or security people of any kind had appeared. All was quiet.

At his apartment he'd studied pictures of the temple, and his on-site inspection earlier had only confirmed his thoughts. He'd brought with him a fifty-foot coil of thick hemp rope, a flashlight, some gloves, and a crowbar. Everything an enterprising burglar might need.

He stepped from the car and retrieved his tools, quietly closing the trunk.

The walk through the woods took ten minutes, the sky clouded over and devoid of a moon or stars. The dark outline of the temple came into view and he strolled up the knoll, dry grass crunching beneath his feet, and stepped up onto the concrete pad. Not much noise in these woods—unlike home where crickets and frogs sang through the night. Sometimes he missed home. After his father's death things had never been the same. Enlisting had been the right call. He saw the world and grew up at the same time. Now he was a U.S. Justice Department agent. His mother had been proud when he told her of the career move, and so had his brothers. He had no college degree, no professional license, no patients, clients, or students.

But by damn he'd made something of himself.

He set the rope and light aside. With the crowbar he began to work the mortar surrounding the center hatch. It chipped away with minimal effort and he was quickly able to wedge the flat end of the iron into the joint. A few pushes and one edge lifted free. A little farther and he exposed an opening in the floor plenty wide for him to fit through.

He laid the square section of concrete down beside the entrance, then tied the rope to one of the columns. He tested the strength and was satisfied it could hold him. He tossed the rest of the rope into the opening.

One last look around.

Still quiet.

He extended his hand with the flashlight into the hatch and switched on its red-filtered light. Darkness dissolved below and he spotted brick walls and a brick floor thirty feet down. As he'd anticipated, the first ten feet would be all rope until the slack hinged inward and his feet found wall. Then he could ease himself down. The same would be true on the way back up. Thank God his upper body was in great shape The climb in and out should not be a problem.

He switched off the light and stuffed it inside his jean pocket. He slipped on leather gloves and down he went.

He marveled at what it would have taken to dig

this pit two hundred years ago, all with only picks and shovels. Of course Madison had owned slaves—about a hundred according to Katie's tour. So labor wasn't a problem. Still, the effort to construct a hole this wide and deep was impressive.

His feet found the wall and he walked himself to the floor.

He glanced back up and imagined the scene from long ago. A lot of ice would have been stacked in here during winter. The lake he'd admired earlier beyond the house would have frozen over annually. Blocks would then be cut away by slaves, dragged to the pit, and packed with straw for insulation. So much ice that it kept itself frozen till the following winter, when the process was repeated all over again. He'd read on the Montpelier website earlier that ice cream was one of Madison's favorite foods. His wife, Dolley, was even credited with popularizing the treat by serving it at her husband's second inaugural ball.

He switched the light back on and surveyed the interior. The red beam shone only a short stretch, and everything was swathed in gray, so he risked it and switched to white. Hard to say how many bricks surrounded him. Certainly in the thousands, their color faded, a yellow moss encrusting the joints and crevices. Impossible to prevent given the porous soil and the length of time the pit had existed. But overall, the walls were relatively clean. Being sealed had certainly helped.

The beam caught something.

He swung back and focused on the brick face.

Faint.

But there.

He stepped closer and glanced upward, focusing through the dimness.

"It's friggin' letters," he whispered.

XIII.

He began a careful survey with the light.

Letters etched on more bricks appeared.

XIX. LXX. XV. LIX. XCIX.

He was no student of Latin. Sure, he knew the obvious Roman numerals. The Super Bowls had taught him that. He'd never figured out why the NFL chose to use those over good old-fashioned American numbers. Maybe it classed things up?

He continued his scan and noticed that there were duplicates scattered about. He quickly counted five LXXs. Eight XVs. He recalled what Stephanie had showed him from Madison's note. Scrawled at the bottom was IV. He searched, whipping the light around the cylindrical walls.

And found it.

IV.

Near the top, maybe six feet down from the opening.

He decided to see if his hunch was correct. A further scan revealed not another IV anywhere.

Good enough for him.

He would need the crowbar for further investigation. But it lay up at ground level. He switched off the light, gripped the rope, and climbed. At the top he pulled himself up through the hatch and was just about to retrieve the tool when something caught his attention.

In the distance.

Beyond the mansion.

The night broken by the rhythmic flashing of blue lights and the wail of sirens. Then he saw two more sets of flashing blue lights.

All coming his way.

"Ah, crap," he whispered. "That can't be good."

FORTY-ONE

✦

Washington, D.C.
1:40 a.m.

Rowan stepped from the cab. Across 1st Street the white façade of the Capitol was lit bright. He'd worked through the night many times when Congress was in session, especially years ago during his first two terms. Not so much anymore, though occasionally some issue of importance mandated the show of a national legislature that refused to sleep.

But that's all it was.

Show.

The real work never happened on the legislative floor. That was accomplished in closed offices, or at restaurant tables, or during a walk on the National Mall. The federal government was fatally flawed and had been for a long time. It no longer possessed the ability to actually do anything constructive. Instead, what it did best was suck away resources from both the people and the states. It could do little to solve any problem, and refused to allow anyone or anything else to do so, either. What he'd read yesterday morning from the Texas petition on secession had stuck in his mind. **Given that the state of Texas maintains a balanced budget and is the 15th largest economy in the world, it is practically feasible for Texas to withdraw from the union, and to do so would protect its citizens' standard of living and re-secure their rights and liberties in accordance with the original ideas and beliefs of our founding fathers which are no longer being reflected by the federal government.**

Perfectly said.

He could not recall the precise moment when he became a secessionist, but he was utterly convinced that his position was correct. **Whenever any form of government becomes destructive, it is the right of the people to alter or to abolish it, and to institute new government, laying its foundation on such principles and organizing its powers in such form, as to them shall seem most likely to effect their safety and happiness.** Thomas Jefferson and the fifty-five other patriots who signed the Declaration of Independence were right. Interesting how those men supposedly possessed the natural and inalienable right to violently rebel against an oppressive England. Yet if their descendants tried to do the same against the United States of America, myriad federal statutes would be brought to bear against their every act. When did Americans lose those "natural and inalienable rights"?

He knew.

1861.

With Abraham Lincoln.

But he intended to reclaim them.

The entrance of Stephanie Nelle into the fray was unexpected. One of his legislative aides had briefed him about the swirling rumors. Nothing definitive, only that questions had arisen about her, and the White House was trying to handle the problem in secret. No one wanted any scandal this late in the term. Had his requests for information accelerated things? Or was he actually responsible? Hard to say. All he knew was that Nelle had appeared, knew he'd been searching for classified records, then offered to provide exactly what he was after.

So he'd taken advantage of the situation.

He climbed a granite staircase past the Neptune fountain to the entrance of the Library of Congress.

Trust Nelle?
No way.
Use her?
Absolutely.

✹ ✹ ✹

STEPHANIE WAITED INSIDE THE VESTIBULE OF THE
Great Hall at the Library of Congress. Ordinarily,
the building would be sealed for the night, only
security guards present. But after leaving Rowan
she'd called the White House. Fifteen minutes
later the library director contacted her. Thirty
minutes after that an older gentleman distinguished by a warm smile, thinning gray hair, and
steel-rimmed spectacles met her at the library. He
introduced himself as John Cole and, though it
was the middle of the night, wore a suit and tie
and seemed quite chipper. She'd apologized for
disturbing his sleep, but he dismissed her concerns
with a wave of his hand, saying, "The director says
I'm to do whatever you ask." After explaining what
she had in mind, he disappeared into the bowels of
the building, leaving her alone in the Great Hall.

Two marble staircases flanked her, the sparkling
white walls towering seventy-five feet to an ornate
stucco ceiling centered by stained-glass skylights.
A large brass sun-shaped inlay highlighted the
marble floor, surrounded by more inlays of the zo-

diac. The sculptures, murals, and architecture combined into a grand European style.

Which had been the whole idea.

Built in 1897 as a showcase for the art and culture of a growing republic, a place to store the national library, the domed Jefferson Building had evolved into one of the world's great repositories. Cherubs sprang up along both staircases and she knew their symbolism. They represented the various occupations, habits, and pursuits of modern life. She spotted a musician, a doctor, an electrician, a farmer, a hunter, a mechanic, and an astronomer, each complete with the tools of the trade.

It was appropriate that the building had eventually been named for Jefferson as, after the War of 1812—when the British burned Washington, including the library at the time—he sold the nation 6,400 of his personal books to form the nucleus of a new collection. That modest beginning had grown into hundreds of millions of objects. She once read that around 10,000 new items were added each day. Nearly all of it was open to the public, available for inspection. All you needed was a library card, which was easy to obtain. She'd maintained one for years. When she lived in D.C. she'd often enjoyed roaming the exhibit rooms, or attending a presentation in the auditorium.

Something was always happening at the library.

Some of the materials, though, were restricted, ostensibly because of their fragile state or rarity, kept in a special collection room on the upper floor.

What Rowan sought was held there.

ROWAN APPROACHED THE THREE BRONZE DOORS, representing tradition, writing, and printing. Like the temple in Salt Lake, the Library of Congress was replete with symbolism. The voice message from Stephanie Nelle had told him to bypass the usual visitor entrance one flight below and knock on these doors.

He did.

One opened and he saw Nelle.

He stepped inside the Minerva foyer, named for the eight statues bordering the ceiling representing the goddess of universal knowledge. Her symbol, the owl, repeated throughout.

They entered the Great Hall.

"I thought it better you come inside here than downstairs," she said. "No security cameras."

He appreciated her discretion. "I'm always impressed when I visit this place."

"It is a magnificent creation. We're alone, except for one curator, who is retrieving what it is you wish to see. I'm curious, though. Surely you could have gained access to the rare collection room without my help."

"I probably could. But only in the past two days have I discovered the book's relevance, and I would prefer not to draw attention to my inquiries. Lucky for us both you came along."

"I told the library that this was a matter of national security you and I were handling. They did not question. Nor will anyone note our visit in any logs. I had the volume brought down to the Congressional Reading Room. I thought you might be more comfortable there."

She motioned to their right and they found a long richly decorated gallery. Sets of double doors opened off it into an equally long room. Oak floors and half walls, together with a paneled ceiling inset with colorful paintings, created a regal atmosphere. Wall sconces burned softly and illuminated oak scrolls. A marble fireplace, adorned with mosaics, anchored each end. He knew this room's former pedigree. Once it had been kept open when Congress was in session, staffed by a librarian, messengers available twenty-four hours a day. Back in the 1960s and '70s, when long filibusters were common, staff would sleep here on cots, then ferry books by the hundreds across the street to keep the stall alive. The cots were gone, the room used now for ceremony.

"It's there," she said.

He caught sight of the treasure lying on a table surrounded by a sofa and upholstered chairs before one of the fireplaces.

He walked over and sat on the sofa.

The book measured about four inches by six inches, a little over an inch thick. Its tan leather bindings were in remarkably good shape.

He opened it and read the title page.

BOOK OF MORMON
Translated By
JOSEPH SMITH JR.

Third Edition
Carefully Revised By The Translator

Nauvoo, Illinois
Printed by Robinson and Smith
Cincinnati, Ohio
1840

A bookplate affixed to the cover sheet noted an identification number and that the Library of Congress had acquired it on December 12, 1849.

He felt awed to be in its presence.

In 1838 the Saints were headquartered in Missouri. But on October 30 a rogue militia attacked the peaceful village of Haun's Mill and massacred most of the inhabitants. Fearing more violence the

Saints fled to Illinois, where a need developed for more copies of the Book of Mormon, the original 1830 printing exhausted. The $1,000 it would have cost to print new copies was nonexistent, but a divine revelation told them what to do. Circulars were sent throughout the church, and for every $100 sent toward the printing costs, a branch would receive 110 copies. Prophet Joseph himself endorsed the financing plan and set about revising the text, correcting errors. Money flowed in and five thousand new copies were eventually produced, one of which lay before him.

"This edition was so successful," he said, "that from that point forward this book has never been out of print."

"I read the library's record on it," she said.

He smiled. "I would have expected no less."

"The registers indicate that Abraham Lincoln checked this book out on November 18, 1861, and returned it on July 29, 1862. He also borrowed three other books the library had at the time on Mormonism."

"He was the first and, to our knowledge, the only president ever to read the Book of Mormon. We Saints hold Lincoln in high esteem."

He'd yet to delve any deeper than the title page.

"If you'll excuse me," he said to her. "I need to examine this in private."

FORTY-TWO

★

ORANGE COUNTY, VIRGINIA

LUKE SCRAMBLED OUT OF THE OPENING AND quickly untied the rope from the column. Blue strobing continued in the distance, the sirens growing louder. He slid the concrete hatch back into place and stuffed mortar chips into the joint. Then he swiped away all remnants from the concrete floor. If no one came too close, the dark should provide enough cover to prove that all was okay. He grabbed the rope and tools and retreated into the woods, twenty yards away.

The police arrived at the mansion and within two minutes three flashlights appeared, heading his way. He hid among the thickets, his dark clothes providing plenty of cover in the moonless night. He heard voices as the flashlights fanned out and approached the temple.

But no one stepped onto it.

The officers seemed satisfied that all was calm. The flashlights stayed fifty feet away. What had spooked them? Why had they come? Some sort of video surveillance with night-vision capability?

He doubted that. Listening to Katie at dinner he knew the estate was strapped for money, barely enough coming in to make ends meet. And why have such elaborate security? There was little of real value here. Certainly not enough to justify hundreds of thousands of dollars in surveillance.

The flashlights loitered a bit longer. He could hear men talking but couldn't make out what was being said. He watched, lying on his belly, through gnarly branches. Luckily the air was cool enough for it not to be a snake night, though he wouldn't be surprised if a raccoon or two appeared.

The flashlights departed.

He saw all three retreat from the knoll to the house, heading around to its front. He stood and listened as the cars drove off, three sets of head-lights fading away.

Time to finish.

He hustled back to the temple and retied the rope. He freed the hatch and tossed the slack back down. This was risky, but that was what he was paid to do. He'd learned during Ranger training to think, assess, then act under pressure, all with a clear goal in sight. Whatever it took, no matter the odds. Get the job done.

He grabbed the crowbar and with one gloved hand gripped the rope, adding a twist around his wrist for extra security, keeping it taut. He lowered himself, allowing his body to drop the ten feet needed to find the two letters.

IV.

He came to the approximate spot he remembered, then slid the crowbar into the top of his boot. He fetched the flashlight from his pocket and located the marked brick. Then he regripped the crowbar and popped the façade with the crook in the handle.

The clay held.

Again, but harder.

The brick cracked.

What the hell?

He slammed the iron bar into the surface, which shattered, revealing a dark hole. He switched the crowbar out for the light and shone the beam inside. Something glittered back.

Like glass.

He regripped the bar and carefully broke away the rest of the brick labeled IV. His right hand was beginning to ache from supporting his weight, though his feet, locked together around the rope, bore the brunt. He stuffed the crowbar back into his boot and swiped away the remaining fragments. Before he stuffed his hand inside he used the light one more time to see what awaited him.

A small object.

Maybe eight inches wide and a couple of inches tall.

Definitely glass.

He clenched the small flashlight between his teeth and removed the prize. He angled his chin down and the light reflected off the glass. He could see something sealed inside. A quick check with the beam showed the hole in the wall was now empty.

Mission accomplished.

He walked through the woods at a leisurely pace, allowing his right arm and hand to relax after their strain. That shouldn't have taxed his muscles so much. He was going to have to increase his workouts.

The rope was coiled over his shoulder. One hand held the crowbar, the other the glass receptacle. Definitely something sealed inside but he was not tasked with determining what. Stephanie had told him to retrieve and return whatever was there to her. Fine by him. He wasn't upper management, and he liked it that way.

He'd replaced everything at the temple. Surely, either tomorrow or soon after, someone would notice the broken mortar joints. They'd raise the concrete hatch and discover the hole in the wall. What it all meant would simply be a mystery. No answers, no evidence. Nothing to point to any culprit. All in all a good night. He'd not only struck pay dirt in the ice pit, he had Katie's phone number. He just might take her up on her offer and connect. He was due some downtime in another week.

He found his car and tossed the rope and crowbar into the trunk. He slipped back inside the Mustang, no cabin light betraying his presence. He laid the glass on the passenger seat and inserted the key in the ignition.

Something moved in the backseat.

He came alert.

A head appeared.

Then a face in the rearview mirror.

Katie's.

She was holding a gun—the one he kept in the glove compartment—aimed at him.

"You know how to use that?" he asked, not turning his head around.

"I can squeeze a trigger. The back of your seat is a big target."

"You turned me in?"

"I knew you weren't any army man. You're a thief. I followed you back here and waited for you to make a move. Then I called the sheriff."

"Now, darlin', that hurts to the core. And I thought you and I were gettin' along real good." Then it hit him. "That phone number you gave me ain't real. Right?"

"I only went to eat with you because I wanted to see what you were up to. I'm not a tour guide. I was just filling in today. I work on the restoration staff. I have a master's degree in American history, working on my doctorate. Madison is my specialty. That house is important. Thieves like you ruin it for all of us. And what do you think? That phone number is for the local sheriff."

Her being here was a big problem. What had Stephanie said? **Don't get caught**. "I'm not a thief."

"Then what's on the front seat?"

He lifted the hunk of glass and handed it back to her.

"Where'd you find this? I've never seen it before."

"That's because Madison hid it in his ice pit."

"How did you know that?"

He did not answer her.

"We're going to the sheriff," she said.

"Unfortunately, I can't do that. You might be some bigwig academic, but I'm an agent for the U.S. government and we need what you're holding."

"You don't expect me to believe that."

He heard sirens. Again.

"Come on, Katie. What did you do now?"

"I called the sheriff back when I saw you coming."

He turned around and faced her. "You're rapidly becoming a pain in my ass. Look, I'm telling you the truth. I have to take that back to my boss. You can come with me, if you want, to make sure it's cool."

The wail grew closer.

"Did you tell them where we are?" he asked.

"Of course. How else are they going to find you?"

This just kept getting better and better.

"Make a decision, Katie. Shoot me, get out, or come with me. Which is it?" He saw the indecision in her eyes. "I really am an agent and this is damn important. Tell you what. If it makes you feel better, keep the gun and that hunk of glass back there with you."

She said nothing.

The sirens kept coming.

"Go," she finally said. "Get us out of here."

He fired up the Mustang's engine.

Tires spun, then grabbed a firm patch, and they sped away.

"Where are we going?" she asked.

"Now that, darlin', is going to blow your mind."

FORTY-THREE

★

WASHINGTON, D.C.

ROWAN WAITED UNTIL STEPHANIE NELLE HAD
left the reading room and the doors were closed
before he focused on the book. He felt awe that
Lincoln himself had held what lay on the table
and pondered the meaning of lessons from long
ago.

> It shall be brought out of darkness unto light, ac-
> cording to the word of God. Yea, it shall be brought
> out of the earth, it shall shine forth out of the dark-
> ness and come unto the knowledge of the people,
> and it shall be done by the power of God. For the
> eternal purposes of the Lord shall roll on until all
> of his promises shall be fulfilled.

A prophecy, voiced just before the sacred golden record was hidden in the earth, where it was found centuries later by Joseph Smith and converted to the book before him.

Rowan had dedicated his life to his religion. His parents and theirs before them had all been Saints. Rowans had served the prophets, enduring both good and bad. Many had died to preserve what those before them had created. Why should this generation be any different? Charles R. Snow had done nothing but retreat and conform. His leadership had been irrelevant and uninspiring. The church remained fractured, with offshoots in Missouri and Pennsylvania, and smaller ones scattered around the world. Each believed in Joseph Smith as prophet and founder. They accepted the Book of Mormon. But they disagreed on many fundamental issues.

And they were not wrong.

So many tenets Joseph Smith and Brigham Young instituted had been either abandoned or repudiated by later leadership in Salt Lake.

Most prominent was the belief in plural marriage, which many fundamentalists still held as central to their religion.

As he believed.

The prophet Smith decreed the practice essential, and no later decision made for political and public relations reasons could reverse that. For Rowan, personally, monogamy was fine. But a Saint should have the choice, as the Prophet Joseph decreed.

The time had come to reassemble as many of the faithful who wanted under one banner. But that could not be done while the U.S. government still wielded power. Each state should be free to chart its own course, especially in matters of faith and religion. Congress had no business in the hearts and minds of individuals.

If the people only knew.

He'd served thirty-three years in the Senate. Sadly, nothing ever seemed to get done unless it benefited a select few, the government as a whole, or both. Nothing ever passed simply because it was good for the country, or the states, or the people. Those were the farthest things from most legislators' minds. Every congressman quickly learned that his or her only goal was to gather enough resources for the next election. Beyond that? Not a worry, until the **next** election was over. How many times had he watched as one lobbyist after another metamorphosed a good bill into a bad one. He'd never accepted one penny from a lobbyist. He rarely talked with them, and when he did, it was always in a group so there'd be no misunderstanding as to what was said. His reelections were paid for by individual donations from constituents inside Utah, all of which were reported in minute detail. If the voters were dissatisfied with that arrangement, they were free to elect someone else. But for the past thirty-three years, the people of his state had chosen him.

He stared down at the book.

Brigham Young had written in the note sealed within the cornerstone that Lincoln **told my emissary that he had read the Book of Mormon.** As a young legislator in Illinois, Lincoln had known Saints. He actually helped obtain approval for the Nauvoo city charter, which granted them unprecedented autonomy. For thirty-two years, starting with Franklin Pierce and ending with Chester Arthur, presidents of the United States showed nothing but harshness toward the church. Lincoln's five years were the sole oasis. In death his stature with Saints only grew. He emerged constantly at conference talks, in lesson manuals, in anecdotes. Rowan never realized the full extent of the connection until he began this quest.

But now he understood.

Did this book hold the key?

The moment he'd read Brigham Young's note he knew where he had to look. **Two months after our bargain was sealed Lincoln sent me a telegram that said Samuel, the Lamanite, stood guard over our secret, among the Word, which** gave me great comfort. Three words—among the Word—had made him immediately think of the book kept safe in the Library of Congress, the one Lincoln himself had read.

He opened to the first few pages and studied the tiny print. Nothing unusual had appeared on the front endpapers, so he checked the back ones.

All blank.

He could thumb through every page, but there were hundreds and that would take time. So he allowed the tissue-thin pages to slip past his thumb as he rifled through in rapid succession, his eyes scanning for anything unusual.

He saw something.

He stopped and found the page.

Part of the Book of Helaman. More precisely, chapter 13. The prophecy of Samuel, the Lamanite, to the Nephites. He knew the story, from around five hundred years before the coming of Christ. It told of the righteousness of the Lamanites and the wickedness of the Nephites. In no uncertain terms Samuel predicted the destruction of the Nephites, unless they repented.

Atop the type on the page, penned in ink, was a drawing.

He found the copy of the map from the temple cornerstone, which Snow had provided to him. They were the same, except this one had writing.

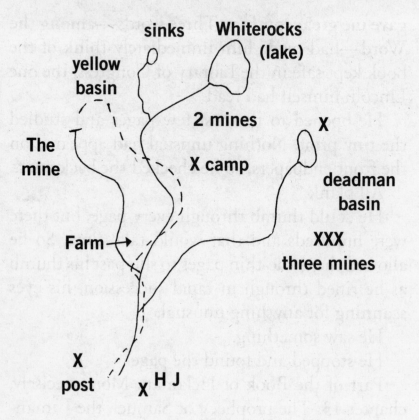

He noticed the printed passages that lay beneath the drawing.

**19 For I will, saith the Lord, that they shall
hide up their treasures unto me; and cursed
be they who hide not up their treasures unto
me; for none hideth up their treasures unto
me save it be the righteous; and he that
hideth not up his treasures unto me, cursed
is he, and also the treasure, and none shall
redeem it because of the curse of the land.**

20 And the day shall come that they shall hide up their treasures, because they have set their hearts upon riches; and because they have set their hearts upon their riches, and will hide up their treasures when they shall flee before their enemies; because they will not hide them up unto me, cursed be they and also their treasures; and in that day shall they be smitten, saith the Lord. 21 Behold ye, the people of this great city, and hearken unto my words; yea, hearken unto the words which the Lord saith; for behold, he saith that ye are cursed because of your riches, and also are your riches cursed because ye have set your hearts upon them, and have not hearkened unto the words of him who gave them unto you.

He smiled.

Lincoln had chosen his page with care.

The Nephites rejected Samuel and ultimately stoned the prophets.

A warning?

Perhaps.

But he had no choice. He had to move forward.

He noticed that something was missing from the map. One location unidentified. That could be problematic. He'd already recognized some of the locales. They were in the mountains northeast of

Salt Lake, in an area long suspected of holding secrets. But the area contained thousands of miles of wilderness, with few or no markers, and the omitted reference seemed to be an end point.

Lincoln had hedged his bets and not revealed all.

At the bottom of the page was scrawled **Romans 13:11**. He could not recall the gist of the passage.

Why had it been included?

He stared past the open blinds, out the window, at the illuminated Capitol dome. He needed time to think and could not leave this evidence.

Heavenly Father forgive him.

Never had he defaced the scriptures.

But he carefully tore the page from the book.

FORTY-FOUR

✦

3:50 A.M.

LUKE HAD FLED MONTPELIER QUICKLY, FINDING the highway and speeding north out of Virginia to Washington, D.C. Katie had sat in the backseat, quiet for the most part, only occasionally engaging in conversation. She'd kept the gun, but obviously knew little about it. He wasn't stupid enough to leave a loaded weapon around for anyone to get hold of. He kept the magazine beneath the driver's seat, easy to get, if you knew where to look. Which she didn't. He'd checked and was comforted to discover it was still hidden away.

They were now off the highway, headed into the city, the streets devoid of cars at this godforsaken hour. Luckily he'd always been a night person, so his mind was alert.

"You ever watch **The Andy Griffith Show**?" he asked her.

"Sure. Who hasn't?"

"Remember how Barney wanted to carry a gun. Made a big thing out of it. But Andy made him keep the bullets in his pocket."

Katie said nothing.

"The gun's not loaded," he told her.

"I don't believe you."

"Pull the trigger."

He watched her in the rearview mirror.

She did nothing.

"You said you knew how to use one. So use it."

He heard a click. Then another. And another.

Damn. She actually did it.

She tossed the gun over the seat. It thumped to the floorboard on the passenger side. "You think you're so damn smart."

He chuckled. "I don't know about that. You with your master's degree, working on your doctorate. I thought maybe you might figure it out on your own."

He stopped for a red light. "And you really gave me the sheriff department's number as your own?"

"I thought maybe you might turn yourself in."

"That just wasn't nice. I was so looking forward to calling you back."

"My loss," she said. "I think I'll leave now."

"I wouldn't do that."

"And why not?"

"'Cause you're going to miss out on somethin' really cool. Might even help that education of yours along."

She made no attempt to open her door and he accelerated through the intersection. It was an easy matter to cut across town, find Pennsylvania Avenue, and approach the guard gate for the White House. Before he'd left for Virginia hours ago, Stephanie had called and told him to come here when he was done.

He wasn't looking forward to the family reunion.

"What the crap?" Katie muttered.

He rolled down his window and prepared to identify himself. "I told you it would blow your mind."

They entered through the visitor entrance, a Secret Service agent waiting inside. Katie still carried the hunk of glass, her eyes alight with anticipation.

"I've never been here before," she said.

"Neither have I," he said.

"You really are an agent?"

"That's what they tell me."

Their escort led them through a marble hall. Cut-glass chandeliers lit everything in a daylight glow. They passed a portrait of Eisenhower. More presidential images hung at the far end. Kennedy. Johnson. Ford. Carter. Like a recent greatest hits parade.

They stayed on the ground floor and entered a room with walls sheathed in a red twill fabric. Gold scroll formed a border. The furniture was all upholstered in the same red shade with patterns of gold medallions and more scrolls. The carpet was beige, red, and gold. Another chandelier burned bright. Waiting there were Stephanie and good ol' Uncle Danny. He hadn't seen him in thirteen years, not since his father's funeral. He told himself to be respectful and mind his manners. His boss would want that, no matter what he might feel.

"Who is this?" Stephanie immediately asked.

He realized that protocol was being waived tonight. Usually, no one came close to the president without being vetted.

But this situation was anything but usual.

Katie, though, seemed remarkably composed, as if she met the president of the United States every day.

"A problem that occurred too quickly for me to solve, so I brought it along. This is Katie—"

He suddenly realized he did not know her last name.

"Bishop," she said. "Katie Bishop."

And she extended her hand for the president to shake.

"It's a pleasure to meet you," Daniels said. "Now could you answer the lady's question and tell me what you're doing here?"

"Show him," Luke said, motioning to what she held.

Katie handed over the hunk of glass.

"That came out of the ice pit," Luke said. "Hidden behind a brick with IV marked on it. I got it out, but Katie here managed to call the locals on me. They were closing in, so I had no choice but to bring her along."

"She one-upped you?" the president asked.

"I know it may be a little hard to believe. I'm having trouble with it myself. But stuff happens. As you certainly know."

"I see you still have that smart mouth," the president said.

"Probably a family trait. You think?" He caught Stephanie's glare. "Okay. I'll stop. Look, I didn't have a lot of choice. I also thought she might be helpful. She tells me that she has a master's in American history, and she also knows a lot about Madison. It was either that or get caught, so I took the lesser of two evils."

"Okay," the president said, "Katie Bishop, with your degrees in American history, where are we standing?"

"The Red Room. Dolley Madison used to have her fashionable Wednesday-night receptions here. That was the place to be in those days. Since then it's been a parlor, sitting room, music room. Unfortunately, the walls are reproductions, done when Truman gutted the White House. Hillary Clinton changed things to pretty much what you see now. This furniture, if I remember right, is from Madison's time. What's really cool is what happened during U. S. Grant's term. He was afraid there'd be a problem with Rutherford B. Hayes' inauguration, since he was elected after a trumped-up commission awarded him twenty disputed electoral votes, so he had him sworn in right here the night before."

"You know about the Compromise of 1877?"

Katie smiled. "Now you're being silly. One of the great backroom deals of all time. Hayes lost the popular vote in the 1876 election to Samuel Tilden, and neither one of them had enough electoral votes. So southern Democrats allowed those twenty disputed votes to go to the Republican, Hayes, in return for all troops being withdrawn from the South, a railroad built west through the South, and legislation to help rebuild what the war destroyed. Finally, they had a bargaining tool and they used it to its max. Grant immediately honored the deal and withdrew some of the troops. Hayes got rid of the rest. With them gone, the

Democrats took total control of the South, which they kept until the late 20th century."

"Not bad. Pretty good, in fact." The president motioned with what he held. "Now tell me what this is?"

"We've known about symbols on the bricks in the ice pit for a long time. No one ever figured out their implications. We thought it was just something Madison did. Decorative. Or an idiosyncrasy."

"Is that why there are no pictures of the pit on the Internet?" Stephanie asked.

Katie nodded. "The curators didn't want any of that **Da Vinci Code** kind of press, so they sealed it up."

"And it's a good thing they did," Daniels said. "But you haven't answered my question. What is it I'm holding?"

"I've been considering that all the way from Virginia. And I think I know the answer."

STEPHANIE WAS CLOSELY WATCHING BOTH DANNY and Luke. She'd arrived at the White House an hour ago, after finishing with Rowan at the Library of Congress. The senator had spent thirty minutes alone with the Book of Mormon. She'd watched every moment thanks to a closed-circuit feed from a hidden camera used for security in that part of the library. She and John Cole had witnessed Rowan tear a page from the 1840 edition. Cole had winced when that happened, but there was nothing either of them could do. Thankfully, Cole had already examined the book and photocopied the page with the writing. He told her that anomaly had been known for some time, but no one had any idea what it meant. It was one reason why the book was kept in the restricted access collection. Now, it seemed, the mystery may have been solved.

"Why don't you have a seat," the president said to them all. "I want to hear more of what Ms. Bishop has to say."

Stephanie was a little perturbed at Luke for involving an outsider. But she'd learned long ago to choose her battles when questioning her agents' decisions. They were the ones putting their butts on the line. All were highly trained, smart people. Luke had apparently weighed the options and made his call.

The president carefully laid the glass receptacle on a table.

"In the early 19th century," Katie said, "vacuum sealing didn't exist. Canning technology was just beginning to be explored. Preserving something like paper was tough. The first cans were actually made of glass, but tin eventually replaced that. To save fragile things, they would sometimes seal them in glass."

The hunk on the table clearly held something that resembled a small book.

"Madison was good friends with Thomas Jefferson. Monticello sat only thirty miles away, which in those days was like next door. Jefferson knew all about glass sealing. So maybe he told his good friend James Madison about the technique."

The president sat silent.

So did Luke.

Unusual for them both.

Not a word of affection had passed between them.

Two peas in a pod.

LUKE WAS DETERMINED TO WAIT HIS UNCLE OUT. Danny had always been a cold one. Interesting how brothers could be such polar opposites. He knew all about his uncle's sad past, and sympathized some—emphasis on **some**. Luke's family had always been close. He and his three siblings got along, brothers in the truest sense of the word. All three of his brothers were married, with children. He was the only one still wild and single.

"Good job getting this," his uncle said to him.

Had he heard right? A compliment? From the

great Danny Daniels? For the first time, their eyes met. "That pain you?"

"Luke—," Stephanie began.

But the president held up his hand. "It's all right. We're blood. And I probably deserve it, anyway."

That admission shocked him.

"You're related?" Katie asked.

The president faced her. "He's my nephew. He probably would never admit to that, but that's what he is."

"Aren't you just full of surprises," Katie said to him.

He wasn't interested in mending family fences. He really didn't give a damn about his uncle at all. He had to be careful, though, around his mother, as she'd always liked her brother-in-law.

The president motioned to the hunk of glass. "Do the honors, Luke. Break it open."

He wondered about all of the kindness but decided now was not the time to fight. He tested the weight. Maybe two or three pounds. Thick glass. A hammer would be good, but his boot might do the trick. He laid the receptacle on the floor atop a rug and popped his heel down hard. Nothing happened. He repeated and the glass cracked. A third jab and it broke away in chunks.

Carefully, he fished out the small book.

"Let our historian take a look," the president said.

He handed it to Katie.

She opened its cover and scanned a few of the pages. After a moment she glanced up and said, "Wow."

FORTY-FIVE

✦

Salzburg
9:50 a.m.

Cassiopeia sat in her suite, her mind in turmoil. Everything around her would normally be enticing. The wooden beams, embroidered linens, painted Bavarian chests, teakwood furniture. The Goldener Hirsch seemed an homage to history. But none of it mattered. What consumed her was how she'd managed to embroil herself in such an awful mess.

Her father would be so ashamed. He'd liked Josepe. But her father, though smart in so many ways, had been so naïve in others. Religion being his main fallacy. He always thought there was a divine plan, one that each person had little choice but to follow. If followed correctly the reward was eternal bliss. If not, then only cold and darkness awaited.

Unfortunately, her father was wrong.

She'd come to that realization shortly after he died. For a daughter who'd worshiped her father, that had been hard to accept. But there was no divine plan. No eternal salvation. No Heavenly Father. It was all a story, concocted by men who wanted to fashion a religion where others would obey them.

And that galled her.

Mormon doctrine taught that neither sex should be upset if privileges and responsibilities were bestowed on one but not the other. That seemed especially true when it came to women. Every woman was supposedly born with a divine purpose. Foremost was her role as mother. Serving in the home was tagged the highest of spiritual callings. She assumed such rhetoric had been designed to mask the fact that women could never attain the priesthood, or any position of church leadership or authority. Those were exclusively bestowed on men. But why? It made no sense. What was she, twenty-six, when she realized the implications? Just after her mother died. Men had created her religion and men would dominate it. God's plan? Hardly. She was not going to dedicate her life to raising children and obeying a husband. Not that there was anything wrong with either. Just that neither was right for her.

An old intentness burned inside. She thought back to a concert in Barcelona. Josepe had chosen the place. El Teatre més Petit del Món. Once the private home of a renowned artist, it had become the world's smallest theater—Chopin, Beethoven, and Mozart played in a romantic candlelit garden with 19th-century ambience.

It had been lovely.

Afterward, they'd dined alone and talked of the church, as Josepe liked to do. She recalled how, increasingly, that topic came to repulse her. But she'd indulged him, as she'd then thought was her place.

"There was an incident last week, in southern Spain," he said. "My father told me of it. A member of the church was attacked and beaten."

She was shocked. "Why?"

"When I heard I thought of Nephi, who came upon a drunken and passed-out Laban, lying on the streets of Jerusalem."

She knew the story of Laban, who refused to return a set of brass plates, which contained the scriptures needed for Nephi's family to remain obedient.

"Nephi realized the fallen drunk was Laban himself, and he felt commanded by the Spirit to kill him. Nephi struggled with that feeling. He'd never shed blood. But the Spirit repeated the order twice more. So he killed Laban and wrote that it was better that one man should perish than a nation should dwindle and perish in unbelief."

She could see he was troubled.

"Why would Heavenly Father order Nephi to do that?" he asked. "It seems contrary to all that is good and right."

"Perhaps because it is merely a story."

"But what of Abraham's attempted sacrifice of Isaac? He was commanded to offer his son, even though it was written, Thou shalt not kill. Abraham did not refuse. He was ready to kill Isaac, but an angel stopped him. God, though, was proud of his obedience. Joseph Smith himself spoke of that."

"Surely you see that as a parable, not an actual event?"

He stared at her, perplexed. "Nothing in the Book of Mormon is without truth."

"I didn't say it was false, just that it might be more a story with a lesson than an actual occurrence."

She recalled his reluctance to bend.

For him the Book of Mormon had been absolute.

"I'm not saying that I would have killed my son," he said. "But Abraham was brave to obey

Heavenly Father. He was prepared to do as commanded."

Cotton and Stephanie both had said Josepe killed an American agent.

Was it possible?

She'd not heard much of the conversation in the Salzburg chapel, except the last few words spoken just before she made her appearance. Never had Josepe been violent. As far as she knew, that simply wasn't his character. His forceful denial about killing anyone sounded true. So she had to wonder if she was being manipulated. She wasn't happy with either Cotton or Stephanie. One had no business being here, treating her like she was helpless—and the other was a liar. She'd hated the friction last night when she went to see Cotton, regretted calling him an ass, but she was angry then and remained so now.

She loved Cotton.

But she'd once loved Josepe, too.

How had she allowed this chaos to gather?

Part of her own arrogance, she assumed. A belief that she could handle whatever life threw her way. Yet she was not as tough as she wanted everyone to think. Her father had been her rock. But he'd been gone a long time. Maybe Josepe was intended to be his replacement, but she'd ended that relationship. Cotton was a little like her father, but also vastly different. He was the first man since

Josepe that she'd thought about in terms of permanency.

Yet she'd walked away from Josepe.

And Cotton? What of him? He should go home, but that wasn't going to happen. Stephanie had now involved him, so he would do his job.

As she should do.

She reached for her phone.

A check-in call with Stephanie was scheduled shortly. No way. Not anymore. She deleted all references to Stephanie from her phone.

Something was wrong here, of that there could be no doubt. Josepe traveled with armed men. Danites? The government, the president in particular, was apparently focused on him—something that also involved a U.S. senator. An American agent was apparently dead.

And Josepe was the prime suspect.

How it all fit together she did not know, but she intended to find out.

With one change.

She would handle it her way.

FORTY-SIX

★

Washington, D.C.

Saturday Sepr 15th 1787. In Convention

The main session having adjourned for the day the delegates reassembled after the evening meal for further discussion on a separate point.

Doc. FRANKLIN rose to confess that there are several parts of this constitution which I do not at present approve, but I am not sure I shall never approve them. For having lived long, I have experienced many instances of being obliged by better information, or fuller consideration, to change opinions even on important subjects, which I once thought right, but found to be otherwise. It is therefore that the older I grow, the more apt I am to doubt my own judgment, and to pay more respect to the judgment of others. Most men indeed as well as most sects in Religion, think themselves in possession of all truth, and that wherever others differ from them it is so far error. Steele a Protestant in a Dedication tells the Pope, that the only difference between our Churches in their opinions of the certainty of their doctrines is, the Church of Rome is infallible and the Church of England is never in the wrong. But though many private persons think almost as highly of their own infallibility as of that of their sect, few express it so naturally as a certain French lady, who in a dispute with her sister, said "I don't know how it happens, Sister, but I meet with no body but myself that's always in the right." In these sentiments, Sir, I agree to this constitution with all its faults, if they are such; because I think a general Government necessary for us, and there is no form of Government but what may be a blessing to the people if well administered, and believe farther that this is likely to be well administered for a course of years, and can only end in Despotism, as other forms have done before it, when the people shall become so corrupted as to need despotic Government, being incapable of any other. But I am not unmindful of the caution that our recent conflict has bred within us all. True, I doubt whether any other Convention we can obtain, may be able to make a better constitution. For when you assemble a number of men to have the advantage of their joint wisdom, you inevitably assemble with those men, all their prejudices, their passions, their errors of opinion, their local interests, and their selfish views. From such an assembly can a perfect production be expected? So the concerns of those who fear a perpetual, unbending, unbreakable association of States is well taken. We must be mindful that all that is created comes with an end.

Mr. GERRY stated his objections which determined him to withhold his name from the constitution. 1. the duration and re-eligibility of the Senate. 2. the power of the House of Representatives to conceal their journals. 3. the power of Congress over the places of election. 4 the unlimited power of Congress over their own compensation. 5. Massachusetts has not a due share of Representatives allotted to her. 6. 3/5 of the Blacks are to be represented as if they were freemen. 7. Under the power over commerce, monopolies may be established. 8. The vice president being made head of the Senate. He could however he said get over all these, if the rights of the Citizens were not rendered insecure 1. by the general power of the Legislature to make what laws they may please to call necessary and proper. 2. raise armies and money without limit. 3. have a union to which there be no withdrawal. What say all of you if there comes a time when a State no longer desires to be part of this grand association?

Col. MASON noted that any Government that proclaims itself perpetual becomes dangerous, concluding that it would end either in monarchy, or a tyrannical aristocracy. Which one, he was in doubt, but one or other, he was sure. This constitution had been formed without the knowledge or idea of the people. It is improper to say to the people, take this or nothing and take it forever. As the constitution now stands, he could neither give it his support or vote in Virginia; and he could not sign here what he could not support there.

Mr. RANDOLPH rose to the indefinite and dangerous power given by the constitution to Congress, expressing the pain he felt at differing from the body of the Convention, on the close of the great and awful subject of their labours, and anxiously wishing for some accommodating expedient which would relieve him from his embarrassments. His concern was shared by many others present in that the States might well reject the plan if there be offered no way to leave. What would happen if the national government becomes oppressive? What would prevent it from doing so if no State was allowed to withdraw? Some accommodation must be made and should this proposition be disregarded, it would he said be impossible for him to put his name to the instrument. Whether he should oppose it afterwards he would not then decide, but he would not deprive himself of the freedom to do so in his own State, if that course should be prescribed by his final judgment.

Mr. PINKNEY. These declarations from members so respectable at the close of this important scene, give a peculiar solemnity to the present moment. He too is concerned about a plan that must be accepted in its entirety, with no alterations, and, once accepted, a State is bound by the decision forever. A suggestion was made that another Convention could solve any disputes. He descanted on the consequences of calling forth the deliberations and amendments of the different States on the subject of Government at large at another gathering. Nothing but confusion and contrariety could spring from such an experiment. The States will never agree in their plans, and the Deputies to a second Convention coming together under the discordant impressions of their Constituents will never agree. Conventions are serious things and ought not to be repeated. He was not without objections as well as others to the plan. He objected to the contemptible weakness and dependence of the Executive. He objected to the power of a majority only of Congress over Commerce. He was not content with silence on the issue of the length of any union. He wondered if there might be a solution that could avoid the danger of a general confusion and an ultimate decision by the sword.

The circulating murmurs of the States indicated that thought was being given to Mr. Pinkney's question. In order to gain the dissenting members it was agreed to put the issue into the hands of informal discussion so that it might have the better chance of resolution.

Stephanie had listened to every word Katie Bishop had read, cognizant of the fact that she, Luke, and the president were the first people in over two hundred years to hear the account.

"This is incredible," Katie said. "I've read Madison's notes. Part of my master's thesis dealt with them. None of this is there."

And Stephanie knew why since Madison himself had said that the record was **in addition** to the main body, hidden away, for presidential eyes only.

"Tell me about this notion of a second convention," Daniels asked.

"It was talked about a lot. Several of the delegates worried that they were ramming an all-or-nothing proposition on the states. You've got to remember, they were sent to Philadelphia only to revise the Articles of Confederation, not throw them out and start over."

"So they thought a second convention would solve that?" Luke asked.

"Not solve it, but soften it. Their Constitution would be out there, every word debated. If it failed to be ratified, then the backup plan was to call a second convention and work through the disagreements."

The president chuckled. "That's like saying, **Let Congress solve the problem.** You get 535 different opinions. Eventually they'll compromise, but the country in 1787 didn't have that kind of time. The world was a tough place then. The French, the Spanish, and the English all wanted us to fail. They were just waiting for an opportunity to pounce."

"The convention had to act definitively," Katie said. "They knew there was only one chance to get it done. They couldn't kick the can down the street for long, and they didn't. Listen to this."

Mr. SHERMAN preferred the option of a State being allowed to leave if that state so desired. Having just thrown off the yoke of an oppressive tyranny through the shedding of much blood, he harbored no desire to create a new oppressive government from which there would be no relief. He doubted any of the states would ratify the document if that was not allowed.

Col. MASON agreed and observed that the States being differently situated such a rule ought to be formed as would put them as nearly as possible on a level. Small states would be more inclined to ratify if they were allowed the act of withdrawal as a check on any oppression by large States. Such a reservation to the States would likewise be a check on the national government, one that would restrain tyranny since a

State could withdraw if disagreements between that State and the national government became so grand and permanent as to warrant a separation. Otherwise, a majority of States could impose whatever they desired onto the minority.

Col. HAMILTON urged that there ought to be neither too much nor too little dependence on popular sentiments. The checks in the other branches of Government would be but feeble if the association of States was deemed forever. He noted that no empire has lasted. Not the Egyptians, the Romans, the Turks, or the Persians. They all failed and that was because of overreaching, complexity, domination, inequality, and stratification. He expressed his belief that the States are merely delegating certain powers to the new national government, not their sovereignty. To think otherwise would be an evil complained of in all of the States.

"They're debating an out clause," Katie said. "A way for a state to leave the Union. That's never been discussed before in the context of the Constitutional Convention. From everything I've read, that subject was never openly discussed."

"That's because Madison left it out of his notes," the president said. "And he modified the rest of his remembrances. He had fifty-three years to jiggle those notes, make them read however he wanted. We have no idea what happened at that convention. We only know what Madison wanted us to know. Now we learn that he hid this part away."

"So secession could be legal?" Katie asked.

"You tell me," Daniels said.

"What we're reading is dated September 15, 1787. The convention was over. The final session came on the 17th with the signing. They're doing this at the end, probably to counter lingering fears from the delegates that their states might not ratify. States were important entities to those delegates. Maybe the most important, even over the people. That was the way these men thought. It wasn't until 1861 that Lincoln changed all that."

"So you've read his first inaugural address?" the president asked.

"Of course. To Lincoln, the states were never sovereign. He said the Continental Congress created them, not the people. They were meaningless to him. He believed that, once made, any constitutional contract among the states was irrevocable."

"Was he right?"

"Jefferson and Madison would say no."

Stephanie smiled. This young lady knew her stuff.

"According to their theory the states existed long before 1787, and the Continental Congress had nothing to do with them. And, by the way, they're right. The Constitution is clearly a compact among sovereign states. Each one, by ratifying, delegated certain powers to the federal government as their agent. The rest of the powers were reserved to the people **and** the states. The Ninth and Tenth Amendments make that point. Secession would not only be legal under that view, it would be sacred."

The president pointed to the journal. "So what do the Founding Fathers have to say about that?"

Mr. L. MARTIN contended that the general government ought to be formed for the States, not for individuals. It will be in vain to propose any plan offensive to the rulers of the States, whose influence over the people will certainly prevent their adopting it.

This discourse was delivered with much diffuseness & considerable vehemence, which others likewise stated.

Mr. WILLIAMSON thought that if any political truth could be grounded on mathematical demonstration, it was that if the States were equally sovereign now they would remain equally sovereign.

Mr. SHERMAN. The question is not what rights naturally belong to men; but how they may be most equally & effectually guarded in Society. And if some give up more than others in order to attain this end, there can be no room for complaint. To do otherwise, to require an equal concession from all, if it would create danger to the rights of some, would be sacrificing the end to the means. The rich man who enters into Society along with the poor man, gives up more than the poor man, yet with an equal vote he is equally safe. Were he to have more votes than the poor man in proportion to his superior stake, the rights of the poor man would immediately cease to be secure. This consideration prevailed when the Articles of Confederation were formed and should prevail now. The best protection from tyranny is the right to escape it. There should be no need for another revolution. No blood should be spilt. If a State wishes to no longer be part of this association, it should be free to withdraw.

Col. MASON notes that for the States to know that the new association could be so easily dissolved might be both good and bad. As in a marriage, for a political union to succeed there must be a perpetual element or one party to the union could chose withdrawal instead of diligence and compromise. He agreed that a State should possess the right to leave, but it should be tempered with the realization of the hard work from the past few months and grand plan that has been conceived. It must have a chance for success equal or greater to that of failure.

Mr. MADISON proposed a solution. A document, signed by all who support the new constitution, which provides that the States have the right, in perpetuity, to withdraw from the union. He urged that this be in a separate writing since, if such provision were expressly incorporated, the ratification of the main document as a whole would be unlikely. What be the point of forming an association, if it be so easily dissolved. Further, once formed, if the States knew they could just as easily withdraw then the strength of any such union would be brittle at best. Instead, a separate agreement would be executed in private as clear intent from the delegates of their belief that a State remains sovereign in all respects. The document would be given to Gen. Washington to hold and utilize as he deemed appropriate. The desire being that its existence need not be revealed unless necessary to secure the ratification of a State, or to later sanction the withdrawal of State from the association. On the whole, he expressed a wish that every member of the Convention who may still have objections would, with him, on this occasion doubt a little of his own infallibility and put his name to this instrument.

Mr. MADISON then moved that the document be drawn, signed, and offered the following as a convenient form viz. "Done in Convention by the unanimous consent of the States present the 15th. of Sepr.—In Witness whereof we have hereunto subscribed our names."

FORTY-SEVEN

✦

SALZBURG

SALAZAR STOOD IN THE OUTER ROOM OF HIS SUITE, one floor above where Cassiopeia was awaiting him. He was still shocked by the angel's revelation that he was Joseph Smith. The honor that had been bestowed upon him weighed heavily. He'd come to rely on the emissary, but now to know that it was the Prophet Joseph himself seemed glorious. He'd prayed for nearly an hour after the vision departed before falling asleep, managing his usual four hours of rest. He'd wondered what was next, and the call he'd just answered from Elder Rowan seemed to be answering that inquiry.

"Much has happened here," Rowan said.

He listened as his superior explained what was found last night in the Library of Congress.

"It was amazing," Rowan said. "Lincoln himself left the map. Everything we suspected about the Prophet Brigham has now been confirmed. I'm convinced that what we're after still exists."

He could hear excitement, which was rare for the senator.

"The map is identical to the one Young left in the cornerstone," Rowan said. "Except that Lincoln's is labeled, save for the missing end piece. I suspect the reference to Romans 13:11 will fill in that blank."

He knew the passage.

And that, knowing the time, that now it is high time to awake out of sleep: for now is our salvation nearer than we believed.

"Any thoughts?" Rowan asked.

"The passage speaks of time and salvation."

He stepped to his laptop and typed LINCOLN and ROMANS into the search engine. Nothing relevant appeared on the first few pages.

He knew Romans 13:11 taught that the journey for salvation was coming to an end. Time to make yourselves ready. The night was far spent, the day at hand. Time to cast off the sinful works of darkness.

So he tried LINCOLN and TIME.

More unimportant sites were referenced until he

scanned the fourth page into the search engine and noticed a headline. SECRET IN LINCOLN'S WATCH IS OUT. He clicked on the link and discovered that for 150 years a story had circulated about some sort of hidden Civil War message inside Lincoln's pocket watch. The timepiece was now part of the collection at the Smithsonian's National Museum of American History. Responding to the rumors, a few years ago curators allowed the watch to be opened and found a message. APRIL 13 — 1861. FORT SUMTER WAS ATTACKED BY THE REBELS ON THE ABOVE DATE. J DILLON. THANK GOD WE HAVE A GOVERNMENT.

It seemed that the watchmaker had worked on Pennsylvania Avenue, the only Union sympathizer in the shop. He was repairing Lincoln's gold hunting-case, English-lever watch on April 12, 1861, the day the first shot was fired at Fort Sumter. Upset, he scrawled his message of hope inside. During the 18th and 19th centuries professional watchmakers often recorded their work inside a watch, but such messages were typically seen only by other craftsmen. No one knew if Lincoln was aware of the message. The president had purchased the watch in the 1850s, supposedly the first one he ever owned.

He read more from the site, which noted that the watch came to the museum as a gift from Lincoln's great-grandson. But what appeared at the end of the article piqued his interest.

> The watch was made in Liverpool, but the maker is unknown. Some sources reported that the watch never ran properly. Not surprising given that, once opened, the 3rd and 4th wheel jewels were missing. Lincoln also owned and carried an 18-size, 11-jewel, Waltham "Wm. Ellery" model, key wind, in a silver hunter case. That watch was also donated to the Smithsonian, where it is part of their American history collection.

He told Elder Rowan what he'd found.

"A fine gold watch was a symbol of success in Lincoln's time," Rowan said. "Both my father and grandfather carried one. Lincoln, as a prominent Illinois lawyer, would have, too."

He found images of Lincoln, some of the earliest photographs ever taken, and noticed that in most a watch chain was visible. Then he searched for the second timepiece and discovered that it had never been opened, currently part of a traveling Smithsonian exhibit on Lincoln.

Now in Des Moines, Iowa.

"You think, perhaps, there's a message inside that watch, too?" Rowan asked.

"Lincoln chose his biblical passage with care.

There are distinct references to time in Romans 13:11. Salvation being near. And Lincoln would have worn his watch every day."

"Brigham Young wrote in his message," Rowan said, "that Lincoln kept the most important part of the secret close to him every day. Two days ago I would have said all of this was a far-fetched notion. But not anymore. It seems that both Brother Brigham and Mr. Lincoln reveled in their mysteries. Can you go to Iowa and see for sure?"

"It may require the theft of the watch."

"Normally I would say no, but we're reaching a critical juncture and need answers fast. Do whatever is necessary. But proceed with great caution."

He understood.

"If it turns out to be a dead end," Rowans said, "we will regroup in Salt Lake and decide what to do next."

He abridged a report of what had happened the night before, saying only that he'd been able to determine that the Americans were intently focused on precisely what they were after.

"Though I'm still unclear as to how much they know," he said.

"I believe I can determine that from this end," Rowan said. "There's no need for you to deal with them anymore. Can you slip away?"

"I'll be in the air in the next two hours."

✦ ✦ ✦

CASSIOPEIA SAT IN SILENCE. WHAT WAS GOING TO happen next? How much worse could this get? A gentle rap brought her back to reality. She opened the door to find Josepe and invited him inside.

"We have to leave," he said.

She caught the **we**.

"I need to travel to the United States. Iowa."

She'd never visited that state before. "Why?"

"That project I told you about for Elder Rowan. There is an artifact I must examine." He hesitated. "It might be necessary to steal the object, just temporarily, so it can be studied."

"I can manage that."

He seemed surprised at her complicity.

"Stealing is a sin," he said.

"You said you were merely borrowing it for a short time. I assume it will be returned?"

He nodded.

"Then that's not theft."

"Elder Rowan says it's necessary. This mission is of tremendous importance. As you've seen, the Americans are trying to stop us. So we need to leave quickly and quietly."

She wondered about Cotton. He would not give up. And Stephanie. No retreat there, either.

"I'll tell you more during the flight," he said. "I

promise. It's another Great Trek. Perhaps the Saints' greatest journey ever. More exciting than you can imagine."

The first Great Trek had started in 1847. Wagons, handcarts, and, for many, their own two legs were used to make the thousand-plus-mile trip west. The route along the north bank of the Platte River, over the Continental Divide, through the valley of the Sweetwater River, then into the Salt Lake basin became known as the Mormon Trail. Her father had spoken of it many times with reverence. From 1847 to 1869, 70,000 of the faithful made the journey, each one labeled a pioneer.

He gently grasped her hand. "We, too, are pioneers. But in a new and exciting way. I'll tell you everything on the way."

He swept her into his arms and they kissed.

She felt his intensity.

"I love you," he said.

His eyes confirmed his words.

"I have since we were young," he said. "Our parting—broke my heart. But I respected your decision. I must confess something. I keep a photograph of us in my house in Spain. I found it a few years ago, after my wife died. When my heart was sad and empty, I found that the picture brought me joy."

Why was it that every man who showed her interest came with his own assortment of problems? It had started with Josepe and his religion, then continued through a litany of suitors, all of them wonderful in one respect, awful in another. Now she seemed to have come full circle. Back to the beginning. Part of her cared for this man, part was repulsed. And she was not sure which side of her should prevail.

But she had to find out.

"This time I will not force a choice," he said. "You can decide in your own way and in your own time. That lesson I did learn long ago."

She appreciated that on a multitude of levels. "Thank you."

"I need your help," he said.

"It's significant that you trust me enough to include me. I won't let you down."

He smiled.

"You never have."

FORTY-EIGHT

✶

Salzburg

Malone was four hundred feet above Salzburg, atop the pine-clad escarpment known as Mönchsberg. The air was cold, his exhales rising in white columns. Hohensalzburg's gray hulk rose to his right, the local museum of modern art, clad in minimalist white marble, to his left. Beyond the museum stood the Mönchstein—a former castle, now a luxury hotel. Rays from the morning sun blazed off its shiny windows in brilliant reds, golds, and yellows. He knew this mound of rock, made of crushed river stone deposited for eons, liked to fall away in avalanches. One in the 17th century killed a couple hundred townspeople as they slept in their beds. Today there were inspectors who made sure the cliff face remained free of danger, and he'd spotted the mountaineers at work on his way up.

He'd risen early and walked from his hotel, approaching the Goldener Hirsch with caution. High above, among the trees on the Mönchsberg plateau, he'd caught sight of a man keeping watch. He'd thought at first it was simply another early riser, but when the tiny figure never moved from his perch he decided that one of the Danites had decided to make use of the high ground.

The Goldener Hirsch was directly below, the entrance to the restaurant visible, as was a busy boulevard with cars winding a path around the pedestrian-only old town. He assumed the other Danite was watching the hotel's second entrance onto Getreidegasse.

Tall lime and chestnut trees formed an unbroken canopy above him, providing shade. He'd made his way up using the same footpath as last night, rounding the fortress and walking the quarter mile across the top of the escarpment. Below him, cut through the rock, was the Sigmundstor, a four-hundred-foot-long tunnel with elaborate Baroque portals on both ends. Cars whizzed in and out of the entrance on this side of the Mönchsberg, stopping occasionally at a traffic signal directly in front of the Goldener Hirsch.

Surrounding him was a manicured wilderness park of trees, grass, and shrubs. He'd managed to close within fifty yards of the Danite, close enough to the edge that he could also see below. What happened last night surely had spooked Salazar, so he was apparently taking no chances, his men ready for anything. He was still in the dark as to what was going on, but none of that really mattered anymore.

Cassiopeia was the problem.

Her visit had haunted him.

She was not the same.

The last time they were together, three weeks back, had been so different. They'd spent the weekend in Avignon, enjoying the old city, dining at cafés lining its cobbled streets. They'd stayed in a quaint inn, an iron terrace offering stunning views of the former papal palace. Everything had been wonderful. Just like other times they'd spent together, outside some crisis.

Maybe that was it?

Too many crises.

That he could understand. Like him, Cassiopeia seemed to thrive on adventure.

But at what price?

He huddled close to the trunk of a massive chestnut tree, the young Danite's attention remaining downward. He, too, glanced out at the city, preparing itself for another busy day. Salzburg was a town of walkers, each seemingly with little time for dawdling.

A siren wailed in the distance.

He spotted the footbridge that led from the old to the new city, spanning the river. He knew what adorned its railings. Tiny locks, all shapes and sizes, each clamped tight to metal fencing. On each was scrawled some form of affection signifying a union of two people. Usually initials joined with **and** surrounded by hearts. Symbols of love, hundreds of them. A local tradition. Like the way folks in the South carved hearts into trees.

He'd never really understood any of that sentiment—until recently.

He felt a strange uneasiness coupled with a touch of anger. He was glad to be alone, since he was not in a talkative mood. Silence enveloped him, which he welcomed. He liked to think that he wasn't cynical. More pragmatic.

But maybe he was just a fool.

He thrust his hands into his jacket pockets.

Below, he spotted Cassiopeia emerge from the hotel.

Then Salazar.

Behind them came two bellmen carrying their bags.

A car eased from the street and parked in one of the empty spaces facing the hotel.

They both climbed inside.

He heard the growl of an engine nearby and spotted a light-colored Audi negotiating the paved lane that bisected the woods. It was possible to drive to the top from the mound's far side, the one facing Salzburg's eastern suburbs. He used the tree for cover and watched as the Danite fled his post and broke into a sprint.

The young man climbed inside and the vehicle sped away.

Seemed everyone was leaving.

No surprise.

Which was why his own bag was packed at his hotel.

STEPHANIE WAITED AS DANNY DANIELS DIGESTED what Katie had read to them. The implications were beyond dispute. The Founding Fathers had expressly fashioned a way for a state to withdraw from the Union, if that state so desired. But they'd been smart and not included the language in the Constitution. Instead, a separate agreement had been executed that could be used, if needed, to ease any apprehension a ratifying state might have on losing its sovereignty.

What had the Supreme Court said in **Texas v. White?**

Our conclusion therefore is, that Texas contin-ued to be a State, and a State of the Union, not-withstanding the transactions to which we have

referred. And this conclusion, in our judgment, is not in conflict with any act or declaration of any department of the National government.

But it was.

It directly conflicted with the founders themselves.

"The whole convention was held in secret," the president said. "They changed everything behind closed doors, going against the entire intent of why they were there. That's bad enough, then they go and do this."

"The Civil War was fought for nothing," Katie said. "All those men died for nothing."

"What do you mean?" Luke asked.

"It's real simple," the president said. "Lincoln decided the Union was forever. You can't leave it. No discussion, no debate. He made that call himself. Then he fought a war to prove his point. But guess what. You actually can leave. It's not forever. Which makes sense. I've never believed the founders forged a Union that could never be dissolved. They'd just fought off totalitarianism. Why would they then create a whole new version?"

Stephanie asked the question she knew Danny was thinking. "Did Lincoln know this?"

"Mary Todd seemed to think so."

And she agreed, recalling the former First Lady's letter to Ulysses Grant.

His anguish during the war was deep and pro-

found. I always thought it a consequence of being the commander in chief, but once he told me that it was because of the message.

"Yet he fought the war anyway," she said.

Daniels shrugged. "What choice did he have? It was either that or shut the whole damn country down."

"He should have let the people make that call."

"This journal is useless," Katie said.

Daniels nodded. "You got that right. It's a good starting point, shows intent, but it's not enough for anyone who wants to prove the point. To conclusively show that secession is legal, you'd need what they signed."

The president's eyes said what Stephanie was thinking.

And it was sent to Brigham Young.

She faced Luke. "Which you're going to find."

"And where do I look?"

Her phone vibrated.

She checked the display.

"I have to take this. It's Cotton."

She stood to leave.

"Take this one with you," the president said, pointing to Katie. "I want to speak with my nephew alone."

MALONE HELD HIS iPHONE IN ONE HAND, THE other propped against the side of a building. He'd made his way down from the Mönchsberg and back to his hotel, taking a cab to the Salzburg airport. He'd been fairly sure Salazar would be bugging out today. Not so clear, though, was his own destination.

"Cassiopeia and Salazar have left," he told Stephanie.

"She failed to check in with me."

"She's pissed. I imagine she's gone off the grid."

He reported what happened with her visit to his room.

"I lied to her," Stephanie said. "I didn't tell her about you."

"Which she clearly didn't appreciate."

"I don't have time to worry about her feelings. We have a situation here, and we need her help."

"She doesn't give a damn about your situation. This is about her and dear Josepe. Or at least that's how it appears. She's managed to worm her way close. That I'll give her. But I'm not sure she knows what to do now that she's there. Her head's screwed up."

"Cotton, I can't afford her going Lone Ranger right now. I need a team, working together."

"I'm thinking about going home."

And he was. This wasn't his fight, and he needed to butt out.

"Salazar practically admitted to me he killed your man. I don't think Cassiopeia heard that. If she did, then her head is beyond screwed up. I think she's operating in the dark. She doesn't want to believe that he's a loose cannon. And she wants me out of this. Now."

"Where's Salazar headed?"

She knew him perfectly, knowing he would not have called until he had the answers to all her questions. He'd flashed his badge inside the terminal and obtained the flight plan.

"Des Moines, Iowa."

"Excuse me?"

"My reaction, too. Not your usual destination."

"I need you to stay on this one," she said.

He didn't want to hear that. "Salazar told me that this has to do with something he called the White Horse Prophecy. You need to find out what that is."

"Why do I get the feeling you already have?"

He ignored her observation and asked, "Where's Frat Boy?"

"I'm sending him to Iowa, as soon as we're through talking."

"I should go home."

"It was my mistake involving amateurs. I thought, based on past experience, Cassiopeia could handle this. She was actually the only one who could at the time. But this has changed. Salazar is dangerous. And like you say, she's not think-ing clearly."

"Stephanie, there comes a time when you have to leave it be. Cassiopeia wants to handle this her way. Let her."

"I can't, Cotton."

Her voice had risen. Which was unusual.

He'd debated this decision all night. He'd walked to the top of the Mönchsberg to take out his frustrations on one of the Danites. The plan had been to beat whatever information he needed out of the young man. But Salazar's abrupt depar-ture had quelled the urge. He could easily take a flight back to Copenhagen and sell books, waiting to see if Cassiopeia Vitt ever spoke to him again.

Or he could stay involved—her wishes be damned.

"I'll need a fast lift to Iowa."

"Sit tight," she said. "One's on the way."

PART
FOUR

FORTY-NINE

★

WASHINGTON, D.C.

LUKE SAT SILENT AND WAITED FOR HIS UNCLE TO make the first move.

"How have you been?" the president asked.

"That the best you got?"

"I speak to your mother regularly. She tells me she's doing good. I'm always glad to hear that."

"For some reason she likes you," he said, "I never could figure that one out."

"Maybe it's because you just don't know everything about everything."

"I know that my daddy thought you were a horse's ass and, by the way, that's my opinion of you, too."

"You talk awful tough to a man who could fire you in an instant."

"Like I give a crap what you do."

"You're so much like him, it's scary. Your brothers are more like your mother. But you." His uncle pointed at him. "You're a carbon copy of him."

"That's about the nicest thing I've ever heard you say."

"I'm not as bad as you think I am."

"I don't think about you at all."

"Does all this resentment come from what happened to Mary?"

They'd never had this conversation before. Danny's only daughter, Mary, his cousin, was killed in a house fire when she was a little girl, her father helpless to do anything, listening as she pleaded to be saved. The fire had started from an ashtray where Danny had left a cigar. Luke's aunt Pauline had repeatedly asked her husband not to smoke in the house, but Danny being Danny ignored her and did what he wanted. Mary was buried in the family plot, among the tall pines of Tennessee. The next day Danny had attended a city council meeting as if nothing had happened. He went on to be mayor, a state senator, governor, and finally president.

"**Never once has he visited that child's grave,**" Luke's father had said many times.

Aunt Pauline never forgave her husband, and after that their marriage became something only for show. Luke's father never forgave Danny, either. Not for the cigar, and certainly not for the callous indifference.

"You did good tonight," Danny said to him. "I wanted you to know that I have confidence in you."

"Gee, I'll sleep better knowin' that."

"You're a cocksure little thing, aren't you."

His uncle's voice had risen a few notches, the face scrunched tight.

"Maybe I get **that** from you."

"Contrary to what you might think. I loved your daddy, and he loved me. We were brothers."

"My daddy thought you were an asshole."

"I was."

That admission shocked him. So long as it was confession night, he wanted to know, "Why is it my mama has a soft spot for you?"

"I dated her first."

He'd never known that.

"She dumped me for your daddy." Danny laughed. "She always liked that. And to tell you the truth, I liked it, too. She was too damn good for me."

He agreed, but for once kept his mouth shut.

"I regret what happened between your daddy and me. I regret what happened in my life in general. I lost my daughter." His uncle paused. "But I think it's time my nephews quit hating me."

"You've spoken to my brothers?"

"Nope. I'm starting with you."

"Have you visited Mary's grave?"

His uncle stared back. "Not yet."

"And you don't see a problem there?"

Tension filled the room.

"We lost everything in that fire," Danny said, the voice now low and distant. "Every picture. Every memory. Burned to ash."

"And you acted like it never happened."

For a moment, silence passed between them. Then Danny said, "All I have left is a vision of her in my mind."

Luke didn't know what to say.

The president's eyes glistened.

He'd never seen emotion from this man before.

Danny stuffed a hand into his trouser pocket and removed a folded envelope, which he handed over. On the front, scrawled in blue ink, were the words FOR MY SONS.

Luke's father's handwriting.

Danny seemed to grab hold of himself and stood. "He gave that to me just before he died and told me to give it to his boys—whenever I thought the time was right."

The president walked toward the door.

He watched the big man retreat, the door opening, then closing.

He stared at the folded envelope.

Whatever was inside had been written at least

thirteen years ago. His first thought was that it should be read with his brothers present, but there was no way he could wait that long. His uncle had known he was coming here tonight, this moment apparently chosen to pass it along.

He smoothed the folds and tore open the seal. A single sheet of paper was inside, handwritten by his father.

He sucked in a breath and read.

So that the end would be peaceful and we could focus on saying our goodbyes I decided to say this from the grave. Nearly all my life my brother and I were at odds. Not only age separated us, but so many other things did, too. We never really bonded, as brothers should. What happened with Mary and my reaction to Danny's grief has caused a lot of pain in this family. Your uncle can be tough. Sometimes even cruel. But that doesn't mean he can't feel. All of us deal with grief in different ways. His was to ignore it. My mistake was not allowing him to be himself. I want all of you to know that Danny and I have made our peace. He knows of my illness and, together, we cried at the mess we made of things. I want you to know that he's my brother, I love him, and I want my sons to love him, too. He has no children and never will. The horrible loss he suffered is something I cannot comprehend. I blamed him and he resented me. But what happened was just an accident. I was wrong to think otherwise. We're both sorry for what we did and we forgave each other fully and completely, as brothers should. He told me that there's not a second of any day that he does not think about Mary. Never will that pain leave him. So my sons, let's not add to that. Be good to your uncle. He needs you, though he'll probably never admit that. So do this for me.

Tears dripped from his eyes.

His father was right.

The world knew nothing of Danny Daniels' private pain. He'd always kept that to himself. Luke had somehow sensed that Stephanie might know something, but they'd never discussed the subject.

Danny had faced some tough stuff.

And all of us **do** deal with grief in different ways.

He felt like a fool.

Or more accurately, like a son scolded by his father.

"I did it," he whispered to the page. "I made good. Like you wanted."

The tears came faster.

He hadn't cried in a long time.

He held the letter tight, knowing that his father had actually touched the paper. It was the last physical connection he would ever have. But he realized what his dad had meant. There was still another Daniels alive to whom they all had a connection.

Misunderstanding had kept them apart.

But that had to end.

Sons owed their father obedience.

"I'll do what you say," he mouthed. "I promise. We'll all do exactly what you say."

FIFTY

★

7:30 A.M.

ROWAN STEPPED FROM THE CAB AT 9900 STONEY-brook Drive and paid the driver. Four colleagues waited for him, each representing one of the four congressional districts within Utah. He was the fifth representative, in the Senate. The sixth congressmen, his fellow senator, was not part of the plan, as that man's election six years ago had been a fluke. All five men were Saints, and he was the senior member for both the delegation and the church. He wore an overcoat buttoned tight, but the brittle dawn air was more invigorating than uncomfortable. He'd called the meeting by an email sent out in the early-morning hours after he returned from the Library of Congress.

They stood before the Washington, D.C., tem-

419 / THE LINCOLN MYTH

ple, a soaring edifice sheathed in Alabama white marble, topped by six golden spires. It stood ten miles north of the U.S. Capitol. Its distinctive shape and size, centered within fifty-two wooded acres, had become a landmark along the Capital Beltway, easily spotted from the air in the Maryland countryside each time he flew in and out of Reagan National.

They exchanged greetings and walked toward a reflection pond and fountain that adorned the main entrance. He'd chosen this locale since he knew that no one would be here this early on a Friday morning. The building itself was locked. Which was fine. They would talk outside, with the house of the Lord in sight, so all of the prophets could hear. Both the House and Senate met today, but roll call was not for another two hours.

"We're almost there," he told them, controlling his excitement. "It's finally happening. I need to know that we're ready in Salt Lake."

"I checked," the 4th District representative said. "The count hasn't changed. We have 95 of 104 votes, between the state House and Senate, solid for secession."

What was about to happen had to be done with precision. Utah would be the test case, whose aim would be to overturn the 1869 legal precedent **Texas v. White.** The battle would be fought entirely in the U.S. Supreme Court, and the last thing he wanted was for some minor procedural error to derail the attack. This fight was about a state leaving the Union, not whether a vote here or there had been properly taken.

"And the governor? Is he still okay?"

"Absolutely," the man from the 2nd District made clear. "He and I have discussed it at length. He's as fed up as we are."

He knew what that meant. Reformism did not work. Elections offered no real choices, and third-party alternatives had no chance to succeed. Revolt? Revolution? The federal government would crush either. The only logical way to effect a lasting change was secession. That route offered the most direct path for a state to regain some semblance of control over its destiny. It was nonviolent—a peaceable rejection of policies and practices deemed unacceptable—fitting to the American way. After all, that was precisely what the Founding Fathers had done to England.

He stared up at the grand temple.

One hundred and sixty thousand square feet under the roof. Six ordinance rooms. Fourteen sealing rooms. Its white exterior symbolized purity and enlightenment. Some of the stone had been shaved to just over half an inch thick, which allowed the glow of sunlight to pass through to the interior at certain times of the day.

He loved it here.

"A bill has already been drafted, ready for the state legislature," another of the congressmen said, "that will call for Utah's withdrawal from the Union and an immediate referendum from the people of Utah affirming the act. There'll be opposition, but the overwhelming majority in the legislature will vote for it."

And its terms would be reasonable.

The act of secession would recognize that there were federal properties within the state for which there would need to be reimbursement, most prominent of which were the massive federal land-holdings. Some citizens of Utah might not want to be a part of the new nation, so allowances for them to leave would be made, perhaps even compensation offered for any personal or property losses they would suffer. The same would be true of corporations and businesses, though the new nation of Deseret would offer an environment far more friendly to them than did the United States. Some arrangement for repaying Utah's portion of the national debt—up to the date of secession—would also be detailed, but that would be countered by a credit for Utah's portion of the remaining federal assets spread across the other forty-nine states. His team had studied this ratio and discovered that assets outweighed debt and Utah might actually be entitled to a claim on assets, which would be waived, of course, provided the federal government relinquished its claim on all assets in Utah. To solidify it all, the referendum would pronounce in no uncertain terms what a majority of the people in the state of Utah wanted.

Secession.

Would it all go so smoothly? He doubted that, but Saints had always been good at planning, administering, and improvising.

They'd get the job done.

"Of course," one congressman said, "Washington will just ignore the resolution and the vote. You know that. And that's when we turn up the heat."

This would definitely be a fight of political wills. They'd quietly polled Utah and discovered that nearly 70 percent favored secession, a percentage that had remained unchanged over the past five years. That information had been used to quietly secure legislative support, which had been surprisingly easy to lock down.

People were ready to go it on their own.

But there was still the reality that the United States of America would not go away without a fight.

"We have a plan ready. Utah will immediately default on all federal obligations," one of his colleagues said. "The enforcement of all federal laws and regulations will be suspended. Federal officials will be asked to leave. Nothing Washington says will be respected. We'll take a hands-off approach. After the vote on secession by the people, all of us will walk away from Congress, no longer members. I imagine even our wayward, gentile Senate brother will join us, once he sees the support back home."

He smiled at the thought of that. He and his fellow senator had spoken little during the past six years. "It's a bold move. But necessary. While all of this is playing out, I'll pressure the church to reassure everyone."

"Washington wouldn't dare send troops," another of the congressmen said. "They can't risk somebody getting hurt. That would be an international PR disaster."

And history would work in their favor.

Over the course of a few weeks in 1989, Bulgaria, Czechoslovakia, East Germany, Hungary, and Poland all seceded from their communist regimes with little to no violence. The Soviet Union never invaded, nor pressed the point militarily. It simply let them go. Only in Romania, where both sides had wanted a fight, had bloodshed occurred. The United States could ill afford to conduct itself differently. Invading Utah made no sense.

"No," he said. "They'll turn to the courts."

Which was precisely where he wanted them.

The United States of America would file suit against what it would still label the state of Utah, seeking declaratory and injunctive relief to prevent the state from enforcing any portion of its secessionist legislation. The argument would be that, under **Texas v. White**, the state of Utah had no constitutional right to secede. Since a state was a party to that suit, under Article III of the Constitution, the Supreme Court possessed original jurisdiction. That meant the matter would be heard in a matter of weeks, if not days considering the implications. The last thing the federal government would want is time for more secessionist sentiment to spread.

But it would.

Texas, Hawaii, Alaska, Vermont, and Montana would quickly follow Utah's lead. This movement would be national.

And he'd add the final ingredient.

Startling new evidence.

Enough to win both the legal and the PR battle.

Words from the founders themselves.

"The lawyers are ready," he said. "I just met with them yesterday. And I'm closing in on the final piece. It's merely a matter of hours or days."

What encouraged him was the package that had arrived just before he left his Georgetown residence. A copy of notes, written by James Madison, hidden away at Montpelier, found last night by Stephanie Nelle, every word of which confirmed what he knew to be true.

Secession was legal.

One sentence in particular drove the point home.

The document would be given to Gen. Washington to hold and utilize as he deemed appropriate. The desire being that its existence need not be revealed unless necessary to secure the ratification of a State, or to later sanction the withdrawal of a State from the association.

How much clearer could it be?

Nelle had promised the originals when she had written assurance that Rowan's interest in her department had ended. He needed those, but he needed the actual document the founders signed that Saturday in September 1787 even more. Thankfully, the answer as to its location lay with the church, not the government.

He stared again at the magnificent temple, the first one built by Saints on the eastern seaboard. The first, after the Salt Lake temple, to feature six spires. The tallest worldwide. One of five that featured the angel Moroni holding the golden plates. Its seven floors represented the six days of creation and the day of rest, and beautiful stained glass ran the height of the towers, reds and oranges yielding to blues and violets, all representing the unbroken progress toward the divine. So appropriate, with what was about to happen.

"We will change our world," he said.

The other men seemed pleased.

"We will accomplish what Joseph Smith and Brigham Young, and every other pioneer failed to do."

He paused.

"We shall finally be independent."

FIFTY-ONE

✦

Over the Atlantic Ocean

Salazar settled into the leather seat and began to enjoy the in-flight meal provided by the catering service. A combination of lamb and vegetables, which Cassiopeia had reheated, serving them both in the spacious main cabin. Of all his possessions, the Learjet was his favorite. He spent a lot of time moving from one place to another, so it was important he travel in comfort.

"I promised you an explanation," he said.

She smiled. "You did."

His two associates sat aft, near the galley and restroom, eating their own lunch. He kept his voice low, though the roar of the engines helped with privacy.

"It's hard to know where to start. But the best way to summarize is that we intend to finish the establishment of Zion. What Joseph Smith and BrighamYoung began, we will complete."

"The church is a vital organization," she said. "A worldwide entity. Seems that mission **is** complete."

"Not in the way they truly envisioned. We've always been required to conform—to be like everyone else. We migrated to the Salt Lake valley so we could live by the prophets, following the Book of Mormon, a true Zion on earth. But that never happened."

"To accomplish that would mean having your own country."

He smiled. "And that's precisely what we intend to create. The nation of Deseret, headquartered in Salt Lake, encompassing the boundaries of the former American state of Utah, and other land that may want to join us."

He could see she was intrigued. He remembered when he first heard Elder Rowan's plan. His heart had been filled with joy tempered with confusion. But all doubts had been erased when Rowan described how the White Horse Prophecy would finally come to fulfillment.

"Remember what I read to you from Rushton's journal? The White Horse Prophecy makes clear that Saints hold the key to the Constitution. In

1854 Brigham Young made a speech at the Salt Lake Tabernacle. He said, **Will the Constitution be destroyed? No. It will be held inviolate by this people and, as Joseph Smith said, 'The time will come when the destiny of the nation will hang upon a single thread. At that critical juncture, this people will step forth and save it from the threatened destruction.' It will be so.** Prophet Brigham said that fourteen years after the White Horse Prophecy was revealed and seven years before the Civil War. His words became truth during the Civil War, as Saints did save the nation from destruction."

She listened as he explained about a bargain made between Brigham Young and Abraham Lincoln, one that was sealed by Lincoln when he provided a document, signed by the Founding Fathers, that said individual states possessed the right to leave the Union.

"Prophet Brigham never revealed that document to the South," he said. "Instead, he hid it away and allowed the Union to survive. The American Civil War was fought over whether a state could secede. What would have happened if those wayward states knew that the founders of their nation sanctioned their act? I would say that the Constitution truly did hang by a thread. But the church, as the White Horse, allowed the United States to survive."

"Amazing," she said. "Considering how the federal government had treated them."

"Which only demonstrates our commitment to the Constitution."

"And that doesn't exist anymore?"

"Of course it does. But the White Horse Prophecy makes clear that we should **stand by the Constitution of the United States as it was given by the inspiration of God.** That means the document, in its entirety, as intended by its drafters. The world has changed, Cassiopeia. The American government has changed. From all I've seen and read, there are many in the United States who would love to be rid of their federal government. We are just one group, but the time has come for the church to go a separate way. Elder Rowan will lead the secession of Utah. Those states you noticed on the map in my study? They will follow our lead."

She stopped eating and seemed to focus on what he was saying. "What will you do if you're able to actually leave the United States?"

"We shall live as the prophets intended. We have managed our resources wisely. The church owns billions of euros in assets all around the world, with little to no debt. We are smart, capable, and self-sufficient, more solvent than any government in the world. We also have extensive management expertise. It will be nothing at all for us to take charge of our own government."

"And who will head this?"

"The prophet, of course. That man is, and will remain, our leader on this earth. Soon that will be Elder Rowan."

He reached for his briefcase and found a sheaf of papers.

"All of this was foretold long ago. In 1879, by the third prophet, John Taylor. Listen to what he said. **The day is not far distant when this nation will be shaken from centre to circumference. And now, you may write it down, any of you, and I will prophesy it in the name of God. And then will be fulfilled that prediction to be found in one of the revelations given through the Prophet Joseph Smith. Those who will not take up their sword to fight against their neighbor will flee to Zion for safety. And they will come, saying, we do not know anything of the principles of your religion, but we perceive that you are an honest community, you administer justice and righteousness, and we want to live with you and receive the protection of your law. But as for your religion we will talk about that some other time. Will we protect such people? Yes, all honorable men. When the people shall have torn to shreds the Constitution of the United States the Elders**

of Israel will be found holding it up to the nations of the earth and proclaiming liberty and equal rights to all men, and extending the hand of fellowship to the oppressed of all nations. This is part of the program, and as long as we do what is right and fear God, he will help us and stand by us under all circumstances.

"I didn't make this up. Taylor said it, in public. Now Elder Rowan will fulfill this prophecy." He paused. "But not without our help. We're headed at this moment to find the last piece of the puzzle to make it all happen."

He told her about Lincoln's watch and what may await inside.

"It's a long shot," she said.

He nodded. "One we have to take. If it proves false, we'll try another tack."

"I can get it for you," she said.

"You?"

"Certainly not you. What would Elder Rowan say if a respected member of the First Quorum of the Seventy is caught trying to steal a historic artifact? I have no connection to him or the church. I can make it happen. And I won't get caught."

He loved her confidence. His mother had been a gentle, kind, quiet woman concerned only with her family. Cassiopeia was so different. There was an intense energy about her he found irresistible. She would make a fitting start to his burgeoning new family. With all of the changes coming, he'd decided to practice plural marriage, since he doubted the angel, Joseph Smith himself, would expect anything less. But with Cassiopeia's re-awakening he would now have a faithful partner, a true believer, to ensure that their extended family would be forever together in heaven.

"Think of it," he said. "We will finally have a land that is ours. The nation of Deseret, as Prophet Brigham intended. We will be free to make our own laws and live in our own way. It will be a good, fruitful place, one where people will flock to live among us and all will be right."

✶ ✶ ✶

CASSIOPEIA COULD HARDLY BELIEVE WHAT SHE was hearing, but the simple force of Josepe's words was proof enough that this was real. Apparently, though, neither Josepe nor this Senator Rowan had considered the international ramifications from the dissolution of the United States. And how would Washington respond to a secession? Threats? For sure. Force? That would have to be carefully thought through. Most likely, the response would come in court.

"You realize that the federal government will try and stop Utah," she said.

"Certainly. But what we seek will ensure that

legal battle will be lost by them. And how could it not? The American Founding Fathers' own words on the subject would be decisive. A document, signed by them all, that says secession is allowed. That would carry the same weight as the Constitution itself."

"Except that it apparently wasn't ratified by the states."

"But it is their written intent, and that cannot be ignored. We have teams of lawyers who have studied this from every angle. They are convinced this will succeed. The U.S. Supreme Court itself disallowed secession long ago, but that entire opinion was predicated on there being nothing contrary in American jurisprudence. Yet actually, there is. Something directly contrary. Americans place great faith in what their founders intended. Their constitutional precedents are all based on that intent."

What he said was true.

Stare decisis.

To stand by that which is decided.

"It will prove impossible for the courts to ignore reality. Then look at what President Abraham Lincoln did. Instead of telling the nation that states had a choice as to whether they wanted to be part of the Union, he hid the evidence of that away and fought a war to prove the contrary. How do you suppose that will be viewed?"

Not good. "Does this document actually exist?"

"That's what you and I are going to determine. It did once, and we think it still does."

She now understood why Stephanie Nelle had been so tense. Sure, political unrest existed in the United States, as it did in other parts of the world. Calls for radical change were nothing new. But having the legal means to actually effect that change was an entirely different matter.

She got it.

This was a problem.

But knowing its extent changed nothing.

She still intended to do this her way.

FIFTY-TWO

★

MALONE WAS STRAPPED INTO THE REAR SEAT OF AN F-15E Strike Eagle, cruising over the southern tip of Greenland. An air force pilot out of Germany occupied the front seat, flying the aircraft. But Malone had taken the controls a bit, once again in command of a fighter. It had been twenty years since he last flew one, thanks to a switch in career paths while in the navy that sent him to the JAG corps.

Stephanie had arranged for a helicopter ride from Salzburg to Ramstein Air Force Base in Germany. There the Strike Eagle had waited, engines running, and they'd immediately headed west across Europe toward the open Atlantic. It was 4,600 miles to Des Moines but, at Mach 2 the flight time was less than five hours. Of course, that meant an in-flight refueling, and a KC-10 Extender tanker now hovered ahead of them, its aerial boom captured by the fighter's probe.

"I appreciate this ride," he said into his mouthpiece.

Stephanie was on the radio's other end. "I thought you'd like that."

He listened as she told him about what they'd found at Montpelier. The channel was scrambled and secure, the best place for them to talk, the pilot's headset switched off for the time being.

"Rowan is trying to dissolve the United States," she said. "And he just might be able to do it."

She filled his ears with more bad news about what Rowan and Salazar were after. A document signed by the Founding Fathers.

"The White Horse Prophecy," he said. "Did you check it out?"

"I did, as I'm sure you did, too."

"The whole thing is regarded as crap by the Mormon Church. It was officially disavowed in 1918. The church today doesn't even recognize it as credible. Just a fable, nothing more."

"But Rowan believes it's real, and what he's after is also real. Unfortunately, the Mormon Church knows more about this than we do."

He agreed. That was a problem.

"We've done some research on this end," she said. "We think Salazar may be after something in a traveling Lincoln exhibit that's currently in Des Moines."

"Research my ass. You tapped somebody's phone."

She chuckled. "Of course we did. Rowan and Salazar spoke about the exhibit a few hours ago. They think a watch owned by Lincoln might hold the key."

He gave that some thought. "The reference to Romans 13:11 is all about time. And I specifically remember reading a few years ago about a Lincoln watch in the Smithsonian with something etched inside."

"That memory of yours comes in handy sometimes. The watch in Iowa is a second Lincoln timepiece the Smithsonian owns. It's never been opened. It's on exhibit at a place called Salisbury House, until tomorrow."

He checked his own watch. "We're going to be on the ground there, with the time difference, around 1:00 P.M. Salazar's Learjet won't make it until around 5:00 P.M. Iowa time. That gives us a chance to scope things out."

"Luke's there by now. I'll have him meet you."

"We're going to land north of Des Moines at a place called Ankeny Regional Airport. Its runway is only 5,500 feet. This fighter requires 6,000 feet, but we'll do it. We're going to need a waiver so we can land there."

"I'll handle it. They'll be no problem. Luke will be waiting.

"We've studied the images Luke made of the Rushton journal," Stephanie said. "Research tells me that it was probably written post-1890. That's fifty years past when Smith first uttered the White Horse Prophecy. So you're right. The whole prediction about the Constitution is suspect, most likely written long after everything happened."

"When you read the prophecy, it's just too right. The references are nearly dead-on. Like at one point it specifically says that **You will go to the Rocky Mountains and you will be a great and mighty people established there, which I will call the White Horse of peace and safety.** Why say **Rocky Mountains**? Why not **you will go west.** Supposedly, Joseph Smith said that years before anyone thought of migrating. No seer is that good."

"But finding that journal is significant since, before now, all the Mormon Church had was other accounts of what the prophecy entailed. Now Rushton's own words give new credibility to things. We can't ignore this."

And one other thing. "The Constitution actually is hanging by a thread, and the Mormon Church holds the key."

"We followed Rowan this morning to a meeting with the Utah congressional delegation and listened in. They're ready to move on Utah's secession. They have the votes and the political support. The people themselves may well sanction the move. All they need is that document signed in Philadelphia."

But that wasn't the only thing dangling.

"Any word from Cassiopeia?" he asked.

"Nothing. You're going to have to lasso her in. She could screw all this up."

"She's a pro, Stephanie. No matter what, if she realizes the implications, she'll handle it."

"That's just it, Cotton. We have no idea what Salazar has shared with her. It might not be enough for her to know what's at stake. We need her out of this."

He knew what that meant. "I'll take care of that. No need to involve other agents. Let me handle her."

"Can you?"

"What is it with you and Frat Boy? Both of you seem to think I'm some lovesick puppy. I can deal with Cassiopeia."

"Okay. You get first crack. If she doesn't stand down, then it's my turn."

LUKE DROVE HIS RENTAL CAR THROUGH THE streets of Des Moines. The day was overcast, temperatures in the midsixties. He'd slept nearly the

entire flight west on a military transport from An-
drews Air Force Base to an Air National Guard
facility outside town. His body was seriously jet-
lagged, but he was accustomed to that feeling.

Stephanie had already informed him that they
thought a place called Salisbury House may be
Salazar's destination, so he was driving there to
give the locale a quick once over. She'd told him
that Malone was on his way, but she'd yet to say
when and where he was to meet the old-timer.

He followed the map app on his phone and entered a quiet neighborhood west of downtown.
Salisbury House sat on the crest of a hill among a
forest of oaks. The manor looked like something
from the English countryside, built of flint, stone,
and brick, with gables and a tiled roof. A placard
out front detailed how it had once been a private
residence, built by a wealthy Des Moines family.
Now it was owned by a foundation.

Nobody was around.

But it was just after 10:00 A.M. He knew the
Lincoln exhibit inside did not open until 6:00 P.M.,
this its last day before moving on to its next location.

He wheeled the car past the house. He was hungry and decided some pancakes and sausage would
be good.

But first he had to make a call.

He eased the car onto the street's grassy shoulder, trees casting the pavement in deep shadows. He found his phone and dialed his mother. When she answered he said, "I need to know something. Were Dad and Danny okay when Dad died?"

"I've wondered when we would have this talk."

"Seems everyone was in the know but me and my brothers."

He told her about the envelope.

"I made sure your father and his brother made their peace."

"Why?"

"Because I did not want him to go to his grave with that unresolved. And neither did he, by the way. He was glad it was done."

"Why didn't he tell us himself?"

"There was too much happening. My God, Luke, he died so quickly. We decided to leave that till later."

"It's been thirteen years."

"It was for your uncle to decide the time. We all agreed on that."

"Why were Dad and Danny never close?" He truly wanted to know.

"Since childhood, they never were like brothers. Just not close. No one thing kept them apart. Over time, the distance between them grew and they both became accustomed to it. Then Mary died. Your father and your aunt blamed Danny."

"But not you."

"That would have been wrong. Danny worshiped Mary. She was everything to him. He didn't kill her. It was a terrible accident. And Danny dealt with his pain by ignoring it. That's not healthy, but it's Danny's way. I know, though, how much he's suffered."

He recalled what his uncle had said. "Danny said you dumped him."

She laughed. "That I did. He and I dated a few times. But once I met your father that was it for me. Another man never entered my thoughts. I always understood Danny, though. I may be one of the few who do. Your cousin's death sucked the life from him. Then he watched as his brother raised four strapping boys in a happy family. That had to be tough. Jealousy is not Danny's style, but every time he looked at us he had to think of what might have been—if he'd just smoked outside."

He could only imagine that guilt.

"Danny chose to deal with his loss by looking the other way. That's why he never went to the grave. He simply couldn't. Your father came to understand that. God bless him. He was such a good man. I was there when he wrote the note. There when he and Danny said their goodbyes. That happened just before we told you boys that your father was dying."

His contact with his uncle had always been minimal, little to nothing in fact, the talk earlier their first since he was a boy.

"Luke, Danny is not a bad man. He's looked after us, made sure everyone got what they wanted."

"What do you mean?"

"He's helped out with your brothers, when needed, though they have no idea. You wanted to be an intelligence agent. He's the one who had you steered to where you are. He and I spoke. He told me the Justice Department was the best place for you and he'd take care of it."

"Sonovabitch," he whispered. He never knew that.

"Don't get the wrong idea. He didn't order any-body to hire you. That was earned, by you. And he and I both agreed that if you couldn't cut it then out you went. No favors. No special privileges. Nothing. Yes, he got you in the door, but you kept yourself there."

"Does that mean I owe him **or** you?"

"You only owe yourself, Luke. Do your job. Make us all proud."

She'd always known exactly what to say to him.

"I'm glad you called," she told him.

"So am I."

FIFTY-THREE

✦

Des Moines, Iowa
6:40 p.m.

Cassiopeia settled into the driver's seat while Josepe climbed into the passenger side. His two associates occupied the rear seat. Josepe had arranged for a rental car to be waiting for them at a private terminal adjacent to the main airport. Before landing, she'd changed into a dark pantsuit with comfortable shoes, ready for what might lie ahead. The Learjet had been equipped with sophisticated communications equipment, so she was able to learn all about Salisbury House.

It was built by Carl and Edith Weeks in the 1920s, after an overseas trip ignited their passion to re-create an English manor house. They bought fourteen acres of timberland and built 28,000 square feet of house, 42 rooms, for them and their four boys. Inside they decorated with 10,000 pieces of art, statuary, tapestries, relics, and rare books, collected from their many travels. There were Tudor fireplaces, 15th-century oak paneling, and ceiling beams from a demolished British inn. Title to the house had been lost during the Depression, then passed through a succession of owners, until a foundation finally took control. Now it was a cultural center, museum, and rental space, a local landmark that was currently hosting a traveling Smithsonian exhibit that dealt with Abraham Lincoln.

She was able to download a PDF brochure on the house, which included a map of the two floors open to visitors. The exhibit was spread out between the Great Hall and the Common Room, both on the ground floor and near each other. She'd reserved a ticket online for the exhibition, then studied Google Maps to learn the local geography. Salisbury House was situated in a quiet residential neighborhood, surrounded by winding streets and older houses. Trees and gardens enclosed it on all sides. The plan was to drop Josepe and his men off at a hotel, then head for the exhibit, arriving after sunset, giving her the opportunity to reconnoiter the site and decide how best to accomplish her task.

"I can't imagine the security is anything elaborate," she said to him. "From all I read about the exhibit, nothing contained within it is particularly precious or valuable. Just a few historic artifacts. My guess is there will be some private security guards, maybe an off-duty policemen, but that's about it."

"You speak as if you've done things like this before."

"I told you that I have some specialized skills."

"May I ask why you developed these?"

She could not tell him the truth, so she said, "Mainly to protect my business interests. Then it was to protect my reconstruction project. We've had theft and vandalism. I learned that to handle things myself was best."

She hated herself for telling more lies. When would they stop? Impossible to say. Especially with the leap she was about to make.

They found the hotel where Josepe had booked three rooms and said their goodbyes.

"Be careful," he told her.

"I always am."

★ ✳ ★

LUKE STARED ACROSS THE CAR'S INTERIOR. HE'D just spent the past four hours with Cotton Malone and learned that the ex-agent's mood had not changed since Denmark.

He'd been waiting at the regional airfield north of Des Moines and watched as an F-15E Strike Eagle dropped from the midday sky and powered to a stop on the field's short runway. He'd never flown in a fighter and envied those allowed the privilege. He knew from Stephanie that Malone was a trained fighter pilot who'd abandoned that career to become a Navy lawyer. She hadn't explained why he made the transition, but he assumed there'd been a good reason, since he doubted Malone did anything he didn't want to. They'd eaten lunch, then scoped out Salisbury House, learning all they could about its layout.

"She's pullin' out," he said as he watched Cassiopeia Vitt leave a downtown hotel and ease back into traffic, minus Josepe Salazar and the two others.

He and Malone had been waiting at the Des Moines airport, near the terminal that accommodated private aircraft.

"She's headed in the right direction," he said to Malone.

"Just don't let her make you. She's good at paying attention."

Usually he'd have some snappy comeback, but he decided to not aggravate the old-timer. Instead he asked, "What do we do if she goes to where we think she's goin'?"

"You'll deal with her. She's never seen you. So you can blend right in."

449 / THE LINCOLN MYTH

"And you?"

"I'll watch your back and try to anticipate her. I have some experience with the way she thinks."

"Stephanie says we're to get that watch, no matter what."

"I know. She told me, too."

He liked the element of not knowing that came from developing a plan as you went along. There was a thrill about it, especially when everything went right. Like at Montpelier. Katie Bishop was now ensconced at the White House, Uncle Danny telling her that she wouldn't be heading back to Virginia. Instead, her employer would be told that she was needed in Washington for a few days, her job secure. Katie had seemed thrilled, and Stephanie had asked her to explore the Madison journal in detail.

He kept a quarter mile back from Cassiopeia's vehicle, plenty of cars in between. The road west out of central downtown was a busy boulevard, no way anyone would ever notice a tail.

She was still headed in the right direction.

"It's going to get more difficult once we get back into that neighborhood near Salisbury House."

They'd already made the trip, prior to Salazar landing. No danger had existed of missing anybody since the U.S. military was tracking the Learjet across the United States. Stephanie had called in the troops, as this was a top priority.

Ahead, Cassiopeia made a left turn exactly where she should.

"Give her space," Malone said, his voice remaining deadpan.

He'd already intended to do just that.

SALAZAR ENTERED HIS ROOM AND CLOSED THE door. He immediately fell to his knees and prayed for the angel to appear. To his immense relief, the apparition hovered above the bed, the same gentle gaze he'd come to expect smiling down at him.

"It is as you commanded. I've trusted her."

"She will not disappoint you."

"Help her be successful. I want no harm to come her way."

"She is to be of your body. To become your wife. Together you will start a family that will grow and emerge in the fullness of heaven. Know that to be true."

He was grateful for the angel's vision. It calmed him. He'd wanted to go with Cassiopeia, but knew that her caution was wise. He could not risk exposure. For now, Cassiopeia's skill and independence were assets. But once this threat passed and the promise of Zion fulfilled, there would be changes. Leading and supporting a family was a father's duty. Mothers raised children. That was the way it had been in his parents' family, and it would be the same in his own. For both parents to be devoted to something outside the home was a detriment to children, and he wanted good children. At least one from Cassiopeia, more from other wives. His and Cassiopeia's ages would be a factor, so any other unions would have to be with younger women. He firmly believed that a mother at home improved children's school performance, enhanced their attitude toward life, stimulated a healthier work ethic later in life, and forged stronger morals.

He wanted that for his children.

He'd been patient finding a new wife.

So he intended to do it right.

"Heavenly Father and Heavenly Mother were married. As parents they bore the spirit children, which meant that all of the people who ever lived are literally the children of God, brothers and sisters to one another. Soon you will add to their number."

He liked hearing that.

But for now, he bowed his head and prayed for Cassiopeia's success.

FIFTY-FOUR

✦

LUKE ENTERED SALISBURY HOUSE THROUGH ITS north door, following a group of excited visitors. Malone had dropped him at the end of the drive and he'd walked the rest of the way. They could not afford to have their car parked in some restricted lot, subject to a valet. Instead Malone kept it a few streets over, past the house's rear garden, through the trees. They'd chosen a suitable locale earlier.

He checked his watch: 7:25 P.M.

Darkness had arrived, a tame crowd of maybe a hundred milling about through the ground floor and onto a lit back terrace. The front doors opened into what appeared to be a grand hall, where half-timbered beams held the ceiling high overhead and an enormous medieval-style fireplace anchored the opposite wall. Above him, a railing crowded with visitors protected an exposed second-floor balcony that overlooked the hall.

Malone had described Cassiopeia Vitt and Stephanie had emailed a photograph. He saw no one matching her description admiring the glass cases of Lincoln artifacts displayed in the Great Hall. The only security was a uniformed city policeman, no sidearm, standing near the fireplace, surely here to earn a few bucks from an easy off-duty gig.

Sorry to mess up your night, he thought.

He wandered from the hall down a short flight of stairs and entered what a placard called the Common Room. More halogen-light-displayed exhibits were here, as were more people.

One of the patrons caught his eye.

Long dark hair, with a hint of curl. Killer body. Gorgeous face. Like a model, but he could tell that she was in shape. She wore a clingy silk pantsuit that clung to all of her curves.

He liked what he saw.

No wonder Malone was freaked out.

Cassiopeia Vitt was hot.

✮ ✯ ✰

CASSIOPEIA ADMIRED A MAGNIFICENT STEINWAY grand piano. On the walls of the Common Room she'd already noticed a Van Dyck portrait dated to 1624 and an elaborate crest of the Armand Cosmetics Company, which had been founded at the turn of the 20th century by the house's original owner. The center of the long room was dotted with lit glass cases, each displaying some object dealing with Lincoln. There was an iron wedge used to split wood, various clothing, books, writings, even the top hat worn the night he was assassinated. The idea seemed to present an intimate portrait of Lincoln's life and legacy. The case that drew her attention stood third from the end and contained a silver pocket watch. The information card inside confirmed that this was her prize.

She'd already taken a look at the ground-floor rooms.

Lighting was ambient, intentionally low so as to highlight the brightly lit displays. That would help. She'd only seen two security men, both wearing local police uniforms. Neither appeared especially interested, nor a threat. Maybe a hundred people were present, scattered about, making for plenty of distractions.

She ambled from the Common Room back to the Great Hall, admiring the three-quarter-scale suit of armor that sat near stairs leading up to a balcony. She'd only need a minute or so to acquire the watch. The glass in the case was not thick.

Breaking it would be an easy matter that would not damage the watch. Besides, according to Josepe, what they were after lay within the timepiece.

She admired the house's interior style and design. Her trained eye noticed English oak, Elizabethan cupboards, Chinese vases, and the paintings, each old and unique. But she also felt the sense that this had been someone's home. People had lived here. In some ways it reminded her of her own childhood home, though Tudor adornments gave way there to Spanish and Arab influences. Her parents had also decorated it with things that meant something to them. It remained that way to this day, as, like Josepe and his mother's parlor, she'd not changed much.

She wandered outside to the terrace.

A lovely rear garden stretched to a tree line about forty meters away. Her gaze drifted up to the roofline, and she saw where electrical cables entered the main house. She followed the wires to an outbuilding among the trees. She'd expected that to be the case. Through decades of modifications and upgrades, eventually everything became centralized. It happened with her château in France and at her parents' home. Here, the location was a cottage with a gabled tile roof.

All she had to do was get inside.

Unnoticed.

✯ ✯ ✯

LUKE KEPT BACK, AMONG THE VISITORS, EVEN chatting with a few as if he belonged there. But he kept one eye on Cassiopeia Vitt, who was clearly scoping things out. He'd lingered inside while she explored the terrace, then drifted out into the garden.

She was noticing something.

He reentered the house and twisted on the radio in his pocket. He'd brought with him from D.C. communications equipment, which came with a lapel mike and ear fob, Malone wearing its counterpart.

"You there?" he whispered.

"No, I left," Malone said in his ear.

"She's casing the joint."

"Let me guess. She's outside, checking the roof."

"You do know your girl."

"Get ready, 'cause things are about to go dark."

"What do you mean?"

"You'll see."

✯ ✯ ✯

MALONE STOOD IN THE SHADOWS OF THE TREES behind Salisbury House. He'd parked their car a hundred yards away on a side street that paralleled the estate's rear property line. The lack of fencing had made it easy to hike back to a place from which he could spy the house's illuminated terrace and the people milling about, enjoying the cool night. Soft lights burned in the ground-floor windows. He'd watched as Cassiopeia exited and casually strolled the gardens. She'd have to improvise, and the best way to gain an advantage was to take away the other side's ability to see.

Just for a few minutes.

Which was all she'd need.

He, too, had spotted the electrical wires on the roof, their path leading to an outbuilding. If he was right, that was where she'd head.

The trick was to figure out how far to allow this to go.

He needed her to steal the watch, but he could not allow her to escape. He studied the woman he loved. She looked great, as usual, strolling confidently. They'd saved each other's hides more times than he could count. He trusted her. Depended on her. And he'd thought she felt the same toward him.

Now he wasn't so sure.

Interesting how his life had turned 180 degrees over the course of two days.

For what?

And why?

No answer would come until he and Cassiopeia could sit down and talk. But what was about to happen would surely stick a spur in that.

She would not be glad to see him.

But see him she would.

FIFTY-FIVE

✦

ROWAN APPROACHED BLAIR HOUSE. SINCE THE time of Franklin Roosevelt the property had been owned by the United States, used exclusively by presidential guests. Now the government also owed the three adjacent town houses, and many foreign dignitaries had stayed within the 70,000 square feet of elegance. Truman had lived here while the White House had been extensively renovated, walking each day across the street to his office. Just outside the front door, on November 1, 1950, an attempt to assassinate Truman had been foiled by a Secret Service agent, who lost his life in the process. A bronze plaque adorned the iron fence in that agent's honor, and Rowan had taken a moment to pay his respects to the hero.

The call had come to his Senate office two hours ago. The president of the United States wanted to see him. How quickly could he be there? One of his aides had found him and passed along the message. He realized that there was no way to dodge such a summons, so he'd agreed on 9:00 P.M.

Interesting, though, the choice of location.

Not the White House.

Instead, the guesthouse. Off premises. As if Daniels was saying that he was not welcome. But maybe he was reading too much into things. Danny Daniels had never been regarded as a great thinker. Some feared him, others ridiculed him, most just left him alone. But he **was** popular. His approval ratings remained surprisingly high for a man in the twilight of a political career. Daniels had won both presidential elections with solid majorities. If truth be known the opposition was just glad to see him go, content to allow the old man to simply fade away. Unfortunately, Rowan did not have the same option. His presence had been commanded.

He was shown inside and through a maze of rooms into a space with yellow-striped walls, anchored by a portrait of Abraham Lincoln, which hung above a mantel adorned with red Bohemian crystal lamps. He knew the room. This was where officials were ushered before calling on foreign leaders staying at Blair House. A few years ago he'd waited here while paying his respects to the queen of England.

He was left alone inside.

Apparently the president was showing him who was in charge. Which was fine. He could indulge such pettiness, at least for a while longer. Once the state of Deseret came into being, with him as its secular head, presidents would wait on him. No longer would Saints be ignored, repudiated, or ridiculed. His new nation would be a shining example to the world of how religion, politics, and sound management could mesh into one.

The door opened and Danny Daniels offered him a fiery gaze.

"It's time you and I speak," the president said, his voice low.

No hand was offered to shake.

No seat offered.

Instead they stood, Daniels a foot taller, dressed in an open-collared, long-sleeved shirt, no jacket, and dress trousers. Rowan had worn his customary suit.

Daniels closed the door. "You're a traitor."

He was ready with his response. "Quite the contrary. I'm a patriot. You, sir, and all the presidents who came before you, back to that man himself"—he pointed at Lincoln's portrait—"are the traitors."

"How would you know that?"

Time for truth.

"Within the church we have long known that there was more to the Constitution of the United States than what Lincoln wanted us to know."

"Lincoln trusted the Mormons, as Brigham Young trusted Lincoln."

He nodded. "And look what it got us. When the war was over, the threat past, Congress passed the Edmunds-Tucker bill that criminalized polygamy and this government prosecuted hundreds of church members. What happened to all that trust?"

"Polygamy was contrary to our society," the president said. "Even your own leaders finally realized that."

"No, we were forced to realize that, as such was the price of our statehood. At that time all believed statehood was the route to safety and prosperity. That is no longer the case."

Thinking about what happened so long ago disgusted him. The 1887 Edmunds-Tucker Act had literally dissolved the Church of Jesus Christ of Latter-day Saints. Never before or since had the Congress directed such venom toward a singular religious organization. The bill provided not only for the end of the church, but a confiscation of all its property. And the devil-ridden Supreme Court of the United States in 1890 validated those acts as constitutional.

"What are you after?" Daniels asked.

"I only want what's best for the people of Utah. I personally could not care less about the federal government. It has outlived its usefulness."

"I'll remind you of that when your borders are attacked."

He chuckled. "I doubt anyone, besides you, would ever want to invade Deseret."

"Is that the name you've decided on?"

"It means something to us. It's what the land should have been called in the first place. But this government insisted on Utah."

All part of the despicable concessions demanded and provided. The day still disgusted him. September 25, 1890. When a declaration was issued by the then-prophet accepting obedience to all federal law and announcing the end of plural marriage. Six years later, statehood was granted. Property was slowly returned, including the Salt Lake temple. But the church had taken a beating. Heavily in debt and divided over both theology and finances, it would take decades to recover.

But recover it did.

Now it was worth billions. No one outside a handful of apostles and a few high-level administrators knew the exact amount.

And he'd keep it that way.

"We will be able to buy and sell every remaining state in your Union," he said, "and many of the nations of the world."

"You're not out yet."

"It's only a matter of time. Obviously you know what the founders left behind, what they signed in 1787."

"I do. But I also know things you don't know."

He could not tell if Daniels was serious or merely posturing. The president was known as an excellent poker player, but something told him this was not a bluff—instead, this was the reason he'd been summoned.

"Your church," Daniels said, "was trusted with something that could have, at that time, destroyed this nation. Instead the United States survived, partly thanks to what Brigham Young did not do with what he had. Thankfully, after Lincoln was killed, and no one contacted him for the document, Young still did nothing."

"He foolishly trusted that the federal government would continue to leave us alone. But it didn't. Twenty years later you all but destroyed us."

"Yet no one within the church brought out the document. Quite a bargaining chip to never use."

"No one knew. Young was dead by then, and he took the secret to his grave."

"That's not true. People **were** aware."

"How would you know that?"

Daniels stepped back and opened the door.

Charles R. Snow appeared, standing on his frail legs, dressed in a suit and tie, looking every bit the head of Zion. The prophet stepped inside, his steps short but firm.

Rowan was taken aback, unsure what to say or do.

"Thaddeus," Snow said. "I can't express in words how disappointed I am in you."

"You **told** me to search."

"That I did. The disappointment is with your motives and judgment."

He was not in the mood for any criticism from this imbecile. "You're so weak. We cannot afford any more like you."

Snow crept over to a pale green sofa and sat. "What you are about to do, Thaddeus, will destroy a hundred years of hard work."

FIFTY-SIX

✶

DES MOINES, IOWA

CASSIOPEIA STUDIED THE COTTAGE, WHICH RE-
minded her of something from the English countryside. Everything else at Salisbury House carried
a similar look and feel. No one had paid her any
attention as she drifted from the garden, following
a pebbled path that wound through autumn grass
and fall flowers. A couple of times she'd stopped to
admire the foliage, checking to see if she was alone.
The cottage stood about thirty meters from the
main house, electrical wires entering through a
conduit projecting from a gable. Thankfully the
entrance was away from the terrace and garden,
where the darkness was nearly absolute.

The wooden door was secured by a single pin-

and-tumbler lock mounted above the knob, an obvious addition. Luckily, she'd come prepared, picks always at the ready in her makeup bag. Cotton had found that so amusing—traveling with burglary tools—but he was just as bad—a small pick stayed hidden inside his wallet. She liked that about him. Always prepared.

She found the picks in her clutch bag and worked them into the lock. No need to see anything, more a matter of feel. Both hands had to sense the inner workings and feel for the tumblers.

Two clicks signaled success.

She worked the bolt free from the jamb, then entered and closed the door, relocking the latch on the inside. As she suspected, electrical boxes dotted one wall. Lawn and garden equipment filled about a third of the space. Light spilled in through four windows. Her pupils were wide to the night, and she found the main breaker on the outside of one of the boxes.

Switch that off and she'd have maybe five minutes before somebody checked the circuits, especially once they noticed through the trees that houses in the distance remained lit.

But that's all the time she'd need.

She found a dirty rag near a lawn mower and used it to wipe the lock latch clean, then to grip the electrical cutoff.

MALONE SMILED AS SALISBURY HOUSE WENT dark.

"What the hell, Pappy?" Luke said in his ear.

"She's making her move. Your turn, Frat Boy."

"Bring her on. I'm ready."

Yeah, right.

LUKE STOOD IN THE GREAT HALL WHEN THE house lights extinguished. There was at first just a low murmur from those around him. Then, once folks realized the electricity was not returning, voices rose. He immediately turned and headed back for the Common Room, where the pocket watch waited. Darkness inside ran deep, the going slow as he had to be careful of others and constantly excuse himself.

"She's back inside," Malone said in his ear. "Have fun."

He could almost see the smirk on Malone's face. But he'd not met a woman yet he couldn't handle. Katie Bishop was a perfect example. He'd certainly turned those lemons into lemonade.

He found the short flight of stairs that led down to the Common Room. Luckily the corridor was wide and not as populated as it had been at the Great Hall. He entered the main room and noticed shadows moving toward the walls, a male voice asking everyone to inch that way until they found it. Smart move. Protects the cases in the middle. Keeps people controlled and contained. Shows that somebody is in charge. Of course, he ignored the instruction and eased toward the third case.

Cassiopeia Vitt was already there.

"I don't think so," he whispered.

"Who are you?" she asked.

"The guy that's here to keep you from stealing this watch."

"Bad move, Frat Boy," Malone said in his ear. "Don't give her a heads-up."

He ignored the advice and said, "Move away from the case."

The black form stood still.

"I don't stutter," he made clear. "Move away from the case."

"Is there a problem?" a new male voice said, the same one who'd been directing traffic a few moments ago. Probably one of the cops.

Cassiopeia moved fast.

One leg came into the air and clipped the cop in the chest, sending him sprawling backward, crashing into an adjacent display case, which slammed to the wood floor, glass obliterated in a shattering crescendo.

People on the perimeter gasped in surprise.

Before Luke could react a second kick caught him square in the crotch. Breath spewed from his lungs. Pain burst upward and outward.

Mother of—

His legs collapsed.

Down he went.

He tried to gather himself and stand, but the pain was too intense. He grabbed for his aching midsection, fighting nausea and helpless to do anything as Vitt shattered the display case's glass cover and claimed the watch.

"What's happening?" Malone asked in his ears. "Talk to me."

He tried, but nothing came out.

He'd played a little football in high school and had been racked before. It even happened a couple of times in the army.

But nothing like this.

Vitt vanished into the darkness, amid the chaos.

He drew a breath and staggered to his feet.

People were trying to flee the room.

Suck it up, he told himself.

"She's got the watch . . . and . . . is leaving," he reported into the mike.

He started after her.

★ ★ ★

CASSIOPEIA WAS BAFFLED AS TO HOW THAT MAN knew what she was after. He'd obviously been waiting for her to make a move. The voice had sounded younger, with a touch of the American South she'd come to recognize from Cotton. Had Stephanie tracked her here? That seemed the only explanation, which meant the younger man was not alone.

She kept moving through the dark mass of people, edging herself toward the front door. Her car waited only a few hundred meters behind the house. Getting there from here through the house could be a problem.

Rounding the exterior would work much better.

So she found the door latch and eased it open, slipping out into the night.

✯ ✯ ✯

LUKE HEADED BACK TOWARD THE MAIN ENTRANCE and the Great Hall. The folks remaining in the Common Room had determined that glass was now everywhere on the floor, caution being advised, so he'd used that momentary distraction to slip away, finding his way through the dark.

His crotch ached, but the pain had eased.

No matter, he wasn't going to allow Cassiopeia Vitt to get away. He'd never hear the end of it from Malone or Stephanie, especially after the old-timer had warned him. He turned a corner and felt his way along the wall to the short flight of steps that led up to the entrance foyer.

He heard the front door open, then close.

Was that her?

It made sense.

So he headed for the exit.

He opened the door and stepped outside.

Ahead he saw nothing.

Then he caught a glimpse of Cassiopeia Vitt, near the house wall, turning a corner, heading back toward its rear. This time he provided her no warning, but said into the mike, "She's coming your way, Pappy."

Then he followed.

FIFTY-SEVEN

★

RICHARD NIXON ENTERED THE CONFERENCE
room and shook hands with the Prophet Joseph
Fielding Smith, his two counselors, and all of
the Quorum of the Twelve Apostles. The president of the United States had come to Salt Lake
campaigning for local Republican candidates
in the congressional midterm elections. He'd
brought his wife, daughter Tricia, and two cabinet members—George Romney and David
Kennedy—who were both Saints. The customary public appearances had all been made, and
now they were safe inside the church's main administrative building, behind closed doors, paneled walls and a coffered wood ceiling enclosing
them. Nixon and Smith sat at one end of a pol-

ished table, the rest of the apostles occupying its sides.

"I've always found my visits to Salt Lake City to be extremely heartwarming," Nixon said. "Your church is a great institution that has played a part in this administration."

The date was July 24, 1970. Pioneer Day. An official Utah state holiday, designated to commemorate the entry, in 1847, of the first wave of people to the Salt Lake basin. Parades, fireworks, rodeos, and other festivities traditionally marked the day. Like July 4 for Latter-day Saints. Later, Nixon himself was scheduled to attend the famous Days of '47 Rodeo at the Salt Palace.

"I don't know of any group in America that has contributed more to our strong moral leadership and high moral standards—the spirit that has kept America going through bad times as well as good times. No group has done more than those who are members of this church."

"Why are you here?" Smith asked.

Nixon seemed taken aback by the abruptness of the question. "I just told you. I came to offer my praise."

"Mr. President, you personally requested this private audience with myself, my counselors, and the Quorum of Twelve. No president has ever asked that of us before. Surely you have to understand why we would be curious. So here we are. Just us. What is it you want?"

Smith, though a consummate gentleman, was no fool. He was the tenth prophet to lead the church, his father had been the sixth, and his grandfather had been the brother of founder Joseph Smith. He became an apostle in 1910, at age twenty-five, and had only six months back been elevated to prophet at the age of ninety-four, the oldest man ever selected. He was the only one in the room who'd actually been present when the temple in Salt Lake had been dedicated in 1893.

He bowed to no one.

Not even presidents of the United States.

Nixon's face changed, shifting from a countenance of congeniality to one of a man on a mission. "All right. I like directness. Saves time. Something was given to you in 1863 by Abraham Lincoln, something you never returned. I want it back."

"Why is that?" Smith asked.

"Because it belongs to the United States."

"Yet it was given to us for safekeeping."

Nixon studied the men around the table. "I see you know what I'm talking about. Good. That'll make this simpler."

Smith pointed a wizened finger at the president. "You have no idea what it says, do you?"

"I know that it caused Lincoln great anguish. I know that he sent it away for a reason. I know that, as part of the bargain, Brigham Young provided Lincoln with the location of a mine, one that people have sought for a long time. A place where a lot of your gold may be hidden away, gold lost during the Mormon War when 22 wagons disappeared."

"None of that gold was lost," one of the apostles said. "Not one ounce. All of it was reintroduced into our economy, after the threat of war from the federal government waned. Prophet Brigham made sure that happened. There is no mystery there."

"Interesting you would say that," Nixon said. "I had that researched. Brigham Young sent the gold away to California. But according to your own written records, those wagons were attacked and men were killed, the gold stolen and lost. Are you saying your prophet was involved with that theft?"

"We're not saying anything," another of the apostles said, "except that no gold was lost."

"Does not the White Horse Prophecy mean anything to you? Were you not to be the saviors of our Constitution?"

A few of the apostles chuckled.

"That's a fable," one of them said. "A story made up by the early church fathers as a way to bolster our new religion. Just hearsay and misinterpretation that spread, like rumors do. Every theology has such stories. But it's not real. We disavowed its language long ago."

Nixon grinned. "Gentlemen, I've played many a hand of poker, and I've played against the best. I'm not fooled here by your bluff. Brigham Young made a deal with Abraham Lincoln, and both sides, to their credit, kept it. I've read a note that survived from Lincoln's time. A handwritten message from James Buchanan, sent to Lincoln, that provided him with a document. More papers I've seen indicate that the document was ultimately sent here, as Lincoln's part of the bargain. But thanks to Lincoln's sudden, untimely death you still have that document."

"For sake of argument," Smith said. "If such a document were returned, what would you do with it?"

"That depends on what it says. My guess is that it concerns the Founding Fathers and what they may, or may not, have done in Philadelphia."

"The Constitution is, to us, a glorious standard, one founded in the wisdom of God," the prophet said. "It is a heavenly banner. To all those who are privileged with the blessings of liberty, it is like the cooling shades and refreshing waters of a great rock in a thirsty and weary land."

"Wonderful analogies," Nixon said. "But you have yet to answer my question."

Smith faced the apostles around the table. "You see here an example of what we've faced since the beginning. The arrogance of a federal government, come here, to our home, demanding that we obey its commands."

A few heads bobbed in agreement.

"I indulged this request for a private audience hoping that this president would be different." Smith's gaze locked on George Romney and David Kennedy. "Two of our own serve in this administration, which we took as a good sign." The prophet paused, as if gathering himself. Smith had served for many years as church Historian and Recorder. If anyone would know what the records held, he would.

Finally, Smith faced Nixon.

"We are indeed the custodians of something given to us long ago. But Brigham Young made the decision to keep what he'd been given, and every prophet since has likewise done the same. That decision is, therefore, mine. So I decline your request."

"You're refusing a direct demand from the president of the United States?"

"In our Doctrine and Covenants, 109:54, it is said Have mercy, O Lord, upon all the nations of the earth; have mercy upon the rulers of our land;

may those principles, which were so honorably and nobly defended, namely, the Constitution of our land, by our fathers, be established forever. **That is what I obey . . . Mr. President. Not you.**"

Rowan stared at Charles Snow and Danny Daniels.

He'd listened as Snow told him what happened over four decades ago.

"I was there," Snow said. "Sitting around that table. A relatively new apostle, but I watched as Joseph Fielding Smith dealt with Richard Nixon. That was the first time I became aware of our great secret."

"And the others knew?"

Snow nodded. "Some of the most senior were aware."

"Charles," Rowan said. "You sent me to find it. You told me to look."

"No, Thaddeus. I showed you what came from the record stone simply as way to provide you with enough rope to hang yourself. President Daniels and I have been speaking on this for many months now."

He could not believe what he was hearing. The prophet himself a spy? A traitor? Placing the interests of gentiles above those of Saints?

"Joseph Fielding Smith," Snow said, "was a brilliant man. He served this church for three-quarters of the 20th century. After Nixon left that day, we were all briefed on some of what happened in 1863. But it was only when I became prophet that I learned the rest. Each prophet since has passed that information on to his successor. All of the men there that day with Nixon are now dead. Only I remain. But the duty of passing on ends here and now. I will tell you nothing."

"We can do this, Charles," Rowan said. "We can leave this godforsaken country, with all of its laws and rules and taxes and problems. We don't need it any longer. We've done polls. The people are solidly behind secession. Utahans will approve any resolution calling for it."

"Do you realize what will happen," Daniels asked, "if you go through with this? The United States is a world power."

"And losing Utah will change that?" he asked. "You're being ludicrous."

"Unfortunately, it won't stop with Utah. Which is your plan. Other states will follow. You're right, our problems run deep. People are ready to flee. They think there's something better. But I'm here to tell you there's not. For all its faults this is the best damn political system man has ever conceived. It does work. But only as a unit of fifty states. I can't allow you to destroy that."

"Even if the founders themselves said it was okay?"

Snow sighed. "Thaddeus, our own founders said a lot of things, too. Some of it was wise, some nonsense. It's our duty, our responsibility, to ignore the bad and keep the good. Times have changed. What may have worked in 1787 no longer works today."

"That's not for us to decide." His voice rose. "It's for the people to choose. They have a right to know everything."

"If that's the case," Daniels said, "then why do we classify information? Why do we meet in secret to make national security decisions? Because it's up to us, as the people's representatives, to make smart decisions. They elect and trust us to get it right. And every few years they have chance to tell us how we're doing. Senator, we're asking you to stop this, both your president and your prophet are asking you to stop."

His first thought was about what was happening in Iowa. Did the Lincoln watch hold the final piece of the puzzle? He also wondered about Stephanie Nelle and her complicity. She'd offered him vital information. But what had Snow just said about his own offered cooperation?

Enough rope to hang yourself.

"You sent Stephanie Nelle to me, didn't you?" he asked Daniels.

"I sent no one. She's a thief and a traitor. I'm going to fire her, then put her sorry ass in jail. That's where you're going, too, if you don't stop."

He faced Snow. "We have a right to live free, as we please, according to the prophets. We've earned that. **Our** founders envisioned that."

"We **are** free, Thaddeus."

"How can you say that? It's our duty to fulfill the White Horse Prophecy."

"That's a fantasy. It always has been."

"No, it's not. We were told to **stand by the Constitution of the United States as it was given by the inspiration of God.** That means **in its entirety.** And that's what I'm doing. The founders themselves said a state could leave, if it wanted to. I'm prepared to see if Utah wants that."

Then something occurred to him.

"You lied to Nixon about the prophecy, didn't you?"

Snow stared back.

"That's exactly what you did," he said again. "You told him it was fantasy."

"We simply reiterated what the church has publicly said of that pronouncement," Snow made clear.

"Which was a lie. You just said every prophet since Brigham Young was aware of the truth. What we held for the United States."

"Which has nothing to do with that prophecy," Snow said. "It has everything to do, though, with the future of this nation. We simply chose not to destroy this country. The Constitution would, indeed, hang by a thread if you're allowed to proceed."

"Where is it, Charles?" His body shook with intensity. "Where is that document hidden? Tell me."

Snow shook his head. "That will not be passed from this prophet to the next. And I assure you, I'm the only one who knows."

"Then you have betrayed your faith, and all that it stands for."

"I'm prepared to answer to Heavenly Father. Are you?"

"Absolutely. I know Lincoln fought a war that never should have been fought. The South had a right to leave, and he knew that. He made a personal choice to wage that war. Hundreds of thousands died. What do you think the American people will say when that's revealed?"

"That he chose the Union," Daniels said. "He chose this country. I would have done the same."

"Then you're a traitor, too."

"Lincoln decided that the **United** States was more important than the individual states," Daniels said. "Granted, times have changed. The same pressures he faced we don't. But we have pressures that are just as immediate. Worldwide concerns. It's important that this nation survive."

He leveled his gaze at the president of the United States. "It. Will. Fall."

"I'm releasing you from your calling," Snow said. "I want your resignation as an apostle."

"And I want you out of the Senate," the president said.

"You can both go to hell."

Never before had he uttered such derogatory words. Swearing was contrary to all that he believed. But he was angry. And he had to hope that Salazar was successful. Everything now depended on that.

He turned for the door, but could not resist a parting shot.

"This Lincoln myth will end. The nation will see him for what he was. A man who fought a war for nothing, who hid away the truth for his own purposes. Unlike either of you, I trust the judgment of the people. They'll decide if this Union is forever."

FIFTY-EIGHT

✦

MALONE KEPT WATCH ON THE DARK OUTLINE OF Salisbury House. The electricity had been down about fifteen minutes, and he finally spotted flashlights streaking through the cottage where Cassiopeia had done her damage. A couple of minutes later the lights inside and out came back on. Surely it was clear now that someone had intentionally tripped the breaker. It would not be long before police would be everywhere.

"She's coming your way, Pappy," Luke said in his ear.

He fled his post and headed back through the trees to where he'd parked the rental car. It sat on the shoulder of a tree-lined street, the houses around all set back from the road a hundred-plus feet. One of those older neighborhoods built when people craved privacy and land was cheap.

There was no telling what had happened inside Salisbury House. Frat Boy had kept the details to himself. The fact that Cassiopeia now possessed the watch meant Luke had underestimated her.

Big mistake.

LUKE HASTENED HIS PACE, HIS GROIN STILL ACHing. He owed her one for that. He found the edge of the house and turned the corner. Trees, shrubs, and woods nestled close to the side wall. A rustling noise up ahead confirmed that Vitt was still on the move. The lights had returned inside, the ground-floor windows now illuminating this side of the building.

He pushed his way through the foliage.

Malone should be somewhere behind the rear garden, Vitt heading straight toward him.

CASSIOPEIA STAYED IN THE TREES AND PASSED THE edge of the rear garden. Her car was waiting fifty meters away on a street labeled Greenwood Drive. She had the watch. Josepe would be pleased. Maybe once she handed it over she could learn its significance. All Josepe had mentioned was that it might be the final piece of a much larger puzzle. Would she tell Stephanie Nelle?

Probably not.

Sirens could now be heard.

With the lights back on in Salisbury House, the theft would be evident.

Time to be far away, and fast.

"SHE SHOULD BE RIGHT ON YOU," LUKE SAID INTO the mike.

No reply.

"Malone."

Still silent.

Where the heck was the old-timer?

He decided to take matters into his own hands. The pain had finally subsided, and his hard-trained muscles were ready, nerves alert.

So he sprang ahead.

CASSIOPEIA HEARD THRASHING RAPIDLY COMING her way.

She increased her pace and came to the end of the rear garden, rushing ahead through the woods toward her parked vehicle. Someone was closing in. The car doors were unlocked, the keys in her purse along with the watch, which she held tightly.

The woods ended at the edge of the road.

She spotted her car and raced over, climbing inside, stuffing the key in the ignition and firing the engine. She shifted into drive, foot on the accelerator, and was about to speed away when something pounded the hood. Through the windshield she spotted a man sprawled out and a face. Younger. Late twenties, early thirties.

"Going somewhere?" he asked her.

The man's left arm came up from his side, the hand holding a semi-automatic, which he aimed straight at her.

She smiled and kept her eyes locked on his.

Then her right foot floored the accelerator.

LUKE HAD EXPECTED SOMETHING, WHICH WAS why his right hand was vised onto the hood's lip at the base of the windshield, where the wipers were hidden.

The car lunged forward, tires spinning in the dirt and grass, then grabbing pavement.

She swung the wheel left, then right, trying to dislodge him.

He held tight.

She increased speed.

"Pappy," he said. "I don't know where you are, but I need you. I'm going to have to shoot this crazy bitch."

Stephanie's orders were clear.

Get the watch.

At any cost.

CASSIOPEIA DID NOT WANT TO SERIOUSLY INJURE the man on her hood, but she also needed him to go away. He surely worked for Stephanie Nelle. Who else would be here?

They were on a dark side street with no traffic, woods on both sides between an occasional driveway.

Ahead, something emerged from the trees.

Another vehicle.

Blocking both lanes, perpendicular to her path.

Its driver's-side door opened and the outline of a man emerged.

One she knew.

Cotton.

She slammed on the brakes and skidded the car to a stop.

Malone stood his ground.

Luke dropped himself off the hood and yanked open the driver's door, his weapon pointed at Cassiopeia.

She did not move.

The cabin light revealed her face, another mask of stone, like in Salzburg, her gaze locked on him. Luke reached in and switched off the ignition.

"Get the hell out," Luke yelled.

She ignored him.

Malone walked toward her, his steps slow and steady. He came close and spotted the small purse on the passenger seat. Black. Chanel. Adorned with iconic charms that had served, in years past, as symbols of the brand. He'd bought it in Paris, a Christmas present last year, for the woman who quite literally had everything.

He stepped to the passenger door, opened it, and retrieved the purse. Inside lay the watch, which he removed, tossing the handbag back inside. He was as pissed with her as she was with him and, like her, said nothing.

He motioned that they should leave.

"You sure?" Luke asked.

"Leave her be."

Luke shrugged, then tossed the keys into her lap.

Still, not a speck of reaction from her. Instead she slammed the door shut, fired up the engine, and spun the car around 180 degrees before speeding away.

"That wasn't good," Luke said.

He watched as the vehicle faded into the night.

"No," he whispered. "It wasn't."

FIFTY-NINE

✫

MARYLAND

ROWAN SAT INSIDE THE TEMPLE.

Ever since childhood, he'd felt safe within a temple's walls. Then it had been the temple in Salt Lake. Since coming to Washington, he'd made this temple his home. Here, behind thick masonry and locked doors, Saints could practice as they pleased. No one but Saints who'd achieved temple recommend could enter. Only during the weeks prior to its consecration were a temple's doors opened to gentiles. In 1974 nearly a million had walked through this magnificent structure in the Maryland countryside. **Time, Newsweek,** and **U.S. News & World Report** had all published stories on it. Open houses had been the norm since the early days, a way to counter the wild rumors and misconceptions about what lay inside. But once a temple was consecrated it became the exclusive realm of Saints.

He'd fled Blair House and taken a cab straight here, his second visit of the day. Earlier, outside in the morning chill, he'd planned with his congressional colleagues what was to happen next.

Now he was unsure of everything.

Charles R. Snow himself had entered the fray.

An extraordinary occurrence, one he'd never anticipated. Actually, he'd been counting on Snow's death. Once he was ordained as prophet, which was a given, he'd have the entire church at his disposal. Instead Snow had released him, demanding a resignation. That was unprecedented. Apostles kept their jobs until death. He'd currently served the longest, rising through the hierarchy, now one heartbeat away from becoming prophet.

And not just any prophet.

The first since Brigham Young who would lead both the church and the government. And the first to do such with the status of an independent, viable nation.

Deseret.

True, a vote of the electorate and a court fight lay ahead, but he was confident both could be won.

Now the dream seemed in dire jeopardy.

Both Daniels and Snow knew everything. Had

Stephanie Nelle sold him out? Was she a spy? Her appearance had been most fortuitous.

Paranoia was setting in.

Just as it had after the Civil War and before the turn of the 20th century, when Saints were prosecuted and jailed under the anti-polygamy Edmunds-Tucker Act. When the church itself was declared illegal. When one turned on the other. Spies were everywhere. The Time of Troubles, it had come to be called. Which only ended when the church caved and conformed.

He was alone, inside one of the celestial rooms.

He had to think.

His cell phone vibrated.

Usually the devices were not allowed inside the temple. But this was far from usual. He checked the display.

Salazar.

"What happened?" he asked, after answering.

"The watch is gone. The government now has it."

He closed his eyes. The evening was turning into a disaster. Nothing had gone right.

"Head to Salt Lake," he ordered. "I'll be there in the morning."

"They knew we were here," Salazar said.

Of course they did. Why wouldn't they?

"We'll talk in Salt Lake."

He ended the call.

CASSIOPEIA SAT IN JOSEPE'S HOTEL SUITE AND watched as he spoke on the phone.

The call ended.

"Elder Rowan sounded defeated," he said, his voice not much above a whisper. "I have to say, I echo his feeling. We've been at this for several years. But only in the past few months has the goal come into sight. It's been a long hard struggle to get this far."

"I'm sorry I lost the watch."

"It's not your fault. It's mine. I should have anticipated problems and been ready to act. I could have sent my associates with you."

"They would have been in the way. I'm the one who didn't see it coming."

Josepe let out a long exhale. "How about this? No more talk of defeatism tonight. Let's have dinner somewhere."

She was not in the mood, role or no role.

"I'm pretty jet-lagged. Would you mind if I just went to sleep?"

STEPHANIE HAD SET UP A MAKESHIFT HEADQUARTERS inside her room at the Mandarin Oriental, her laptop connected to the Magellan Billet's secured server, her phone on ready. She'd brought with her Katie Bishop, who was in an adjacent room combing through Madison's secret notes, harvesting every piece of relevant information that she could. The young woman was bright and articulate and had apparently taken a shine to Luke Daniels. On the cab ride over from the White House there'd been lots of questions on that subject.

And now they had the watch.

Luke and Cotton had been successful.

She stared at her screen and the video feed from Luke's laptop in Des Moines. Katie had consulted the appropriate websites and talked with a curator at the Smithsonian's National Museum of American History, who'd explained how the first Lincoln watch had been opened.

Really simple.

The back screwed off, right-to-left, counterclockwise, exposing its inner workings. The only trick would be to loosen the threads from corrosion, since they hadn't seen any action in a long time. A few gentle taps in the right places was what worked the first time.

Which had all been passed on to Iowa.

MALONE LIFTED THE WATCH FROM THE DESKTOP. He and Luke had obtained a room in a downtown hotel away from where Salazar was staying, a video link established to Stephanie in DC.

He admired the timepiece, which was in excellent condition.

"Let's try and not destroy it," Stephanie said from the screen.

He smirked her way. "Is that directed at me?"

"You do have a tendency to harm things."

"At least it's not a World Heritage Site."

From past experience, those seemed his favorite targets.

The encounter with Cassiopeia weighed heavy on his mind. They had a problem, and no amount of talking was going to make for an easy fix. He'd done exactly what she asked him not to do, and there'd be consequences.

He handed the timepiece to Luke. "You do the honors."

Luke gripped the watch and tried to loosen the back plate. Stephanie's instructions had said it could be difficult, and it was.

Three more attempts produced no results.

"It won't turn," Luke said.

They tried a few gentle taps to its side, as recommended, but still nothing. He recalled years ago that he'd liked a particular brand of citrus salad, oranges and grapefruit, peeled, packed in water, and sold inside a plastic screw-top container. The lid was always tough to get off the first time. Finally one day he discovered the secret: Don't grip it so hard. In his frustration he tended to squeeze the plastic so tight that it would not unscrew. So he gently grasped the watch's edges, holding just tight enough that his fingers wouldn't slip.

He turned, feeling resistance from the tiny threads.

Another try and movement.

Slight.

But enough.

He regripped, kept his touch light, and freed the back plate.

He laid the watch down, and Luke pointed the laptop's camera at the exposed gears and springs. Stephanie had forwarded an image of the inside of Lincoln's other watch when it had been opened at the Smithsonian, and he expected to see the same array of etchings on the inner structure.

But there was nothing.

He and Luke seemed to have the thought at the same time.

So he nodded to the younger man.

Luke flipped over the back plate.

ROWAN SAT IN THE SILENCE OF AN EMPTY SEALING room. People had come to the celestial room, and he was not in the mood for company, so he'd left. He wondered how many marriages had been performed here. He recalled his own, inside a sealing room at the Salt Lake temple. Bride and groom kneeling, facing each other over the altar, their families seated behind them on either side. Both held hands and pronounced a covenant to be faithful with each other, and to God, and to keep His commandments. To be sealed in Jesus' name, by priesthood authority in a temple, was to be joined for all eternity—not just "till death do they part." Here, as in most sealing rooms, mirrors placed on the walls allowed the couple to symbolically see themselves through their many reflections, together for all eternity.

And I will give unto thee the keys of the kingdom of heaven: and whatsoever thou shalt bind on earth shall be bound in heaven.

Matthew 16:19.

To believe that marriage was forever only strengthened the earthly bond between husband and wife. Divorce, though allowed by the church, was frowned upon. Commitment was taught and expected.

And nothing was wrong with that.

He'd been praying for the past half hour, unsure what to do. He could not believe Heavenly

Father had taken him this far, only to deprive him of the moment of glory.

His cell phone vibrated in his pocket again.

He checked the display.

An unknown number.

He decided to answer.

"You didn't think I would actually trust you," Stephanie Nelle said in his ear.

"You set me up."

"Really? And how did I do that?"

"I have neither the time nor the inclination to explain myself to you."

"I want your committee's interest in my department officially withdrawn. I want you off my back, Senator. I want you out of my life."

"I frankly don't care—"

"I have the watch."

Had he heard right?

"I sent my people in to get it, and they did."

"How did you know I wanted it?"

"I read what Lincoln left in that book, too. I made a copy of the page before you tore it out."

A reprieve? Second opportunity?

"Do we have a deal, Senator?"

No choice. "We do. I will have a letter drafted tomorrow. My committee will say that we have no need of anything from you."

"That's what I want. Except I want the letter

drafted and signed within the next hour, the original delivered to me."

"Done. Now I'm waiting."

"Open your email. I sent some pictures along with the address of where to send the letter. If I don't get it within the hour, your little scheme will come to an abrupt end. You understand?"

"I do."

"Goodbye, Senator."

He tapped the screen on his smartphone and found the email. Two images downloaded. The first was of an open pocket watch. The second was a close-up of the watch's back plate, inner side, two words etched into the silver.

FALTA NADA.

Missing Nothing.

He thought of the map Lincoln had scrawled into the Book of Mormon, how every site had been labeled save for one.

And here was that omitted piece of information.

He smiled, stared up at Heavenly Father, and whispered, "Thank you."

His prayers had been answered. Where a few moments ago he was stuck, literally at the end, now he was on the move again. Even better he didn't need Charles Snow, Stephanie Nelle, Danny Daniels, Brigham Young, or any map Lincoln had left behind.

He knew exactly where his prize waited.

SIXTY

✫

10:00 P.M.

STEPHANIE LEFT THE MANDARIN ORIENTAL AND rode in a taxi toward the White House. She'd done exactly as Danny Daniels had requested, funneling to Rowan the information acquired from the watch. To further bolster her credibility, an image of the watch's exposed interior had also been sent. Rowan, to his credit, had signed the letter of withdrawal and delivered it to the hotel, as she'd insisted. By now Salazar and Cassiopeia would know what Rowan knew. She understood the wisdom in what the president had wanted done, but she did not like the implications. Nearly twenty years in the intelligence business had taught her when to recognize an endgame.

The cab deposited her near Blair House and she

walked the remainder of the way, ushered inside by the Secret Service and led to a room with yellow walls and a portrait of Abraham Lincoln. Waiting were Daniels and Charles R. Snow, 17th Prophet of the Church of Jesus Christ of Latter-day Saints. She'd already been told by Danny, on the phone, what had happened here a few hours ago with Rowan.

Both men appeared agitated.

"On December 20, 1860, less than two months after Abraham Lincoln was elected president, South Carolina seceded from the Union," Daniels said. "The first state to ever do that. Over the next sixty days Mississippi, Alabama, Georgia, Louisiana, and Texas did the same thing. Then, on April 12, 1861, Fort Sumter was attacked. Five days later Virginia, Arkansas, Tennessee, and North Carolina left the Union."

She listened to his voice, returned again to the same quiet monotone from yesterday.

"Right here, in this room," the president said, "a few days after Sumter was attacked, Francis Preston Blair sat down with Robert E. Lee. Lincoln wanted Lee to lead the Northern forces and asked Blair to see if it was possible. Lee being Lee, declined. **How can I draw my sword upon Virginia, my native state?**"

"That war challenged everyone's loyalty," Snow said. "Saints, too, had to make choices. Though we were far away, in the Salt Lake valley, the war found us."

"Lincoln trusted you enough to send that document."

"I'm not sure it was from trust. He had to quiet Brigham Young and secure the west for the North. He knew Young would never just take his word, so he sent something of enough value for Young to see he was serious."

"But Young could have given it to the South," she said. "And ended it all. From everything I've ever read, Mormons of that time hated the federal government."

"That's true. We felt it had abandoned us. But it's equally true that we cherished the Constitution. We never saw it as our duty to destroy the nation."

"You don't believe the White Horse Prophecy, do you?" Daniels asked.

"If you had asked me a few days ago I would have said no. Now I'm not so sure. So much of it is becoming reality."

The president looked tired. "Six hundred thousand people died in the Civil War. More than all of our other wars combined. That's a lot of American bloodshed."

And she heard what had not been uttered.

Probably for nothing.

"But we can't blame Lincoln for what he did," Daniels said. "He had a difficult decision, and he made it. We're here thanks to that call. The world is a better place, thanks to that call. Exposing that document would have ended the nation right then. If that had happened, who knows what the world would be like today." The president paused. "Still, he suppressed the will and words of the founders. He chose, on his own, by himself, to determine what was right for this country."

And now she realized why she was here. "A choice you may have to make soon, too."

Daniels' eyes found hers. "If that document still exists, I'll have the same decision. Madison's notes are a problem, but they're only notes. His reputation for altering and editing makes them suspect. Not near enough proof to dissolve the country. But the document itself, signed and sealed, that would be a deal breaker. Who knows what the courts will do with it. That ball could bounce in any direction. And public opinion? It won't be good."

She faced Snow and decided to take advantage of this opportunity. "What is the significance of **Falta Nada**?"

"It's a place, one Rowan will be familiar with."

She caught something in Snow's eyes. "You want him to go there?"

"It's **necessary** that he go there. But it's important that it be on his own initiative. He cannot sense he's being led."

"Do you know much about the man who first owned this house?" Daniels asked her, breaking the moment.

Actually, she did. Francis Preston Blair. Part of Andrew Jackson's informal group of advisers, the so-called Kitchen Cabinet, publisher of an influential Washington newspaper. He eventually sold the newspaper and withdrew from politics, but returned to the forefront in 1861, becoming one of Lincoln's trusted friends.

"Lincoln sent Blair to Richmond," Daniels said, "as an unofficial envoy, to set up peace talks. Those talks happened, at Hampton Roads, in February 1865. Lincoln himself went, but when the South insisted on independence as a condition to peace they reached no agreement. The Union was non-negotiable, as far as Lincoln was concerned. Right to the end, he stuck to his guns."

"You never finished your answer," she said to Daniels.

His eyes focused tight. "I don't want to be forced to make a decision as to what to do with that document. I don't ever want to see it."

"Then why tell Rowan what was inside the watch?"

"He and Salazar have to be stopped," Snow

said. "If I die, which could at be any time, Thaddeus Rowan will be the next prophet. That is our way. He is senior in line. Once he's the prophet, he'll answer to no one."

"We tried to get him to quit," Daniels said. "But you can guess what he said to that."

Yes, she could.

"Right now"—Daniels held up his fingers— "we have ten people who know of this. Of those, we control all but three—Rowan, Salazar, and Cassiopeia. We're not sure how much Cassiopeia Vitt knows, but I'm assuming it's enough. I'm not worried about our people—or you, me, and the prophet here. We all know how to keep a secret, and none of our folks knows it all anyway. But those other three? They're wild cards."

She understood. "Even if we manage to get control of the document, Rowan, Salazar, and Cassiopeia can talk."

Daniels nodded. "And one of them will become the next supreme head of a wealthy and influential religious organization. Rowan has a solid reputation and national credibility. Every indication is that Salazar will be at his side. That's a dangerous man who we know has murdered one of our own."

The implications were becoming clearer.

"Have you ever heard of the Mountain Meadows massacre?" Snow asked her.

She shook her head.

"A shameful chapter in our history. A wagon train from Arkansas, bound for California, passed through the Utah Territory in 1857. This was at the height of tensions between Saints and the federal government. An army was on the way to subdue us. We knew that. Fear was rampant. The wagons stopped in Salt Lake, then traveled south, pausing at a place called Mountain Meadow. For reasons that are still not known, local militiamen attacked the wagons and slaughtered 120 men, women, and children. Only 17 youngsters, below the age of seven, were spared."

"Horrible," she said.

"It is," Snow said. "But it's a sign of those turbulent times. I don't defend what happened, but I understand how something like it could have happened. Paranoia had taken over. We'd traveled west to be safe, to be left alone, yet we were still being attacked by a government that should have protected us in the first place."

Snow paused, as if gathering himself.

"It took seventeen years but, finally, in 1874, nine people were indicted for the murders. Only one man was eventually tried. John Lee. It took two trials, but an all-Saints jury finally convicted him and he was executed. To this day many believe Lee a scapegoat. Some say Brigham Young himself was involved. Others say that's not possible. We'll never know."

"Because the truth was covered up?"

Snow nodded. "Time allowed everything to muddle. But Brigham Young, as prophet, made sure that the church survived. That is my task, too."

"But at what cost? People died back then for that to happen."

"And it seems we have come full circle."

"Except," Daniels said, "an entire nation has to survive this crisis."

She got it. "You want Rowan and Salazar dead?"

Snow bristled at her directness, but it had to be asked.

"The United States of America does not assassinate people," Daniels said. "Nor do we condone political murder. But—if the opportunity for Rowan to not survive presents itself from a third party, there's nothing to say we have to interfere."

She caught the message. **Find an acceptable way.**

"Now, Salazar?" the president said. "He's an entirely different matter."

And she agreed.

The United States of America did avenge its own.

"Elder Salazar," Snow said, "worships an idol that I'm afraid never existed. Joseph Smith, our founder, had many good ideas, and he was both bold and brave. But men like Salazar refuse to acknowledge any flaws. They see only what they want to see. These Danites he's organized are a dangerous group, just as they were during Smith's time. They have no place in our church."

"Did you know the Danites existed before I told you?" Daniels asked.

"I had heard a rumor. Which is why I've been watching Rowan and Salazar."

She recalled what Edwin Davis had said. **We were hoping that time had taken care of things. But we've received information indicating that this is not the case.** And she realized something. "You kept us informed?"

Daniels nodded. "For over a year. By then we were already watching Rowan, too. So we shared information. Each of us knew things the other didn't."

"Now you two are the only ones who know it all?"

No reply came to her inquiry.

"The fact that Salazar killed one of your agents saddens me," Snow finally said. "But it does not surprise me. Once, in the beginning, we believed in blood atonement. Killing was rationalized, even legitimized. We repudiated such barbarism long ago. Our church does not, in any way, condone murder, for any reason. My heart aches for that dead man."

"This has to stop," Daniels said, his voice stronger. "We've discovered secessionist movements scattered all around the country, and Rowan is stoking those fires. He has people ready and waiting to exploit what will happen in Utah. As we learned this morning, he has a majority of the Utah legislature, along with the governor, supporting him. It will be just like in 1860. South Carolina led the way, and other states quickly followed. We certainly cannot use violence of any form and, considering what we know about the founders, we may not legally be able to prevent it."

A moment of strained silence filled the room. They each seemed to be considering the consequences of what had to be done.

"I want you to accompany the prophet back to Utah and find a way to stop Rowan and Salazar at **Falta Nada**." The president paused. "Permanently."

But there was something else.

She asked, "And Cassiopeia?"

Cotton had been provided a chance to handle her in Iowa and failed. Luke's field report was not encouraging, either. Cassiopeia was far too close to the situation to be effective any longer.

She knew what had to be done.

"I'll handle her, too."

SIXTY-ONE

★

Malone admired Temple Square. He'd never visited before, but he'd read about what had long ago been accomplished here. A bronze plaque attached to the high stone wall that rimmed its outer perimeter noted the origin.

Fixed by orson pratt assisted by henry g. Sherwood, august 3, 1847, when beginning the original survey of "Great Salt lake City," around the "Mormon" temple site designated by brigham young july 28, 1847. The city streets were named and numbered from this point.

A concrete monument stood beneath the marker, upon which was chiseled BASE AND MERIDIAN. Here was the starting point from which everything around him—an entire city, home now to two hundred thousand people—had been built.

Hard not to be impressed.

He and Luke had flown out of Des Moines just after dawn in a Department of Justice plane sent by Stephanie. They'd been told that Salazar and Cassiopeia were likewise headed their way. Senator Thaddeus Rowan had left Washington, D.C., late last night, back now at his Utah residence.

Stephanie's instructions were for them both to be here at 10:00 A.M. All would be explained, she'd said. The placard and monument stood adjacent to busy South Temple Street, just across from a downtown shopping complex and the Deseret Book Company. Both he and Luke were armed, carrying Magellan Billet–issued Berettas identical to the one back in Copenhagen beneath his bed. He'd called the bookstore earlier, after they'd landed, to see how things were going. Luckily he employed three ladies who treated the store as their own, so all was under control. He appreciated all that they did, and rewarded them by paying a high wage and sharing the profits. Considering the mayhem the bookstore had endured over the past few years, it was amazing they stuck around.

A black Lincoln Navigator with tinted windows

emerged from traffic and stopped at the curb. The rear window lowered, and an older man's face appeared.

"Mr. Malone. Mr. Daniels. I'm Charles Snow, here to retrieve you."

The front passenger door opened and Stephanie emerged.

"Why am I not surprised you're here?" Malone said.

"'Cause this isn't your first rodeo."

He stared at Luke. "I assume you knew."

"I am on the payroll, Pappy."

The driver, a younger man, left the car and offered a set of keys.

"I thought, perhaps, Mr. Daniels could drive," Snow said. "And you and I could sit back here, Mr. Malone."

He knew both the name and the face, recognizing Snow as the current leader of the Church of Jesus Christ of Latter-day Saints.

He climbed into the Navigator's rear seat, Luke and Stephanie into the front.

"It's important that I come with you," Snow said. "My legs are weak, but they'll have to work. I'll make sure of it."

He wanted to know, "Why is this so important?"

Snow nodded. "It is, for both **my** church and **our** country."

"We're going to **Falta Nada**?"

"That we are. Mr. Daniels, if you will engage the navigation, the route is already programmed. It's about an hour's drive." Snow paused. "But in the old days it was a good two-day ride by horseback."

Luke drove the car away, the navigation screen lit with a map, an arrow pointing the way.

"Ms. Nelle tells me you were once one of the government's best agents," Snow said.

"She's been known to exaggerate."

"President Daniels said the same thing."

"He can tell a few whoppers himself."

Snow chuckled. "He's a tough man. My heart hurts for him. He may have some difficult choices to soon make."

He thought he understood. "Salazar?"

Snow nodded. "Evil. But I've only learned the extent of how bad over the past two days. He killed one of your agents. I have prayed for that departed soul."

"Not much consolation to his widow and children."

The older man appraised him with a hard glare. "No. I imagine not."

He understood about killing. Never a good thing. But there was a difference between the heat-of-battle self-defense, and in-cold-blood, one Josepe Salazar seemed to not care about.

"I need to know what **Falta Nada** is."

He noticed that Stephanie had not turned back and joined the conversation. Instead she kept her gaze out the front windshield, her mouth closed.

"I never thought I would again travel to the high country," Snow said. "You see, Mr. Malone, I'm dying. You can look at me and tell. But of late a new strength has found its way into me. Maybe it's the last bit of life before death begins to take hold. I can only hope it lasts until we finish this."

He knew enough about the situation to say, "This mess was sown a long time ago. You merely inherited it."

"That's true. But Thaddeus Rowan is **my** problem. The president and I tried to coerce his resignation, but he rejected that. I can't challenge him publicly because of his standing and the overall sensitivity of this. Instead, **we** have to deal with him. Today."

Only a few men rose to lead the world's great religions. Catholic popes. Orthodox patriarchs. Protestant archbishops. Here was the prophet of the Saints. Malone sympathized with both the man's health and his difficult situation, but they were headed into a perilous unknown.

And he had to prepare.

"**Falta Nada,**" he said. "Tell me about it."

Utah was settled two years before the 1849 California gold rush. The Church of Jesus Christ of

Latter-day Saints opposed gold prospecting in all forms, since it distracted members from concentrating their labors on building Zion. In 1847, when the pioneers first arrived, most were penniless. Yet by 1850, Saints were minting gold coins and furbishing their new temple in gold leaf. Where had the wealth come from?

The Salt Lake basin had long been occupied by Utes. Surprisingly, these Natives welcomed the religious immigrants. Wakara, their chief, developed a close relationship with the newcomers, especially a Saint named Isaac Morley. Eventually Wakara admitted to Brother Isaac that years ago he'd received a vision from Towats, the Ute word for "God." In that vision, the chief was told to give gold to "tall hats" who would one day come to his land. The Saints fit that description perfectly, so Wakara led Brother Isaac to Carre-Shinob, a sacred place supposedly build by the ancestors. There Morley collected 58 pounds of refined gold and sent it to Brigham Young in Salt Lake City. A deal was struck for more of the cache, which Wakara agreed to provide with two conditions. Only one man would know the mine's location, and that man had to be equally trusted by both parties. Brother Isaac was chosen for the task, but eventually he became too old to make the yearly trip.

In 1852 a new man was selected.

Thomas Rhoades.

From his first journey to the secret mine, Rhoades returned with 62 pounds of gold. More trips were made in subsequent years. Wakara died in 1855 and his son, Arapeen, succeeded him as chief. At the same time Rhoades also became sick and could no longer make the annual trip into the mountains.

So Brigham Young had a problem.

He wasn't even sure if the new chief would honor the agreement. If he did, Young needed Arapeen's permission to allow Caleb Rhoades, Thomas Rhoades' son, to take over the gold extractions. This was tentatively agreed to, provided that a Native escort Caleb on his visits. Eventually Caleb became trustworthy enough in Arapeen's eyes to go alone and made many trips. Arapeen's successor ended the deal, but Caleb Rhoades continued to make covert journeys. He even petitioned Congress for a land lease, but the petition was denied. The federal government eventually chartered other companies to survey and mine the area. Government-paid geologists came and scouted, but never found the fabled Rhoades Mine.

Brigham Young knew that if word got out that Utah possessed such a treasure, it would cause a gold rush bigger than the one in California. That was the last thing he wanted, as Saints had fled west to escape gentiles. So he forbid all talk of the mine. Any Saint who participated in prospecting would be excommunicated.

"The Rhoades Mine is one of our legends," Snow said. "Few facts exist about it thanks to Young's order of silence. Just a lot of wild stories. But it's not all a lie."

"Interesting to hear you admit that," Malone said.

"Until now it was just a harmless legend. Now, though, things have changed."

To say the least.

"Brigham Young had a difficult job," Snow said. "He was nation building **and** faith building. His Saints were living in one of the harshest places imaginable. Money was nonexistent. So he did what had to be done."

He was watching their route as Luke merged onto Interstate 15 north, leaving Salt Lake, heading toward Ogden. He also noticed the younger man's eyes watching them in the rearview mirror.

Still only silence from Stephanie.

"There was refined gold in the sacred mine Wakara showed Isaac Morley," Snow said. "Most likely brought north by Spaniards from Mexico centuries ago and secreted away. Bars, coins, nuggets, dust. The Utes discovered this, but gold was not precious to them. So Wakara made the deal thinking he was pleasing not only the newcomers, but his own God. Contrary to the legend it was Young, not the Utes, who insisted that only one person have access. For ten years he milked that cache, allowing that gold to slowly make its way into our economy. Coins were minted, wages paid with coin, goods bought with those wages. Nobody ever questioned the source. All just appreciated its presence. Remember, we were a closed society. That gold just moved about in circles, never leaving, always benefiting each person who held it. Then, in 1857, with the coming of war with the United States, the threat existed of losing that wealth. So Young ordered everyone to repatriate their gold. Everything was melted down, loaded onto wagons, and supposedly sent to California for safekeeping until the threat was over."

Snow reached into his pocket and removed something, handing it over.

A gold coin.

On one side were clasped hands surrounded by capital letters G S L C P G and the value amount of five dollars. On the obverse was an all-seeing eye surrounded by HOLINESS TO THE LORD.

"Those letters stand for Greater Salt Lake City Pure Gold. A bit of a misnomer as the coins were fashioned from bullion metal that contained silver and copper. It's about 80% gold. That's one of the coins minted by Brigham Young, included in a time capsule Young created inside a record stone at the Salt Lake temple. We opened it in 1993. The coins were all the same, only differing in value from $2.50 to $20. The so-called Mormon Money."

"That's part of what got him in trouble with the federal government," Malone said. "The Constitution says only Congress can mint money."

"Brigham Young tended to ignore those laws he did not agree with. But in his defense, we were a long way from the United States and had to survive. To do that we needed an economy we could control. So he created one."

"Except those wagons never made it to California," Luke said from the front seat. "In fact, they were just found a few days ago, in Zion National Park, hidden in a cave with four skeletons."

"That's right," Snow said. "By 1857 the Utes' sacred mine was tapped out. So Young made the decision to replenish his supply with the gold from the wagons. The same wealth, back where it started. But this time it wasn't hidden in the sacred mine. Instead Young arranged for a private land grant from the territorial legislature and created a new place, his own, where he was in charge. **Falta Nada**."

"Missing Nothing. A touch of irony?"

"I've always thought so. Slowly, over the next two decades that gold filtered its way back into our community."

"But not to its rightful owners."

Snow paused, then shook his head. "I'm afraid not. Another one of those difficult decisions by Young. But it turned out to be brilliant. Our economy flourished. We prospered greatly after the Civil War ended, and especially so as the 19th century gave way to the 20th."

"Four men were dead in that cave with the wagons," Luke said from the front seat.

"I know," Snow said. "Fjeldsted. Hyde. Woodruff. Egan. Their names have been known to us for many years."

"What did the message in the cave mean?" Luke asked. "**Damnation to the prophet. Forget us not.**"

No one had told Malone about any cave, but he let it pass.

"I'm afraid the implications are hard to ignore. Young was the prophet at the time, and they blamed him for their deaths."

"It seems like they had good reason," Luke said.

"What I've told you so far has been passed from prophet to prophet, for their ears only. But when those wagons were found, I learned a new aspect of the story. Four men murdered was never part of what was passed down."

"Does Rowan know any of this?"

Snow shook his head. "He knows of the wagons, but I did not tell him any of these other details, and I will not."

The car continued to speed down the interstate, the landscape becoming more rural and rugged.

"**Falta Nada** eventually became a place for prophets," Snow said. "The gold was exhausted, its smelting furnace removed. So it evolved into a place of refuge in the wilderness."

He did not like the continued silence from the front seat so he asked, "Stephanie, where are Salazar and Cassiopeia?"

"Ahead of us," she said, her eyes still facing the windshield. "They should be at the site by now, with Rowan."

He caught the deadpan tone. Troubling—on many levels. He knew enough about the situation to know that none of this information could ever see the light of day. Too explosive, the implications too profound. Not only for the Mormon Church but for the United States of America.

Salazar?

Rowan?

They were one thing.

But Cassiopeia.

She was quite another.

And this time she was in deep.

SIXTY-TWO

✦

CASSIOPEIA STOOD BESIDE THE CAR. SHE AND JO-sepe had made the journey northeast from Salt Lake City in a little over an hour, and they'd been waiting in the morning mountain air for twenty minutes. The peaks surrounding her were not especially high, but glaciers had performed their sculpting, the evidence clear from deep scars and dark canyons. The two-lane highway east from the interstate had woven a path through a spectacular wilderness thick with poplar, birch, and spruce all dressed in autumn gold. Another two miles on a graveled lane led them to a clearing among the trees, where they parked. A posted sign proclaimed

PRIVATE PROPERTY
Do Not Trespass
Grounds Patrolled

Josepe had remained quiet both during the flight from Iowa and on the car ride north from the airport. She'd preferred the silence as her own rage was becoming increasingly hard to control. Somebody was funneling information to Thaddeus Rowan. Somebody who'd been provided that information by Cotton. How else would anyone know what had been inside that watch? Cotton had surely opened it and reported what he'd found to Stephanie. Then that had been passed to Rowan. She'd finally pressed Josepe, who'd called Rowan, and the senator revealed that he had a source inside the government, working as his ally.

But why trust such a source?

The answer was easy.

Rowan **wanted** to believe. So did Josepe. They'd lost all objectivity, willing to take chances that otherwise cautious souls would never risk. They were fools. But what was she? A liar? A cheat?

Worse?

She was angry at Cotton. She'd asked him to stay out of this, but he'd ignored her. He'd been ready and waiting in Des Moines, seemingly knowing her every move. But why wouldn't he? They knew each other. Loved each other.

Or so she thought.

But she also had to tell herself that this involved **his** country, not hers. The threat was far more real and immediate for him. And that clearly made a difference, at least in his eyes.

"This is a beautiful place," Josepe said.

She agreed. They'd risen in altitude, the brisk crystalline air refreshing, reminding her of Salzburg. Snow dotted the distant peaks, a high forested plateau stretching out before them for miles, the scars from past wildfires still visible. A morning sun shone across the surface of a nearby lake. The two Danites had traveled with them and kept close watch on their employer. She assumed both were armed. As was Josepe. She'd caught sight of a shoulder holster beneath his jacket.

Interesting that she'd not been offered a weapon.

SALAZAR HAD NEVER BEFORE VENTURED BEYOND Salt Lake into the wilderness the pioneers had traversed. But here he was, among the trees and mountains of Deseret, where the first Saints had passed on their way to the promised land. Those early settlers were so different from other western immigrants. They employed no professional guides, preferring to find their own way. They also improved the route as they traveled, making it better for the next group. They were cohesive, moving as one, a culture, a faith, a people—modern pilgrims, routed from their homes by intolerance and persecution—intent on finding their salvation on earth.

It took two years for the first group to trek 1,300 miles from Illinois to the Great Basin. Eventually, 1,650 made it to the valley in 1847. That first year had been tough, but the next was tougher. Spring plantings had looked promising, but hordes of crickets soon invaded—**three to four a leaf,** as one Saint described—and began to devour the crops. They fought back with brooms, sticks, fire, and water. Anything and everything. Prayers, too. Which were finally answered by a sight from heaven. Seagulls. Which swooped in by the thousands and devoured the insects.

The Miracle of the Gulls.

Some say it was exaggerated. Others that it never happened. But he believed every word. Why wouldn't he? God and the prophets always provided—so why would it be impossible that help would appear at just the right moment? The seagull remained Utah's state bird, and he was sure that would be the case with the soon-to-be independent nation of Deseret.

He felt invigorated.

Soon, once again, all of this would be theirs.

"This is a special place," he told Cassiopeia.

"There's nothing here," Cassiopeia said.

"We have to hike. **Falta Nada** is nearby."

He heard the growl of an engine and turned to see a small red coupe approaching. The car stopped and Elder Rowan emerged, dressed in boots and jeans, ready for the wilderness.

They greeted each other with a handshake.

"It's good to see you again, brother," Rowan said. "This is a great day, equal to the moment when the pioneers first arrived. If we're successful, everything will change."

He, too, was energized by the possibilities.

Rowan noticed Cassiopeia. "And who is this?"

He introduced them. "She's been invaluable the past few days. She's the one who obtained the watch, only to have it stolen back."

"You haven't mentioned her," Rowan said.

"I know. Her involvement came about quickly."

He explained how he and Cassiopeia had known each other since childhood, how they'd once been close, drifted apart, and were now reuniting. Rowan seemed pleased with her reawakening, and the fact that her family were among the early European converts.

"I actually recall your father," Rowan said. "In the 1970s I was working with the church in Europe. He headed the stake in Barcelona, if I recall. A truly spiritual and dedicated man."

"Thank you for saying that. I always thought so, too."

Where at first there'd been apprehension in the elder's eyes at Cassiopeia's presence, now there was calm. Perhaps from knowing that she was a Saint by birth?

"Cassiopeia is aware of what we're doing. She also helped fend off the Americans in Salzburg. She and I are discussing a personal future together."

He hoped he wasn't being too presumptuous with the revelation.

"I'd like her to be a part of this," he said.

"Then she shall," Rowan said. "We've come a long way, brother. There were times when I doubted we'd make it this far. But we're here. So let us all go and claim our prize."

Salazar faced his two men. "Stay here and keep watch. We can contact each other by phone, if need be."

The two Danites nodded.

None of what was about to happen was for their eyes.

He turned toward Elder Rowan.

"Please, lead the way."

ROWAN HAD VISITED HERE BEFORE, ONCE, YEARS ago. The prophet who'd served before Charles

Snow had held a retreat for the elders. They'd spent three days praying, making decisions that would govern the church for years to come. Since then, he'd heard little about the site, though he knew it was still maintained. The house had been built about fifty years ago, remodeled several times since. Two hundred and forty acres of forest surrounded the building, all owned by the church. As best he could recall a private security firm kept an eye on everything, so at some point he might have to deal with them. Unlikely, though, they would give the second-highest-ranking church official any trouble.

He led the way into the trees, following a defined path that wound through the woods, climbing in elevation. Saints had mainly settled along the western front of the Wasatch Range, where the rivers drained, founding 25 towns against a hundred miles of mountain frontage. Eighty-five percent of Utah's population still lived within fifteen miles of the Wasatch Range, two million people, on what was simply called the Front. The eastern slopes were gentler, home to ski resorts. Here, on the western edge, the terrain was far more rugged and 5,000 feet higher than in Salt Lake. The idea of **Falta Nada** had been to fashion something reminiscent of the early days, and through the trees he caught a glimpse of the three-story house. Massive hand-hewn logs had been notched and fitted together, mortar filling the cracks and outlining the aged timber with thick gray lines. Large bay windows dotted the ground floor, more windows above, the house a pleasing mix of wood, stone, and glass. It sat within a hundred yards of a mountain, a zigzag trail winding upward through the trees.

"The house is not **Falta Nada**," he told them. "It was built after the refuge was discovered."

"So where are we headed?" Salazar asked as they kept walking.

He pointed at the mountain. "Inside there."

SIXTY-THREE

✦

LUKE ROUNDED A CURVE IN THE DIRT ROAD AND spotted two cars parked ahead. They'd left the interstate thirty minutes ago and an asphalt road a couple of miles back, following the Navigator's GPS. Stephanie had sat beside him the whole way and said little. Malone and Snow in the backseat had likewise been quiet for a while. Everyone seemed anxious. He was just ready to get on with it. Ahead he spotted two men standing near vehicles.

"Those are the same two guys from Salzburg," Malone said. "I doubt they'll be happy to see me."

"I can handle them," Snow said. "Ease close on my side."

Luke brought the car to a stop, and the prophet lowered his window. Both Danites stood ready, hands beneath their jackets surely on weapons. Luke's right hand found his own automatic.

"Do you know who I am?" Snow asked.

They nodded.

"Then you will do exactly as I say. Is that clear?"

Both remained silent.

"I am your prophet," Snow said. "You are sworn to protect me, are you not?"

The men nodded again.

"**Dan shall be a serpent by the way, an adder in the path, that biteth the horse's heels so that his rider shall fall backward.** You know the significance of those words?"

"From Genesis," one said. "We are sworn to live by them."

"Then remove your weapons and drop them to the ground."

They did as Snow ordered.

"Stand back and wait."

The window whined closed.

"I shall pray with these poor sinners for forgiveness," Snow said. "You three have a job to do."

Luke caught Stephanie's glare, the first time she'd looked his way. They'd talked on the phone earlier, just after he and Malone had arrived in Utah. She'd told him what had to be done, none of which he particularly liked. Her stare now asked if he understood that—like the Danites outside—he, too, was sworn to duty.

He gave a nod.

"I will pray for your success," Snow said.

Luke turned and faced the prophet.

"Old man, you're foolin' no one. You led Rowan and Salazar here because this godforsaken place is in the middle of nowhere. Now you want us to go and do your dirty work. So let's don't cast this with any sense of righteousness. There's nothin' right or sacred here."

"I must apologize," Stephanie said, "for my agent's rudeness."

"He's correct," Snow said. "There is nothing righteous about this. It is a despicable business. I've wondered all night if this is how Brigham Young himself felt when he ordered those wagons taken and the gold returned? He had to have known that men would die. But he had no choice. And neither do I."

Luke opened his door and stepped out.

Malone and Stephanie followed.

The two Danites reacted to Malone's appearance, retrieving their weapons.

"He is our enemy," one of them said.

"No, he's not," the prophet said. "Your enemy is far more complex."

Neither man backed down.

"I will not say it again," Snow said. "Drop those guns and do as I say. Or pay the price in heaven."

The two tossed the guns back down.

Snow motioned for them to leave. "Go ahead. I'll catch up."

Stephanie led the way toward the trail.

"You're not going to hurt her," Malone said.

Stephanie stopped and faced her former employee. "And you think I would?"

"Depends on what happens."

"I've been ordered to make sure that nothing leaves this spot that could jeopardize the future of the United States of America."

"Fine. Do your job. But you and Frat Boy here better know, right now, nobody is going to hurt her. Period."

"I also have a job to do," Luke said.

"Do it. But if you make a move on Cassiopeia I'll kill you."

Luke did not like to be threatened. Never had. But Stephanie had also ordered him not to provoke Malone. They would deal with Cassiopeia as the situation developed. She'd warned him that Malone would know the score, better to rock him to sleep than challenge him.

They weren't here to win battles, only the war.

MALONE MEANT EVERY WORD HE SAID. HE'D shoot the Frat Boy dead if any harm came to Cassiopeia. He'd sensed the gravity of the situation from Stephanie's silence, knowing that every loose end of this operation had to be snipped tight. Stephanie, Luke, himself? They were pros. Sworn to secrecy. No danger of them revealing anything. But Rowan, Salazar, and Cassiopeia? They were an entirely different matter. Especially Cassiopeia, who was not thinking like herself. He possessed the greatest respect for Stephanie, even understood her quandary—orders were orders—and the stakes were the highest he could ever remember. But that changed nothing. And if Cassiopeia was too involved to look after herself, he'd do it for her.

She'd many times done it for him.

Time to repay the favor.

Whether she wanted it or not.

☆ ☆ ☆

STEPHANIE WAS ARMED. UNUSUAL FOR HER. A BEretta was nestled in a shoulder harness beneath her coat. Surely Malone had seen that. Before leaving Blair House, Danny Daniels had taken her aside, outside of Charles Snow's presence.

"We have no choice," he said to her. "None at all."

"There's always options."

"Not here. You realize there are a crap load of people in this country who would take secession seriously. And God knows it's our own fault. I've tried for eight years to govern, and it ain't easy, Stephanie. In fact, it might be damn well impossible. So for a state to opt out? I could understand why it might. And it doesn't matter if the effort succeeds. The existence of that document alone is enough to jeopardize the future of this nation. Things will never be the same with it around, and I can't allow that to happen. We've managed to maneuver all of our problems to one spot. So you and Luke. Handle it."

"There's Cotton."

"I know. But he's also a pro."

"None of us is a murderer."

"Nobody said you were."

He gently grasped her arm. A chill shot through her.

"This is exactly what Lincoln faced," he said, his voice barely a whisper. "He had to choose. Only difference is that, for him, the states were already seceded, so he had to fight a war to win them back. It's no wonder every one of those war casualties took a toll on him. He, and he alone, made that call. He had to ask himself, Do I do what the founders said? Or do I ignore them? It was his choice, right? Damn straight. But America survived and became what we are today."

"Broken?"

He stared at her with pain in his eyes. "Best damn broken system on the planet. And I'm not going to let it just dissolve away."

"The founders of this country thought otherwise."

"Actually, so did Lincoln."

She waited for more.

"He gave a speech in 1848. Edwin found it. He said that any people, anywhere, have the right to rise up, shake off their government, and form one that suits them better. He called it a valuable and sacred right. Even worse, he said that right wasn't confined to the whole people of a government. Any portion of those people, like a state or a territory, could make their own way. The son of a bitch said, flat out, that secession was a natural right.

"But then, thirteen years later, as president, when the time came to allow those states to go, he chose the country over states' rights. I'm making that same call. Every president, in the twilight of his term, thinks of history. I'd be lying if I said I wasn't. My legacy, Stephanie, is this. Not a soul will know, besides us, but that's okay. Like Lincoln, I choose to save the United States of America."

She'd listened to what Malone had said to Luke and knew the threat was directed her way, too.

Malone's nerves were frayed, his patience at an end.

But he wasn't in charge.

"Cotton," she said. "We're going to do what we have to."

Malone stopped walking and stepped close. They'd known each other a long time, been through a lot. He'd always helped her when she'd really needed it, and she'd repaid each of those favors as friends do for friends.

"Stephanie, I get it. This fight's different. But you're the one who roped Cassiopeia into this, and lied to keep her in it. Then you drew me in. So I'll tell you again. Leave. Her. Alone. I'll handle Cassiopeia. She won't be a problem."

"And if you're wrong?"

Malone's face hardened. "I'm not."

And he walked off.

SIXTY-FOUR

⋆

CASSIOPEIA ADMIRED THE SWEEPING UPLAND scenery. Everything seemed so peaceful and pleasant, rather than frightening and foreboding, which was far closer to the truth. They'd rounded the huge house and found a rocky trail that zigzagged upward. Scarlet bunchberry lay scattered over a thick carpet of green moss. Fir, maple, and oak trees engulfed them with a canopy, leaves falling in waves. Two deer emerged from the foliage, then meandered off, seemingly unafraid.

"We don't allow hunting here," Rowan said. "We've left it all to nature."

She was trying to assess the senator. He was a handsome, older man with plenty of vigor. He easily handled the inclined trail, barely breaking a sweat or struggling for a breath. He carried himself like a man in charge—which, according to Josepe, fit him, as this was the second-highest-ranking official in the church. The next prophet. She'd caught the wariness in his eyes when they met. She could recall, as a child, many men in dark suits, white shirts, and thin ties coming to their house. She'd always known that her father was a church leader, and her mother had explained that the visitors were other leaders from far and wide. But those men had made her feel uncomfortable.

And now she knew why.

They were followers.

Blindly plowing along on a path forged by others, hoping, along the way, to garner some favor for themselves. Never did they decide things for themselves.

Rowan and Josepe were different.

Their path was their own.

And they were nearing its end.

A ten-minute climb up the trail brought them to a black gash in the mountainside. A tin placard warned trespassers not to enter the cavern since it was private property. An iron grille barred entrance, and was secured by a padlock.

A few tugs and Rowan tested the gate.

Secure.

Then the senator motioned to Josepe, who removed his weapon and fired three rounds into the lock.

STEPHANIE HEARD THREE SOUNDS THROUGH THE woods.

Gunshots.

Malone and Luke quickened their pace, and she followed suit. Never had she felt so distant from Cotton. But she had no choice. What she'd do once confronted with the problem, she had no idea. This was all being invented as she went along.

But one thing was absolute.

She agreed with Danny Daniels.

The United States had to survive.

SALAZAR FREED THE REMNANT OF THE LOCK AND opened the iron gate. A few feet inside the tunnel he spotted an electrical box with a heavy cable protruding from its bottom, leading down into the ground, then disappearing ahead. Rowan stepped past him and worked the lever on one side upward.

Lights sprang on, dissolving the darkness.

"This is **Falta Nada**," Rowan said.

He and Cassiopeia followed the elder into a wide tunnel that led into a small chamber. Stalactites, stalagmites, and flowstones twisted and turned before them, defying gravity, each as delicate and fragile as blown glass. Color abounded from prisms created by the lights through the crystals. A stunning scene, carefully illuminated to maximize the effect.

"It's breathtaking, isn't it?" Rowan asked.

Cassiopeia was studying some drawings on the rock wall. Salazar examined them, too, and saw strange pack animals, like llamas, led by a man dressed in what appeared to be armor.

"The Spanish," Rowan said, noticing their interest. "They found this cave when they came north from Mexico in the 16th century and mined these hills, looking for gold." Rowan stepped to a pile of white quartz and lifted one of the rocks. Stringers of yellow could be seen. "These were found along with tool marks on the walls from shovels and picks. The Spanish were here long before Saints ever came."

Rowan motioned to a passageway.

"There's more."

ROWAN ALLOWED SALAZAR AND CASSIOPEIA VITT to go first, then he laid the quartz back down and followed. He'd been coy when Josepe introduced his companion, feigning ignorance, and ultimately offering his acceptance.

But he knew all about Cassiopeia Vitt.

"She works for the president," Stephanie Nelle said.

The call had come just before he'd left his house to drive north from Salt Lake City.

"She's been embedded with Salazar for some time. They were lovers once, in their youth, so it was thought she could make inroads where others couldn't. And she did. He has no idea."

He'd listened with a mixture of anxiety and anger. How many times had the federal government interjected itself into church business? How many spies had there been? Too many to count. Everyone said that sort of violation was a thing of the past. How wrong they were.

"She was sent by Daniels. He's been watching you and Salazar for over a year. Your prophet, Charles Snow, has been working with him, too."

That he knew.

"I found out about Vitt and Snow a short while ago."

"Why tell me?"

"Because I need you to succeed in whatever it is you're doing. That helps me in what I'm doing. So I thought I'd pass this along."

"I'm glad you did. But what do you expect me to do with it?"

"I don't give a damn. Just finish whatever it is you're doing and keep the president occupied. That's all I need."

He actually still did not know what to do. His own prophet an enemy? His president against him? Now his chief ally had a spy in their midst? He wasn't sure as to the solution, but knew that once the truth was exposed Josepe would know what to do. Danites were resourceful like that. Never had anything been said to him that even remotely implicated anything improper or illegal had ever occurred. So his heart was pure. The details had been left to Salazar, who to his credit had always handled them.

And that's what would happen today.

Here, at **Falta Nada**.

The name appropriate.

Missing Nothing.

SIXTY-FIVE

★

MALONE RACED UP THE TRAIL IN THE DIRECTION of the three retorts, Luke quick on his heels. Around a bend a huge house came into view. A mixture of timber and stone, three-story, with large-bowed windows and a steep gabled roof. Two stone chimneys stretched skyward. Trees rose on all sides, a mountain behind, a grassy clearing leading up to its front entrance.

Stephanie trotted up behind them.

"That's it," she said. "They're in there."

"I'll go in the front," he said to Luke. "You take the rear." He stared at Stephanie. "You wait here."

She nodded.

Luke darted right, gun in hand, and wove a path through the trees.

He kept down and hustled to the base of a redwood staircase that led up ten feet to the front door. He stared back to see Stephanie take cover behind a tree trunk. He started up the stairs, the wooden risers cushy at spots from years in the elements. The house itself appeared in good shape. Somebody had been doing regular maintenance. He made it to the porch, which seemed to wrap itself completely around the exterior.

The door was a solid slab on a wood frame.

He carefully tested the knob.

Locked.

There were more windows and he carefully spied into each one, listening carefully, hearing nothing.

LUKE STOOD OUTSIDE THE REAR DOOR, BENEATH A covered terrace. A mountain rose a hundred yards away, dense forest extending upward. He tried the latch and discovered it locked. Windows were adjacent to the rear entrance, and he stared inside to see a great room, the wood unpainted, the tones of pine and spruce blending with the bland columns and beams that supported a high-pitched ceiling. The furniture was simple and functional, a splash of color emerging from the fabrics on sofas and chairs. Another window opened into a kitchen equipped with stone countertops, wooden cupboards, and stainless-steel appliances. From beyond the deck he heard the gurgle of a stream and caught sight of a spinning waterwheel.

Something about this wasn't right.

He heard no voices from inside.

He'd have to kick the door from its jamb in order to enter, which wasn't a problem except that it would announce his presence loud and clear.

He heard movement on the deck.

And felt a vibration across the wood floor.

MALONE STARED THROUGH THE WINDOWS AS HE rounded the covered porch. Everything inside had the look and feel of a typical mountain retreat, its size and furnishings signaling affluence. Still not a sound from anywhere in the house. Had they seen them coming and retreated to safety?

He didn't think so.

His hunch had been confirmed by the wood floor inside, where a layer of dust coated the planks. Unmarred. No sign that anyone else had entered and walked about.

This was a dead end.

"Luke," he said.

The younger agent appeared from around the corner. "I was hoping that was you. Nobody's here."

He shook his head in agreement. But Stephanie

had specifically said this was where Rowan, Salazar, and Cassiopeia had gone.

"She lied to us."

They both darted toward the front porch. Stephanie was nowhere to be seen. He leaped down the stairs two at a time and ran for the tree where he'd last seen her.

Gone.

A noise on the trail behind him caught his attention. He whirled and leveled his gun. Luke did the same. Charles Snow appeared, helped with his steps by the two young Danites.

They lowered their weapons.

"What's happening?" Snow asked as he dislodged his arms from his helpers' shoulders.

"Stephanie's gone," Malone said.

"The house is empty and locked tight," Luke noted.

"She didn't tell you? The house is not **Falta Nada**."

That information grabbed Malone's attention.

"It was built later." Snow pointed to the mountain. "**Falta Nada** is up there, a cave, you can't miss it."

⭐ ⭐ ⭐

STEPHANIE HUSTLED UP THE ROCKY PATH, CLIMBing the forested ridge. The air was noticeably cooler. She'd misled Cotton and Luke to provide herself an opportunity to slip away. Snow had told her the details on the flight west last night.

"There is something you need to know about this place," Snow said. "There will be a dwelling at the location, but it is not Falta Nada. The site is above the house, inside the mountain. The trail is easy to spot. One of the early settlers discovered the place. The story goes that he was cutting timber when he spotted mountain lion tracks. He followed them to a high ledge and found a gash in the rock. A cave opened beyond, which he explored. Fifty years ago we wired that cave with lights and the power remains. It is a place only a few have seen. Once special, now forgotten. The fact that Brigham Young chose it as his vault for both the gold and what Lincoln sent him is no surprise."

Malone was right. She'd created this mess and it was up to her to fix it. How to accomplish that was still a mystery, but she'd figure it out. Doubtful either Luke or Cotton would find her, since they had no idea of the real locale. True, Charles Snow could tell them. But by the time they retreated to the cars, learned the truth, and returned it would all be over.

Ahead she spotted the cave entrance, framed by a doorway of pine poles iced with green moss. An iron gate at its center hung half open, a destroyed padlock on the ground. She retrieved it and saw the damage. Now she new why three shots had been fired.

She tossed the lock aside and found her gun.

Ahead was a lighted passage.

Time to practice what she preached.

Two steps and she was inside.

MALONE WAS FURIOUS.

He'd pushed Stephanie, and now she was walking into something that she was ill equipped to handle.

"Pappy, nothin' about this is good," Luke said as they raced up the trail.

"She's going to get herself killed."

"Let's not let that happen."

"That's certainly the plan. Unfortunately, we have no idea what's up there. Unless you know something I don't."

"Not this time. She kept me in the dark."

He stared up the trail. Everyone had a head start on them.

"It's just you and me," he said to Luke.

"I get that. And I'm with you, all the way."

SIXTY-SIX

✯

CASSIOPEIA WAS IMPRESSED. THE CHAMBER THEY
stood inside was twenty meters across, that much
and more wide, and that tall. Stalactites hung like
icicles. Needlelike crystals and smooth and spiral-
ing helictites corkscrewed downward. Draperies of
orange calcite stretched down, thin as paper, which
allowed light from the incandescent fixtures to
shine through to a spectacular effect. Popcorn
clumps of white rock dotted the walls. Toward the
center was a pool of still green water, its surface as
flat and reflective as a mirror. On one edge stood a
plinth that displayed an enormous statue of the
angel Moroni. Four meters high, sculpted from
stone, in the familiar pose of blowing a trumpet,
everything sheathed in gold leaf.

She stepped close to the image.

"**Having the everlasting gospel to preach unto them that dwell on the earth, and to every nation, and kindred, and tongue, and people,**" Rowan said. "Revelation 14:6. Moroni is our messenger from heaven. This is the plaster original from which the hammered copper statue atop the Salt Lake temple was fashioned. Brigham Young himself brought this here."

Josepe was clearly in awe. "He is the angel of light, who wore a loose robe of most exquisite whiteness. A whiteness beyond anything ever seen. His whole person glorious beyond description."

Rowan nodded. "You quote the prophet well. That is exactly how Joseph Smith described Moroni, and it's how we try to depict him."

"But he's golden, not white," she said.

"Our way of accentuating the brightness."

But she wasn't so sure.

She'd read once that Smith may have come across the name Moroni from reading the treasure-hunting stories of William Kidd. Legend held that Kidd buried his treasure on the Comoros Islands. Moroni was the capital city of the Union of the Comoros. Smith also named the hill where he found the golden plates Cumorah. Coincidence? If so, she wondered about the odds.

"This is an underground temple," Rowan said. "Created long ago by the prophets as a place of worship inside the earth. Few come here anymore. But this is where Prophet Brigham hid what Abraham Lincoln gave him."

She'd already surveyed the chamber. Except for the statue and the artificial lighting, there was nothing else man-made in sight.

"The one time I came," Rowan said, "there were artifacts on display from the Spanish. Pieces of bone, buttons, bits of iron, and shoulder yokes. The yokes were cut from cedar, about three feet wide, with a curve in the center to fit the bearer's neck. There were notches on each end to secure heavy, rawhide ore sacks. I was amazed how they'd survived the centuries."

But no artifacts were here now.

"Where do we look?" Josepe asked.

"In a moment," Rowan said. "First, there is a matter we must deal with."

The senator pointed a finger her way.

"This woman is a spy."

SALAZAR WAS SHOCKED BY THE APOSTLE'S DECLARATION. "A spy? You're mistaken."

"Am I? Ask yourself, Josepe, how did she reenter your life? After so many years, and at this precise moment."

"She's been nothing but helpful."

"As spies are. How else can they ingratiate themselves? You pressed me yesterday about how I learned of this place. I finally revealed that I possessed a source within the government, one who is close to our enemies. That source told me not only this location, but that this woman is working for the president of the United States."

"And you believed that?" Cassiopeia asked. "Of course your enemies want to create confusion in your ranks. What better way than to provide false information."

"How did that source know your exact name?" Rowan asked. "How did the source even know you existed?"

Salazar waited for a reply.

"I can only assume," she said, "that your source is in the intelligence business, aware of what that man Malone has been doing."

"Interesting you mention his name. My source also said you not only know Cotton Malone, but that you are romantically linked with him."

"Is that true?" Salazar demanded, his voice rising.

CASSIOPEIA FELT CAGED.

Stephanie had intentionally compromised her,

surely in response to her breaking off all contact and stealing the watch.

She heard the anger in Josepe's question.

Two options.

Lie or tell the truth.

SALAZAR WAITED FOR AN ANSWER, UNSURE WHAT might come from Cassioepia's mouth. The fact that she'd not instantly denied the accusation gave him pause. His heart thudded, and his breathing had gone shallow. His head spun.

The angel appeared.

Hovering near the statue of Moroni, the face unadorned with its usual reassuring smile.

"We might have been wrong about her."

He could not reply, so he simply shook his head, ever so gently, refusing to acknowledge the fact.

"Do not be ashamed, Josepe. The time for pretense is over. Reveal me to them. Let them know that the prophets are with you."

He'd never spoken of the angel to anyone.

"What are you looking at?" Rowan asked him.

He ignored the elder and focused on the vision.

"Protect me."

And he saw something on the angel's face he'd never before seen.

Concern.

His right hand plunged beneath his jacket and found the gun.

⋆ ⋆ ⋆

STEPHANIE HAD SLOWLY WORKED HER WAY through the passage, following lights toward voices. She'd traversed one small chamber, then found a larger one, slipping inside unnoticed among more illuminated rock formations. She'd listened as Rowan, Salazar, and Cassiopeia talked, Salazar angry over what Rowan had revealed.

"Josepe," Rowan said. "I speak the truth. This woman is a spy. She's no different from those who turned on us during the Time of Troubles. How many of our brothers went to prison thanks to spies? I'm your elder. I have never lied to you, and I am not lying now."

But Salazar's focus was not on the senator, but toward the statue on the plinth, his eyes far off, head toward the cavern ceiling.

Odd.

Salazar's right hand held a gun.

Stephanie found her own weapon.

No.

That would only inflame the situation.

There was just one way. She'd been unsure what to do when she entered, but now the path was clear. She laid the gun down, stepped from her hiding place, and called out, "He's telling the truth."

All three whirled her way.

"I'm his source."

Rowan was shocked at Stephanie Nelle's appearance.

She had no business here.

He watched as she slowly approached. Salazar's weapon was now trained on her, and he did not like the wild look in the Spaniard's eyes.

"Who are you?" Salazar demanded.

"Stephanie Nelle. United States Justice Department. Tell him, Cassiopeia. Tell him the truth."

"What truth?" Salazar called out.

Nelle kept her eyes locked on Vitt. "Tell him what you've wanted to say to him."

"Rowan is right. I am a spy."

An incredulous look came over Salazar's face. "That can't be. I refuse to believe that."

"It's true," Vitt said. "This woman asked me to make contact with you on behalf of the American government, and I did. But I stayed on my own." She paused. "I remember you as a good, kind, gentle man. Those memories were dear and precious. What happened, Josepe? What changed your soul?"

Salazar did not answer. Instead his attention seemed again diverted to the statue, lips moving but no sound emanating.

"What is it you see?" Vitt asked.

"Brother Salazar," Rowan said.

"The Prophet Joseph is here. He has been with me for some time." Salazar pointed with his gun at Vitt. "He, too, was deceived by you."

"She's not the only one who fooled you," Nelle said, pointing his way.

"The senator is a spy, too."

SIXTY-SEVEN

⭐

LUKE MEANT WHAT HE'D TOLD MALONE. HE HAD his back. Stephanie had misled them both and was now in deep trouble. They had to work this together. No bickering, no debate. Malone had read Cassiopeia Vitt perfectly in Iowa, staying one step ahead. He also knew Stephanie better than Luke did. Unfortunately for them both, they were now at least two steps behind the pack.

They'd jogged up the forested incline. Inside the tunnel they'd quickly reconnoitered a small lit chamber, then fled out another tunnel that led to a second interior hall. Everything was surreal, the rock formations like works of art, the lights working as paint on a canvas.

Malone raised a hand and signaled for them to stop.

Voices could be heard beyond the tunnel's exit.

They crept close to the end and he could see Vitt, Rowan, and Salazar, a gun in Salazar's hand pointed directly at Stephanie, who stood twenty feet from the Spaniard, her arms in the air.

His first instinct was to burst in.

They had two guns to Salazar's one.

But Malone seemed to read his mind and shook his head.

MALONE DID NOT LIKE ANY OF WHAT HE WAS seeing.

Stephanie had either been compromised or had compromised herself. He opted for the latter, especially after spotting her Beretta lying on the floor nestled close to a large boulder, hidden from view. She'd deliberately misled him and Luke to buy herself enough time to get here. She would have to assume that they would head back to Charles Snow, where they'd learn about the cavern, counting on the fifteen to twenty minutes of time she'd bought herself.

Thankfully, they'd cut that in half and were already here.

Think.
Be right.

✦ ✦ ✦

STEPHANIE STOOD WITH HER HANDS IN THE AIR and faced Salazar. She was not afraid, though she should be. Danny Daniels had told her that if a third party happened to intervene and cause havoc, who were they to interfere? But she'd understood what the president of the United States had not said. **And if you can cause that havoc, so much the better.**

"What do you mean Elder Rowan is a spy?" Salazar asked.

"He's a long-standing member of the U.S. Senate. He's taken an oath to uphold the laws and Constitution of this country. He is one of the most powerful men in Washington."

"I'm also a Latter-day Saint," Rowan said. "A duty I take even more seriously than my oath to this country."

She had to work this carefully.

Timing was everything.

"What the senator said about Cassiopeia is true. When I learned of the photograph you kept of you and her, I realized you might still care. I asked Cassiopeia if she would be willing to approach you and she agreed."

"Is that true?" Salazar asked.

Cassiopeia nodded. "I was told you were involved with some illegal activities. Even murder. I wanted to clear your name."

"Murder?" Rowan asked.

Stephanie said, "He murdered a man in Michigan for a Mormon journal. Then he killed one of my agents."

The senator seemed genuinely shocked by the information.

"Josepe," Rowan said. "Please tell me she's lying."

SALAZAR LOOKED TOWARD THE ANGEL FOR GUIDANCE.

"They know not what we face. We guard Saints and all they hold dear. Elder Rowan wanted that done. He cannot complain as to the methods."

"Their agent was sent to destroy us," he said. "My task was to not allow that to happen. The agent was not murdered. He was properly atoned, now with Heavenly Father enjoying his reward."

"You beat him," the new woman said. "Then you shot him. He had a wife and children."

"This woman's fault. Not yours."

"Josepe," Rowan said. "Is what she says true?"

"**Be not afraid.**"

"It is."

"Then you have greatly sinned."

"It has always been our way to offer atonement to our enemies. It was that way in the beginning, and remains so."

"No," Rowan declared. "We renounced violence long ago. Never is that a means to an end. I've spent my life working for a way for Saints to be independent, to be free of outside influence, with**out** violence."

Was he hearing right? He was being chastised for doing what was expected. And Cassiopeia?

"Why did you lie to me?" he asked her. "Why would you do such a thing?"

"It was necessary. What you've done is wrong."

"**How dare she. She must know her place.**"

"I am sworn to obey the prophets, and that is all I have done."

"When you suggested the formation of Danites," Rowan said, "never did I imagine you would go this far."

"**He is weak, Josepe. A fool, like all of the others. Do not tolerate it. We cannot tolerate it. Not any longer.**"

The angel was right.

"Prophet Joseph tells me that you are wrong," he said.

"Joseph Smith has been dead for over 150 years," the new woman said.

"Shut up," he yelled, jutting the gun her way, leveling the barrel at her chest. "Never say such a thing. He lives."

"Find out about the elder. We must know where he stands."

"Is he a traitor?" he asked her, motioning toward Rowan with the weapon.

ROWAN HAD ALLOWED SALAZAR A FREE REIN AND asked precious few questions, but he'd honestly never factored murder into the equation.

"Did you kill that man in Michigan, as Ms. Nelle says?" he asked.

"We needed his journal and he would not sell it. So he was atoned for his sin."

"Which was?"

"Greed. What else? And we're here today partly because of my act of kindness toward him."

"Is that how you describe murder?" he asked. "Kindness?"

"It is as the prophet declared." Salazar's attention returned to Nelle. "How is this apostle a traitor?"

"You're here to find a document Abraham Lincoln entrusted to the Mormons. So ask him, where is it?"

A question Rowan had been asking himself. He'd assumed that things would be obvious once here. But there was nothing inside **Falta Nada** except rocks, the pool, and a statue. Yet this was where Lincoln had directed. He'd seen the inside of the watch. But that was assuming both the watch and the image were genuine.

He pointed at Nelle. "She told me this was the place."

"And it is," she said. "This is the location Brigham Young gave Lincoln. Where the Mormon gold was stored. Lincoln etched it inside the watch. So where's the document?"

She'd posed the question straight to him.

He saw that Salazar was waiting for an answer.

But he had none.

Nelle lowered her arms. "He has no answer because there's nothing here. He's not your ally. In fact, he's your enemy. He tells you it's okay to form the Danites, then is upset how they operate. He wants results, but complains how they're obtained. He's a respected member of the U.S. Senate. Part of the government of the United States. Do you think for one moment he's going to assume any responsibility for any illegal acts you might have committed?"

She was baiting Salazar.

"Quit listening to her," he yelled.

Salazar faced him. "Why? Because she speaks the truth?"

"This has to end, Josepe."

"And it's about to get much worse," Nelle said. "There are more agents on their way here. All of this will soon be over. Senator Rowan knows that. We planned it together."

Rowan advanced toward Salazar.

The gun swung his way, halting his approach.

"Josepe," Rowan said in a calm voice. "You must listen to me."

CASSIOPEIA STOOD SILENT, LISTENING, TRYING TO gauge the depth of Josepe's madness. He claimed to see Joseph Smith, right here, right now. But she'd also caught the hurt in his eyes when, for a second time in his life, she'd wounded him.

"None of you move," Josepe said to Rowan.

"Is the prophet still here?" she asked.

"He watches all of you, as he watches over me."

"How long have you seen him?"

"Many years. But only recently did he reveal his true nature. I always thought him Moroni."

"Did the prophet tell you to kill my agent?" Stephanie asked.

Josepe threw her a glare. "He told me to offer

him an atonement for his sins so that he might enjoy eternal happiness. And that is what I did."

"You've been played for a fool," Stephanie said. "By Rowan and by Cassiopeia."

"Yet here I am, with a gun on you."

Cassiopeia realized that Stephanie was trying to provoke a reaction and, if she kept pressing, she'd get one. "Josepe, I'm asking you to lower the gun and end this. It's over."

"Over? It's only begun. Tell her, **Elder** Rowan. Tell her of the grand vision that is to become reality."

"Yes, Senator," Stephanie said. "Tell us of the coming glory. Of course, you'll need the document, signed by the founders, to make that happen. Have you remembered where it is yet?"

"You set me up," Rowan spat out. "You led me along and set me up."

"I told you the truth—every step of the way. **Falta Nada** was written inside Lincoln's watch. Mary Todd's letter was real, as were Madison's notes. I provided all of those to you. And by the way, did you share any of that with your cohort here?"

"Stop it," Cassiopeia yelled.

"Really?" Stephanie said. "You want to stop now? You certainly didn't want to stop when you went to Austria. Or when you flew to Iowa. Of course, your ex-lover didn't know the truth. You were lying to him. Using him. Doing **my** bidding."

"Shut up."

Stephanie homed in on Josepe. "Ask your prophet what the penalty is for lying."

SALAZAR DID NOT WANT TO LISTEN BUT HE COULD not block out the words. Cassiopeia herself had admitted that she lied. And Elder Rowan had no idea why they were actually here. All of that made him wonder. Was he being set up? Nelle had proclaimed that more agents were on the way. Perhaps he should leave and call his two men. But that could not be done from inside this cavern. Then there was the matter of Cassiopeia, Nelle, and Rowan.

"She's right, Josepe. The punishment for lying is severe. An atonement is in order. All three of these lost souls require your benevolence. Killing for the sake of the soul is no sin at all."

SIXTY-EIGHT

★

MALONE HAD HEARD ENOUGH. SALAZAR WAS nuts, that was clear. But the man was also armed. They could shoot their way in and be done with it, but that came with a risk of collateral damage.

Or they could finesse it.

He'd listened as Stephanie kept trying to provoke Salazar, confusing him with both Cassiopeia's and Rowan's betrayals. He had a good idea what she was doing, but he wasn't going to sit back and allow her to keep placing herself and Cassiopeia in the line of fire.

He whispered to Luke, "We have to go in there."

The younger man nodded.

He motioned with his gun and shook his head. "Not with these."

Luke seemed to understand.

But he wasn't foolish.

"I assume you carry two guns?" he whispered.

Luke slid up his right trouser leg to reveal a small revolver strapped to his lower leg. There was a time when he'd done the same thing. Luke freed the weapon and handed it over. He tucked it snugly at the base of Luke's spine, tight behind the belt.

Stay in front of me, he mouthed.

★ ★ ★

STEPHANIE KNEW THAT THIS PLACE HELD NOTH-ing. Before leaving Blair House the last thing Danny Daniels had told her was that the document had indeed once been housed here, during Lincoln's time, but not since. Charles Snow had told the president everything, and he'd passed the information on to her. She'd omitted giving those details to Rowan because she wanted him here, with Salazar and Cassiopeia. If she was right—and twenty years of second-guessing people had made her an expert—Cotton and Luke were now nearby.

"The penalty for lying **is** severe," Salazar said. "It always has been."

"I'm **not** lying," Stephanie said. "In fact, I'm the only one telling the truth. Senator Rowan still has not told you where the document is located. He can't, because he doesn't know. I'm the only one who knows. The idea was to get you here, so I could deal with you. He was a party to that."

"Deal with me?" Salazar asked.

She leveled her gaze. "The penalty for killing my agent is severe, too."

"Brigham Young made a mistake trusting the federal government," Rowan said. "Lincoln was truly different, but the presidents who came after him were not. They were all snakes. This woman is just like them, Josepe. I've never trusted the government. You know that."

"Reveal the document," Salazar said.

Stephanie heard a new resolve in the voice.

A test?

"FEDERAL AGENTS," MALONE CALLED OUT, keeping himself and Luke concealed in the passageway. "It's over, Salazar. You're finished."

He peered past the tunnel's edge and saw the Spaniard react, lunging toward Stephanie, wrapping an arm around her neck, jamming the gun into her jugular.

"Come out," Salazar screamed.

He motioned and Luke led the way.

They both held Berettas, their arms in the air, weapons clearly visible. He was hoping Salazar was not thinking clearly and the obvious would be enough.

"Toss those guns into the water," Salazar demanded.

They hesitated a moment, then obeyed.

"Is that all of you?"

"Just us two amigos," Luke said. "But that ought to be plenty."

He nearly smiled. Had to love that cocksure can-do.

He kept Luke ahead of him, the gun in sight, only a foot or so away. He caught Stephanie's gaze and tried to register what she was thinking. He glanced at Cassiopeia, who stared at him with vacant eyes. Nothing about this had gone right, as far as she was concerned.

"I should have shot you in Salzburg," Salazar said to him. "When I had the chance."

"Who stopped you?" Stephanie asked.

Salazar said nothing.

Stephanie pointed at Cassiopeia. "She did."

CASSIOPEIA KNEW ENOUGH ABOUT COTTON TO realize that he hadn't appeared without a fail-safe. Both he and the younger man, the same one from Iowa, had too freely relinquished their weapons.

They could have just as easily kept themselves hidden and attacked at will. Instead, now they stood with their hands in the air, vulnerable.

Or were they?

"Josepe, please, I beg you," she said. "Lay down your gun. Don't do this."

"Do you know Malone?"

She nodded.

"Are you . . . involved with him?"

She hesitated, but there was no way out.

Another nod.

"You lied to me about everything," he yelled. "You've not experienced any reawakening. The words of the prophet haven't moved you. You mock all that is holy."

"You're not the man I once knew."

"I'm exactly the same man. I was then, and am now, a devout follower of the Prophet Joseph Smith. Heavenly Father has sent the prophet to me. He is here now, watching all of you. He is my guidance. **He** never lies."

"It's not real," she told him.

The gun shifted among them all, staying aimed, a shaking finger on the trigger. She knew Josepe was an expert marksman, but his mind was wavering.

"Brother Salazar," Rowan said. "I'm leaving. I will no longer be a part of this."

"See. He leaves you to do the dirty work," Stephanie said. "That way he can deny any involvement. Ask the vision if that's what **he** wants this apostle to do."

Josepe's gaze darted toward the statue, where he stared for a moment.

"Do you really see him?" Cassiopeia asked.

He nodded. "A wondrous sight."

"Josepe," Rowan said, his voice filled with pity.

"See what he thinks of you," Cotton said. "He allowed you to kill that agent in Denmark. Fine by him, as long as it's you pulling the trigger. Now he doesn't care what you do to us, just so long as he's not a part of it."

Rowan turned and started to walk away.

"Stop," Josepe screamed.

The senator hesitated, turned his head, and said, "And what will you do? Shoot me? I'm a member of the Quorum of Twelve Apostles. You profess so much obedience. So I assume that means something to you."

"He's abandoning you," Stephanie said. "Leaving you to us. But you can't kill us all—not before we get you. Do you really think I brought only two agents?"

Actually, Cassiopeia believed just that.

Bad enough what Josepe had already done.

She could not allow him to do any more.

⭐ ⭐ ⭐

SALAZAR'S MIND REELED.

He stared again at the angel.

"I was the prophet, the seer, the revelator. I was the dictator in the things of God and it was the duty of the faithful to listen to me and do as I told them."

That he knew to be true.

"It was my plan to form a temporal kingdom that would be subject to no laws of any government. We would make our own laws and have our own civil officers to execute them. When their edicts were sent forth they would be obeyed, without a murmur."

That was his dream, too.

"Brother Salazar," Rowan said. "Look at me."

He turned from the vision.

"There is nothing there. Joseph Smith is dead. He's not providing any guidance."

"He speaks blasphemy. He insults me. I am his prophet. Make him obey."

⭐ ⭐ ⭐

LUKE KEPT EVERY MUSCLE LIMBER, READY TO react, his nerves electrified. Salazar could go any which way and he had to be ready to counter. He could feel the gun pressed at his spine. Malone stayed just behind him, to his left, where a right hand could easily retrieve the weapon. But not with Salazar's gaze tight on them. They'd need a distraction, preferably one that did not entail anyone getting shot.

"Brother Salazar," Rowan said. "I will pray to Heavenly Father for your soul, for you have lost your way."

"If he did," Stephanie said, "it was because of you. Tell me, Senor Salazar, who encouraged you to form the Danites? Who directed you every step of the way? Who gave all of the commands? And who obeyed? Now ask yourself, is this man, this **United** States senator, with you or against you?"

Salazar was obviously rattled.

"Which one?" Salazar asked Rowan. "For? Or against?"

SALAZAR WAITED FOR AN ANSWER TO HIS QUES-tion. As did the angel, who watched Elder Rowan with a stern gaze.

"I did not encourage or condone murder," Rowan said. "I never have."

"**We murdered no one**," the angel said. "**We saved those sinners from the cold and the dark-**

ness. **That is good and just and right. He is against us, Josepe. The woman speaks the truth.**"

"I did not commit murder. I atoned sinners. That is our way."

"No," Rowan said. "It is not. No one and nothing in our church condones such an atrocity. What you did is wrong in every way."

He was hurt by the rebuke.

"We had a grand vision," Rowan said. "A new Zion. Just as Prophet Joseph wanted. That is still within our grasp. But you, and your foolishness, have placed it all in jeopardy."

"Where is the document?" he demanded.

"I thought it was here. I was wrong."

"And now he intends to leave you to these enemies."

Rowan turned and walked away.

The others stood and watched him.

He still held the gun, finger on the trigger, Cassiopeia's eyes pleading with him.

"Do it."

I can't.

"Then you are no better than him. You have failed me."

That rebuke he could not bear. The angel had been with him a long time, never yielding, guiding him to this precise moment when he must decide what was more important.

Now or eternity?

He'd always thought the choice clear.

More than anything else, he was loyal to the prophets.

So he swung the gun around and fired.

ROWAN HEARD THE BLAST THEN FELT THE BULLET as it pierced his right shoulder from behind. At first it was as if someone had shoved him with violence, then a searing pain exploded upward and out, an agony he'd never felt before.

He staggered a few steps, then turned.

Pain both weakened and alarmed him.

Salazar still had his gun aimed.

He opened his mouth to protest, to ask why, to question the foolishness of such an irrational act, but another blast filled his ears.

And the world ended.

SIXTY-NINE

STEPHANIE WATCHED AS SENATOR THADDEUS Rowan died.

Neither she, Luke, Cotton, nor Cassiopeia moved.

Everyone kept still as Salazar ended a problem.

One down.

Two to go.

CASSIOPEIA WINCED AS JOSEPE COMMITTED MURder. Her first thought was revulsion, her second anger.

"You did this," she screamed at Stephanie. "You pushed him."

"This man is a murderer. Even worse, he's a delusional murderer. He actually thinks he's doing good."

"I am a warrior of God. Server of the prophets," Salazar said, the gun now aimed straight at Stephanie. "Get. On. Your. Knees."

"Is that what the angel wants?"

"You mock him?"

Cassiopeia decided to try, "Josepe. Please. Leave these people be and let's you and I go."

"**You** lied to me. You used me. You're as bad they are."

"I'm not like them at all."

Josepe gestured with the gun at Stephanie. "I told you to kneel."

✷ ✷ ✷

MALONE REALIZED THIS WAS GOING TO BE TRICKY.

Salazar was deranged. But that didn't mean he could not be led. In fact, it might make the task easier. He caught Stephanie's gaze and gave her a slight nod of his head, enough for her to know he was with her.

So she knelt on the dry ground.

Luke stood in front of him, both of them holding their arms at their sides, the gun no more than a foot away, hidden from everyone's view but his. He searched his eidetic memory for what he'd read in the book back at his shop. Salazar clearly lived in the past, so the past would be his weapon.

He said, "**Wherefore, this is the land of promise and the place for the city of Zion. And thus saith the Lord your God, if you will receive wisdom here is wisdom.**"

"You know the Doctrine and Covenants?"

"I've read it. **Verily this is the word of the Lord that the city New Jerusalem shall be built by the gathering of the Saints.**"

"And we built it. In Ohio. Missouri. Illinois. And finally in Salt Lake. If you know our teachings then you know that the Prophet Joseph declared that the redemption of Zion comes only by power."

"Yet you have none."

"I have this gun. I have my enemy on her knees. I have the rest of you at my mercy."

"**You elders of Israel, have you not entered into a covenant with God that you never would betray one another? A covenant not to speak against the anointed.**" He was quoting more of what he'd read, a statement made by one of the early church elders.

"Every Saint pledges that," Salazar said. "We must stay together. We draw our strength from being together."

"Yet you were surrounded by liars," Stephanie said.

★ ★ ★

SALAZAR TRIED TO KEEP REALITY IN FOCUS, BUT too much assaulted him. Luckily the angel had remained, watching, staying silent, allowing him time to think. He was angry at everyone, Cassiopeia included. Elder Rowan lay on the ground, his body still, almost certainly dead.

"Shedding human blood is necessary for the remission of sin," the angel said. **"The apostle sinned. He is with Heavenly Father now, happy, and will thank you one day. His tortured soul could only be saved through the shedding of his blood."**

He felt comforted by the knowledge.

Still, Rowan had been a chosen man.

Had he done wrong atoning him?

"Don't be alarmed if there be curiosities in Zion. If I wished to find the best men in the world, I should go to Zion to find them. If I wished to find the biggest devil, I would also look in Zion. For among the people of God there I can find the greatest scamps."

Which surely explained Rowan's betrayal.

What now? he asked in his head, staring at the apparition.

His enemy still knelt before him.

"She must be atoned."

He agreed.

"All of them must be atoned."

Including Cassiopeia?

"Her most of all. She betrayed you to our enemies."

"Salazar."

Malone's voice jarred him from the vision.

"It's done."

"No, it's not."

"Yes, it is," Cassiopeia said.

He swung the gun her way. "Don't say that. Don't ever say that. You have not earned the right to pass judgment on me, or anyone else."

"Are you going to shoot me?" she asked.

"Atone her."

"I can't," he called out. "I can't."

STEPHANIE WAS CONCERNED FOR CASSIOPEIA. Salazar was now not only seeing things, he was talking to them. There was no telling what he would do next. She assumed Luke and Cotton had things under control. They'd freely shed their weapons, which meant that at least one of them was still armed. She'd noticed how Cotton stayed close to Luke, keeping him to his right, in front of him, never far away.

That could not be unintentional.

And thankfully, in his present state Salazar was incapable of noticing anything.

CASSIOPEIA TOOK A STEP TOWARD JOSEPE.

He reacted by re-aiming the gun her way, his eyes alight with rage.

"Remember when we were young," she said, her voice low. "When we were together. When you first loved me."

"I think of it every day."

"Those were innocent times. We can't ever go back to them, but we can have something new and different. Lay down your gun and give this up."

"The prophet commands me to fight."

"There is no prophet here."

"I wish you could see him. He's so beautiful, bathed in light, full of goodness. He has never led me astray."

"Josepe, they won't hurt you if you're unarmed."

"They can't hurt me."

She stared at Cotton and the younger man. "I'm afraid they can. They're just waiting for the chance to kill you."

Not a hint of fear filled any of the eyes that watched her. Instead she read calculation in the cool gazes that came from all three professionals. Josepe was no match for them. They knew it. He didn't.

"Please," she said. "I beg you. None of them will shoot an unarmed man."

Josepe seemed puzzled.

"Don't you see," she said. "They came here to kill you. Neither you, nor Rowan, was going to leave here alive."

"How do you know that?"

"Because it was her job to lead you here," Stephanie said.

LUKE CRINGED AT STEPHANIE'S WORDS. ON HER knees, with no weapon, but still on the offensive. Gotta give it to her. He formed a new respect for his boss.

"She's only trying to antagonize you," Cassiopeia said. "She can't, if you lay down the weapon and surrender."

"You have no power over me any longer."

"Josepe, you have to listen. These people know what they're doing. You're not in control."

"They don't seem like a problem to me," Salazar said. "Killing them would be easy."

"Then do it," Luke said.

"I might just blow your knees away and let you

live as a cripple the rest of your life. That's what you deserve. Death may be too good for any of you."

"Does that include me?" Cassiopeia asked.

"Your thoughts are impure. Your motives tainted. You played with me years ago, and again over the past few days. So yes, it includes you."

★ ★ ★

MALONE SPIED THE DISTANCE BETWEEN HIS RIGHT hand and the gun nestled at Luke's spine. Eighteen inches. Tops. It rested facing away, making it easy for his hand to secure a grip. But that had to be done quickly and carefully, signaling nothing to Salazar. Cassiopeia had read their intentions. Thankfully, Salazar was confused enough to not know exactly who to believe.

"Josepe," Cassiopeia said. "I want you to lay the gun down and come with me. You and I can work this through."

"How?"

"I don't know. We'll figure it out. Don't make it any worse. There's no escaping here."

Salazar chuckled. "You underestimate me. My two men are out there waiting. I think this is all of the government we're going to see. I would imagine if there were more we would have seen them already."

Salazar aimed the gun at Stephanie.

Cassiopeia stepped in between, daring him to fire.

Malone's hand eased toward the gun.

"I'm not going to allow you to do this," Cassiopeia said. "You're going to have to shoot her through me."

"I feel nothing for you," Salazar made clear. "Not anymore."

SALAZAR FOUGHT TO KEEP HIS COMPOSURE.

"She should expect no more protection from you than the wolf might find or the dog the shepherd finds killing the sheep. It is our duty to wipe all of the unclean from our midst. Let Heavenly Father deal with them."

The angel glared at him.

"When a man prays for a thing, he ought to be willing to perform it himself."

That he should.

"Kill them all. Start with the lying temptress."

MALONE'S HAND WRAPPED AROUND THE GUN. HE felt Luke tense as his finger found the trigger. Cassiopeia had diverted Salazar's attention enough to allow the move to go unnoticed.

589 / THE LINCOLN MYTH

"If you turn and trample the holy commandments of God," Salazar said to Cassiopeia, "and break your sacred and solemn covenants, becoming traitors to the people of God, would you not be worthy of death?"

"You cannot do—"

"You have committed a sin that cannot be forgiven in this world."

Salazar's voice rose.

"Let the smoke ascend that the incense thereof may come before God as atonement for your sins."

Malone heard the magic word.

Atonement.

His grip on the gun tightened, but he hadn't yet freed it from Luke's belt.

"Stop this," Cassiopeia said. "Stop it now."

"You are no different from Judas, who deceived and betrayed Jesus Christ."

Salazar was yelling.

Working up courage.

"No different at all. The prophets say that we should suffer our bowels to be taken out before forfeiting the covenant we have made with God. Judas was like salt that had lost its saving principles, good for nothing but to be cast out and trodden under the foot of man."

He slid the gun free.

"One," he whispered to Luke, his lips not moving.

"I love you, Josepe."

Cassiopeia's words sliced his heart.

Was it true, or simply designed to stand Salazar down?

"You're not worthy of love," Salazar bellowed back. "You are not to be believed."

"Please."

Tears streamed down her face.

"Please, Josepe."

The Spaniard's attention was totally on her. Stephanie remained on her knees, back straight, head high, watching. The gun was leveled at Cassiopeia's chest. Malone resented the hell out of being placed in this position. Stephanie had come to end the problem.

But the task had fallen to him.

"Two," he breathed.

SALAZAR STEELED HIMSELF.

"If the gentiles wish to see a few tricks," the angel said, "we can perform them. They call you a devil. That is not an insult. We Saints have the meanest devils on the earth in our midst. We cannot attain our endowment without those devils being present. We cannot make progress, nor prosper in the kingdom of God, without them. We have always had a need among us for those who steal our fence poles, or the hay from a neighbor's stack, or the corn from a field. These men have always served a need. As you do."

He resented being called a devil, but understood what the vision was saying. Tough jobs had always required tough men. He watched as Cassiopeia's tears increased. He'd never seen her cry before, and the sight was disconcerting.

And those words.

I love you.

They gave him pause.

"Heavenly Father will have mercy on all of their souls."

That he liked.

"We shall possess the earth because it belongs to Jesus Christ, and he belongs to us, and we to him. We are all one and we will take the kingdom and possess it, under the whole heavens and reign over it forever and ever. All ye kings and emperors and presidents help yourselves, if you can."

"That is true," he said to the vision.

"Nations will bow to our kingdom and all hell cannot stop it. Do your duty. Do it now."

"THREE."

Malone swung the gun around as Luke dropped to the ground.

He aimed the weapon.

Salazar reacted, shifting left.

"No," Cassiopeia screamed.

"Drop the gun," Malone yelled. "Don't make me do it."

Salazar's arm never stopped, the black dot of the barrel homing in on him.

No choice.

Malone fired.

The round found Salazar's chest, staggering him backward. Salazar regained his balance and never hesitated, again re-aiming his weapon.

Malone fired a second time.

To the head.

The bullet entered through a neat crimson hole, then exploded out the back, blood and brains splattering on the rocks.

SALAZAR LOOKED FOR THE ANGEL. BUT THE VI-sion was gone.

He still held the gun, but no muscle in his body seemed to work. He lingered for a moment, his muscles shutting down, yet he was still aware of the surroundings.

Blackness enveloped.

The world blinked in and out.

The last thing he saw was Cassiopeia's face.

And his last thought was a wish that things had been different between them.

CASSIOPEIA RUSHED TO JOSEPE AS HE DROPPED TO the hard earth. No question he was dead. Cotton had shot him twice, once in the chest, once in the head. Just like she knew would happen.

Stephanie stood.

Contempt filled Cassiopeia's eyes and she glared at Cotton. "Are you satisfied now?"

"I gave him a chance to stop."

"Not much of one."

"He would have shot you."

"No, he wouldn't. You both should have let me handle this."

"That was impossible," Stephanie said.

"You're murderers."

"No, we're not," Stephanie said, her voice rising.

"You tell yourself that. Make yourself feel better. But you're not a damn bit different than he was."

SEVENTY

★

Washington, D.C.
Monday, October 13
4:50 a.m.

Stephanie followed Danny Daniels as they climbed the steps inside the Washington Monument. The president had walked from the White House in the predawn chill. She'd been waiting for him outside the lower entrance. He'd called her yesterday, on the flight back from Utah, and told her to be here.

She and Luke had returned alone. Cotton had taken another flight overseas to Copenhagen. Cassiopeia had stayed, intent on returning Salazar's body to Spain. At **Falta Nada** the air had been tense afterward, Cassiopeia refusing to speak to any of them. Malone had tried to approach her, but she'd rebuked him. Wisely, he opted to leave her alone. Cassiopeia had been partly right. They **were** murderers. Only with a free pass to stay out of jail. She'd always wondered why it was right to kill in her business. All that **greater good** crap, she supposed. But killing was killing, no matter where, how, or why.

"My boy did good, didn't he?" Daniels asked her, as they climbed.

She knew who **my boy** was. "Luke handled himself like a pro."

"He's goin' to be fine. You're going to be glad you have him. I even think he and I might make our peace."

She was glad that Danny had settled another score.

One more step toward retirement.

She'd never been inside the Washington Monument. Strange, considering she'd seen it thousands of times. Just one of those visits that had always been delayed. Made entirely of marble, granite, and bluestone gneiss, the 555-foot obelisk carried the distinction of being the tallest stone structure in the world. It had stood since 1884, when its capstone was finally laid. A rare East Coast earthquake a few years back damaged its exterior, which took three years to repair.

"Any reason why we can't use the elevator?" she asked him.

"You'll see."

"Where are we going?"

The Secret Service waited at the bottom of the staircase, which right-angled its way from the ground to the top—a long climb, 897 risers, as the site superintendent had explained below.

"Only about halfway up," he said. "What is it? You out of shape?"

She smiled. He seemed back to his old self. "I can keep up with you anytime, anywhere."

He stopped and turned back. "I'll hold you to that."

"I sincerely hope so."

They were alone, both of them comfortable with the other. Soon he would not be the president of the United States and she would not be his employee.

She pointed to what he was holding.

A laptop computer.

"I was unaware you could use one of those?"

"I'll have you know that I'm actually quite good on one."

He offered nothing more as to why he'd brought it along, but she'd expected little.

They started to climb more stairs.

Along the way, embedded into the exterior walls were commemorative stones, carved with patriotic messages from donors. She'd noticed references to particular towns, cities, and states, many countries, Masonic lodges, Bible verses, maps, military regiments, colleges, a bit of anything and everything.

"Were these all donated?" she asked.

"Every one. All in honor of George Washington. There are 193 of them inside."

They hadn't spoken of Rowan or Salazar, beyond her curt report that both had died, neither at the hand of anyone officially connected to the U.S. government. Charles Snow had been waiting for them outside the cave, a sad, forlorn look on his face. U.S. Army personnel were dispatched to remove the bodies. All evidence of a gunshot was removed from Rowan's remains, the wound erased by an extensive autopsy performed by military pathologists. The senator's family had been told that he died of a heart attack while on church business with the prophet. He would be given an elaborate funeral in Salt Lake sometime this week. Salazar's body was released to Cassiopeia, who flew to Spain aboard Salazar's jet.

Daniels stopped ahead of her on the next platform. "This is the 220-foot level. My thighs actually do ache. I'm not accustomed to that kind of workout."

Hers were throbbing, too.

"We're here for that," he said, pointing to another of the commemorative stones.

She studied the rectangle, this one featuring

what appeared to be a beehive resting atop a table. Above the hive was an all-seeing eye that radiated downward, revealing the words HOLINESS TO THE LORD, which crowned the hive. Beneath the table was carved DESERET. An assortment of three-dimensional trumpets, flowers, vines, and leaves sprang from the stone.

"This was donated in September 1868 by Brigham Young himself. The stone was quarried in Utah and carved by a Mormon pioneer named William Ward. The beehive was the symbol for the state of Deseret, which is what Young wanted to call his new land. Of course, we had other ideas. It would be nearly thirty years before statehood came their way, but this clearly illustrates Young's early intentions."

Daniels hinged open the laptop and laid it on the steps leading up from where they stood. The screen came to life with an image of Charles Snow.

"It's real early out where you are," the president said to the prophet.

"That it is. But I haven't slept much these past few days."

"I know the feeling. Me either."

"I've been praying for Elder Rowan and Brother Salazar. I only hope Heavenly Father is kind to them."

"We did what had to be done. You know that's true."

"I wonder how many of my predecessors said the same thing. They did things, too, that they thought had to be done. But does it make them right?"

"They gave us no choice," the president said. "None at all."

"I see the stone behind you. It's been a long time since I gazed upon it. I visited the monument once, long ago, when you could still climb the stairs and see them."

She wondered what was happening. Why the cyberlink to Utah, which she assumed was on an encoded line?

"Our church has always cherished stone," Snow said. "It is our preferred building material. Maybe because it is harder to destroy. Our wooden temples never stood for long, most burned away by mobs. Finally, once we began to construct them of thick rock, they endured. To this day, nearly all of those early structures remain."

She stared again at the donation from Utah.

"Stone has also held another special purpose," Snow said. "Joseph Smith first glimpsed the golden plates inside a stone box. On October 2, 1841, Smith placed the original manuscript of Book of Mormon inside the Nauvoo Hotel cornerstone. Brigham Young sealed documents and coins inside the cornerstone for the Salt Lake temple, a practice that has been repeated many times at other temples. For us, sealing things inside rock is a sign of reverence."

It hit her. "The document from the founders is here?"

"Brigham Young thought it only fitting that it be returned to Washington," Snow said. "So he sealed it inside his gift for the monument. This he told to John Taylor, the man who ultimately succeeded him, and the secret has been passed from prophet to prophet. We revere this nation, and are honored to be a part of it. Only a few, like Rowan, thought otherwise. But these men were anomalies, no different from the radicals of any other religion. The men who ultimately rose to lead this church realized the gravity of what they knew, so they kept the secret. As they should."

"Is that why Nixon was rebuffed in 1970?" Daniels asked.

"Precisely. There was no way the information would be revealed. Rowan, to his credit, is the first to ever learn as much as he did. But being next in line gave him access few others had ever possessed. Being a senator opened up even more resources."

She stepped to the commemorative stone and lightly caressed its pale gray surface. Behind the façade hid a document that could dismantle the United States of America.

"Why am I here?" she asked. "Why allow me to know this?"

"Those deaths weigh on us all," Daniels said. "You have a right to know that what they died for actually exists."

She appreciated the gesture. But she'd been around the block too many times to count. A lot of people had died on her watch. None of the deaths was easy, and none was forgotten.

"Abraham Lincoln's reputation remains intact," Snow said from the screen. "As it should. Every nation needs its heroes."

"The greatest enemy of truth is often not the lie—deliberate, contrived and dishonest—but the myth—persistent, persuasive and unrealistic."

She was impressed with Daniels' statement and asked about its source.

"John Kennedy. And he's right. A myth is so much harder to counter than a lie. We'll allow the Lincoln myth to continue. It seems to have served this country well."

"Within the White Horse Prophecy," Snow said, "the people of the Rocky Mountains, Saints, were described as the White Horse. It was said they will establish Zion and guard the Constitution. The people of the United States were the Pale Horse. The Black Horse was the force of darkness threatening the Constitution. Then there was the Red Horse, not specifically identified, but noted as a powerful force that would play a key role."

Snow paused.

"Ms. Nelle, you, Mr. Malone, and the young Mr. Daniels are that Red Horse. Joseph Smith said that he **loved the Constitution. It was made by the inspiration of God and it will be preserved and saved by the efforts of the White Horse and by the Red Horse who will combine in its defense.** We've always thought that prophecy suspect, created long after the Civil War, more fiction than truth, but everything played out exactly as predicted. So whoever may have created the prophecy was right."

"What do we do about what's inside this stone?" she asked.

"Nothing," Daniels said. "There it will stay."

"And Madison's notes on the subject?"

"I burned them."

She was shocked to hear that, but understood the necessity. Katie Bishop had already been sworn to secrecy, on threat of criminal prosecution. But with no tangible evidence, anything she might say would never be believed.

"All is as it was," Daniels said.

But she wondered about that.

CASSIOPEIA ENTERED THE SMALL GRAVEYARD ADjacent to the Salazar estate. About fifty graves filled the grassy space. Sacred ground, where for over a century Salazars had been laid to rest. She'd arrived yesterday and arranged for Josepe's body to be cremated. True, that was not the Mormon way, but little Josepe had done fit into that category. Even if heaven existed and there actually was a God, she doubted Josepe would be in His presence.

The sins had been far too great.

Though Josepe had several siblings she'd contacted none of them. Instead, she'd arranged for people from her estate to be at the airport and transport the body to a local crematorium, which accommodated her request for a quick incineration. She'd decided that it was far too complicated to explain to brothers and sisters as to how one of their own had spiraled into insanity. And she certainly could not tell them the U.S. government had sanctioned their brother's death.

Her anger remained hot. There'd been no need to kill Josepe. She could have wrestled him under control. Apparently, the threat he posed was so great that murder had become the only acceptable option.

Some of that she could understand.

But not enough to make it right.

Cotton should not have pulled that trigger.

And not just once.

But twice.

Unforgivable, no matter what Josepe had done.

That's why there were courts. But Stephanie never could have allowed him to speak publicly. Instead, he had to be silenced.

One of her employees had already dug a hole large enough for the silver urn. She would place Josepe there and, eventually, explain to his family what happened, leaving out the awful parts, noting that their brother had simply crossed a line from which there'd been no return.

But that would be another time.

Today, she would say her own goodbye.

★ ★ ★

MALONE STEPPED FROM BEHIND THE COUNTER IN his bookshop. Business was light, usual for a Monday morning. He'd arrived home twenty-four hours ago after an all-night flight from Salt Lake City through Paris. He could not remember when he'd ever been this rattled. Cassiopeia had said little to him, storming off from **Falta Nada.**

He was frustrated, tired, and jet-lagged.

Nothing new, except for the frustrated part.

His employees had, once again, done a masterful job of keeping the store running. They were the best. He'd given them all the day off, deciding to handle things himself. Which actually helped his mood, as he didn't feel like socializing.

He stepped to one of the plate-glass windows and stared out at Højbro Plads. The day was wet and stormy, but people still hustled back and forth. It had all started right here, in the shop, five days ago with a call from Stephanie. He wondered about Luke Daniels and what the young man would do next. He'd wished him well in Salt Lake and hoped that, maybe, one day their paths might cross again.

His thoughts were interrupted by the opening of the front door.

A FedEx deliveryman entered with a package that required a signature for acceptance. He signed the electronic pad and ripped open the box's perforated tab as the courier left. Inside was a book sheathed in bubble wrap. He laid the bundle on the counter and carefully unwrapped it.

The Book of Mormon.

Original edition, 1830.

The one he'd bought in Salzburg, stolen back by Cassiopeia and Salazar.

Protruding from the top was a slip of paper. He removed it and read a note written in black ink.

This was found in Salazar's plane after it
was searched. I decided that you should
have it as compensation for all that you
did. You shouldn't work for free. I know
this was tough and I'm told there might be

consequences. God knows I'm not one to give anyone woman advice, but tread light and be patient. She'll come around.

Danny Daniels

He shook his head and smiled. He'd paid over a million dollars for the book. Worth about a quarter of that, but still not a bad payday. Reality was that the bills did have to be paid, and gallivanting across the globe rarely did the trick.

So he was grateful for the gesture.

He'd miss Danny Daniels.

He approached the front window and watched the storm.

And wondered what Cassiopeia was doing.

Cassiopeia deposited the last shovelful of dirt into the hole and gently patted it into place.

Josepe had been buried. Her father, mother, and first love were gone. She felt alone. She should not be so sad, considering the awful things Josepe had done. But a melancholy had taken root inside her and she doubted it would fade anytime soon.

No love filled her heart.

Despite what she'd said to Josepe in that cave.

Instead, she was angry with both Stephanie and

Cotton and wanted nothing more than to be left alone by them both.

Time for a clean break.

A new life.

Fresh challenges.

She stabbed the shovel into the moist earth and retreated to the gate.

The Spanish countryside was so peaceful, the day cool and sunny. Her own family's estate was not far away. She'd many times visited this place. Now this would be her last. Another link to her past severed.

She found her phone, located her contacts, and scrolled to Cotton Malone.

Everything was there.

Mobile number, bookshop phone, email.

All were once something special to her.

Not anymore.

She hit DELETE.

The phone asked—ARE YOU SURE?

She was.

MALONE STILL HELD THE BOOK OF MORMON.

He'd place it up for auction and convert it into cash. Its words held no special significance for him, as they did for millions of others. Five days ago he'd thought his life pretty much in order. Now there'd been a 180-degree shift. He hadn't been in love for a long time and he was just becoming accustomed to the feeling, adjusting to its demands. He'd killed Salazar because one, the SOB deserved it, and, two, there was no choice. He'd given the man a chance to stand down. Not his fault that it had not been accepted. **Never** did he like killing. But sometimes it just had to be done.

The United States of America was safe and secure.

Threat averted.

Justice had been done.

All was right, except for one thing.

He stared out at the rain.

And wondered if he would ever see Cassiopeia Vitt again.

WRITER'S NOTE

This book involved several field trips. Elizabeth and I visited Washington, D.C. Des Moines, Iowa. Salt Lake City, Utah. And Salzburg, Austria.

Now it's time to separate the real from the imagined.

The meeting described in the prologue between Abraham Lincoln and Mrs. John Fremont happened. The location (the White House's Red Room) is correct, and most of the dialogue is taken from historical accounts. General Fremont did indeed overstep his bounds, and Lincoln ultimately fired him. What Lincoln tells Jesse Fremont about freeing the slaves or saving the Union is taken verbatim from a reply Lincoln sent to a letter from Horace Greeley, the editor of the **New-York Tribune,** published in 1862. The note from James Buchanan and the document Lincoln reads from George Washington are my inventions, though Buchanan did say that he thought he might be the last president of the United States.

The Church of Jesus Christ of Latter-day Saints figures prominently in this story. It is a quintessential American religion—born, bred, and nurtured here. It is the only religion that includes the Constitution of the United States as part of its philosophy (chapters 37, 57). Without question, Mormons have played a role in American history, rising from a modest beginning to a church that now supports over 14 million members worldwide. They literally created and built the state of Utah.

Throughout the novel the words **Mormons** and **Saints** are used interchangeably. There was a time when **Mormon** would have been considered offensive, as that was a label applied in the 19th century by those who persecuted them. But that is no longer the case, and **Mormon** is now an accepted description. Even so, I allowed devout believers, like Rowan and Salazar, to keep to the word **Saints** when referring to their brethren. A modern term, **LDS** (Latter-day Saints), is common, but I decided not to use it here. Also, the head of the Church of Jesus Christ of Latter-day Saints is called either the president or the prophet. I kept to the latter so as not to create any confusion with presidents of the United States.

Apostles of the church are expected to devote themselves full-time to their duties. Thaddeus Rowan, though, remains a U.S. senator. While that arrangement is an extraordinary one, there is precedent. Reed Smoot (chapter 11) served both as an apostle and senator in the early part of the 20th century.

Blood atonement, first described in chapter 2, was once a part of the Mormon community—or at least the idea of such. It grew in response to the violence those early believers were subjected to. Whether it was actually practiced is a matter of debate. One thing is certain—any thought or application of it disappeared long ago, and it is no longer part of Mormon theology. The same is likewise true for Danites (chapter 8), a group that no longer exists. What Sidney Rigdon is quoted as saying in chapter 8 was true then, but no more. Plural marriage was officially abandoned by the church on September 25, 1890 (chapters 18, 55).

Throughout the novel Josepe Salazar is visited by an angel, a figment of his disturbed mind. Nearly everything the angel says was taken from 19th-century Mormon doctrine, speeches, and sermons and, as with blood atonement and Danites, reflects the hostile world in which those people found themselves. None of that applies today. The angel Moroni, though, remains a centerpiece of Mormon theology (chapter 39).

Zion National Park (chapter 3) is accurately described. The legend of the 22 lost wagons is part of

Mormon lore (chapter 11), but no trace of them has ever been found. The 1857 Mormon War happened, and Lincoln did in fact make a deal (as related in chapter 9) with Brigham Young. His words are quoted there exactly. Both sides honored that deal. The anti-polygamy 1862 Morrill Act was never enforced, and the Mormons stayed out of the Civil War. The supposed collateral for that deal (provided by both sides) was my invention.

The locales in Copenhagen, Kalundborg, Salzburg, Iowa, Washington, D.C., and Utah all exist. Readers of prior Cotton Malone adventures may recognize the Café Norden (chapter 10), which anchors Højbro Plads in Copenhagen. The vice president's residence on the grounds of the Naval Observatory stands as depicted (chapter 25). The Hotel Monaco in Salt Lake City (chapter 26) and the Mandarin Oriental in the nation's capital (chapter 38) are wonderful places.

The Washington, D.C., temple is a prominent Maryland landmark (chapters 50, 59). The Salt Lake temple (described in chapter 14) is an iconic monument, as is Temple Square surrounding it (chapter 61). The song quoted in chapter 11 is real, and where the prophet lives in Salt Lake City is accurately noted.

The record stone (mentioned in chapter 14) was excavated from the Salt Lake temple in 1993. Inside were various objects, left there by Brigham

Young in 1867. The inventory provided in chapter 14 is accurate, except for the addition of Young's message. History notes that Joseph Smith first glimpsed the golden plates inside a stone box. On October 2, 1841, Smith placed the original manuscript of Book of Mormon inside the Nauvoo Hotel cornerstone. What Brigham Young did—sealing objects, documents, and gold coins inside stone—became a sign of reverence (chapter 70), repeated at temples across the globe. That's why it made sense to seal the collateral Lincoln sent west within the stone plaque Young donated to the Washington Monument (chapter 70). That gift is still there, mounted inside at the 220-foot level.

The murder of Joseph Smith and his brother on June 27, 1844, is fact (chapter 16). Edwin Rushton also existed, as did his journal. The White Horse Prophecy, quoted throughout (chapters 17, 18), was once part of Mormon folklore. No one knows when the prophecy was first memorialized, but most agree that it was long after its first utterance by Joseph Smith in 1843. The text in chapter 17 is quoted from Rushton's journal, dated in the 1890s. The prophecy itself is so accurate, so detailed, that it begs the question of whether it was embellished after the fact. No matter, it was repudiated by the church in the early part of the 20th century (chapter 52), though mentions of it still exist in various Mormon texts.

What Brigham Young said in chapter 51—**Will the Constitution be destroyed? No. It will be held inviolate by this people and, as Joseph Smith said, "The time will come when the destiny of the nation will hang upon a single thread. At that critical juncture, this people will step forth and save it from the threatened destruction"**—is true. As is the prophecy of John Taylor, first announced in 1879 (chapter 51), which is also uncannily on target.

The original 1830 Book of Mormon described in chapters 20 and 30 is rare and valuable. The 1840 edition found in the Library of Congress (chapter 41) is there. Lincoln remains the first (and only) president to read it, and the dates of him having the book in his possession (noted in chapter 41) were taken from the records of the Library of Congress. All of the handwritten notes added to that book are fictional, but the passages quoted in chapter 43 are exact. The visit by Joesph Smith to President Martin Van Buren happened as told (chapter 21).

Salzburg is a marvelous city. The Goldener Hirsch has welcomed guests for many centuries (chapter 27), and the Hohensalzburg fortress still keeps guard overhead (chapter 30). St. Peter's graveyard, the catacombs, and the Gertraude Chapel are accurately portrayed (chapters 34, 37), as is the towering Mönchsberg (chapter 48). Dorotheum (chapters 20, 30) is an actual European auction house of long standing.

Mary Todd Lincoln was dealt many tough blows. She lost nearly all of her children and her husband to early deaths. Her letter contained in chapter 28 is false, but its wording is drawn from her actual correspondence. Lincoln's watch (as described in chapter 47) is on display at the Smithsonian's National Museum of American History. The inscription noted within was found when the watch was opened in 2009. The addition of a second timepiece was my creation. Salisbury House, in Des Moines, Iowa, is truthfully described—its grounds, geography, and furnishings (chapters 53, 58). Only the addition of the garden cottage is fictional. Likewise, Blair House in Washington, D.C., exists, as does the parlor with the Lincoln portrait (chapters 55, 60).

Richard Nixon did meet privately with the leadership of the Mormon church in July 1970 (chapter 31). An unprecedented thirty-minute session behind closed doors. No one to this day knows the substance of that conversation, and all of its participants are deceased.

Montpelier, its garden temple, and its ice pit are real (chapters 33, 35, 40, 42). The pit itself is sealed, and I could find no photographs of its interior. So the addition of Roman numerals there was easy to concoct.

The Rhoades gold mine is, to this day, a part of Mormon history. The story of the mine, how it was found and exploited, is faithfully told in chapter 61. Such legend is attached to the mine that it's hard to know what, if anything, is real. The map shown in chapter 18 is one of countless versions of the "real thing." The story of Brigham Young melting all of the Mormons' gold and transporting it west to California (chapter 61) for safekeeping is fact. Those 22 wagons did disappear. For this novel I merged the Rhoades Mine with the story of the lost Mormon gold and hypothesized that Brigham Young simply confiscated that wealth and recycled it back into the community (chapter 61), using the mine as a cover. It seemed logical, but there is no way to know if it is true. Gold coins, like the one described in chapter 61, were minted and still exist today. The place known as **Falta Nada** is wholly my creation.

This book deals with secession, an issue upon which the U.S. Constitution is silent. No mention is made anywhere of how a state could leave the Union. The definitive record of the constitutional convention is James Madison's **Notes of Debates in the Federal Convention of 1787**. The speeches quoted in chapter 46 are from those notes. The wording is 90 percent accurate, the only addition being comments of a way out of the Union.

But Madison's notes are indeed suspect.

They were not published until 53 years after the convention, once every participant in that gathering had died, and Madison openly admitted that he altered the account (chapter 25). What actually happened at the Constitutional Convention we will never know. So to say that secession is unconstitutional, or that the founders did not contemplate such a possibility, would be wrong. Yet that is exactly what the U.S. Supreme Court said in **Texas v. White** (1869). The portions of that opinion quoted in chapter 19 are excellent examples of this poorly reasoned opinion. But what else could the High Court have done? Rule the entire Civil War a waste of effort? That 600,000 people died for nothing?

Hardly.

The justices literally had no choice.

We, though, have a greater luxury.

The American Revolution was clearly a war of secession (chapter 9). The colonists' goal was not to overthrow the British Empire and replace that government with something new. Instead, they simply wanted out. The Declaration of Independence was a statement of their secession (chapter 26). Why would the Founding Fathers fight a long bloody war and shake off the yoke of an autocratic king only to establish another autocracy under their new government?

The answer is clear.

They would not.

What preceded the Constitution was the Articles of Confederation and Perpetual Union, which lasted from 1781 to 1789—when they were summarily discarded and replaced by the Constitution of the United States.

What happened to that **perpetual union**?

Even more telling, the new Constitution mentions nothing about **perpetual**. Instead, its Preamble states: **We the People of the United States, in Order to form a more perfect Union.**

Was a **more perfect Union** meant to be nonperpetual?

An interesting question.

And, as noted in chapter 26, Virginia, Rhode Island, and New York, in their ratification votes for the new Constitution, specifically reserved the right to secede, which was not opposed by the other states.

Secession remains a hot topic, and all of the arguments Thaddeus Rowan considers in chapter 26 make good sense. The language quoted there from a Texas petition, signed by 125,000 supporters, is exact. And 125,000 real Texans signed that document in 2012. All of the polls noted can be found in news accounts. The actual legal path to secession—how it might be accomplished, as well as its political and economic ramifications (as described in chapter 50), were drawn from authoritative texts that have considered the issue. If a state seceded there would indeed be another court fight, a test of **Texas v. White**, but a decision this time could be vastly different, especially without a personality as strong and determined as Abraham Lincoln to navigate the outcome.

Lincoln is truly a man more of myth than fact.

The quote in the epigraph of the novel is a good example. There, he made clear that **any people anywhere, being inclined and having the power, have the right to rise up, and shake off the existing government, and form a new one that suits them better. This is a most valuable—a most sacred right—a right, which we hope and believe, is to liberate the world. Nor is this right confined to cases in which the whole people of an existing government may choose to exercise it. Any portion of such people, that can, may revolutionize, and make their own of so much of the territory as they inhabit.**

Lincoln absolutely believed secession legal.

At least in 1848.

But the myths about him say otherwise.

Every schoolchild is told that Lincoln freed the slaves with his Emancipation Proclamation. But nothing could be farther from the truth. What is said in chapter 7 about that effort is historical fact. At the time of that proclamation slavery was both recognized and condoned by the Constitution (chapter 7). No president possessed the authority to alter that. Only a constitutional amendment could make that change. And one eventually did, the Thirteenth Amendment, ratified long after Lincoln's death.

Then there is the reason why Lincoln fought the Civil War in the first place. Myth says it was to end slavery. But Lincoln made his position clear in 1862 when he said, **My task is to save the Union. I would save it the shortest way under the Constitution. If I could save the Union without freeing any slave, I would do it. If I could save it by freeing all slaves, I would do it. If I could save it by freeing some and leaving others alone, I would also do that. What I do about slavery, and the colored race, I do because I believe it helps to save the Union. What I forbear, I forbear because I don't believe it would help to save the Union.**

Again, his intent is beyond question.

And directly contrary to myth.

As president, Lincoln totally ignored what he said in 1848 and fought to establish, beyond question, that the South had no right to leave the Union. The peace talks referred to in chapter 60, at Hampton Roads in February 1865, happened.

Lincoln himself was there, and when the South insisted on independence as a condition to peace he ended the discussion.

For Lincoln, the Union was non-negotiable.

John Kennedy said it best: **The greatest enemy of truth is often not the lie—deliberate, contrived and dishonest—but the myth—persistent, persuasive and unrealistic.**

The idea of an indivisible, perpetual union of states did not exist prior to 1861. No one believed such nonsense. States' rights ruled that day. The federal government was regarded as small, weak, and inconsequential. If a state could choose to join the Union, then a state could choose to leave.

As noted in the prologue, James Buchanan, Lincoln's predecessor, actually did pave the way for South Carolina to secede, blaming that act on the **intemperate interference of the northern people with the question of slavery.** Buchanan also voiced what many in the nation regarded as true: that slave states should be left alone to manage their domestic institutions in their own way. Northern states should also repeal all laws that encouraged slaves to become fugitives. If not, then, as Buchanan said, **the injured states, after having first used all peaceful and constitutional means to effect redress, would be justified in revolutionary resistance to the government of the Union.**

Strong words from our 15th president.

But things quickly changed.

Our 16th president believed in a **perpetual union**. One from which no state was free to leave.

Here's a fact, beyond the myth.

Lincoln did not fight the Civil War to **preserve** the union.

He fought that war to **create** it.

ABOUT THE AUTHOR

STEVE BERRY is the **New York Times** and #1 internationally bestselling author of nine Cotton Malone adventures, four stand-alone novels, and four short story originals. He has seventeen million books in print, translated into forty languages and sold in fifty-one countries. With his wife, Elizabeth, he is the founder of History Matters, a foundation dedicated to historic preservation. He was awarded the 2013 Writers for Writers Award from **Poets & Writers Magazine,** has twice acted as national spokesman for the American Library Association's Preservation Week, and is a member of the Smithsonian Libraries Advisory Board. He is a founding member of International Thriller Writers and served three years as its co-president. To learn more, visit www.steveberry.org.

LIKE WHAT YOU'VE READ?

If you enjoyed this large print edition of
THE LINCOLN MYTH,
here are a few of Steve Berry's latest bestsellers
also available in large print.

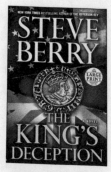
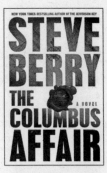
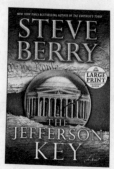
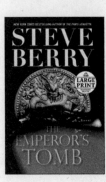